THE LAST VAMPIRE

THE LAST VAMPIRE

Book I of the Annals of Alchemy and Blood

PATRICIA ROSEMOOR & MARC PAOLETTI

BALLANTINE BOOKS • NEW YORK

The Last Vampire is a work of fiction. Names, characters, places, and incidents are the products of the author's imagination or are used fictitiously. Any resemblance to actual events, locales, or persons, living or dead, is entirely coincidental.

A Del Rey Books Mass Market Original

Published in the United States by Del Rey Books, an imprint of The Random House Publishing Group, a division of Random House, Inc., New York.

ISBN 978-0-345-50104-2

Printed in the United States of America

www.delreybooks.com

OPM 9 8 7 6 5 4 3 2 1

I would like to thank my critique partners Sherrill Bodine, Rosemary Paulas, Cheryl Jefferson, Jude Mandell, and my long-distance critique buddy Ruth Glick/Rebecca York for their continuing and valuable support while working on this new venture. Kudos to my agent Jennifer Jackson, for finding a home for this work. And thanks to my partner Marc Paoletti for challenging me to write something different that rekindled the joy of writing for me.

—Patricia Rosemoor

I would like to send endless love and thanks to Mom, Dad, Marilyn, Mostafa, Stephen, Frances, Alyssa, Ken, Audrey, Allyn, Elizabeth, Nyle, Caroline, Colin, Ramsay, Laura, Robert, Cole, Lena, John, ChiSook, and Mina. I'm so lucky to have you all in my life. Thanks as well to Ray and Renee, cherished friends, for your warm and constant influence. Deepest gratitude to Jennifer Jackson, step-agent, who helped make this novel possible, and has great taste in scotch. Thanks to Bean Addiction Coffee and the two Starbucks Coffees on Clinton Street for the constant flow of caffeine. Special love to Tracy, who makes every day memorable in profound and unexpected ways. Finally, love and kudos to Kimberly, Avery, Sawyer, and Sadie—the true action heroes.

—Marc Paoletti

Prologue

Cueva del Diablo, Texas, 1993

"Don't do it, Leah. I'm warning you! Dad told us to wait up for him."

Stopping, Leah Maguire glared at her big brother Gabe, her helmet's lamp making his maturing face glow eerily pale against the enveloping dark. The only light in the cave came from their headlamps and flashlights and a single thin beam from the narrow fissure overhead. Right now, everything looked flat, colorless, including his green eyes so like her own. Behind him, the maw leading to the chamber they'd just passed through was still dark, void of movement.

"Dad should be back with another lantern by now." She couldn't believe he'd dropped his into a narrow crevasse where it had gotten stuck. "He said it would only take a minute to catch up to Mr. Anderson's group and borrow one of theirs."

"Maybe he took the wrong tunnel or something, but he'll get it straight. Be patient, would you?"

Hating it when Gabe got so bossy—he was only three years older, after all—Leah glanced back at the small opening with longing. "You just don't want me to go in because *you* can't fit."

Her brother had grown and filled out in the last year. His shoulders were so broad he barely made it through a doorway anymore. They sure wouldn't get through the small opening.

"No, it's not that," Gabe said, his voice sounding odd enough that it sent a shiver up Leah's spine. "Something feels strange about this place."

Though she didn't say so, Leah sensed it, too. Lately, she'd been experiencing a lot of things she couldn't understand. Things that frightened her, made her feel like a little kid or something.

Shaking off the frisson of fear that radiated from Gabe, Leah started to get angry with him. Her big brother was putting her on, that was it, because he didn't want her beating him out at anything.

She turned back to the opening, her ginger braids flying, saying, "Oh, I'm so sure you're worried. What's the matter, Gabe? Afraid your little sister's the better spelunker?"

"I'm telling you—"

"I'm going to get the most awesome shots of limestone formations that *you'll* never get to see!"

Before Gabe could stop her, Leah found footing in the wall and boosted herself up and through the opening and under a ragged limestone shawl that dripped like dozens of yard-long fingers. Good thing she was still scrawny, as Gabe liked to remind her. For once not having breasts or hips like her friends played to her advantage.

Negotiating any cave without public access took some amount of expertise, and Leah was a natural. Her pulse always thrummed as she found new flowstone formations—limestone canopies and shawls and curtains—but she especially liked the more uniquely formed stalactites and stalagmites. Always champing at the bit to make new discoveries, she couldn't wait another minute.

"Leah Maguire, get back here!" Gabe called.

"Bite me!" she yelled in response.

On her hands and knees in a tunnel, she felt the walls

close in around her, hugging her with their cool, damp breath. Her camera had a wide-angle lens and was rigged to a front jacket pocket so she could take photos right from there. She'd gotten a lot of good shots already; a lot of formations that shone an extraordinary bright white. The cave deposits were translucent because of the purity of the limestone. She couldn't wait to see what lay ahead.

From behind, she heard Gabe's voice. "I told her to wait, Dad. She's in there."

"Leah?" came the voice deep and firm enough to put the fear of God in anyone. "Get back here."

Sighing in frustration, Leah stopped. She was almost there, almost to the next chamber. Her headlight picked up the ragged edges of a limestone canopy, and halfway there, seemingly embedded in the limestone, a soft red glow. What the heck was that? A dropped light? A rock of some kind? Another few feet wouldn't hurt anything. She'd check it out, take her photo, and then go back.

"Coming, Dad," she fibbed as she crept forward, her gaze intent on the red glow.

She sensed movement ahead.

Whipping her head up, she stared at the opening of the other chamber. A tickle of uncertainty crawled through her, pebbling the flesh along her spine. Then a scrabbling sound stopped her again, and her pulse picked up.

More movement . . .

Bats?

She moved her head so her light went straight through the opening. For a second, nothing. Then more movement. A flurry. Two spots glowed at her like eyes in the dark.

Her heart leaped to her throat, its beat filling her ears. What the heck was that? Not bats.

A click of her camera and bright white flashed down

the tunnel for a quick glimpse of something dark moving fast out of the light. Something dark and scary that made her squirm inside. A strong sense of danger whipped through her and took her breath away.

Her throat tight, Leah averted her eyes and began backing up the way she'd come. Waves of what felt like anger pulsating from the other cavern pushed her faster. When she looked up again, a whirl of dark movement like a stream of those supposed bats seemed to be coming down the tunnel after her.

Gasping, she crabbed backward faster toward the cavern and Gabe and Dad.

"Leah, come on!"

"Coming, Gabe, and something's coming after me!"

"Well, hurry!" Dad yelled.

She *was* hurrying, and the whirling darkness was hurrying to overtake her. A rush of blood filled her ears and her throat again went tight. Suddenly her feet shot out into nothingness—the chamber—and her body followed, tumbling downward, her right hip hitting the cavern floor hard and the breath whooshing out of her even as the black mist shot right over her head.

An agonized scream raised the hair on the back of her neck. She twisted and a gush of something wet hit her. Her brother . . . her big, strong, wide-as-a-doorway brother . . . was on his knees, gagging, trying to avoid the dark silhouette that seemed to be attacking him.

"Gabe!"

His only answer was a strangled gurgle.

Oh my God . . . oh my God . . . oh my God . . .

Her mouth rounded into an O and she panted to get air as she prayed to the God that Mom assured her always listened.

Help Gabe . . . help him . . . help . . . !

The words screamed through Leah's mind if not

through her throat as Gabe slid onto his back. Then her father was there, lifting her to her feet.

"Leah, get out now! Run!"

Leah couldn't move as her father came at the black force, only to be struck to his knees, too.

No, no! Please, God, please . . . do something! Help them! Please!

But her prayers went unheard. Dad collapsed in a heap a few feet from Gabe.

Then the thing that attacked them turned to *her,* twin spots glowing against the dark her only warning.

Leah turned to run.

A narrow shaft of light guided her to the fissure in the earth, so it was right above her. She could climb to get to it . . . she could find little chinks in the limestone wall for her toes and fingers . . . she could get help to save Gabe and Dad . . .

Before she could try, long fingers manacled her thin arm, bringing her flight to an abrupt halt. A dark river of evil rushed through her like an extra pulse, and for a split second she saw Gabe and Dad in her mind. Stumbling, she whirled and fell backward, the foreign hand plunging with her straight into the light.

The creature yelled, the sound filling the cavern and nearly splitting her eardrums.

Her arm was on fire.

No, its hand—smoke was rising off it.

She slapped at the putrid flesh to get it off her, then screamed herself at contact. The thin leather of her glove was smoking and her palm felt seared by flame.

The manacle fell from her arm as if useless, and Leah fell to the ground, surrounded by nothing but a thin stream of sunlight. Then she could see things. . . her clothing . . . her hands . . . all covered in blood.

"Dad! Gabe!" She sobbed, brokenhearted at what she had caused.

Her brother and father didn't respond. They lay as still as death, separated from her by the creature.

No escape . . . there was no escaping the fate she'd brought on them all.

Wrapping her arms around her head and closing her eyes so that she couldn't see what was coming next, Leah rolled into a tight ball of pain and waited to die.

Chapter 1

**Louis Armstrong International Airport,
New Orleans, 2010**

The white airline catering van lurched to a stop.

Captain Scott Boulder crouched in the dim, hot cargo area behind the driver's seat with the three other members of his assault team. They wore black tactical hoods, fatigues, Kevlar vests, and combat boots, and carried MP5s and flexicuffs. The bare minimum so they could move. Fast.

Scott spoke into his headset, "Team Ultra to base. We've reached the target."

"We read you, Team Ultra," came the crackling reply. "Spotter reports four, repeat, four hijackers aboard the aircraft."

Men of unknown nationality had hijacked an Airbus A320 on the ground and demanded the release of military prisoners from Guantánamo Bay. How the assholes got AK-47s and grenades on board was anybody's guess. Officials had three hours to meet their demands or the hijackers would start killing a passenger every fifteen minutes.

The U.S. government didn't negotiate with terrorists, at least not directly. More often than not, they sent a team like Boulder's to do the "talking" for them, to fight fire with fire. In a situation like this, it was the only realistic response.

"Where are the hijackers now?" Scott asked into his headset.

There was a pause before the answer came back. "Locations remain unchanged. One in the cockpit. Two in the forward galley beyond the main door. Another in the passenger cabin. Execute in thirty seconds."

"Thirty seconds, on your mark," Scott said into the headset, and felt a deep weariness in his muscles, his bones. He'd seen many people die at the hands of fanatics like these. Too fucking many. Innocent civilians and men he'd served with . . . their bodies torn apart by bullets and bombs, their families left behind to suffer. He'd proudly protected his country for the past eighteen years, but lately he felt like he was drowning in blood. He should have quit months ago when he'd had the chance, but he'd enlisted for one more tour of duty. And now he had to live with that decision.

Scott forced himself to concentrate. He didn't have the luxury to indulge his fatigue. As always, success today would depend on *control* . . . on his controlling the team, and on the team wresting control from the hijackers.

The latter wouldn't be easy. Airplane incursions were a tactical nightmare. You had tight quarters, sharp corners, interrupted lines of sight. Not to mention every row of seats was a potential barricade for the bad guys to hide behind. It didn't help that his team had been assembled only six weeks ago. They'd been successful thus far, but lacked the cohesion of a team that had spent real time together in the field.

Then again, they had a few tricks up their sleeves that other teams didn't.

"Let's do this by the numbers," Scott said.

The two men across from him nodded to indicate they understood. Scott traded places with them, positioning himself in front of the van's sliding door and gripping the handle, ready to throw it open when the time came. If the hijackers expected water and peanuts from this catering van, they were in for one hell of a surprise.

Scott glanced at the third man on his right, who was making a last-minute adjustment to his gear. "You okay?"

"Yeah."

"Sure about that?"

The man glared, amber eyes flashing. "I said I was."

Scott wasn't convinced. Eric had been acting strangely these past few days. Distracted, contentious. This was just more of the same. "I never asked you to look out for me," added Eric.

"It's my job to look out for you," said Scott, suppressing an urge to bounce his younger brother from the mission right then and there. Eric's disrespect to a superior officer notwithstanding, the action would hardly be appropriate minutes before go time. He had to make sure Team Ultra maintained discipline and focus, acted as a unit. But Eric was still obviously in pain, and as his older brother, that meant Scott felt some of it, too. "What the hell is up with you? This is a mission."

A look of pure resentment crossed Eric's face. "Why not worry about yourself for a change?"

Scott was about to reply when the voice in his headset returned. "Ten seconds."

"Ten seconds," Scott repeated to his men, and made a mental note to bring up the personal issues with Eric later. He had to keep his mind on the matters at hand. "Remember, fire only if necessary and at what you can see. Drew and Jonas, you're up first. Eric, you're with me. By the numbers, gentlemen, do you hear me?"

Eric flashed him another "fuck you" look. Scott glared back in reply—*You're on thin ice, little brother*—and then it was time.

"Mark," came the voice on his headset.

"Mark," Scott said, then wrenched open the side door; it slammed open with a rolling bang. Sunlight and swampy New Orleans air flooded the back of the van as Drew and Jonas leaped past him onto the tarmac. Scott moved to follow, but Eric rushed past him. Scowling, Scott let the transgression go. He didn't want to break the rhythm of the team in the middle of an op.

Outside, the airbus loomed, its aluminum skin gleaming in the morning sun.

"Cockpit!" Scott yelled to Drew.

Drew sprinted beneath the nose section, and looked up at the cockpit's side window. Earlier, one of the hijackers had shot it out and stuck out his arm to wave a pistol around, demonstrating that the pilot was no longer in control of the airplane. A stupid move.

Drew stood ramrod straight with his arms at his sides, cutting a lean profile, and then the entire surface of his body—flesh, clothes, equipment—began to whirl, colors and textures mixing, until the framework of flesh and bone fell into itself with an implosion of gray mist.

The transformation took less than two seconds, and never failed to make Scott a little queasy. Seeing Drew's body evaporate was too fucking weird.

The gray cloud stretched and flowed up through the side window as quickly as a waterfall in reverse, then a scream issued from the cockpit. From the sound of it, the hijacker holding the pilot found the transformation disturbing, too. A Special Forces commando materializing from thin air is not something they prepare you for in terrorist school.

Scott turned to see Jonas already at the top of the air stairs that had been wheeled into place earlier under the pretext of delivering food and water. Jonas had anticipated his order. Good. With each mission, the team's cohesion was improving.

"Stay on my six," he said to Eric.

"Go to hell," Eric growled, and rushed past him up the stairs, taking them two at a time.

Not completely improving, Scott thought grimly, and followed. He no longer cared about what his brother was going through; this was crossing the line.

At the top of the stairs, Jonas punched his fingers into the metal seam on either side of the locked forward main door, and pulled. With a screech of rending metal, he ripped the massive door from its mooring and pitched it over his shoulder. Scott ducked instinctively as the door passed over his and Eric's head with a slip-stream *whoosh,* and crashed onto the tarmac below.

Two hijackers with AK-47s waited inside the forward galley. They were young, probably mid-twenties, and wore dirty white T-shirts with American logos on them, blue jeans, and tennis shoes. Red bandannas covered the lower halves of their faces, but their confused eyes said it all: *What just happened?*

Scott felt much the same way. Jonas was a tall, lantern-jawed Swede who was thick with muscle, al-ready plenty strong, but his enhanced strength was downright scary.

Jonas grabbed the hijackers by their shirts and knocked them together. Hard. They crumpled to the ground, and then he rolled them onto their stomachs and pressed a knee into their backs to make sure they didn't get up again.

Barely nine seconds had elapsed.

Scott followed as Eric ran headlong past Jonas through the greeting area and took a hard right, leading with his MP5. Scott glanced into the cockpit as he passed and saw a reconstituted Drew hog-tying his hi-jacker with flexicuffs. A grenade lay harmlessly on the floor. The pilot appeared uninjured, and sat wide-eyed in his seat, staring at Drew. Apparently, the pilot had witnessed Drew's transformation, too.

Scott moved smoothly into the main cabin behind Eric. Eighty-two passengers stared at them, faces frozen in uniform terror. The sharp scent of urine wafted into Scott's nostrils. Some of the passengers had no doubt wet themselves in fear.

The remaining hijacker was in the aisle about ten rows away, using a woman as a shield. Pressing a gun to her temple, he yelled in a thick accent, "Get back! Get back!"

"Drop the gun!" Scott yelled. "Now!"

Scott knew there was no way the guy would comply. He was too freaked out that his comrades had been taken down in less than ten seconds; freaked out that Team Ultra was more than human. He was about to pull the trigger, and there was no way any of the team could draw a safe bead on him before he did.

"Hey!" Eric yelled. The hijacker looked at him, finger tightening on the trigger. Eric stretched out his right arm as though he were trying to touch the man across the rows that separated them. "Put down the gun."

The hijacker frowned, obviously confused at Eric's audacity, then his eyes went completely white, like they'd been replaced with cue balls. Scott didn't know which he found more disturbing: Drew's and Jonas's overt physical powers, or Eric's sublime power of Suggestion.

"Put down the gun," Eric repeated, keeping his arm outstretched.

The hijacker began to tremble, and then the pistol fell away from the woman's temple. Scott began to breathe easier. Mission accomplished. He slung the shoulder strap of the MP5 over his head when he saw the hijacker's pupils and irises reappear, disappear, and then flicker like an out-of-tune television station.

Eric placed his hand on the top of a nearby seat to steady himself. Although Scott couldn't see his brother's expression from where he was standing, he could tell something was wrong.

"Eric!" he said.

Eric didn't reply as he continued to waver. Something was very, very wrong.

Heart hammering in his chest, Scott leveled the MP5 at the hijacker. Eric looked pale. "Eric, what the hell?"

Eric didn't reply. He just kept muttering, ". . . the gun . . . the gun . . ."

Scott wanted to push Eric from harm's way, but he dared not leave the hijacker uncovered. He squared the man's head between his sights. Took a deep breath. Another. He forced himself to forget about Eric and concentrate on his aim. If he was even a fraction off target, he could hit a passenger.

". . . the gun . . ." Eric muttered, and dropped to his knees, breaking whatever connection he'd had. The hijacker's eyes cleared, and he raised the gun back to the woman's temple.

Scott fired.

A red mist blossomed behind the hijacker's head and he went down. Scott looked at the man's supine body. A spray of brain painted the aisle behind his head as blood trickled from the tiny bullet wound. There'd been no other way.

So much blood . . .

Eric struggled back to his feet, his face a mask of rage. "I had him!"

Scott ignored him and said, "Ladies and gentlemen, if you'll please remain seated, we'll have people on board in just a few minutes to escort you from the aircraft."

The danger suddenly over, some passengers wept in relief. Others broke into applause.

"I told you I fucking had him!" Eric said.

Scott regarded him evenly, if not incredulously. "You lost hold of the guy."

Clearly, Eric was beyond listening, because he pushed roughly past, exiting the cabin.

Chapter 2

Santa Maria Pueblo, New Mexico

Wind whistled over the mesa and pummeled the striated red and brown canyon walls with sand—not so different from the landscape in Texas where Leah had begun this emotional journey seventeen years before. They'd come to this high desert outcropping on foot along a wash through a narrow canyon where lava had once scorched the walls.

They'd come to this particular spot because it had been here where twelve-year-old Isabel Yepa had lost her voice, Leah Maguire knew.

Two months before, Isabel had disappeared from her home, only to be found wandering alone in this area the next morning. Her eyes had been wild, her temper unpredictable, and she'd been unable or unwilling to speak. A physical examination had confirmed that she'd been raped, but there was no medical explanation for the silence. A therapist specializing in trauma had worked with the girl with no results.

While Isabel didn't try to run back to where her mother waited for her—crying silently, brown face wet with tears—the girl was making sounds of her own. Pitiful mewling sounds, sounds of fear that had no shape. Hair hung loose over her high forehead and cupped her round cheeks. Her dark eyes were wide, rolling, showing the whites, as if she could feel evil pressing down on her.

Leah felt it, too. She felt everything the girl did, as if what had happened to Isabel had happened to her. Though she was used to feeling the emotions of another, that didn't make doing so any easier for her.

"Relax, Isabel, I'm here with you." Kneeling on the ground, Leah reached out and gently touched the girl's arm, her fingers pale against the brown skin. The contrast made her wonder how this girl could relate to—how she could trust—a woman like her, with her freckled pale skin, spiky red hair, and eyes shaded by sunglasses. They were so different on the outside, but inside they were the same—suffering from a horror they couldn't prevent, couldn't stop. Not that the girl would know it. Knowing too much about people was Leah's curse. And, if she could ever harness it constructively, her gift. "I won't let you face this alone."

Isabel jerked her arm away, her anguished sounds making Leah want to take the girl in her arms and hold her until she was better.

Stomach tightening, Leah said, "Let me help you free your spirit and find peace."

As a cultural anthropologist who specialized in apotropaic magic—rituals that turned away evil—Leah had studied white and black magic of various cultures. While intellectually she understood the theories and the reasons people believed they worked, putting them into practice was such a scary proposition for her that she rarely tried.

This time was different.

This time she'd agreed because of her instant bond with Isabel, because Leah, too, had once gotten lost inside her own head after her father and brother had been slaughtered. In many ways, she still was.

She looked to Javier Estes, her mentor trained in *curanderismo*, the Aztec healing tradition of caring for the body, mind, and spirit as one. Dressed in dusty work pants and a light woven cotton shirt, a brimmed hat sheltering his seamed, leather face, he sat cross-legged on the ground nearby, feet encased in huaraches.

"You can do this, *chica,*" he assured her. "Believe that you can and you will."

Leah nodded, but inside she wasn't so sure.

The girl's mother—a mestizo who'd married a Pueblo man—had decided her daughter's soul had been infected by evil and had turned to someone from her own culture to help. But Javier had thought it fitting that Leah perform the soul-retrieval ceremony under his guidance. He'd insisted that the universe worked in mysterious ways, bringing together people who needed one another. It had been no accident that Leah had come to him for instruction, he'd told her.

Leah had observed Javier at work many times in the past weeks, and had seen the results. It was hard to believe, but more often than not, *curanderismo* seemed to work where modern medicine failed.

Hard to believe . . .

Javier nodded at her in encouragement, and Leah turned to the makeshift altar before them—a rock set with a hand-embroidered cloth, fresh flowers, and representations of the four elements. Stones, crystals, and copal stood for the earth. A clay pitcher held water. Candles when burning would represent fire. An eagle feather symbolized wind or air.

Leah lit the candles—the glass holders painted with pictures of the Catholic saints. Then she lit the copal and brushed the blue smoke over the other objects on the altar. The copal burned for protection, cleansing, purification, and spirituality.

Handing Isabel the pitcher, she said, "Drink a little."

The girl's hands shook as she lifted the pitcher to her mouth—more water got on her than in her. Leah took the pitcher and set it on the altar, then lifted the eagle feather and swept it around Isabel.

"Close your eyes . . . that's it . . . I'm clearing the space around you, blowing away your fear." Her pulse trilled with trepidation as she murmured, "We are going on a journey together. Just relax. Let go of the tension, starting with your arms and legs."

Her tone seemed to quiet the girl down a bit, so Leah kept it up.

"They feel light . . . floating . . . the feeling spreads to your body . . . open your mind and see yourself in a pure blue sky, holding my hand . . ."

Leah recognized the moment Isabel relaxed and gave herself over to the ceremony. Swallowing hard, she glanced at Javier, who watched the proceedings with the attention of a hawk. Too bad the *curandero* nodding his approval didn't settle her down inside. Javier would do this with prayers, but Leah continued to use a familiar relaxation technique instead.

"Feel yourself moving on an air current . . . dreaming in the clouds. . . all the beauty of the world wrapping around you . . . your mother's arms . . . the arms of Isabel, your patron saint . . ."

Closing her own eyes, Leah attempted to float along with the girl so she could guide Isabel as Javier had coached her to do, but try as she might, the trance eluded her. No matter the pretty pictures she painted for Isabel, her own mind was stuck in the dark matter of the girl's rape. Her screams echoed through Leah's mind.

She tried not to panic.

What was she doing, involving herself like this? She'd come to Santa Maria Pueblo with Javier as an observer, but he'd told her she *needed* to be a participant, that her own soul demanded it.

Pulse surging, Leah tried again, forcing herself deeper this time. In her mind, she finally caught onto a cloud in a pure blue sky, and for a moment, she felt the darkness scatter . . . felt Isabel's hand in hers . . . felt the girl squeezing tightly. The clouds raced overhead faster and faster until Leah began to feel giddy and Isabel began trying to tug free.

"No, wait, don't go. It's too soon. Don't be afraid. You're surrounded by beauty that fills you . . ."

But Isabel tugged even harder, and started making those sounds of fright again until her fear chased Leah and began to swallow her. She suddenly felt like she was drowning, and above, the sky dimmed and went gray.

No, no, she couldn't lose the girl now!

"Just a little longer . . ."

The clouds faded, scattered. Darkness was there.

Waiting for her.

Always waiting . . .

Leah did her best to fight being sucked into the frightening whorl. "You can face it, Isabel . . . face *him,* the man who hurt you, with me at your side . . . expose your soul just for a moment so I can chase away the evil and you can find your voice . . ."

Leah's eyes shot open when she realized she'd let her mind wander off. Isabel sat there . . . frightened . . . agitated. But no matter how hard Leah tried, the trance state and Isabel's soul now eluded her.

She shook her head—she couldn't help the girl. She'd let down not only Isabel but also Javier, who had put his trust and the girl's soul in her hands.

A mistake.

She'd failed.

Leah looked to Javier, silently pleading with him for help. Nodding, he took Isabel's other hand, and from his pocket removed a small crucifix.

"In the name of God, the All-Powerful, let the evil spirit that silences this girl be removed so she can speak.

Let the evil pour from her and let her see the mercy of God."

Leah allowed her mind to drift away. She didn't move and still held on to Isabel's hand, but she felt oddly removed from the ceremony, as if she were watching it from a distance.

Javier worked his magic and then brought Isabel back to the present.

Leah was thankful when the girl opened her eyes and called out, "Mami!" and got to her feet and ran to her mother, who caught the girl and wailed in relief.

Javier followed and the adults spoke for a few minutes in Spanish, while Leah began dismantling the altar. She never should have tried it herself.

She'd known better.

Packing the crystals and pitcher into her satchel, she was aware of Javier returning and standing over her without passing judgment.

"I couldn't do it." Exactly as Leah had known when she'd agreed to try. "It simply couldn't be done, not by me."

"You're wrong, Leah. You could have done it. You *can* turn away evil, if first you open your mind and heart."

"I tried."

"You'll be able to do it when you choose to believe in yourself . . . and give yourself over to something even greater."

"You mean God?" she asked with a sharp laugh.

God had deserted her father and brother in that cave. He'd turned deaf ears to her frantic prayers for their salvation . . . and had let her live with the memories.

"Your soul is sick, *chica*. You need to find a way to heal yourself."

"How do I do that?"

Javier simply looked at her.

Maybe he could help her if she could only talk honestly about what had happened all those years ago. But she couldn't. Wouldn't talk about her inexorable guilt. Wouldn't stop punishing herself. Something made her keep evil locked up tight inside her.

Like Isabel, she had lost her voice.

Chapter 3

Miescher Laboratories, Bayou Foncé, Louisiana

Still dressed in black fatigues but now without his hood, Kevlar vest, and gear, Scott walked down the hallway, which opened up into the main lab, a circular room five hundred feet in diameter with polished steel walls and a sixty-foot ceiling.

The place hummed with activity. A small army of men and women wearing white lab coats buzzed around tables that held intricate pieces of high-tech equipment, and a dizzying array of beakers and test tubes that bubbled with colorful liquids and emitted sharp chemical odors. Numerous experiments and tests were being conducted here, all pertaining to Team Ultra, which was the current flagship project of the Defense Advanced Research Projects Agency, aka DARPA, the central research and development organization for the Department of Defense.

Located down an isolated dirt road about thirty miles outside New Orleans, the sprawling DARPA facility might have looked like a civilian lab if not for the ten-foot Cyclone fence that encircled its border with a hanging placard that read: DEADLY FORCE PERIMETER. UNAUTHORIZED PERSONNEL WILL BE FIRED UPON.

Crossing the room, Scott approached a wiry scientist holding a clipboard. His name was Darryl Adams, but Scott affectionately called him "BB," short for Big Brain. At only thirty-one years old, the guy was a bona fide phenom from MIT, and head researcher on Project

24. In fact, he'd helped pioneer the DNA-splicing technique that had made Team Ultra what it was. DNA research had progressed rapidly over the last several years, the main reason that BB had been brought in, and Project 24 had been given the green light. BB sported a shock of fiery red hair, a red goatee, and one hell of a sarcastic streak. The sleeves of his white lab coat were pushed to the elbows, revealing forearms tattooed with Celtic symbols.

When Scott got close, BB looked up from his clipboard and smiled. "Nice job today, Scott. Way to lower the genetically modified boom on the hijackers."

"Yeah," Scott grunted, still thinking about his brother's strange behavior on the plane. A passenger could have been killed. His *brother* could have been killed. He should kick Eric's ass for being so reckless.

"That doesn't sound like the Type-A captain I know and love," BB said, continuing to take notes on his clipboard as they talked.

"Nothing I can't handle," Scott said wearily, hoping it was true. "Though I'm sure Major Ackart will give me an earful. She here yet?"

Major Wallas Ackart was in charge of Team Ultra—their boss—and had convinced legions of military brass that the unconventional and unprecedented could be accomplished. After the team had returned to base a short time ago, he'd found himself on Ackart's shit list, thanks to Eric. Yet another reason to kick his ass. In fact, he planned to do just that after incurring the major's fury.

"On her way," the scientist said, shaking his head. "I ever tell you that woman scares me?"

"Many times."

"She scares me like jungle rot scares me, pal. Like cruel shoes scare me. Remember *Cruel Shoes* by Steve Martin?"

"I hear you," Scott said, then indicated the massive Plexiglas chamber in front of them, trying to distract himself from the coming storm. "How's the mummy?"

"We're about to mine Sleeping Beauty for more DNA samples." BB gestured with his head. "See for yourself."

Scott peered more closely into the climate-controlled chamber, a huge twenty-foot by twenty-foot cell with three-inch-thick walls. A pair of scientists fussed with several opaque tubes, which drooped from the ceiling and connected to the top of a ten-foot-long case on a waist-high pedestal.

Inside the case was the desiccated mummy of a man that had been recently discovered in a Texas cave and carbon-dated back to the fifteenth century—the source of Team Ultra's extraordinary powers.

Scott felt a whisper of unease, as he always did, when regarding the mummy.

It lay on its back, eyes and mouth closed, arms by its sides. Although it was clearly dead, its shriveled muscles and brown leathery flesh seemed to hold just enough residual elasticity to make it look like it was only sleeping. The guy had been pretty big in life, judging from his large head, yawning barrel chest, and broad hands and feet. And tall, too. Over six feet. There were no scraps of clothing, but, oddly, there was a ring on the left hand. Made of silver, it was round with a raised symbol: a triangle inside a square, and inside the triangle an open eye. Nobody knew what the symbol meant, at least not yet. BB had explained the ring was permanently affixed and couldn't be removed without risking damage.

What made the body truly extraordinary, however, was the number of chromosomes it possessed. BB had explained that human beings normally had twenty-three pairs of chromosomes, while the mummy, inexplicably, had twenty-four. When strands from this twenty-fourth pair were fused with the DNA of his men, the impossible suddenly became possible. Why different powers developed for different members of the team was still a mystery. But that didn't seem to matter. All that mattered for now were results.

Scott considered the strange corpse with its extra pair of chromosomes an unknown variable—and he disliked unknown variables. If you gave up control, you invited disaster.

Eric's behavior today was only the latest example of that. Sometimes just thinking about Eric consenting to the DNA splicing made his chest tighten. "Listen, BB, about Eric—"

"Say no more, pal," the scientist said. "I heard what happened and checked Eric out myself when he arrived back ahead of you. Sure, he could use a couple shots of scotch, maybe some Jacuzzi time with Naomi Campbell, but hey, so could I. Physically, though, as far as I can tell, he's fine."

Scott wasn't convinced. Eric was erratic. Not himself at all. "Could he be having an adverse reaction to the splicing?"

BB placed a consoling hand on his shoulder. "Trust me, Scott. There's no sign of rejection or side effect. Whatever your brother is going through, it's not due to the procedure."

Scott felt some relief. At least his brother's genetic makeup was stable. "Where is he now?"

The scientist pointed to a far, tucked-away area of the huge lab where Eric, clad in blue shorts, ran on a treadmill with wires trailing from his bare chest and arms. Around him, men and women in lab coats consulted flatscreen monitors beeping with multiple readouts. "My people are conducting a few backup tests to make absolutely sure." He cleared his throat. "Actually, Eric snapped at me before, so . . . um . . . I might have prescribed sixty minutes on the treadmill that weren't entirely necessary."

Before Scott could reply, he heard a woman's voice behind him, accompanied by the clack of heels on tile. "Hello, Captain."

"Yeah, well, I know you two have a lot to talk about," BB muttered, and then scooted away. Out of the blast radius. Scott could hardly blame him.

Scott turned as Major Ackart approached. She was dressed in formal army blues, jacket and knee-length skirt impeccably pressed, long blond hair done up in a tight bun underneath a blue service cap. Gold maple leaf pins denoting her rank gleamed on her lapels. Around her neck hung a caduceus pendant on a thin metal chain. In a rare moment of humanity, Ackart had told him it was a gift from her grandmother who'd served as a medical researcher in World War II.

"I'm on my way to debrief the generals on the mission this morning, and wanted to stop by first for a word," Ackart said. "Relax, Captain. I think your team performed well."

"Thank you," he said, and thought, *Uh-oh.* Ackart wasn't one to dole out compliments. Male officers tended to let their guard down around her because of her blond hair and good looks, but they did so at their own risk. Ackart was intelligent, fiercely ambitious, and didn't let anyone stand in her way when she set her sights on a goal. Or an enemy.

She regarded him, green eyes flashing. "Did my support staff perform to your satisfaction?"

"Your people were good," Scott said, and meant it. Team Ultra was still in the test phase, a blacker-than-black op, which meant raiding the plane had been an exposure risk. But Ackart's staff had taken every precaution, immediately closing off the runway to unessential personnel, and were now debriefing the passengers and pilot, no doubt convincing them that whatever they'd seen had been delirium caused by severe shock. Only the hijackers really saw anything, but who was going to believe the ravings of religious fanatics?

"I heard from the debriefing team that Eric was a little shaky on the plane," she said.

"He was in the process of Suggesting a hijacker and lost the connection. But the passengers were never at risk." Scott knew he was stretching the truth. Although technically the last passenger had been put at risk by Eric's failure, the woman would have certainly been killed had Eric not kept the hijacker from pulling the trigger long enough for the takedown. "I noticed the break and took over."

She nodded. "That's what teams are for."

He looked at her warily. Normally she was more exacting. "To cover for one another, yes."

"The debriefing team described something else. An outburst. Is Eric all right?"

Scott regarded her again. Was that real concern in her voice? Though unlikely, it wasn't outside the realm of possibility. Since Team Ultra was her baby, she might have a sincere interest in the well-being of its members.

"Eric briefly lost his temper after we took down the last hijacker," Scott conceded. "But everything turned out for the best."

"I see." Her voice took a slight edge. "Let me ask the question another way: Would the Eighty-second Airborne accept that sort of behavior? How about the Rangers or Delta Force?"

Scott felt a pit in his stomach as the trap was sprung. She was dragging out his military history to prove a point. No other SPECWAR leader would allow such an outburst from one of its members. He'd underestimated her like so many other officers had done, and knew where the conversation was headed.

But for a moment, he entertained the notion of letting Ackart dismiss Eric from the team.

With the genetic modification, high-risk missions, and the twice-normal, four-year commitment, serving on Team Ultra was more dangerous than serving on any other Special Forces unit. Far more dangerous. He'd tried to keep Eric from applying, but the punk was always trying to prove himself. So Scott had applied, too . . . this when he'd planned to retire from the Rangers last year and reenter civilian life. He was tired of war, tired of violence, no matter how justified it might be. But there was no way in hell he'd let his little brother face the extreme risk alone.

Now Ackart was providing a legitimate way out. All he had to do was tell her that Eric wasn't fit for service, and that would be it. He could keep his brother safe. The notion made him feel lighter, like a huge weight had been lifted. Maybe he could convince Eric to give up the military completely after that, and maybe they could start a business together. Run a blues club, maybe even become musicians themselves. The corners of Scott's mouth turned up slightly at the thought, and then settled into a hard line again.

Who was he kidding? Eric would be devastated. Utterly fucking miserable. The guy relished his position on Team Ultra, felt like he was part of something truly special for the first time in his life. Scott couldn't take that away. He couldn't. Not when they'd both lost so much in their lives already. He felt his shoulders tighten again as he made his decision.

Of course, it meant he had to eat steaming shit right now, and do it with a fucking smile. "You're absolutely right, Major," Scott said. "The behavior is unacceptable. I guarantee it won't happen again."

"How can I be sure that Eric isn't revealing deeper tendencies? Nearly perfect is not acceptable when people's lives are at stake, Captain."

"I couldn't agree more."

"I'm not going to give Eric special treatment just because he's your brother, and neither should you."

Now she was just making it clear who was in charge. The woman never failed to live up to her reputation. "The problem is fixable," he said.

Ackart looked at him evenly. He could see her mind working, as though considering the consequence of forcing him to kick his own brother off the team. Finally, she cocked an eyebrow, her decision made. "He's got one more chance to shape up, Captain. One."

Scott knew Ackart was as good as her word. She was nothing if not consistent in her ultimatums. If Eric screwed up again, he'd be out. Scott would have to convince Eric of this, but as he crossed the lab to where Eric was jogging on the treadmill, he noticed that his brother's face was set like concrete, obviously ready to deflect anything he had to say.

Looking at Eric was like looking at a younger version of himself. Amber eyes, cleft chin. Eric had shaved his dark hair so short that Scott could see the white scar running above his left ear, a trophy he'd picked up as a kid while jumping a fence. Scott flashed a wry smile. No matter how old the two of them got, they always seemed to revert to childhood habits when shit hit the fan.

Scott reached the head of the treadmill, and the medical staff immediately took the hint and left them alone. "Are you going to tell me what's wrong?" he asked. After the outburst on the plane, he wasn't in the mood to play nice. Eric needed to man up and come clean.

"I told you, it's nothing," Eric said.

"Bullshit. I know something is going on."

"Always the older brother."

"I'm speaking as your team leader, not your brother. Ackart is threatening to kick you off the team."

"So let her."

Now Scott knew something was seriously wrong. Again, he was tempted to take Eric at his word, but knew his brother would sorely regret the knee-jerk bravado once whatever was bothering him passed. "You don't mean that."

"Maybe I do. I joined this team to get respect, and clearly don't get that from you."

"Every member of the team gets the respect they deserve."

"Nice dodge. Very politically correct for a team leader." Eric's lip curled while mentioning rank. "For you it's always been about rules and teams, everything by the numbers. But for me? How can I earn this supposed respect when you're talking to Ackart behind my back? Or when you're going out of your way to 'protect' me? Keeping me in your shadow is more like it."

"How can you demand respect when you're disrespecting other people with your actions? You're not the only one taking risks."

"What do you know about risk, Scott? You're the fucking Ghost."

The comment stung, as Eric knew it would. Scott was the genetic straight man—the Ghost—assigned to lead the team precisely because he hadn't been altered. That way, if something went wrong, if a common pathogen struck down the team, he would be left behind like a spirit to initiate an evac. In fact, he'd volunteered to stay clean of the genetic alteration. The procedure presented too many unknown variables. But sometimes, he felt like he wasn't pulling his weight.

"Are you listening to me, Eric?" Scott said, trying to guide the conversation back on track. "Ackart sees you as a liability. You don't get nine lives with her. You get one."

"Liability? That's a fucking laugh." Eric glared at him, and picked up his pace on the treadmill. His feet slapped the quickening belt as a few monitors beeped in more rapid succession. "This from the guy whose heart isn't in the fight. I can see you struggling, Scott. Every day I see it. You know you gotta pull the trigger, you know it's the only way to get the job done, yet part of you doesn't want to. A large part. If anything, *you're* the liability, not me."

"I didn't lose it today, Eric. You did."

"Piss off."

Scott looked at his brother, trying like hell to figure out the problem. The guy's face was a mask of rage, and his aggressive responses were way over the top. Growing up, Scott could tell by the way Eric looked at him when he was pleading for help even while he pushed Scott away. The pull-push between them was nothing new. Yet this was different. Eric's anguish seemed to come from a deeper place, seemed to possess his very soul. It was almost as though he knew he was about to do something terrible, yet couldn't muster the control to stop himself.

"You haven't been yourself lately," Scott whispered. "I just want to help."

"Start with an apology for riding me these past few days."

"If you weren't so goddamn stubborn, you'd know I was looking out for you."

Eric jumped off the treadmill, fists balled. "How many times do I have to tell you? I don't need you to look out for me!"

Scott stepped back in alarm. "Eric, don't."

Too late. Eric's eyes went white—and then Scott heard a thundering hiss of static in his head, and he knew that his own eyes had gone white, too. His brother was trying to control him.

Scott sank to his knees as the deafening sound of static thundered in his head, a drilling, swirling cacophony cut only by Eric's command: *Apologize to me, big brother.*

Cold sweat soaked Scott's body as every muscle trembled. He fought to control his own movement, but he felt like a marionette on a string. His lips twisted to form the words. "I'm sor . . . I'm sorrrr . . ."

He felt a pair of hands roughly grab his shoulders from behind and drag him away from Eric. The din of static in his head went silent. The connection was broken.

Scott sucked in a breath, then turned to see BB behind him.

The scientist glared at Eric. "What are you doing? You know better than to use your power on a member of the team!"

Eric stormed past them and away.

"You okay?" BB said, helping Scott to his feet. "That guy needs a *serious* time-out."

"I'm fine," Scott replied, muscles still trembling. Looking after Eric, he thought about how he and Eric had fought in the past, as all brothers did. But this crossed the line. Suggestion was an invasion of his very person.

What bothered him just as much was that Ackart's assessment of Eric may have been correct, and if that was the case, like it or not, he knew what he had to do.

Chapter 4

New Orleans

Located in a restored antebellum mansion, Magic Nights was the class act gentlemen's club of Bourbon Street. Mahogany wainscoting and flocked gold paper covered the walls. The old-fashioned, hand-carved bar with a large inset mirror in back was mahogany, as well. Even with an outrageous entry fee and high drink and food prices, the club was packed, filled with tourists and locals who sat at small tables or in areas filled with leather club chairs and sofas. The entertainment was a bevy of dancers wearing scanty if expensive costumes and performing on the bar.

Rebecca Dumas looked out one of the windows at the revelers on Bourbon Street. Most of them men in groups, they carried their takeaway drinks in plastic cups and peered into the doorways beneath cast-iron balconies as they tried to decide if they wanted to dine on fine cuisine, listen to jazz, or ogle the near-nude dancers, many of whom stood out on the sidewalks to entice men inside their clubs.

"Hey, *chère,* what you got for me tonight?"

Rebecca turned to face one of the regulars who kept Magic Nights afloat. Jean Baptiste Neff was a handsome Creole with dark eyes, full lips, and a charming manner. He was also a New Orleans City Councilmember. Some said he would run for mayor next election. If she didn't have other irons in the fire, and if there was something in it for her, Rebecca could make sure he won through use of her black arts.

"I got the same as always," she said, lowering her already husky voice. Raising her head so her carefully straightened waist-length black hair parted perfectly around her face, Rebecca gave him a smile she'd cultivated to seem mysterious. "You know I got the tastiest food, wildest music, and hottest girls in New Orleans."

As owner of the gentlemen's club, she made certain of it.

Sweeping her possessive gaze around her place, Rebecca made sure everything was as it should be.

"I was thinking of something more personal," Jean Baptiste said.

He swooped closer, wrapping an arm around Rebecca's back and pulling her tight enough that she could smell the whiskey on his breath. Already halfway drunk, he pressed his hard-on into the folds of tightly wrapped tiger-striped material around her hips. She was the only woman in the place—other than a few female tourists—who wasn't at least half-naked. She was no longer for sale.

"I already have a date for tonight, *cher.*" She scraped her nails along the seam of his pants and felt his erection stir. "But some lucky girl here will be glad to keep you company."

"None of them are you."

Rebecca laughed and stepped back. "Lucky for you—they're much safer than me."

"Maybe I don't want to play safe."

"I'll keep that in mind. Go on over to the bar, Jean Baptiste, and tell Antoine the first drink is on me." She signaled to the head bartender to alert him. "I'll find you an exotic playmate."

Rebecca kept up the sultry smile until he turned his back on her. Then she signaled to Yvon, a dancer whose kohl-dark skin shone with sweat. Though Yvon was in the midst of a table dance, she nodded. Yvon knew what to do.

Nearly every dancer she employed was on the floor and making money for her. And why not? What club could compete? Just as she had boasted to Jean Baptiste, she made sure she gave her customers the best of everything. If customers wanted more than dancers to entertain them, they could find it in the peep shows and private rooms upstairs.

When she turned back to the door and the incoming customers, *he* was there, making her heart beat a little more rapidly.

"Eric."

Very slowly, Rebecca allowed the smile to creep back onto her lips and up into her eyes. Poor, delusional Eric would think the smile was for him rather than for what he would do for her this night.

"God, I need you. Alone."

"Me, too, *cher.*" She signaled to a blonde in a diaphanous gown to act as hostess. "Let's go."

They cut through the club and left the back way, which took them into a fragrant moonlit courtyard filled with camellias, roses, and wisteria. A large fountain sat in its center and the footpath was of glass mosaic design. Rebecca owned not only the business but the building itself—a gift from a rich, reckless former lover, who'd been killed in a car accident of his own making. Her personal quarters lay to one side of the club away from Bourbon Street, and a flower-bedecked cast-iron balcony overlooked the garden.

They ran up the stairs, and at the landing she swung directly into Eric's arms. Cradling his head with its close-cropped hair, she licked at the cleft in his chin and waited for him to kiss her. When he didn't, she looked deeply into his troubled gaze.

"What's wrong, cher?"

"Nothing."

But she could see that there was. "Something bad happen today?"

He shrugged, and she curved a palm around his cheek. "You can tell me anything. You know that, yes?"

For a moment she thought he was going to stay bottled up, keep whatever it was to himself.

Then he made a sound of disgust and said, "There's a chance I'll be kicked off the team."

Rebecca stiffened. That could ruin everything. "What happened?"

"We ran a mission this afternoon, and I got distracted. I don't know what's up with me. I just can't seem to focus lately. I'm losing my edge." He took a big breath and added, "Scott called me on it, and—"

"Your brother?" Though Rebecca knew exactly what was going on, she sounded indignant. "He did this to you?" Things were spinning out of her control.

"To be fair, Scott's doing what a team leader should."

"It sounds like it's just not working out anymore between you and your brother." Rebecca reinforced the wedge she'd been driving between them for weeks now. "He wants to control you."

"He says he wants what's best for me."

"But he never asks what *you* want, does he? He tells you what to do and when you make a mistake . . ."

Eric hung his head and let go a sigh of defeat. "Maybe it's better that I quit on my own."

"No, no, don't say that. Family is all-important." At least for a little while longer, until she had what she wanted. "Let's go inside. I'll make you feel better and then you'll go back and fix things."

Eric's mind was no longer his own, but it wasn't his brother who was controlling him. He had no idea that she'd caused him to lose focus—no idea of what she would have him do—or he would want to kill her, Rebecca was certain. She was going to have to finish it now—bind him to her completely. At first she'd been cautious, had juggled getting what she wanted with being discreet. But now that Scott was aware that Eric was no longer himself, she had no time to waste. She'd already made up the potion. It was lacking only one ingredient.

Eric drew her into her bedroom, a purple and deep red womb of velvets and satins. He'd never commented on the unusual décor, not even on her altar, which sat to one side. The first time she'd brought him up here, he'd checked out the plaster images of Catholic saints with their Voodoo counterparts, the black cross candles, the pots of herbs and vials of blessed oils. He hadn't seemed put off, not even by her collection of books on all types of magic.

Perhaps her practicing New Orleans Voodoo had seemed innocent to a man who'd gained extraordinary powers after receiving the DNA of a centuries-old mummy; powers Rebecca would love to have for herself.

Little did he know the things she'd accomplished to meet her own needs and those of others who'd come to her as a priestess in the dark arts.

As she kissed Eric, she pulled his shirt free of his waistband, then unfastened his zipper. He was crazy for her, for the things she did to him, which was why she'd been able to control him so easily. Thankfully for Rebecca, he was an attractive man with a body any woman would lust after. Her pleasure this night would be boundless. When she dipped below the band of his briefs, he sprang hard and long into her hand.

He found the fastener at her waist and unhooked it, then tugged. Rebecca let go of him and turned and turned and turned until she was unwrapped of the length of cloth. Oddly pale for someone with Creole heritage, she stood nude but for her body jewelry—a fine gold belt studded with topaz, topaz-studded nipple rings, and a matching ring piercing her clitoris. She knew Eric was fascinated with these ornaments, and that gave her more pleasure than the feel of him pushing himself inside her.

Not that he—or any man she wanted power over—would ever know the truth of the matter. She'd learned to play the game before she'd bled for the first time. But it had taken her many more years and a growing proficiency with Voodoo to learn to control men. Since then she'd used her skills to pay back the men who'd treated her badly.

"You need special attention tonight." Rebecca ran her hand open-palmed over his chest, down to the arrow of dark hair below. "Lie back on the bed and let me see to you."

Eric did as she demanded, giving up control with a groan.

Moving to her altar, Rebecca poured some of the special potion into a goblet, then ran a long red-lacquered fingernail along the spine of the book under a black candle. *Vampyre* had proved fascinating—and essential—reading. She handed him the goblet.

"Have a sip, but go slow. It's very strong and I want you to last."

A prepared oil over his body readied him for sex. She knew he wanted to take her hard and fast, but she wouldn't let him ignore this part of the ritual. She silently prayed to the *loa*—or spirits akin to Voodoo saints—as she worked. When he glistened in the moonlight, she climbed on top of him, let his oiled cock slide up inside her, and coaxed him to use the nipple and clit rings to excite her, so that her vaginal juices thickened and flowed around him. She came without him, froze long enough to let the fluids coat him, then slid away and teased him with her mouth, gathering her own essence with her tongue before lifting the goblet and filling her mouth with some of the potion.

With the final ingredient in place, she leaned over him for an openmouthed kiss that transferred the fluid from her mouth to his. Groaning, he took in every drop and tugged at her.

Rebecca smiled and slid her body back into place over his. She would be more than happy to pleasure him.

He was hers now to do with what she wanted.

After spending half the night finishing them both off until neither could rouse any further sexual interest, Rebecca was eager to send Eric on his way and set her plan in motion.

"You need to do something for me."

"Anything. I'll do anything for you."

His eyes already had gone flat like a zombie's. And his tone was lifeless. Not that he was dead. She simply wanted to use him, not kill him. He'd always been kind to her.

"I know you will."

She brushed her lips over his, then reached for a leather pouch containing a specially prepared gris-gris. Handing it to him, she told him what he needed to do.

"I'll do anything you want, Rebecca."

She smiled and sent him on his way.

After showering to get his scent off her, she slipped into a short leopard-print robe and matching mules and let herself out onto the balcony of the inner courtyard, where she stopped for a moment to take in the fragrant night. If only the Bourbon Street noises coming from the other side of the balcony didn't remind her of where she was, of where she had come from.

But things were about to change.

Approaching another room where the French doors were open to the night, she whispered, "Are you awake?"

"Yes. Come in."

The room was dark but she knew every inch by heart. She'd been spending so much time here lately. But not much longer. Soon the prison of a room would be a thing of the past.

Sitting down on the bed with Danton, she despaired when she noted how thin he'd gotten, how his dark hair clung to his wet forehead. His caramel-colored skin had a grayish tone and he seemed both feverish and chilled at the same time.

Rebecca wrapped herself around him. "Soon," she whispered.

"Good."

Her brother pulled a bony arm up out of the covers and wrapped it around her, then kissed the top of her head.

Rebecca's chest squeezed tight at the thought of losing the only person who had ever truly cared for her. She would find the courage for him as he had done for her so long ago when their stepfather Paul had raped her on a regular basis, and their mother had turned a blind eye to what was happening because she didn't want trouble.

Danton was younger than she, but teenage boys had incredible growth spurts, and the moment thirteen-year-old Danton could look Paul in the eye, he had beat him senseless. He'd threatened him, too, had told Paul that death awaited him if the bastard ever touched her again. Paul hadn't. And she and Danton had been inseparable ever since.

Except, of course, for his hospital stays.

The doctors had tried everything to fight her brother's leukemia, including chemotherapy and a bone marrow transplant. Hers. It should have worked, but it hadn't. A desperate Rebecca had been willing to do anything in her power to save him including turning to Voodoo, which worked for a while. With his remission, she'd realized the true power of her faith.

But now, five years later, Danton was sick once more. For some reason, Voodoo failed her this time. The disease was ravaging her brother, and she was desperate to save him.

As he drifted away, his breathing going deeper, Rebecca felt her eyes sting with tears she could not afford to shed. She had to keep her wits about her. She couldn't allow emotions to take over. She was doing this for Danton, to save him. As soon as he fell asleep, she would leave to execute the next part of her plan.

"Soon," she whispered, stroking his damp brow. "I promise you, everything is about to change."

Chapter 5

"I can't believe you're thinking about keeping Eric on the team after what he pulled today," Jonas said, his Swedish accent edged with frustration.

"I heard you the first time," Scott told him.

Jonas was lying on a specially reinforced weight bench doing a smooth series of chest presses. There were several large black iron plates on either side of the barbell he was lifting. They totaled twelve hundred pounds, the weight he worked out with to break a sweat. His max was seventeen hundred pounds. The man was a blond, seven-foot-tall import from *Fallskarmsjagare*—the Swedish equivalent of the Airborne Rangers—who'd been recruited to Team Ultra after his international training at Fort Benning. An ex–Olympic powerlifter, he'd no doubt been chosen because he was used to the strain that feats of incredible strength could put on his body. The only family he had was an aging mother and father, whom he'd hesitantly left behind in Sweden to train in the United States.

"We keep Eric, we're headed for trouble," Jonas said, refusing to drop the subject.

"I said I heard you."

Eric had stormed off after the fight, and Scott had let him go. The guy needed to cool off, and a night on the town was just the thing. He hoped so, anyway.

"Jonas doesn't mean any harm, boss. He just thinks Eric has lost his grip on things," Drew said, holding up his arms. Where his hands should have been were small, static clouds of gray mist. "Lost his grip. Get it?"

Where Jonas looked like he belonged in the Special Forces, Drew wore black turtleneck sweaters despite the bayou heat and looked more like an art school loner. Pale and lean, he was nevertheless an ex–Navy SEAL who'd seen action all over the world. He was divorced, and carried a photo of his three-year-old daughter in his wallet that he liked to show off every chance he got. The little girl had a full head of curly brown hair, and her father's dark eyes.

"Quite the comedian," Scott said. Although he appreciated Drew's attempt to lighten his mood, the very mention of his brother made his stomach go tight. It never failed—after they argued, no matter whose fault it was, he felt like shit. "On my mark, Drew." He palmed the stopwatch hanging around his neck, then clicked a button with his thumb. "Go."

Drew nodded—and then his face whirlpooled along with his body and he dissolved into a gray cloud as a faint odor of brimstone filled the room. For a moment, smoky Drew hung in midair about two feet off the ground. The next, he flowed quickly through a series of dinner plate–sized rings mounted on poles set in a zigzag pattern on the training room floor. When Drew reached the ring at the middle of the course, large fans set on either side clicked on. Powerful, thirty-miles-per-hour winds buffeted the gray mist, but didn't disperse it. On the contrary, Drew only seemed to move faster with the resistance.

"Nothing but trouble," Jonas grunted between sets, voice edged with menace now. "You're one of the best captains I've had, Scott, but your brother is your Achilles' Heel."

Scott ignored Jonas as he monitored Drew's progress through the obstacle course. Speed and precision were top-notch, and there weren't any apparent side effects from Drew's ultrahuman powers. Good. But as much as Scott tried to concentrate on the task at hand, he couldn't help wondering if Ackart was right.

Maybe Eric's rebelliousness hadn't reared its head in the military until now because they'd never served on the same unit before. Maybe Eric's behavior this morning was a harbinger of things to come.

If so, it would be a natural progression. They'd been abandoned by their parents as young kids, and ever since Eric had been trying to prove he didn't need caring for, even though he craved it much of the time. First their father, who'd left the family when Scott was only two years old, before Eric was born. And then their mother, when Scott had been twelve and Eric had been ten. She'd been a nurse hooked on pharmaceuticals and couldn't take care of herself, much less two boys. Growing up in the North Carolina child welfare system probably had been the better of two shitty options under the circumstances. Even though they'd lived with separate foster families, Scott took over the role of parent in many ways until they both joined the military at eighteen.

But the true turning point for them had been the day they'd woken up on a cold Saturday in October to learn that their mother had left them without a word. He and Eric had spent hours pacing the empty house as cruel reality sank in, repeatedly going back to their mother's room with its empty closet and open, emptied dresser drawers.

Not knowing what else to do, Scott had just about mustered the courage to ask the kind old woman who lived next door for help when Eric bolted out the front door past him.

"Eric!" Scott yelled, but his brother didn't answer, didn't even throw a look over his shoulder. He scampered across the street like a jackrabbit and disappeared into an empty lot choked with five-foot-high long grass and brambles.

Scott took off after him into the field. As he ran, the long grass, wet from rain the night before, slapped water across his face, chest, and thighs. His brother was quick. He could barely keep up with the yellow T-shirt and blue jeans bobbing far ahead through the waving grass.

And then suddenly Eric disappeared. Scott cried out in alarm, thinking his brother had left him forever, too. But a few frantic steps later, he nearly tripped over Eric, who was sitting in the mud, arms crossed over his knees, crying.

"Eric," Scott said, panting. "Where the heck are you going?"

His brother hadn't answered, only shook his head. His cheeks were streaked with tears. His white socks were riddled with stickers.

Scott plopped down into the cold mud next to him. When he did, Eric looked at him with an expression dulled by confusion and pain. "Why did Mom leave?" he whispered. "Did we make her mad?"

The question made Scott's eyes well with tears, but he fought them back. He had to stay in control. He didn't want to scare Eric more than he already was.

It was just the two of them now.

At that moment, a feeling slid into his heart like a dead bolt. He knew he would do everything he could to protect his brother from now on.

"I don't know why Mom left us, but I'll always be your brother, okay?" Scott said, wrapping his arm across Eric's narrow shoulders and holding him tight. Eric hugged back as though he were holding on for dear life. "I'll always be your brother, and I'll always be there for you, no matter what . . ."

"How's the Mist Man doing?" Jonas called, breaking

Scott from his reverie. The big man had moved on to squat thrusts, and was lifting the equivalent of a Volkswagen bus on his shoulders.

"So far, so good," Scott replied, not taking the bait. He knew Jonas wanted to keep pressing him about Eric.

Drew made it to the end of the course, gray mist flowing down onto a single spot as though filling an invisible container in the shape of his body, and then with a miragelike shimmer solidifiing back into his human form.

"Time," Scott said, clicking his stopwatch.

"Nice trick with the fans," Drew said, panting with exertion. "You trying to mess up my run?"

Scott smirked. "Minute and a half. Personal best for you."

Drew nodded, and said, "Jonas, I heard what you said about Eric, and I completely disagree. He should stay."

Jonas breathed through a few more reps, then let the barbell fall back onto its brackets with a *clang*. "You're nuts, Smokey," he grunted, wiping his armpits with a white towel. "We can't afford a loose cannon on the team. It's too dangerous."

"If Eric needs to act out, let's give him a few more rounds with the heavy bag. But we've worked well together so far."

"That so?" Jonas said, standing, his bulk another wall in the room. "The next time he screws up, I'll let you take the bullet."

"Enough, both of you," Scott said. "Now."

Drew and Jonas immediately stood down. They may have had the opportunity for open team discourse, but when it came down to it, they knew who was in charge. But this wasn't good. The question of Eric's departure was driving a wedge between his men.

"We give Eric another shot," Scott told Jonas and Drew, his tone leaving no room for question. The promise he'd made to Eric had meant a lot of things over the years, not the least of which was joining Team Ultra despite his misgivings. But the simple truth was that he wanted the team to work because he believed Eric was good for the team, and the team for Eric.

"And if he flies off the handle again?" Jonas asked.

"I'll can him myself," Scott said, feeling his stomach tighten further. "You have my word on that."

Chapter 6

The faint scent of incense from that morning's Mass reminded Leah of burning copal as she took a seat in the tiny Pueblo Catholic church with its whitewashed adobe walls and viga ceiling. She stared at the altar with its crucifix and behind that, the painting of the baby Jesus holding a peyote button. Amazing how various peoples adapted their religious beliefs when necessary or to suit themselves.

On the surface, the members of the Santa Maria Pueblo were Catholic. But that didn't mean they couldn't pay tribute to their old gods or look to a shaman for their healing. They believed in archetypal deities as visionary beings and in relationships between man and nature and plants and animals. They took whatever good they could find to believe in and made it work for them.

So why didn't that work for her?

A stooped old widow dressed in black lit candles at a small side altar to the Virgin of Guadalupe. Undoubtedly the candles were tributes to people the woman had once loved. Dead people. People she believed were in some better place now.

Leah's mind drifted to her father and Gabe, to the night before their lives had ended . . .

"Chili again?" Gabe complained as she set the coffee can on the grate over the fire.

Leah glared at him. "If you don't like it, then you cook."

"Guys set up tents and gather dry wood and build the campfires. You know, *man* things. Girls are supposed to provide the food—hopefully something other than chili once in a while."

"*Da-a-ad,* Gabe's being sexist again!" Torturing her was his favorite thing.

Their father unzipped the tent and stepped out. "Do I have to referee or can we just enjoy this beautiful night?"

Dad was right—the night was beautiful. The sky was clear and lit with a full moon and a million stars. The perfect night for camping. So perfect they might take their sleeping bags out of the tent and count stars to fall asleep. Too bad Mom hated the outdoors and never came on adventures with them. She didn't know what she was missing.

Leah stirred the contents of her disposable pot. "Gabe's not eating with us."

"Hey, I didn't say that!"

"He's going to go find himself a snake to cook."

"I'm going to find one that has your name on it, Le-e-a-ah."

Leah squealed and launched herself at him. Laughing, Gabe caught her flailing fists and held them away. The next thing Leah knew, Dad was pulling her off her brother and swooping her into a big one-armed hug. He plunked them down next to Gabe and put his free arm around her brother so they were all connected. Gabe might torture her, but she knew he loved her as much as she loved him.

Although she missed Mom, Leah had never felt happier than she did this night. After dinner, she was going to . . .

Returning to the present, Leah blinked.

After dinner what?

Stemming a rising sense of panic, she tried to concentrate, but she couldn't remember what she'd been thinking about. Or what they'd done. She'd gone over that night hundreds of times over the years. Why couldn't she remember now?

"I thought I saw you come in here."

Startled, Leah looked up. Javier Estes stood there, his weathered leather face cracking in a soft smile aimed at her.

"May I sit with you?"

"Of course." Agitated, she slid over and he set himself down next to her, the old wood creaking at his weight.

"Something's bothering you."

"I was thinking about Gabe and Dad and me when we were happy together, and the memory sort of . . . drifted off."

He thought about it for a moment. "Perhaps that's the price of magic for you."

"What are you talking about?"

"Harnessing magic exacts a toll. Everyone who uses it has to pay the price."

"And the price is losing memory?"

"It's different for everyone, and whether it's black or white magic would make a difference, as well. You were attempting to heal through magic and apparently you made a cosmic trade of something you loved. Your memories of your father and brother must be very precious to you."

"I don't want to give them up!"

"You're not ready to give them up, because you don't really want to involve yourself yet."

Memories and a few photos were all she had left of Gabe and Dad. "Maybe I never will be ready."

"Not if you want to live in the past. But you have a future, too, Leah." He turned dark eyes on her and looked so deep into her that she shifted in her seat. "An important future. Talking might help free you from pain so that you can move on."

That's what people always wanted her to do. Talk. Only they wouldn't understand how she felt—perhaps wouldn't believe—so why bother? Even though she suspected Javier might be the exception to the rule, she couldn't bring herself to really open up with him.

She stared down at her palm, at the burn scar, which looked like a triangle inside a square. Perhaps it was because she'd ignored the warnings she'd felt in that cave and had defied the evil that dwelled there. She'd called down a curse not only on her father and brother but also on herself.

Perhaps it would always be like this for her . . . living in limbo.

"I think it's time for me to leave, maybe go home," Leah said.

"Are you sure your work here is done?"

"Aren't you?"

"There is a reason for everything, *chica.*"

"Like my being there for Isabel?"

Leah couldn't keep the bitter tone from her voice. She couldn't save anyone. Not her father or brother from death. Not her mother from giving up on life and waiting to die to join her husband in some heaven that might not exist. Not Isabel Yepa from the earthly nightmare of rape.

"Perhaps the reason was not for you to save Isabel," Javier was saying, "but to find a way to save yourself."

Her smile felt brittle. "Save myself from what?" Helping people in pain might take away some of her own, but she couldn't even do that.

"Only you know the answer. And unless you want to talk about it–"

"I've said all I want."

How could she tell him her thoughtlessness had provoked the attack on her brother and father?

How could she give voice to the knowledge that she was the one who should have died that day, not Dad and Gabe?

How could she admit that she had been the one to break her mother's heart, leaving Mom with nothing but her religion and a wish to die?

Dad's and Gabe's death would always weigh on Leah. They hadn't just been killed, they'd been slaughtered—and not by some escaped convict as the authorities had believed. She'd come to the conclusion that the thing that had killed them hadn't been human. She tried thinking of them as being in a better place—the blue sky version of her trance—but every time she tried, she failed.

"As you see fit," said Javier.

They sat in silence for a moment. If ever there was a good and just man, it was Javier. He wanted to help anyone who needed it. Even her. No matter how hard she tried, she just couldn't talk about it with him.

"What does it all mean, Javier? I've been seeking answers for years." She'd wanted to know what kind of monster had killed Dad and Gabe and what could have stopped it. "I've studied various belief systems from different parts of the world. I know there's something to them all, but I simply can't relate myself to anything I've learned."

"Because you haven't really learned what you need to. You intellectualize. Rather than involving yourself, you've lived your life as an observer."

A more informed observer than most. She felt things, knew things about people that they didn't have to tell her. Strong emotions from others flowed through her, just as Isabel's had. The phenomenon had flickered like a candle as she'd approached puberty. And it had only grown stronger over the years. Her studies suggested she was an empath, which meant she could feel things outside her own skin. The pain people carried with them. The worries. The fear. She also sensed the presence of evil or danger. Not that she'd been able to use these abilities for good, as she'd hoped.

She asked, "What else should I do other than observe? Fail another Isabel Yepa?"

"You're not a failure, Leah. You're simply lost. You need to find a path with purpose. You need to take a leap of faith, *chica.*"

Faith. She'd spent half her life studying the two sides of religion and magic—good and evil—but still she couldn't make the concepts work for her.

"Easier said than done, Javier. I've tried. I swear I have."

"There's one thing you haven't tried," he said and she tightened inside even before he finished it. "You need to face your own fears."

Leah wondered just what it would take to make herself do so.

Chapter 7

At two thirty in the morning Scott wandered the dimly lit halls of the sleeping base, unable to sleep himself. Other than the occasional wandering research tech, he was completely alone. After working out with Drew and Jonas in the gym, he'd changed into a pair of dark blue sweats and a charcoal gray shirt with the emblem of Team Ultra on the breast—a flying black dragon with *TU* in white block letters under the wings.

Team members were free to sleep either at their own apartments or in the barracks on base. Immediately following an op, Scott usually chose the latter in case a team member had a problem, physical or psychological. It just so happened that Drew and Jonas were staying the night, too, though they split their time more evenly between the base and the outside world.

Reaching past the holstered .45-caliber SIG Sauer at his hip, Scott pulled a PDA from his pocket. All Team Ultra members had a GPS chip in their gear so their movements could be monitored during an op. He wasn't supposed to use the chip to find members during off time, but he rationalized bending the rules this once on Eric's behalf.

Bottom line, he was convinced if he found Eric tonight and spoke to him alone—away from Ackart, Drew, and Jonas—they could work things out like they always had growing up. And once they did that, they could meet with Ackart together at a decent hour and settle things.

Scott flipped on his PDA. *I'm not giving up on you, little brother.*

Using a stylus, he opened a pull-down menu, scrolled to Eric's name on the team member list, and activated the ENGAGE command. A satellite map of New Orleans and vicinity came up with Eric's location appearing as a roving yellow blip. Only Eric wasn't in the city.

He was on base.

In the lab.

Scott's dread returned, deep and sharp. There was no reason for Eric to be there alone, much less at this time of night. He didn't know what Eric was up to, but he knew he had to put a stop to it. For both their sakes.

Sprinting down winding corridors, Scott quickly made it across the base and entered the lab. The mammoth room was eerie in darkness, with the only illumination coming from the full moon that shone through several transoms in the ceiling.

Scott scanned the lab, peering through silver light and blue shadows, and found no sign of Eric until he looked in the last place he expected his brother to be—at the door of the Plexiglas chamber. He was dressed in dark slacks and a gray silk shirt, obviously for a night on the town.

"Eric!" he shouted.

Eric didn't seem to hear him. His face remained slack as he opened the door of the chamber and shuffled slowly inside. The door swung closed behind him and locked with an echoing click. It was designed to open from the outside only to prevent scientists who somehow became infected from running out in panic and infecting the rest of the base.

"Eric, can you hear me?" Scott tried again.

His dread grew as Eric continued to ignore him and moved to one of the long, thick hoses that hung from the ceiling and fed into the top of the glass case that held the mummified remains. He grabbed the hose and twisted sharply, detaching it, and then pulled a small brown leather pouch from inside his jacket's breast pocket. The pouch was tied with a thin red drawstring.

Loosening the drawstring, Eric emptied the powdery contents of the bag into the glass case, and then reattached the tube. The swirling, circulating air within the case immediately turned the powder into a sort of thick red fog, which obscured the mummy from view. Eric took a step back.

Reaching the front of the chamber, Scott pounded on it with his fist. His muted, thudding blows were ineffective against the thick Plexiglas. "Eric! Hey!"

Finally, Eric looked past the glass case to meet his gaze. But there was no awareness there, almost as if his brother had been Suggested himself.

Scott moved around to the door of the chamber. He had no idea what the red mist was, and knew walking into the chamber might contaminate him. But he couldn't leave his brother in there alone. Eric was acting outside himself—that much was obvious—and needed help. Once inside, Scott knew he could use his PDA to call for backup.

He reached the door and grabbed the handle. "Eric, I'm coming in—"

Suddenly, the glass case exploded with a thundering crash.

Scott reared back into an equipment console as glass shards peppered the inside walls of the chamber and the entire space flash-filled with the red mist. His brother was swallowed from view.

"ERIC!" Scott yelled, knowing he couldn't open the door now without risking widespread contamination. He turned to the equipment console, scanned it, then slapped his palm down onto a black mushroom-shaped button. Emergency generators snapped on, flooding the lab with harsh white light as an alarm began to blare.

Reinforcements would be here in a matter of minutes. But he wasn't about to sit back and do nothing until they did.

He ran to the door and peered inside the chamber, but couldn't see though the swirling red mist. Suddenly, the flat of a hand slapped the Plexiglas in front of his face, causing the entire chamber to shake. Startled, he jumped back. Thinking it was his brother, Scott's heart leaped, but then he realized the hand didn't belong to his brother at all; it was far too big and the skin was chalky brown.

It's not possible, Scott thought. But part of him knew it was very possible. His men had adopted terrifying new powers, defied every reality he took for granted, achieved the impossible. So why couldn't this be true as well?

The hand disappeared, then reappeared a moment later as a fist, which slammed into the Plexiglas with a reverberating boom.

Scott stepped back and drew the SIG, aiming at where he thought the center of mass of the obscured figure might be. The fist struck the Plexiglas again, and this time a series of large cracks spidered from the point of impact with the sound of fingernails being dragged across a blackboard. Scott retreated farther, holding the pistol steady, when the door exploded.

He ducked as chunks of thick Plexiglas sailed over his head and ricocheted off the lab wall behind him with a series of thuds, and then he saw a figure appear from the red mist.

A man. Huge. Six and a half feet tall, layered with lean muscle and the chalky brown flesh he'd seen before. His head swiveled on a corded neck, whipping long, shoulder-length black hair to and fro, as though he'd just woken from a deep sleep and was trying to clear his mind. His hands were hooked into claws, and there was a gaping hole in the rippling muscles of his torso on the left side, like his body had been patched together and a large piece was still missing. Through the hole, Scott could see gleaming white ribs over a purple lung that inflated with every intake of breath.

Scott stared in disbelief as the man stood a good twenty yards from him, looking around at the unfamiliar surroundings with hooded red eyes, obviously still dazed but radiating incredible strength and power. Scott knew if the man had been at full capacity, he could have broken through the door of the Plexiglas chamber with even greater ease.

His mind reeled. Had Eric somehow reconstituted the desiccated remains of the mummy? If so, what possible motivation could he have?

Eric . . .

Behind the massive figure and through the hazy remains of the red mist, Scott saw Eric lying on his back. His brother's chest bristled with glass shards from the exploding case, and blood seeped across his gray shirt.

Scott's adrenaline kicked into overdrive. He had to get to his brother. "You! Get on the goddamn floor or I will open fire!"

The man canted his head, either not understanding or not caring to obey the command.

Scott squared the assailant in his sights. "On the floor! Now!"

Before he could issue another order, a research tech ran into the lab through a side door a few feet from the destroyed chamber. The tech was a portly man with small round glasses and greasy black hair. He must have been close by, just down the hall. Only seconds had passed since Scott had triggered the alarm, and the base security team was at least another twenty seconds from responding.

"What the heck is going on?" the tech asked.

"Keep back!" Scott said.

The tech nodded, about to comply, when the pale man lunged with such speed that Scott didn't see him actually move. The tech didn't have time to react, either. He simply stared wide-eyed at the figure that suddenly loomed over him, and then the man whipped a backhand past the tech's throat, opening a horizontal, spouting gash below the Adam's apple.

Scott opened fire with his SIG.

The .45-caliber slugs struck the assailant's broad back, punching half-dollar-sized craters into the flesh with thick slapping sounds—but he didn't seem to notice as he clutched the gagging tech by the arms and pressed his mouth against the gushing throat wound, taking several long swallows.

Scott felt the bile rise in his throat as he kept firing. *You've got to be fucking kidding me . . .*

The man chewed into the wound as he continued to drink, causing the tech to convulse horribly. And then Scott noticed that the man's flesh was getting darker—from chalky brown to reddish umber. With each gulping swallow, the flesh color darkened and transformed until it appeared almost olive.

Scott's heart hammered in his chest. What the hell was happening? He witnessed the scene, but his rational mind simply couldn't make sense of it.

He pulled the trigger as fast as he could, rounds striking home to no effect, and then the clip was empty. He didn't have a spare.

"Yo, Captain!"

The voice came from the main door of the lab to his left. Scott risked a look, and sure enough, Drew and

Jonas had responded quickly to the alarm, each in a T-shirt and sweats and wielding MP5s.

"I'm out!" Scott yelled to them, holstering the SIG.

Jonas tossed him his MP5 since he would attack using physical strength, anyway. Scott caught the automatic weapon with one hand and used his other to rack a round into the chamber. He fired the MP5 full-auto, thunder slamming into his ears, punching more holes in the towering figure's back as the clip emptied in seconds. But still the rounds had no effect.

"What the hell?" Drew said, obviously unable to believe what he was seeing.

The man continued to drink blood from the tech's throat, the overflow running from the corners of his mouth.

"Take him down!" Scott yelled.

Without hesitation, Drew whirlpooled into gray mist and streamed high into the air, arcing left in a flanking maneuver as Jonas charged directly in.

Leaving his men to their assault, Scott ran forward, leaped over the jagged remains of the chamber door, and slid to Eric's side. His brother was panting, and his shirt was completely soaked with blood.

"I'm going to get you out of here," Scott told him, trying to control the rising panic in his voice. He clutched his brother's cold hand, and then turned to monitor the progress of his team. Drew was streaming very close to the assailant, a twenty-foot-long snake of mist passing above his head in an attempt to stage a surprise attack from behind.

Something about the maneuver felt strange. Felt wrong.

"Drew! Stop!" Scott yelled. But it was too late.

As though sensing Drew's presence, the man dropped the pale body of the tech, looked up with a blood-drenched face, and shot out an arm, breaking the plane of mist with his fingertips.

With a slavering shriek that Scott would take to his grave, Drew immediately reconstituted, his physical body stretched hideously to conform to the elongated shape that he'd been as a cloud. Scott couldn't see anything recognizable in the terrible form, only a mottled, quivering mass that hung midair for a moment before the overtaxed flesh ruptured in a shower of viscera that splattered the lab floor.

Where the fuck was backup?!

"Jonas! Fall back, that's an order!" Scott cried, but the Swede was already committed to his attack, roaring in anger and horror at witnessing his friend's death.

The assailant stood to meet him and the two slammed into each other, a clash of titans, locking hands with interlaced fingers. Jonas was approximately the same height and musculature as the man, and they pushed and pulled at each other, seemingly an even match, until the man shoved Jonas's hands back over his forearms, sending spears of bone through the flesh at his wrists. Jonas screamed and dropped to his knees. Taking advantage, the man trapped Jonas's head in the crook of his arm and then wrenched it around with a slingshot snap so that Jonas's chin rested between his shoulder blades.

The assailant didn't let Jonas go once he was dead. Instead, he slashed Jonas's jugular with his ring as he had done to the tech, and began to drink.

With the new influx of blood, Scott saw the hole in the man's torso—the one that revealed his rib cage and lungs—begin to iris closed, as did the dozen bullet wounds in its back. With each gulping swallow, the hole and wounds cinched smaller and smaller until they disappeared altogether.

Scott pushed down his feelings of horror and grief. There was no time to mourn his fallen comrades. He had to get Eric out of there.

Scott slung the MP5's strap around his neck, then pulled Eric's left arm across his own shoulder blades and hoisted his brother to his feet as he stood.

"Eric, we have to go!"

Eric moaned, unable to help, deadweight against him. Hauling his brother along, Scott shuffled across the lab toward the door as the man continued to feed on Jonas behind him, the wet tearing sounds echoing against the metal walls, almost too hideous to bear.

Scott kept his eyes on the door of the lab, their portal to freedom and safety. They were almost there, only thirty feet to go, when suddenly the assailant loomed before them. He lunged for Eric, but Scott pivoted, a move in some terrible dance, so that his arm was grabbed instead; it felt like he'd been caught in the gears of a machine. And then the sharp ring slashed his chest and the man pressed his mouth against the bloody wound.

Fear exploded through Scott as he struggled in vain to free himself. Fear and terrible guilt. He was going to die, but worse, he'd failed to protect Eric.

Scott screamed in agony as he felt a snaking tongue probe the edges of the wound and then slide into his chest cavity.

"Drop him, now!"

Scott felt himself whisked around as the man spun toward the voice. His vision was blurred, but he could make out the phalanx of security guards that had arrived at the lab door. They were clad in black, and wielded MP5s. Major Ackart was at the forefront. She'd issued the command.

"I said drop him!" she yelled again.

Scott was then tossed aside and slammed against the floor as the security guards opened fire.

Thundering automatic chatter filled the lab. The man stood straight, arms slightly away from his sides and palms up in what looked like a posture of supplication.

Every other round the security guards fired was a green tracer. Scott could see the emerald filaments streaking from guards to assailant, and then he noticed that every bullet struck its target, even the rounds that flew wide came back in a tight arc like they were meteors sucked in by the gravitational pull of a planet.

Thousands of glowing green filaments boomed and flickered as bullets impacted the large body that absorbed the metal without so much as a flinch—when the man suddenly exploded into what Scott could only describe as a bolt of black lightning that arced up through one of the transoms and disappeared.

The stench of cordite strong in the air, Scott crawled on his elbows toward his brother, leaving behind a thick swath of blood on the floor. His chest burned like it was on fire.

"I'm right here, little brother," he rasped, clutching Eric's hand. "Don't worry, I'm right here . . ."

Chapter 8

Fear coursed through her veins as Rebecca peered out over St. Louis Cemetery No. 2 with its aboveground burial sites, necessitated by New Orleans's high water table. The full moon cast a silver-blue glow over tombs, vaults, and mausoleums—brick covered with crumbling plaster. Most structures were surrounded by decorative rusty ironwork and topped with crosses or statues, making them look like strange little houses. The rows upon rows of houselike tombs resembled streets, the reason New Orleans cemeteries were called cities of the dead.

Upon entering the cemetery grounds, Rebecca had taken a twisted path that dead-ended at a decaying family tomb, which sat canted to one side on its base. This part of the cemetery was eerie and deserted enough for her purposes. Even the gangs who frequented the cemeteries, waiting for tourists to make the mistake of coming here alone, avoided this area.

Not that they would dare bother her, in any event.

She'd chosen this particular tomb for its size and the fact that it had been easy to enter—apparently someone had recently broken into it. Only two members of the family rested in peace at this time, leaving plenty of room for her Voodoo altar.

Rebecca covered one of the coffins with a black cloth embroidered in real gold and on the altar set candles, a cauldron, a chalice, a rattle, and a drum. Clothed in a tight red dress, she wore ju-ju around her neck for protection—a necklace made up of the skeleton of a snake.

Closing her eyes for a moment, she concentrated on Eric. He'd had enough time to return to the base. Getting a sense of him, she looked through his dazed eyes. The city of the dead held no horrors greater than what Rebecca saw.

The creature with a soldier's head in the crook of his arm . . . the chin rested between his shoulder blades . . . the creature drinking from the jugular.

Knowing what he was, she trembled. Vampires were creatures with a thirst for blood, but she hadn't imagined he would be this savage. Part of her wanted to negate the binding spell and forget her plan. Only she couldn't do that. The vampire might be harder to control than she'd ever imagined, but she had no choice. She would use her Voodoo to find a way. He held the elixir of life for her brother.

Eric's gaze was dazed, his eyes hardly open, but still she saw things that made her heart clutch.

The vampire's mouth on another throat, blood running down its face . . . reaching up to touch something that looked oddly human before it splattered everywhere . . . shoving a man's hands back so bone broke through flesh . . .

Her gorge rising, Rebecca fingered the snake bones, worrying that they wouldn't be enough to protect her, that the vampire would resist her spell and take revenge on her.

Fear couldn't stop her. Nothing could. She could do this for Danton!

Lighting the candles, Rebecca was already praying to her own gods as she reached down to a cage at her feet and removed a chicken—alive, if not for long—and set it in the cauldron. She prayed over the sacrifice, then removed a knife decorated with a serpent's head from a sheath at her calf. Her hand shook, making the kill clumsy. After slitting its throat, she asked forgiveness of the chicken and filled her chalice with its blood. Again, she prayed before drinking. Then she carved into the chicken and cut off a piece of flesh. Still warm, the quivering flesh slid easily down her throat.

Fog snaked along the ground and curled up around the iron grillwork, and the wind whistled along the tombs like a warning. She needed all the help from the loa she could get. From the altar, she lifted the *asson,* a rattle made from a dried calabash gourd filled with sacred stones and serpent vertebrae. Shaking it, she called on Legba to protect her and thought today she wouldn't let the loa ride her or speak through her. Today, she needed her wits about her as she peered once more into the slaughter through Eric's eyes.

The vampire stood with arms spread, palms up as bullet after bullet struck . . . his body absorbing the metal . . . then suddenly exploding into black lightning arcing up through a transom.

He was on his way. And he was very angry.

With her.

Sensing the rage building in the vampire as he sought her like a heat-seeking missile, Rebecca wanted to run and hide, but she couldn't, not if she wanted Danton to live. For him, she would risk herself. As a *mambo,* or priestess of the Sect Rouge—a secret society that held the power to create the walking dead—she'd used the black arts to free herself from modern slavery. The sex trade. Now *she* was in charge and she meant to stay that way, even against a raging vampire.

Even so, sweat trickled between her breasts and her mouth went dry. A good thing the creature was weak from years of starvation—although that wouldn't last. The vampire would grow stronger with each kill, with each feed. She could only hope she could control him long enough to save her brother and get them both out of this alive.

The revival spell she'd cast had been a powerful one. The gris-gris bag she'd given Eric had contained her own blood. To control the creature, she'd added her menstrual blood, the most effective way of binding a man to her, vampire or not, she assured herself.

A hissing wind made Rebecca look up. A cloud of black mist swirled in front of the moon before covering it and sending the surroundings into utter blackness, cut only by strange spikes of lightning that reminded her of the lightning in the lab. Perspiration dotted her entire body. The wind grew stronger, tried to knock her off her feet, but Rebecca stood fast even as her insides trembled.

She was afraid, yes, but strangely excited, too. She'd never met a man with so much power. What would it be like to form an alliance with a vampire? Her nipples hardened and the flesh between her thighs quaked with promise that was at once frightening and exhilarating.

Heart pounding against her ribs, she touched her ju-ju with one hand, rattled the *asson* with the other, and prayed for her life as the cloud settled before her and reshaped itself into the body of a naked man.

"How dare you summon me!" he boomed, his voice reverberating along the tomb walls. "Tell me why I shouldn't kill you now."

"Because I know your real name!" Rebecca shouted back. As she had learned in the ancient text *Vampyre,* knowledge of his name was another way to gain power over the vampire. Using some of Eric's hair and skin, which shared the vampire's DNA, she'd cast a complex spell she'd found within the pages. As excited as she was afraid, she intoned, "*With the blessings of the loa, I bind you to me to do my bidding, Andre Espinoza de Madrid!*"

Chapter 9

A grin cut Andre's face. This was a witch, and from the pathetic trinkets that adorned the coffins, he guessed that she practiced Voodoo.

Voodoo was the magic of peasants.

Of slaves.

She would not be able to protect herself with such paltry mysticism.

He took a menacing step forward, the candles throwing his massive shadow against the walls. He would make her suffer for calling him here just as he had made the soldiers who held him suffer. He had felt the pull, yes, and had followed more out of curiosity than anything. Now that his curiosity was sated, he would kill her, drink her blood, and then hunt down the priest who had entombed him in the cave and interrupted his centuries-old quest. Judging from the technology at the military base, Andre guessed that he had been imprisoned for two decades, perhaps three, making it likely the holy man was still alive. However, not for much longer.

Andre took another step forward and the Voodoo witch trembled, but held her ground.

"You will pay for your insolence," he growled and raised his arm to strike, but found that his muscles were frozen when he attempted to follow through. It was as though an invisible hand stayed him. He strained against the invisible force. Normally he could tear her head from her shoulders with a single blow, but now he could not move.

She muttered her Voodoo prayers as sweat poured down her forehead, her neck, down between her breasts.

Howling in rage, he tried to step closer, but found that he could not do that either. The same invisible hand that had stayed his now formed a barrier between them.

But he knew he did not need touch to slay a victim.

Preparing for the kill, he inhaled deeply, the reek of dead flesh around him thick as fog. The smell reminded him of the countless victims he'd had over the centuries, but also, inevitably, took him back to his boyhood in Spain, to when he had lost his mother. He'd lost her over five hundred years ago, and still it felt like yesterday . . .

Mama had lain in bed with a stained sheet wrapped around her waist like a rope. The room had smelled like spoiled meat. Her white bedclothes had been soaked with sweat, and her skin, once smooth and pretty and warm, had been pale and covered with black, pus-filled sores. Papi had told him it was Black Plague.

"I am going to be with God," Mama had said. "When the time is right, you and Papi will join me, and then we will be together again."

"God is hurting you. I hate him."

"Psshht, do not say that, Andre."

"Mama," Andre had begun when she coughed up a thick stream of blood that splashed against her chin. She'd looked at him wildly as she gripped the stained sheet in her fists. Terrified, he'd crushed his eyes closed and pressed his ear back against her chest and listened to her heart.

. . . thump . . . thump . . . thump . . .

And then he'd heard her heart slow, then stop . . .

"Look at me, witch," Andre commanded. She did not, and continued to whisper her prayers, so he repeated, "Look at me!" His voice boomed louder inside the crypt.

She looked at him, clearly startled by his sudden rage.

His power. Peering deeply into her eyes, he felt their gazes seal tightly in mystic, astral connection.

Release me.

He did not speak the words, he willed her to do so. Her eyes turned white as bone, but stayed that way for a moment only before returning to normal. She gripped the snake vertebrae that draped her neck.

Release me, he willed again, pouring his dark energy into the Suggestion. The air between them became charged with malignant power.

But still, she held fast.

He poured his energy into her, and the room crackled with it, lifted her long hair up around her neck as though she were floating in water.

"I will not!" she said, rattling the snake bones violently.

There was an intense flash of black light, and then he fell to one knee, energy drained from his body like radiation from a cracked nuclear core. Despite the feedings at the lab, he was still weak. Too weak to break the witch's grip.

Andre regarded the witch, listening to her beating heart. It thundered loudly in her chest with fear and, yes, desire. As well it should. He was one to be feared and desired, although his appetite for banal human pleasures had been lost, a price of his transmutation. As a result, his other senses had become more acute.

"Why have you brought me here?" Andre said, standing.

"I don't mean you any harm." She knelt before a recently decapitated chicken and cut off its left foot with a knife. She then stepped close, and he looked down at her as she ran her fingertips across her chest.

What did she mean to do with the bloody chicken's foot? He stood fast out of bemused curiosity. Her spell of protection was one thing. Wielding this quaint charm was quite another. The posturing of a slave.

"Do you know who I am?" he said. "What I am capable of?"

"I do," she said. "That is precisely why I summoned you."

Her insolence knew no bounds. She had summoned him like a common dog with her common magic.

"Release me now, and I will kill you quickly. You will feel no pain."

"If I release you without securing your help, I will suffer more pain than even you could inflict."

He furrowed his brow, surprised at her bold answer. Although enraged, part of him admired this seditious witch. "Tell me what you want."

She ignored the question, not yet done with her spell. *"I bind you in the name of the loa, in the name of God,"* she said, and smeared the bloody foot over his chest, painting a trident, a symbol of enforcement.

Andre reared back, howling as the blood burned his skin like acid. Again, he tried to lunge at her, but found once more that he could not move. He could not harm her in any way.

Cursed witch!

With a deft and practiced movement, she took his hand in hers, and slid a long bamboo splinter under the fingernail of his thumb, popping it free.

He roared more in anger than pain as she pulled a small vial of water from the folds in her skirt and dropped the nail inside. The water clouded red. She then tied a cord around the vial and slipped it around her neck.

"We are bound together now, you and I," she said.

When she turned around to grab her knife, he felt her spell weaken momentarily and bolted from the crypt.

His mind whirled with rage—at her insolence, at his own weakness, however temporary.

The stench of death was stronger outside as the moonlight bathed the raised tombstones and swampy grounds in silver light. He moved fluidly, intent on getting far enough away from her circle of influence to mount a counterattack.

Moving past a towering statue of a weeping angel, he felt the witch's mystic leash yank and stop him once again. He turned and she was there, silvery in the moonlight.

"Enough," he said. "Tell me what you want, and then release me."

She turned and walked away. He had no choice but to follow, but also knew that she had no choice but to allow him to continue to feed if she wanted his help.

That meant soon enough he would be able to break free of her pathetic magic, and then he would teach her the true meaning of pain.

Chapter 10

Thankful that she'd driven her SUV rather than her Jaguar, Rebecca sped away from the cemetery and skirted the crowded French Quarter, traveling as fast as she could without being stopped. She could just imagine some cop spotting a naked man in her passenger seat and pulling her over. She could just imagine the vampire grabbing the cop by the throat and draining his blood no matter how many witnesses might be around.

The thought made it hard to breathe. One slip and she would be the vampire's next victim.

As if he heard her thoughts, Andre growled, "I need to feed."

Rebecca shuddered at the demand. "You'll just have to be hungry a while longer." She gave him a quick look. His flesh was paler than it had been when he'd arrived at the cemetery. His limbs were long and thick as was the penis that lay flaccid against one of his thighs. Good. That's the way he should stay, she thought, unease creeping through her. "I need to find you something to wear."

"Do you fear the sight of my flesh will offend my food? Or does it offend you?"

"You don't need to bring attention to yourself!" she snapped, knowing it would be a mistake to let him see any sign of weakness. "You must do as I say."

Though he was physically drained from the night's exertions and from his need for blood, Rebecca felt him battering at her will . . . trying to get inside her mind so he could control her thoughts. Touching the ju-ju hanging from her neck, she offered a quick prayer to the loa and mentally pushed back.

A glance his way didn't reassure her. His eyes glowed red in the night. Sweat rolled down the back of her neck and between her breasts as she imagined his dark thoughts about her. Thankfully, she had all the oils and potions and powders she needed to keep control of him.

She turned east to go through Faubourg Marigny, its Creole and shotgun cottages bearing a history of *plaçage*—where white Creole gentlemen of the early nineteenth century had set up households for their mistresses. Some things never changed. Not all that many years ago, she'd been kept in a house not far from here, a situation she'd vowed never to repeat. No man would ever hold that kind of power over her again.

Andre asked, "Where are you taking me?"

"Someplace where no one will guess to find you."

More specifically, the part of the Marigny away from the touristy area and west of the canal that would separate them from the hurricane- and tornado-devastated Lower Ninth Ward.

"*This* area will do," he said, staring out hungrily at the tourists walking along the still-hot pavement, flowing in and out of restaurants and bars along Frenchmen Street.

Rebecca could imagine the appetite they stirred in him, like deer in a hungry wolf. "Just a little farther."

Water lines from the hurricane still marked some of the buildings here. The Marigny hadn't been nearly as badly hit as the Lower Ninth, where whole buildings had been swept off their foundations. Locals claimed the hurricane had been the work of Loa Agwe, sovereign of the sea, who'd refused the sacrifices of the Voodooists trying to placate him. Their ceremonial barque had floated back to shore, food and drink intact. She herself was a powerful *mambo,* but Rebecca knew some forces of nature couldn't be stopped, not even by Voodoo.

They passed unoccupied buildings—both residences and businesses. Exactly the right area for a hideout. She pulled in back of an abandoned Queen Anne mansion scheduled for demolition. Luckily she had Jean Baptiste Neff in her pocket. The city Councilmember had made arrangements for her to use this building undisturbed by the authorities for the foreseeable future.

"What is this place?" Andre asked.

"Your new home."

"This ruin?"

The Queen Anne had seen better days. The three-story wooden structure had been abandoned for more than a decade. The owners had braced it against an adjacent building to prevent it from falling over. In daylight it still held a certain worn charm with a pillared porch and a turreted peak, not to mention the peeling pink facade. But at night, its walls simply looked scaly, like a disease was eating away its flesh.

"This housing is fit for swine." Andre's voice was thick with disdain. He stood feet firmly planted in the overgrown side garden where he could be seen, a human statue glowing silver in the moonlight.

O Ogoun, give me strength and protect me.

Rebecca prayed the warrior loa would keep her safe. And though for the moment she had ultimate power over the vampire, that didn't mean he couldn't put up such a fight that he would alert others and ruin her plans.

"Say what you will, Andre, this place is safe for now. Being safe is more important than comfort."

Even as she turned her back on him, Rebecca knew she had to be careful how she dealt with the vampire. He needed blood to be strong enough to save Danton. And when she provided the blood, he would gain strength, perhaps enough to break her hold on him. She must find other ways to control him . . . Commanding Oil would help make him do her bidding, but she also must offer him something he couldn't refuse . . . and therefore have something to trade so that he would save her brother.

Unlocking the padlock securing the back door, she hung it from its hook as if it were still protecting the building.

"Follow me," she said, leading the way inside through an alcove off the main pantry.

The mansion might have been crumbling inside as well as out, but the rooms were spacious, and while the furniture might have been dusty, the place was livable for a while. The first floor consisted of three dining rooms, a front parlor, a reception room, and a couple of foyers wrapped around an inner court with what had once been a working fountain. Three sets of stairs led up to the second and third floors and the bedrooms, library, and additional parlors.

Rebecca had equipped the sideboard in the dining room where they entered with a large cooler as well as her herbs, candles, and other tools of Voodoo.

"These trinkets won't hold me."

"They are for your protection. There will be people looking for you. Dangerous people."

Andre's face twisted cruelly. "I am the danger."

Remembering the horrors she'd seen through Eric's eyes, Rebecca shuddered. How could she have known the vampire would be so violent, so unconcerned with human life? If the soldiers had been vile, evil men, their deaths wouldn't weigh on her. She hadn't factored butchery into her equation, but she wouldn't give in to regret or even fear, lest she fail her brother.

Thinking of Danton steadied her inside.

Expression still dark, Andre sat on the mahogany

table, legs spread, penis dangling as if he dared her to look there. Was he taunting her? Could he possibly know what humiliations and brutality she'd been through with her stepfather and other equally cruel men?

"What is it you want of me?" he asked.

Her pulse began to thunder. "My brother's life. He's dying of leukemia. There is no hope. Not from medicine. Not from magic. You can give him his life back."

"Then he would be like me. You would have reason to fear him."

She shook her head vehemently. "Never Danton."

"Power changes a man." Andre seemed amused by the thought. "What makes you think I will do this thing for you?"

"I gave you back your life."

"And I will be happy to take yours."

Her breath caught in her throat and fear warred with anger. He could kill her, probably would try unless she appeased him, but he was underestimating her if he thought her death would come so easily. She was powerful in her own right and had Voodoo at her command.

"I offer you a trade." She'd guessed he would demand more in return. "No one has everything, not even a five-hundred-year-old vampire."

Andre pinned her with his gaze. His face looked ghostly encased by his long dark hair. He did need to feed, Rebecca realized. Blood would give him back his color. She reached for her ju-ju as he tried using what little energy he had left to get inside her mind rather than capitulating.

A frisson of fear whispered through her. For a moment she thought they had come to an impasse. She could feel his hatred for her ooze off him and knew that if she gave him the opening, he *would* kill her. But he needed her, too. His condition weakened by the moment. His limbs were trembling and he was holding himself stiffly as if to try to hide his helplessness.

"I could leave you here," she said. "Just walk away and let you starve for blood." It wouldn't take that long, she thought, and he undoubtedly knew it. "Or I can give you what you need. Tell me what you want in return for saving my brother!"

She watched his face—need warred with his hatred for her.

Finally, he said, "Get me the Philosopher's Stone. Is the power to acquire it in one of your gris-gris bags?"

"Perhaps." The Philosopher's Stone—she'd heard of it, but in what context? He needed the Stone, but for what? "Do you know where to find it?"

"I know who possesses it. Find *him*."

"Then you will save my brother?"

Andre fell silent for a moment, then, his sunken eyes glowing red, looked up at her and nodded.

Yes! She would make a sacrifice to the loa in thanks.

Relieved, she moved to the sideboard and opened the cooler. Inside, immersed in ice, were a half-dozen packets of blood that she'd obtained from a regular client of the club who worked in a hospital. She, of course, had told the man they were for Danton, that she was going to use Voodoo on the blood and then cure her brother.

"Here," she said, tossing a packet on the table so that it slid toward Andre. That would keep him going until she found the Stone.

He stared down at the packet. "What do you propose I do with this?"

"Drink up."

He slid it back at her, contempt ripe in his voice as he said, "I need to *feed*!"

Feed . . . as in fresh blood . . .

Rebecca's chest tightened. She wasn't prepared for

this. Sacrificing innocent lives hadn't been part of her plan.

But Danton . . .

She could see him in his bed, a shadow of his former self, life draining from him with each breath he took.

For Danton, she could do what she must.

Heading for the nearest staircase, she said, "I'll find you some clothes. Then you can feed."

She left him, telling herself that she would get Andre to do as she demanded, that Danton wouldn't lose his life to some blood disease. She wouldn't think about the price, only about the outcome.

Danton had to live.

When she checked the closet filled with musty old garments, none looked big enough. She pulled out a hanger with a graying white suit that would have to do for now. Halfway back down the stairs, she heard a crash of glass that sent her flying the rest of the way.

"Andre Espinoza de Madrid, you are bound to me and cannot leave this house!"

Checking the downstairs rooms, she found the vampire in the front parlor sprawled on the floor near a broken window. Glass lay shattered around him, but her spell had kept him from leaving. The effort seemed to have drained the last of his energy. He wasn't moving. Dropping the suit on a chair, she knelt and noted a large piece of glass embedded in his hand. Apparently he'd used his fist on the window. In removing it from his flesh, she nicked her finger. A single drop of blood bubbled on the tip.

"Andre, get up," she said, but he didn't so much as twitch. Panicking for a moment, she grabbed his face and shook. "Andre!"

Blood from the cut smeared the corner of his mouth and the next thing she knew, he'd latched onto her finger, sucking as if he meant to drain her. Her mind lit with bright lights and a pain so intense it terrified her. Screaming, she pounded her fist against his face and neck until he let go and fell back. Then with a muttered curse, he turned over onto his side and slept the sleep of the dead once more.

Rising on shaky legs, she backed away from him. He needed to feed. Not on her!

What was she going to do?

Rebecca ran to her altar and found her Domination Powder, then returned to a still-sleeping Andre. Opening the jar, she sprinkled a liberal amount in her palm, said a prayer for help to the loa, and blew it over the vampire.

Though that would give her added protection, he would still need to feed, and that would be her responsibility.

Fighting growing nausea, Rebecca remembered a family living in a nearby isolated area where no one would see. But could she really sacrifice them? They were poor the way she and Danton had been poor once. If she thought about that too closely . . .

If not them, though, then who? If she didn't choose, Andre would, and if she didn't allow that, either, Danton would die, and that would be unthinkable. She must maintain her control over Andre.

What if he chose a child?

No, better that she choose *for* him. The Toutants really had no value to anyone. Two parents with no drive to better themselves and the two grown offspring who followed in their footsteps.

Four lives surely would be enough.

Deep down, she knew there would be more, but all she could think about was getting the Philosopher's Stone for Andre. She would fulfill her end of the bargain, and he would cure Danton.

Returning to the other room, she picked out four

black pillar candles, one for each direction. She had to keep her priorities straight: a few *useless* lives for her brother's. Danton had studied to be a linguist, and hoped to work with a world relief organization, because he wanted to help where he could. He'd been writing his dissertation when the leukemia had overtaken him once more. She had done things she hadn't liked to get where she was, but not Danton. Danton was the good one, the one who'd saved her from her stepfather, the one who'd gone out in the midst of the hurricane to save people he didn't even know.

Danton alive.

Danton *cured.*

That was the goal she had to keep clear in her mind. If she thought too much about what she had to do to save him, she might hesitate. And she never could tell her brother that she was forced to sacrifice others to save him. Then he would *want* to die.

Her eyes stung as she whispered, "Anything for you, Danton," and drew a mouth on each candle, then added a name in each mouth's center.

"Adele Toutant . . ." she read aloud, tears brimming to blur her vision.

"Marthe Toutant . . ." Saying the names gave them power.

"Paul Toutant . . ." Saying the names gave her power over them.

"Henri Toutant . . ." Four intended victims to refuel the vampire.

She blinked and tears coursed down her cheeks.

Once her brother was cured, she would send this vampire back to its hell, Rebecca thought, placing a large X over each mouth and name on each candle. She hadn't thought any further than seeing her brother cured, but now it seemed she must.

Drawing the last X, she invoked the loa to do her bidding.

She might have to be there when the vampire killed these innocent people.

She didn't have to listen to their screams.

Chapter 11

Leah set her suitcase on her narrow bed and fetched her things from the *trastero*. Other than the khaki clothing and boots she wore in the field, Leah preferred skirts and blouses and jangly jewelry, remnants of the bohemian look that had been so popular when she'd been finishing up her PhD.

Closing the suitcase, she looked around one last time. She'd only been at the Pueblo for a couple of days, but she would miss the simple room with the dream catcher over the bed, the plaster saints and candles on the small dresser, the window and door frame painted blue to ward off evil. Working on a research grant to study religious beliefs and superstitions of cultures of the Southwest, Leah had rented a studio apartment in Albuquerque, where Javier lived. Now that Isabel was talking again, and it was appropriate for a traditional therapist to work with the girl, the *curandero* was anxious to get home.

They would leave at dawn.

A distant *thwack-thwack-thwack* from outside distracted her for a moment. It sounded like an approaching helicopter. She glanced out the window but couldn't see anything in the dark, so she zipped up her suitcase.

Maybe she'd go home, surprise Mom with an unexpected visit. A thought that didn't bring a smile to her lips. Her mother had given up on life once Gabe and Dad had been killed. It wasn't that she didn't love Leah as much as Leah loved her. The tragedy had simply severed their close connection.

Throwing her tote over her shoulder, Leah picked up her suitcase and left the bedroom, planning to leave her bags in the living area, so that she would be ready to go. The front door stood open. The helicopter noise was getting much louder. And then the room exploded with beaming white light.

Covering her eyes, she ran outside into a whorl of sand as the helicopter came straight down in the middle of the plaza. It was the middle of the night, but people were running from their apartments and casitas.

This wasn't just any helicopter, Leah realized, but a Black Hawk. What was an instrument of war doing here, in a place of peace?

The moment the Black Hawk touched down, a woman wearing a uniform stepped out onto the Pueblo land. Her blond hair was pulled back tight and was half-hidden under a cap. She looked around and it took but a few seconds for her to zero in on her target.

Leah's stomach clutched.

What the hell did Major Wallas Ackart want with her now?

"Dr. Maguire!" Ackart yelled over the sound of the helicopter blades. Her stride purposeful, the major came right at Leah, and stopped only when she was in Leah's face. "I see you're packed to go. Good."

Waves of strong emotion suddenly pummeled Leah. Startled, she dropped her bags and stepped back, her gaze dropping to the chain and pendant Ackart always wore—a caduceus, a medical symbol with two snakes. The major was clutching it like a lifeline.

Not wanting to know why Ackart was there, Leah shook her head and preempted her. "I'm going back to Albuquerque."

The continuing negativity pushing at her from Ackart was distracting.

What the hell was wrong?

"We need to talk in private," Ackart said. "The situation has changed. We have a problem now—a matter of national security."

Leah's chest tightened and for a moment, she couldn't speak.

Pulse thrumming, she fought free of Ackart's influence only with difficulty. She met the other woman's gaze. "I told you I wasn't interested in your experiment."

Ackart had approached her for the first time more than a year ago, just after her dissertation had been published. As head of Project 24, Ackart had wanted her to be part of the team from the beginning.

After surviving the cave attack, Leah had pursued studies that could give her some answers. She'd delved into ritualistic magic, had gone further than the average anthropologist, the reason she'd been able to interpret the religious symbols surrounding the cave. She'd known they were meant to ward off evil, that someone had successfully imprisoned the thing responsible in the cave after the attack. That's where it had been trapped until the military had gotten involved, finding the mummy and discovering the twenty-fourth set of chromosomes. Ackart had been impressed with her abilities.

When Ackart first approached Leah about becoming part of the team, testing had already begun and strands of DNA had been given to animal subjects that had gained some special powers. Leah hadn't been willing to help propagate those powers in human guinea pigs. She sensed that the military was interested in creating a new weapon—a human weapon capable of new and improved means of killing. She couldn't help disseminate the very evil that had destroyed her family.

She'd refused the work on moral grounds, but now this problem . . .

Leah found her voice. "What kind of problem are we talking about?"

Ackart grabbed her arm and rushed her away from the chopper. "The mummy somehow got . . . reconstituted. He killed several of our men and now he's on the loose."

The major quickly gave Leah a more accurate picture of what had happened in the lab. An icy coldness settled through her as she listened, making it difficult to move. To breathe. To think. What felt like an energy field of something dark and thick held her captive, forced her mind to the human destruction in the lab. She could almost see the sprays of blood as the creature slaughtered the men. She could almost hear their death screams echoing through her head.

"Our men shot at the creature," Ackart said, "but bullets were ineffective. They seemed to give it added strength . . . Dr. Maguire, we need you to help us figure out how to capture and contain that monster."

Leah slowly came back to reality. Ackart was fingering the pendant around her neck nervously, waiting for her answer. So Leah's worst fear had come to pass and now she was supposed to help fix it.

"No! I can't do anything to help." She didn't want to deal with more tragedy.

"You know, Dr. Maguire," Ackart said, "if you would have joined the project in the first place, this might never have happened. Men might never have been killed."

"That's not true!"

Even as the words flew from Leah's lips she wondered if she could have prevented this disaster. The deaths of those soldiers already burdened her. Was she responsible? If she ran away, would there be more?

The dark cloud of Ackart's desperation enveloped Leah once more. It came at her in waves, battering her, weakening her.

"You have no choice," Ackart said. "This is a matter

of national security. I can take you in and force you to cooperate."

Leah believed the major was serious. And terrified of what was to come. "You might be able to take me in, but you can't force me to do anything I don't want to do."

"Look, you're the only one who has firsthand knowledge of the creature," Ackart said, her softened voice telling Leah she was changing tactics. "Two of my men survived the attack—*brothers.*" She emphasized the last. "They're in the infirmary, and the younger one is in a coma. Even if they both live, they don't have your expertise."

Expertise was useless, Leah thought, remembering how she'd frightened poor Isabel.

She recognized that the major was trying to hold her hostage by mentioning the brothers. Her instincts screamed that before the emotional blackmail could work she should grab her bags and run in the other direction and never look back. She didn't want to be part of this. She couldn't trust that Ackart would let her use her anthropological expertise without interference. Getting involved in some military snafu was the last thing Leah was willing to do. She'd experienced more violence in that cave than most people did in a lifetime.

But how many more would die if she did nothing?

The weight of responsibility on her shoulders made it impossible for Leah to run away, even as every instinct told her to do so. Where would it get her? She could never outrun what had happened to her and Gabe and Dad. What now had happened to the men in the lab.

In that context, she had no choice.

But if she did this, if she used magic to stop, maybe destroy this creature, what remained of Gabe and Dad inside her could be lost forever. Leah didn't think she could stand it.

Nor could she bear to think the creature would take more lives, not when she might be able to figure out how to stop it.

Gabe and Dad were gone. The men in the lab were gone. If she didn't agree, more deaths would follow.

"All right," she said. "I'll do it. I'll come with you."

And God help her if she failed again.

Chapter 12

Scott woke up in the base infirmary to see BB standing over him, the man's red hair and beard starkly contrasting with the room's sterile white ceiling and walls. He tried to sit up, but soft restraints at his wrists and ankles kept him from doing so.

"BB! What the hell is going on?"

"For your own good, pal," the scientist said apologetically, indicating the restraints. "Your chest was torn up pretty bad. The doc didn't want you opening up the wounds again."

"What about Eric? Is he . . . ?" Scott's throat closed, unable to say the word. The last image he had of his brother was in the lab, pale and bleeding. He struggled against the restraints, and BB gently but firmly pushed him back to the mattress.

"Calm down, man, calm down," BB said. "Eric is alive, thanks to you."

Relief flooded through him. Eric was alive. His little brother was alive. But BB's tone was heavier than it should have been. Something was wrong. "Where is he, BB?"

"You're not going to try to sit up again, are you?"

"Dammit, BB!"

Nodding solemnly, BB walked across the large room to a sheet that hung from the ceiling. He jerked the sheet back with a *swish!* to reveal Eric in his own bed, tubes running into his arms, monitors beside his bed beeping steadily. His eyes were closed.

"Eric!" Scott called out. "Hey, man, you okay?" No response. The pit of his stomach grew icy. "What aren't you telling me, BB?"

"Like I said, he's alive, Scott. But his reflexes are refusing to cooperate, and his neurotransmitter activity is, well, taking something of a break right now."

"You want to translate that?"

BB's expression fell into a rictus of shared pain. "He's in a sort of coma."

Scott's chest went tight as his relief dissipated like smoke. "Sort of? What the hell does that mean?"

BB returned to his bedside and shook his head. "Eric is catatonic, but from what I can tell, it isn't due to his injuries, or from normal reasons like brain damage or a heart attack. That's good news, actually. Based on his vital signs, he should be awake right now."

"But he isn't." Guilt tore at Scott. If only he'd fired Eric when Ackart had given him the chance. Right now the two of them could be drowning their sorrows in scotch, instead of . . . Scott tried to tear through the restraints that held him as pain stabbed through his bandaged chest. "Goddamn it, BB," he hissed through gritted teeth. "Let me up. Let me see my brother."

BB pushed him down again. "What did I tell you about sitting up? Don't make me sedate you. Don't make me sedate *both* of us . . ." BB may have tried to deliver the joke, but it was clear the situation was taking its toll on him, too.

Scott slumped back against the mattress, sweat soaking his body. Even though his forearm was strapped down, he opened his hand wide, strained his fingers like he could reach across the room and clutch Eric's hand. Bottom line, this debacle was his fault. He could have put Eric in his place long ago, long before Ackart had offered the opportunity—back when his brother had first voiced the desire to join Team Ultra a couple years earlier.

Eric had suggested they meet at Briefcase Full of Blues, a famous blues bar in Fayetteville, North Carolina, during a rare instance when they'd been able to take military leave at the same time. Scott remembered feeling confused by the request. He and Eric never visited their hometown if they could help it. Too many bad memories. But looking back, maybe Eric had suggested it because he knew his life was about to change, and instinctively sought the supposed comfort of home, even when their home had brought only sorrow and pain . . .

"I'm going out for Team Ultra," Eric had said across the table. He spoke loudly and deliberately above the blues band that jammed with electric guitars and saxophones on a small stage.

Scott put down his beer, looked evenly at Eric through the pungent, ambient haze of cigarette smoke. "Tell me you're kidding."

"I've given it a lot of thought. It's something I really want to do."

As decorated members of elite Special Forces units, they both had been courted to join the top secret project. Scott had flatly refused. Not only was he about to retire from the military, but the risks far outweighed the benefits, in his opinion. Blew them away, in fact.

"Do you know what they'll ask you to do?" Scott asked, exasperated.

"Yeah, I've read the brochures."

Scott pounded the table with his fist. "This isn't a joke. They'll fuck with your body, man. Turn you into . . ." He paused, searching for the word, gave up. "Turn you into God-only-knows what."

"It's worth the risk."

Scott rubbed a hand over his face. He wanted to shake

his brother. Hard. "What can be worth changing who you are?"

"Maybe I want to change," Eric said simply. "You ever consider that, big brother?"

Scott leaned back in his chair, stunned. His brother's face looked as though it might collapse in on itself at any moment. For whatever reason, his little brother felt like he needed to join this high-risk group, and now sought his approval.

Scott looked down at his beer. He knew he could use guilt as leverage. Or shame. Or blunt-force, older-brother authority. With a few choice words, he could probably override his brother's wishes and keep him safe.

He could.

But didn't. Not when their childhood had denied them so much already. If Eric really wanted this . . .

Scott sighed, peeled the corner of his beer label. "We try for Team Ultra together, you hear me? Together."

Eric glared at him, still angry at having to jump through hoops. But beneath the scowl was the beginning of a smile. "Think you can muster the energy for one more tour?"

Scott pushed away the memory, but barbs of guilt remained. He thought he'd made the right decision that night. How fucking wrong he'd been.

Looking at BB, Scott decided to change tack, see if he couldn't talk the man into letting him up some other way. "Did you get a chance to watch the security tapes?"

"Yeah." BB stared at him as though anticipating his next question . . . a question he was seemingly afraid to answer.

"What the hell happened in there?" Scott went cold as BB frowned. Before today, Scott would have claimed that nothing seemed beyond the man's intellectual reach, yet this was the second aspect of the attack that eluded him.

"The mummy is gone. That's all we know for sure."

"Did the assailant take it?"

"We think it *was* the assailant."

Scott paused, thoughtful. "I saw Eric introduce a substance into the chamber, BB. Maybe it triggered some sort of rapid tissue regeneration."

"No." BB crossed his arms, looked at the tiled floor. "No . . ."

Scott's frustration surged. The man was acting uncharacteristically evasive, like a high school student caught cheating on a test. "What are you talking about? We saw it happen."

"Listen, we kept the mummy under treated Plexiglas because we knew exposure to certain spectrums of light and air would destroy it. Howard Carter had to contend with the phenomenon when he discovered King Tut, as did every archeologist that came before and followed after. Scientific law, okay? So we took extreme measures to maintain the mummy's structural integrity while we collected our DNA samples. But last night . . ." BB glanced around the room as though searching for an answer. ". . . last night we saw the tissue *amplify* when exposed to air. Not only amplify, but return to its natural state with crazy speed . . . like Shrinky Dinks on acid . . . and that was without protein matrices, nanofiber scaffolds, or any other nutrients you need to support growth."

Scott felt a sudden, spiraling sense of disorientation similar to what he'd experienced when he'd first learned the full extent of Project 24. In the beginning, he'd refused to believe such superhuman abilities were possible—the notion struck at the very core of his sense of control.

If he'd been wrong about something as fundamental as the capability of the human body, what else could he be wrong about? But there'd been no denying the results.

BB had eased his disorientation by explaining that the DNA process was based on proven, scientific principle, even if the powers themselves were not explainable by science. BB had compared the entire procedure to exposing plants to classical music. Who knew why the gentle melodies made for fuller, stronger growth? They just did.

Clearly, the mummy's ability to transform into black lightning and seemingly attract bullets through magnetism fell into the same category. But now BB was saying that the mummy's reconstitution—the process itself—defied scientific law.

"There has to be a rational explanation for what happened," Scott said.

"Take away my boy-genius card, but what we witnessed goes against everything I know about science. And I know a lot," BB said, eyes still hazed with confusion. "If the mummy did indeed reconstitute, it did so as if by . . ." His voice trailed off, but the implication was clear.

As if by magic.

Frustration sizzled through Scott's veins. This was bullshit. BB was clearly still in shock from last night's battle to be spewing nonsense while Eric was catatonic and possibly dying. Whatever the explanation, Scott didn't give a rat's ass. All he cared about was Eric. He had no idea how to revive Eric from his mysterious coma, but right now the freak who'd escaped from the lab was his best lead. He'd go after the guy without quarter until he found the answers he needed. First, he had to get off this goddamn bed. "I swear, BB, if you don't let me up . . ."

"Ackart'll have my head if I do. And you know how

she scares me, man. Like those tiny barbed fish in the Amazon that're attracted to the ammonia in your—"

"You're right, BB. If you let Captain Boulder run off half-cocked, I *will* have your head."

Scott looked past BB and saw Ackart standing at the foot of the bed holding a manila folder under one arm. Beside her was a woman with short red hair; artsy type, clearly not military. Was Ackart involving a civilian? Nothing had played out as he expected in these last few days. It was starting to get to him.

Chapter 13

Leah felt hostility bristle from the man in the bed. She didn't blame him for being angry—she wouldn't like being strapped down, either. His anger went beyond his confinement, however. Glancing at the bed across the room where his brother lay in a coma, she could understand his anguish.

Stepping closer, she said, "The major told me about your brother, Captain. I'm very sorry and will hope for the best."

He looked around her as though she weren't there. "Why am I confined to this bed, Major?"

"For your own good," Ackart said. "And ours."

"We still don't know what effect the attack might have on you," BB said before he turned to Leah. "I'm Darryl Adams, the scientist in charge of the project. Everyone calls me BB."

Leah acknowledged him with a nod and turned her gaze back to Scott, trying to connect with him psychically. Though she wanted to see if there was some way she could help him, she kept her probing subtle. Ackart didn't know about her empathic abilities and Leah felt it was in her own best interests that Ackart didn't know everything. The major was like a shark and would eat anything and anyone that would make her stronger, even if that destroyed the men most loyal to her. Leah focused on Scott. At the moment, the captain was scattered. Panicked in his own head.

As if he'd heard her assessment, he looked straight at her and said, "I'm in my right mind."

"Then you understand my reasoning." Ackart spoke from behind Leah, her voice emotionless. "The lab tests are being run now. When you check out, you'll be released. In the meantime, I've brought our new consultant to meet you. Dr. Leah Maguire, Captain Scott Boulder, leader of Team Ultra. Captain, Dr. Maguire is going to want to know everything you know about the attack."

"What kind of consultant?"

"You can speak directly to me, Captain," Leah said, wanting to draw him away from the powers confining him. She wanted him to trust her. Aware that Ackart was backing off and signaling BB to follow her out of the room to watch through the window, she said, "I'm a cultural anthropologist."

His amber eyes narrowed as he assessed her clothing—long, full skirt, flowing blouse, and embroidered vest. Disdain twisted his attractive features, but there was something more. What?

A facade. He wanted to chase her away.

Instead, she stepped closer, sensing something in him deeper than the disdainful military man.

"You're not medical and you're not military?"

She held back her own thoughts about military strikes and violence. "I bring a different perspective to the situation."

A whirlwind of bitterness and raw fear pulsing off the captain made Leah take a mental step back. From her own experience, she knew what he'd gone through during that attack. What he must be going through now with his brother in this mysterious coma. He was suffering. Part of her wanted to put her arms around Scott and simply take away his pain, but it didn't work that way.

He had to live it as had she. She'd been right where he was now. Was still there at times.

He said, "I don't see how a cultural anthropologist fits in here."

"My area of specialty is religion—more specifically, apotropaic magic. Rituals to turn away evil."

"Religion? Magic? We're dealing with a psychotic killer here."

"Maybe." She turned away from him. "But Major Ackart wants to be certain."

"Certain of what?" Scott asked. "What is it Ackart thinks you can do for us?"

"Nothing will bring back lost lives. But I promise you, Captain Boulder, I will do whatever I can to prevent more deaths."

She slipped the folder the major had given her from her briefcase. Taking several eight-by-ten photographs that had been shot inside Cueva del Diablo, she handed them to Scott, who took them reluctantly. She'd first seen the photographs the year before when she'd turned down Ackart about being part of the team.

"What are these supposed to be?" Scott asked.

"Symbols meant to contain evil. This is the tunnel leading to the cavern where the mummy was found. And these symbols surrounded it, undoubtedly meant to keep the evil inside."

"Dr. Maguire—"

"Just hear me out, please. How do you explain what happened afterward . . . when you got hurt . . . what about that?"

"A science experiment gone wrong, I don't know. But if you'd seen what I've seen on the battlefield, you wouldn't be surprised by anything. There's nothing supernatural about the evil people inflict on one another."

Leah nodded. A simple explanation, certainly one that would make her more comfortable than she was feeling now. Javier had been correct about her intellectualizing her work. But now she had no choice. She would have to learn. She would have to make good her promise to save lives.

Taking a big breath, she asked, "Tell me what happened to the best of your memory."

Leah tried to be objective as she listened to the details, but she soon found herself drifting to a dark place that reminded her of her own experience. Part of her wanted to ignore the connection but she was left with no choice. The utter violence of the telling brought tears to her eyes. Years of grief had taught her to hold back what she was feeling, but this was her greatest test. She stared down at the burn scar on her palm and rubbed it with her thumb.

It took a moment for her to realize Scott had stopped speaking. He was staring at the pyramid and square. Color drained from his face as he met her gaze.

"What the hell is that?"

"A scar—"

"I can see that." His voice was intense, as was his expression. "But where did you get it?"

She shook her head and backed off. "It happened a long time ago." Again, she couldn't talk about it, especially not with a stranger. His intense stare bored right into her. Did he sense her fear? "We're not here to talk about me."

Surprisingly, after a moment of indecision, he let it go. He said instead, "My brother is in some kind of coma the doctors can't explain."

Leah followed his anguished gaze over to the bed on the other side of the room. Knowing what he was feeling from her own experience, she moved to the other bed and tried to ignore the machines and tubes and concentrate on the man.

She'd never tried to read a coma patient before. It was

like trying to sift through layers and layers of random thoughts. She would try another method.

Rubbing her hands together, Leah focused on the captain's brother and sought a deeper insight that would let her see his state of being. She moved her palms a few inches above Eric Boulder's heart. As she spread them farther and farther apart, tension pressed back against her flesh. Her pulse kicked and she could feel her heart beating faster, as before her eyes the surface of his body appeared to be cocooned in a field of luminous radiation.

An aura was composed of soul vibrations or *chakras,* reflecting the state of being of the person it surrounded, and Leah knew what she was seeing wasn't good. A dark, muddy gray oozed from Eric's pores and enveloped his head, indicating a residue of fear and sickness. The dirty brown overlay indicated caged energies, understandable since he was in a coma. But there was something more disturbing yet—a thread of darkest purple vibrating around the aura's edges.

"What the hell!" Scott spat. "What are you doing?"

"His aura is tainted."

"His aura?"

"Tainted by black magic."

Leah turned to face the captain and was startled at the glimpse she got of his aura before she lost focus.

The dark and muddied red was caused by his anger and aggression. What she didn't understand were the pulsing sweeps of black surrounding his chest.

What in the world did that indicate?

Chapter 14

Standing in the tree line, Andre turned to Rebecca. In the moonlight, her features adopted an eerie, ephemeral beauty.

"Do you have everything you need?" he asked.

"Yes," she replied.

He noticed that her eyes lingered on his massive nude form, prompting a feeling of bitter sorrow that gusted through him like cold wind. The pain of lost loves over the centuries had hardened his heart, and he intended to apply those lessons against the witch now. Working together—the illusion of teamwork—would go a long way to winning her trust. And then, once the appropriate time came, he would use her trust and growing desire to instigate her final undoing.

Not far before them was a thirty-foot FEMA trailer parked under a massive, skeletal oak. The light inside was the only illumination for at least a mile of devastation. Through one screened window, Andre saw a father and mother washing dishes in a small kitchen; through another, a son and daughter, each in their early twenties, sitting on a couch and watching television.

"Begin lighting your candles," Andre told her. "I won't be long."

He moved quickly from their wooded hiding place to cross the remains of the family's home, now nothing more than a nimbus of shattered walls and mud-caked remains of clothing, photographs, furniture. He inhaled deeply, smelled charred wood, spoiled vegetation, still water, and the acrid smoke of a distant grill or fire pit. But he could sense no living things close by. The family was alone and without protection.

As he drew closer to the trailer, a humid breeze whipped over his marble-cold flesh, causing his muscles to tremble. Although he was still several times stronger than a human being, the warmed-over blood the witch had given him barely kept him upright. He needed more blood—blood from a living, pulsing source—to rebuild his desiccated body. In this way, he knew the family should consider themselves fortunate.

They would serve a greater purpose—*his* purpose. Their sacrifice would provide him the opportunity to grow stronger and test the potency of his powers.

Andre reached the rear of the trailer and crouched beneath the locked living room window as blue light from the television spilled into the darkness and over his naked body. He stood, peered carefully through the screened glass. The brother and sister sat on a couch with their backs to the window, and the room was separated from the rest of the trailer by a drawn privacy screen. A critical factor, he knew. Normally, he would attack without mercy or quarter. But since the witch was conflicted about the use of violence, a chaotic, bloody assault on all four people might alienate her from him. She might then plot to take the Philosopher's Stone for herself, which was something he could not allow. The screen would enable him to divide and conquer cleanly.

Looking back at Rebecca, Andre saw that she had planted four black candles in a wide perimeter around the trailer. She met his gaze, ready. Nodding for her to incant her spell, he saw a tiny flame spring to life at her fingers as she lit the first candle. She then made a quarter circle around the trailer and lit the next one.

Andre was reminded of a distant past, staring at the bobbing orange flames. Papi's eyes had held the same flickering intensity after he'd been unable to purchase absolution for Mama's soul from a greedy Catholic priest—a flickering intensity that had swelled into burning grief and lunacy after Mama's passing shortly thereafter. Though he had been just a boy at the time, he could hear the ghosts of centuries past very clearly, as though he were hiding behind the pew in the old church once again . . .

"My Anna is a loving wife and mother. I beg you," Papi had said, following the robed priest to the altar. "We are poor, but please, accept this as my offering. It will fetch a handsome price."

He'd held out a gleaming rapier with an intricately designed hilt that Andre knew he had spent months forging, and had worked a medallion that belonged to Mama into the hilt.

"A sword cannot keep up this church, nor can it properly compensate me for dealing with such a wretched member of my flock," the priest had replied with disdain, and tore the absolution parchment in two.

Papi had cried out in anguish, and in a rush of fury, ran the priest through with the rapier. "I renounce you!" his father had hissed as the priest slumped to the floor in a pool of blood. "I renounce you and your greed!" He'd then grabbed a candle from the altar and flung it against a hanging tapestry. The threadbare fabric had caught quickly, and soon flames were licking up the wall . . .

Andre felt his own anger rekindle and spread with the memory.

"*For the souls of those we love,*" he growled, as he did before any bloodletting. It was a call to arms, a mantra of strength, a pledge of allegiance to *Los Oscuros*—the secret order Papi had subsequently founded to battle the Church that had robbed him of so much.

Perhaps it was a similar loss, or the threat of it that was driving this witch.

Seeing that all four of her candles were lit, Andre reached out a hand toward the window and concentrated, feeling the air go thick around his fingers as though they were suspended in viscous fluid. He then flicked his finger and watched as the window lock popped free with a soft *click*. Although he still possessed the power of magnetism, his influence was far below what it should have been. Manipulating bullets in the lab had been relatively easy since they'd been streaking toward him—but manipulating an object at rest was another matter entirely. He would need to take steps to increase the power after the attack.

After quietly opening the window, he concentrated on his corporeal form. This is the weight of my body, this is the weight of my blood, he thought, trembling with effort as sweat slid down his forehead. For a moment, nothing happened, and then he felt the weight of his core melt away as his body dissolved into black mist.

Channeling himself like a river, he flowed through the screen and poured slowly into the living room. With feeding, he knew he would be able to control his dissolution with greater agility and speed. He willed his body to become solid again—the muscled weight of his torso and limbs returning with an exquisite tightening sensation—a mere two feet behind the couch. Brother and sister were so captivated by the television that they didn't notice.

Looming behind them, Andre could see that the boy was muscular, a football player, perhaps, and clad in a hooded sweatshirt and khakis. His sister was slight with long brown hair and dressed in a purple blouse and jeans. The boy, a bigger threat, would die first.

"I don't understand what men see in her," the girl said, indicating a slender blond actress on television.

"If you mean big boobs and a nice butt, neither do I,"

her brother replied, smirking. His sister hit him playfully in the thigh.

In a single, smooth motion, Andre gripped the boy's head and wrenched it around with a sharp *crack!* His mouth curled with satisfaction. Perhaps he was not as weak as he believed.

Attracted by the noise, his sister turned and stared, not quite understanding what had happened. A look of confusion crossed her face, followed by one of abject horror.

She scrambled away from her brother's corpse, and screamed—only there was no sound. The witch's spell had kicked in. Andre was impressed with her skill.

The girl's mouth twisted and her neck muscles throbbed with the force of her silent cry, and when she saw Andre, she screamed even harder, eyes bulging, spittle flying from her lips, frozen in place by terror. Still, there was no sound. But the element of surprise was gone, and that meant he would have to be more savage in his attack. Something the witch should not see.

Andre reached out toward a knife that rested on a plate on an end table. Felt the air grow thick. With a grunt of extreme effort, he whipped his hand toward the girl and the knife followed, burying itself hilt-deep in her stomach.

As she doubled over, Andre quickly lowered the window shade. The hiss of falling plastic and the babbling television were the only noises in the room. When he was certain the witch could not see into the room, he leaped over the couch. Yanked the girl's head back by the hair. Raked his ring across her throat.

A fountain of blood shot from her carotid artery, dousing his chest, before he clamped his mouth over the spray.

The kicking girl's lifeblood rushed down his throat and throughout his body, warming his icy flesh for a delicious few moments while his vision swam with brilliant colors and his parched organs swelled with new strength. When he was done feeding, he let her pale, limp body slump to the floor and then slashed the neck of her brother and drank again.

After draining the second corpse, Andre paused at the privacy screen and listened for sounds of alarm from the parents in the kitchen, but heard only the clanking of dishes. Opening the screen, he walked down a dark, narrow hallway past a tiny shower until he reached the doorway of the kitchen. His bare, bloody feet tracked the beige carpet.

His muscles still trembled, but felt stronger now. That was no reason to be careless, however.

Reaching the kitchen, he saw that the wife was in close profile, washing dirty dishes in the sink. She had long black hair and wore a green T-shirt and navy shorts. Her husband, muscular like his son and clad in a New Orleans Saints football jersey and blue jeans, stood near the master bedroom doorway, and dried clean dishes with a towel.

Neither noticed him, when the wife's mouth clearly formed the words, "How much longer can we stay in this trailer, hon? I'm worried about the kids." But there was no sound. She canted her head in confusion. Tried again. Nothing.

Her husband smirked, obviously shrugging off her silence to some joke—and then he saw Andre. His eyes went wide.

Andre charged past the wife, slammed a fist into the husband's chest. With a crunch of shattered ribs, the man pitched back into the master bedroom. Andre then reached out a hand, felt the air grow thick, and slammed the bedroom door closed behind the man, pressing the metal edge deep into the frame. Sealing him in.

The woman cowered against the sink, mouth twisted

in a silent scream. Andre threw her to the floor, away from the window and the prying eyes of the witch.

Since there was no shade on the kitchen window, he knew he would have to kill the mother in a different way, a way that was much less messy. Time to test another ability.

Andre clutched the wife's arm. Transforming his body into a bolt of black lightning at the lab had required blunt effort, yes, but channeling it required lethal finesse and therefore more effort. Gritting his teeth, he summoned crackling blue-black energy from his core and sent it rushing down his arm into her body. She convulsed on the floor, racked by current, as her husband pounded desperately against the sealed bedroom door. The air smelled of cooked flesh.

So his imprisonment had not permanently damaged him after all. And as with his power of magnetism, his control of lightning would improve with the appropriate preparation, no doubt.

The wife writhing weakly in his grip, Andre raked his ring against her throat and drank. Again he relished the spiraling colors that crowded his vision, and the precious, fleeting warmth that infused his skin—until he heard a crash, then a clap of thunder. Then felt a punch in his left shoulder. He whirled, tasting her blood on his lips.

The husband had battered down the bedroom door, and now stood with a smoking pistol clutched in both hands. The man's face was a mask of anguish, his lips twisting with silent curses.

Meeting the baleful gaze, Andre concentrated and imagined the husband turning the weapon on himself. "Now you," he ordered.

Pupils turning pure white, the husband dutifully pressed the gun barrel to his temple and pulled the trigger, a victim of Suggestion—another power that had survived his imprisonment in the cave.

Andre finished feeding on the wife, and then moved to the husband. Finally sated, he exited the trailer and headed toward the witch who was back in the tree line. The candle there flickered and silhouetted her body with orange light.

"Are you sure they're dead?" she said as he approached. "We can't afford any witnesses."

"You need to ask?" Andre scowled, anger flaring, and thought that maybe the witch wasn't as averse to violence as he'd believed her to be, a fact that could make her more pliable—or dangerous.

Chapter 15

Leah found that, beyond the attacks, she and Scott had nothing in common and agreed on little, but when he'd mentioned going to Cueva del Diablo and seeing the Texas cave for himself, she'd known she'd had no choice but to accompany him. Perhaps there in the labyrinth where her father and brother had been slaughtered, she would find the key to undoing the creature responsible.

Early the next morning, the moment Scott was cleared by Ackart and freed of his bonds, they left in a helicopter with the major's approval and with him piloting the craft. Wearing fatigues too big for her with sleeves and pant legs rolled up, Leah sat belted into the cockpit seat next to Scott, her stomach doing a tumble as they lifted off.

They flew in virtual silence, the thunderous noise muffled by microphone-equipped headsets with large earcups. Leah looked at the control consoles between them and overhead, but the array of breakers, dials, and controls that Scott continually consulted and adjusted meant nothing to her.

It was only when they were halfway there that Leah said, "I suppose Major Ackart didn't tell you about what happened to me."

"Ackart doles out information on a need-to-know basis. I needed to know, so of course she told me that you survived an attack in the cave."

Leah never talked about what had happened to her.

Not with anyone, not even with Javier, who might have been able to help her sort out her emotions and deal with them in a healthy way. But maybe Scott was the one person she *could* talk to—having survived the creature's attack as they both had, he might be the only one who could understand how she felt. Sharing could forge some bond between them, she thought, an important factor if they were to work together rather than at cross-purposes.

"You were what . . . eleven?"

She nodded. "An eleven-year-old kid full of herself. I felt like nothing could touch me, like I could do anything, no matter what anyone said."

"Don't do it, Leah. I'm warning you! Dad told us to wait up for him . . ."

Gabe's warning still haunted her. A sick feeling filled her as she saw his face illuminated by her helmet light as clearly as she had that fatal day. Other memories might be less bright, but this one was as vivid as ever.

Scott made some adjustments and angled the helicopter in a slightly different direction. Leah's stomach swirled and her pulse rushed through her at an accelerated pace.

"I didn't listen when I should have," she said. "Dad and Gabe . . ."

Her senses were heightened and yet she suddenly felt detached, like she wasn't even in the helicopter, despite the muffled noise and vibration. For a moment, she was back in the cave . . . seeing the black smoke that reminded her of bats . . . hearing Dad's and Gabe's screams . . . being covered with their blood.

"What happened? I want to hear it from you."

Her eyes filled with tears. "They were slaughtered by that creature, and I couldn't do anything to stop it."

Scott surprised her by saying, "How could you? We

couldn't stop it with an arsenal. But how did you get away from him?"

Leah swallowed hard and went on. Her hand was shaking as she held it out, palm up. "In the infirmary, you asked about this scar. He left me this when he tried to kill me, too. He was hanging on to my arm when I fell into a shaft of light. His hand started burning, and I slapped at it to get it off me." She flexed her hand and her voice grew weaker as she said, "That thin beam of light is the only reason I'm alive."

"Leah . . ."

Scott covered her hand and glanced at her again, obviously full of questions he didn't ask, and for a moment time stood still. At his reassuring touch, Leah felt her pulse speed up and her senses come alive.

But her attraction to Scott warred with something else, something equally disturbing. . .

Remembering the weird aura she'd seen in the infirmary, she slipped her hand free. Why did she have this insistent sense that something was wrong? Was it simply an echo of the attack in the lab or was there more to it?

Realizing she was through talking, Scott let it be and concentrated on the flight.

Trying to ignore the currents of air that rocked the helicopter and threatened her stomach, Leah prepared herself.

She could do this, she told herself. She had to for Dad and Gabe. And for herself.

A while later, Scott landed in a clearing that looked like a parking lot. No vehicles in sight meant they would be alone inside. If anything happened to them, no one would come to their rescue.

Nothing was going to happen, Leah assured herself as she put on her spelunking gear. The creature was loose somewhere in the swamps or back bayous of southern Louisiana. Not here.

Even so, as they faced the entrance to the cave, Leah could hardly breathe. She clung to the soft shoulder bag that held the few simple tools of her trade she would need. She had to go in. Had to. It might be the only way to find something to use against the creature.

Scott dressed more for a military strike—a vest with pockets for ammo and a belt hung with weapons. "Are you ready?" he said as he snapped a light to his tactical helmet.

Leah would never be ready. She didn't say anything. She just stood and stared at the entrance, which to her seemed like the gates of hell.

"C'mon." His hand pressed into the small of her back, he urged her to take that first step forward.

Meeting Scott's gaze, she noted his expression. While previously she'd seen anger or disdain pulling at his features when he looked at her, they now were drawn into something more subtle. Compassion? As if realizing his expression betrayed his thoughts, he covered and went neutral. Leah guessed that a military man like Scott would consider such a soft emotion a weakness.

Her heart thudded against her ribs as she moved through the entrance into the dark and down a tunnel, whose floor was slanted and broken.

"Watch your step," he said. "Lots of loose rocks along the way."

The deeper they moved into the cave, the stronger became her unease. The air grew cooler but her body grew hotter. Sweat licked her flesh and a bead dribbled down her forehead into her eyelashes. Her vision suddenly blurred, she blinked rapidly and stepped wrong. Her ankle twisted and she flew sideways.

Scott caught her arm and steadied her, but grunted with the effort.

Realizing he was hurting, she met his gaze directly and said, "Your wounds—"

"Just a little sore." He looked away first as though admitting any weakness might embarrass him. "I'm fine."

So he didn't want to talk about it, but his stoicism didn't keep her from worrying about him, from wanting to do something to make it better. As they walked on, she watched him carefully for any signs of his being in trouble. If one of his wounds opened, he could bleed out. Not on her watch.

Captain Scott Boulder might be gruff, but he was a good man and probably an even better soldier. He would have to be to do what he did for his country. She might not agree with using violence to solve the world's problems, but war seemed to be a fact of life. She needed to accept that, accept Scott as he was. If there was trouble, she would be glad to have him on her side. They might be coming from different directions in their methods, but their mutual goal to stop the creature was a bond she couldn't deny.

"I know this has to be tough for you—coming back here," he said.

Leah had been so wrapped up in her worry about Scott, she had forgotten about where they were.

Swallowing hard, she forced a smile, pretending she was okay just as he had. "Sometimes we have to do tough things to protect others," she said.

Leah was thinking mainly about Scott. Whatever it was that affected his aura had to be a result of the attack. She was certain it indicated some connection to the creature, though he wouldn't believe as much. And though that connection might help her find what she needed, she couldn't imagine him agreeing to cooperate. So she would have to do what she needed to do without his permission, just as she had in obtaining a vial of his blood from Major Ackart before leaving.

In the large outer cavern now, she took the left branch

as she had seventeen years before, the route forever etched into her memory. Her steps slowed as they neared the next cavern. *The* cavern. The glyphs she'd seen only in photographs surrounding the entryway seemed to glow with an unearthly light under her headlamp's beam.

"What the . . ." Scott stopped beside her and stared for a moment before tracing one of the glyphs with his fingers. "I wonder who did this." Studying them for a moment longer, he then said, "Let's go inside." He motioned her to follow him.

Leah couldn't make her legs work. They felt wooden, frozen in place. Scott stopped and turned to give her a questioning look. Though she could feel his impatience, he kept his own counsel and waited. She tried again, finally forcing herself to take that first step and follow.

Once inside, heart hammering, breath held, she took a quick look around at the limestone formations flat in the spray of white light, then pinned her gaze on the familiar flowstone shawl that dripped dozens of fingers. Again she froze.

"So this is where they found the mummy," Scott said, moving around, inspecting every cranny.

Making herself move, Leah avoided looking at the one place she could never revisit and fumbled with her bag. From it, she removed a green rock and five candles—four white and one green.

"What is all that?"

"The tools of my trade."

Shaking his head, Scott went back to his own search. She set the white candles in the four directions, lighting them as she went, seeing the magic circle forming in her mind's eye. She hadn't known what to expect—to feel her father and brother here, perhaps—but it was just a space empty of anything to do with them but bad memories now. Still, a space that made her pulse rush and her tongue feel thick against the roof of her mouth. She sensed there was, indeed, more—something of the creature's—and she was going to find whatever it was.

Taking the vial of Scott's blood from her bag, she flicked a few drops on the stone. Ready to cast the spell, she found Scott poking his head into a corner several yards away.

"Captain, can you stop what you're doing for a moment and take a couple of steps toward me."

When he turned toward her, a familiar aggravation pulled on his features once more. "What? Why?"

"Please." He needed to be inside the circle. "It's important."

Scowling, Scott stepped toward her until she raised her hand, indicating he should stop. "Now what?"

"Now this." She set fire to the blood on the stone and whispered, "Link all that is connected by blood."

A second later, a ghostly haze of purple made a triangle between the stone and Scott, extending to the far reaches of the tunnel beyond the shawl canopy.

Leah gasped and fought to hold herself together.

Whatever was here was in the middle of her nightmare, a place she wasn't willing to revisit.

Chapter 16

Scott saw a purple flash and instantly brought his MP5 to bear on Leah, wincing as the sudden movement sent a barb of pain through his bandaged chest wound. In that split second, he felt a surge of sizzling fear and regret as he thought she'd triggered an improvised explosive device of some sort. And then he saw the hovering triangle of deep purple light that connected a patch of blood-splashed stone, his chest, and a distant point on the cave wall.

"What the hell?" he said, his heart racing. He sidestepped quickly, but couldn't shake the point of purple light expanding from his chest. The triangle warped as he moved. "Tell me what's going on. *Now!*"

"It's okay, Captain!" Leah said raising her hands. "You're not in any danger, I promise!"

He moved again, but the point of light stayed put. The effect seemed harmless enough, but he kept a tight grip on his weapon just in case. "You'd better have a damn good reason for this. I could have killed you."

"I'm sorry, but I didn't think you'd let me cast it otherwise."

"Cast? What are you talking about?"

"The Finding Spell," she said, indicating the triangle. "Actually, I was hoping we wouldn't need the spell at all, but the cave is much bigger than I remember as a child. Much more complex. We don't have time to search it all if we want to save your brother."

He saw her eyes flicker with remembered pain as she

glanced at the myriad passages that led from the antechamber. He'd empathized with her on the helicopter because her past had been truly horrific. No little girl should experience what she'd experienced. But if she'd shared the information as a ploy to lower his guard . . .

"So this is your 'apotropaic magic'?"

"Yes."

Scott gritted his teeth. If this woman was so concerned with his brother's life, why was she wasting time with parlor tricks? "And what about the blood on the stone?" His finger tightened on the trigger. "Did you get that from Eric?"

"No. That blood is yours."

"Excuse me?"

"From the lab. Ackart gave it to me when you were gearing up."

"Wrong answer, lady. There's no way Ackart would let you take a sample from the lab." He yanked a pair of flexicuffs from his assault vest and stepped toward her. The purple triangle stretched to follow his movement. "I'm placing you under arrest for interfering with an investigation."

"Please, Captain," she said, meeting his gaze in the eerie light. "Please let me put my hands down, and I'll explain."

Despite her plea to stay, he could see that her face was etched with fear—and not entirely because she was staring down the barrel of his MP5. As an expert in battlefield interrogation, he knew well enough when a subject was telling the truth. This woman was telling the truth as she believed it, but she was also keeping something from him. What it could be he didn't know. Playing along might be the only way to find out what it was.

"Go ahead and put down your arms. Slowly." As she did, he put away the flexicuffs and lowered the MP5.

"Now let's assume you're being straight with me. Why does this spell of yours require my blood?"

"Since you made physical contact with the creature, your essence would complete any possible connection."

"Connection to what?"

"Behind you. That was where . . ." Her voice trailed off as she looked away.

He glanced over his shoulder at the spot where the shimmering purple triangle touched the cave wall, but made sure to keep her in his peripheral vision. "Nothing there."

"Yes, there is."

"Don't move," he warned, and then walked to the wall for a closer look. The circle of white light from his helmet washed out the purple haze to illuminate the rock formation before him—a shawl of limestone drippings that concealed a low, tight passageway about three feet off the ground.

"He was there," Leah said softly, approaching. Clearly struggling with memories. "We accidentally let him out. I did . . ."

Scott felt a whisper of compassion, pushed it aside. He still didn't trust her completely, especially not after the stunt she'd pulled with the light. He could have shot her so easily . . . another needless collateral death when he'd already witnessed so many in his Special Forces career. "If you're confident about finding something down there, by all means, lead the way."

A greater dread depressed her features. "I . . . I don't know if I can."

"That's because you know as well as I do that nothing is down there. It's time you dispensed with the bullshit and told me what's really going on."

"I'll go," she said hesitantly and stepped past him. "If we want to know what's really going on we have to go in." But when she stood before the passage—the triangle's light casting her body purple—she began to tremble, unable to move. She glanced back with an expression of such abject terror that Scott couldn't help but lay a consoling hand on her shoulder. He'd felt a similar terror when Eric had fallen in the Plexiglas chamber, and realized now that coming back to the cave was far more traumatic for her than she'd let on. Even though he disagreed with her methods, he respected that she was trying to be brave in the face of her deepest fear.

"Step aside," he said softly as he shrugged free from the assault vest, pulled off his helmet, and yanked the clip from the MP5. If he was setting himself up for a fall, so be it, he thought as he laid the gear on the ground. He had to find out what was down the tunnel for Eric's sake. "If I'm not back in ten minutes, go back to the helicopter and radio for help. Got that?"

Leah glanced furtively around the cavern, still trembling, lost in her terror.

"Dr. Maguire?"

She was beyond hearing him.

"Leah?" He touched her chin and turned her face to his. Her eyes were dark, wild. "I'll be in your ear the entire time, okay?" He gently tapped the earjack of her headset. "Everything's going to be fine. Now try to hold on, and I'll be back in a few."

"Follow the beam," she managed. "It'll guide you."

"A night-light might work better in this case."

He was pleased that she smiled at the joke, and he smiled back before turning and hoisting himself into the passageway, headfirst. He couldn't blame her for her breakdown. She'd experienced more trauma than some of the soldiers he'd worked with.

He crawled the first few feet on his hands and knees as purple light filtered past him, illuminating the tunnel. But soon the tunnel closed in on all sides, forcing him onto his stomach. Eclipsing the light. Pitching him into inky darkness. He made progress now by planting his elbows on the rough stone and pulling himself forward while holding the SIG in front of him as best he could. He wormed forward inch by inch as the rock floor painfully scraped his bandaged chest wound.

"How're you doing back there, Leah?" he asked, his voice a dull echo in the tight space.

"Better," came her crackling reply.

"Good."

"How're you?"

"Making progress." And playing tunnel rat again, Scott thought, tasting gritty cave dust with each writhing inch of progress. He and Eric had done the same many times before, most recently while rooting out Taliban fighters in the mountains of Afghanistan. *Wish you were here right now, bro . . .* He and Eric had been in tight situations before. A lot tighter than this cave. That's why he steadfastly believed Eric would recover. Failure just wasn't an option.

"I'm sorry again for not telling you about the spell." Her voice was stronger now. Nearly back to normal.

"Neat trick with this purple light," he said, still wondering about the effect. "You'll have to tell me how you did it. But next time, try telling me what you're planning to do. It'll be safer for both of us."

As a leader, he knew when to dispense the advice, but he also knew when it fell on deaf ears. She'd probably do what she felt she needed to do, regardless of orders. He only hoped it wouldn't get one or both of them killed.

Scott kept going. Planted his elbows against rough stone, pulled himself forward, ate dust, planted his elbows, pulled himself forward—when the stone before him crumbled, suddenly, and he felt nothing but yawning space.

Before he could shift his center of gravity, he pitched forward and slid from the tunnel, falling for two long seconds before slamming onto the ground with a grunt. He lay on his back, dazed, as purple light flowed unobstructed from the tunnel about six feet above him. It was a miracle he'd been able to hold on to the SIG.

"Scott! Are you okay?!" Leah cried in his ear. Clearly she'd heard the commotion.

"I'm fine," he said, holstering the pistol, then rolling onto his hands and knees. "I'm out of the tunnel now . . . in another cave. What exactly am I looking for?"

"The light should be striking an object of some sort. Do you see it?"

Skeptical, Scott looked in the direction of the beam, still not convinced that the light show would pay off. From his vantage point, the deep purple beam was merely striking the dirt ground. Clambering to his feet, he walked to the spotlight, dropped to his knees, and started to dig—the only action that made sense. But he wouldn't humor Leah for much longer. Not when Eric was fighting for his life.

He'd dug a few inches down when his fingers scratched against something coarse. Cocking his eyebrow, he wiped away the dirt to reveal what looked like a three-foot-long bundle of cloth wrapped in twine. "There's something here," he said.

"What?" she said, voice edged with fear again.

He untied the twine, taking care to disturb the bundle as little as possible in case it was booby-trapped. When he folded aside the dirty cloth, the purple light reflected brilliantly off something inside, making him wince. He glimpsed a narrow edge of steel. "A sword." He took a closer look. The blade was thin, with an intricately designed hilt that would surround the fist of whoever wielded it. "A rapier."

"What does it look like?"

"I'll bring it out."

"Let me warn you," Leah said. "Touch the sword, and you'll bring two points of the triangle together. The Finding Spell will be broken. You'll be in darkness."

"It's okay. I didn't travel far from the tunnel."

"Please be careful."

Scott carefully slid his hand into the gilded hilt, feeling the cool, intricate carvings against the back of his hand—when his entire body convulsed like he'd been given a powerful jolt of electricity. He cried out in surprise and tried to let go of the hilt, but found that he couldn't, as though the hilt were clutching him instead.

"Scott?" Leah's voice crackled in his ear, her terror rising along with his. "SCOTT?!"

Trembling uncontrollably on the cave floor, Scott's vision flashed bright red and then he felt like he was falling through space, as Leah's screams echoed in his ears, fading, fading . . .

At first he thought he'd fallen from the tunnel again, but then he realized the claustrophobic, viselike sensations of the cave had disappeared.

In fact, it felt like he was running now. He could feel his legs pumping, could feel his feet striking soft earth. Soft images crowded his vision—blobs of dark color and shadow—before they sharpened into focus to reveal that he was sprinting down a moonlit trail between trees and fragrant wild grass. Running like his life depended on it as sweat poured down the back of his neck and fear sizzled through his veins.

But even though the fear felt very real, it also felt removed. Distant. Filtered somehow. Almost like the emotion belonged to someone else.

He tried to stop running—no use. Looking down he saw the short legs of a young boy clad in black stockings.

What the hell? He felt a spinning sense of disorientation that was very much his own. Was he still in the tunnel? Had Leah done something else to him?

His vision bounced up and down as he continued along the path toward a small church with cracked stone walls and a splintered cross looming from a wooden roof. He burst through the creaking front doors into a nave cluttered with rotting pews.

Two men were arguing at the altar. One had dark hair and wore a black ironsmith's apron, the other was a priest with white hair and a long brown robe tied at the waist with a rope. Their voices warbled like someone was screwing with the volume control on a television set.

Scott felt growing terror—filtered, distant, not his own—as he hid behind a pew and watched. And then the man in the black leather apron ran the priest through with a sword.

But not just any sword, Scott realized with astonishment as the distant terror blossomed, rushing through his veins. A rapier exactly like the one he'd found at the end of the tunnel.

What the *fuck* was going on? Scott tried to force himself from the scene as he would from a nightmare, but no matter how hard he tried, he couldn't affect what was happening. He felt trapped, out of control. At the mercy of the bizarre vision.

"I renounce you and your greed!" the man yelled at the priest in Spanish, voice suddenly clear.

And even though Scott didn't speak the language, he was amazed to discover he understood every word.

Scott then saw the man fling an altar candle against a hanging tapestry, which ignited into roaring flames. The man almost ran past him on his way out of the church, but spotted him at the last moment. Scott's vision pinwheeled as the man scooped him into this arms and then shouldered his way through the front doors.

"Mama is dead!" This time the voice did not come from the man. The plaintive, pitched cry echoed dully. Close, yet oddly distant.

The man nodded like he understood, and then glanced back at the burning church. Scott saw a disturbing fire in the man's eyes that rivaled the growing flames . . .

Suddenly there was another flash of red, and Scott found himself scrabbling on the dirt floor of the cave again.

"Scott? What's happened? Please answer me!" Leah's panicked voice was back in his ear.

Still trembling but no longer clutching the rapier, Scott wished like hell he could answer that question.

Chapter 17

Her dreams haunted by the Toutant family, Rebecca awoke telling herself that she'd done what she'd had to do for Danton's sake. Tears and regrets were for the weak. Guilt slid through her. No, that wasn't right. She really hadn't wanted innocents to die. Of course she regretted it.

Trying to put the deaths out of mind, she attended to her toilette and dressed for the day, then checked on the one person in her life who mattered to her before going back to the mansion and facing Andre once more. The moment she stepped into Danton's bedroom, he opened his eyes, but they seemed glazed, as if he were feverish again.

Placing a hand on his forehead, she asked, "Didn't you sleep?"

"Off and on all night."

He was warm but not hot. Still, she sat at the edge of the bed and dampened a washcloth in his bedside basin, then ran the cool, wet cloth over his face.

"Having bad dreams again?"

"Some," he admitted.

Though he would never admit to being afraid of dying, she could hear that fear in his voice. It cut through her like a knife. She couldn't lose him. She would do anything she had to if it meant Danton would live.

"It won't be long." At least she hoped Andre wouldn't

be a problem. Her voice was like steel when she said, "I found someone who is going to help you."

Despite his illness, Danton seemed to realize something was wrong. His expression alarmed, he asked, "*Chère*, you're not doing anything that will get you in trouble, are you?"

"No, Danton. No trouble."

"I would never want you to put yourself at risk for me."

The very reason she loved him so much. He'd protected her from the time he was able to beat up their stepfather. Now it was her turn to protect him.

Rebecca had confidence that not only would she succeed in getting her brother a new lease on life, but that she would find a way to gain more power using Andre.

She did have one worry, however, and that was the military. What were they doing to find the vampire? If they got to him before she had succeeded in her plan, Danton would die. How close were they? The night before, she'd tried to connect with Eric to find out, but it had been to no avail.

Was he even still alive?

She would have to use more magic to find out.

Arriving back at the mansion a half hour later, Rebecca first made certain Andre wasn't around to spy on her, then began preparing potions she might need.

She'd gone through her library at home the night before to research the Philosopher's Stone and had found some answers in *The Grand Grimoire*, the definitive book presenting rituals of black magic—the same book that had guided her in restoring the vampire and putting him under her control. According to the *Grimoire*, the Philosopher's Stone could be used to create gold from lead. But in a darker context, if Andre were made one with the Stone, his soul would be restored to him. He would be able to walk in sunlight, wouldn't *need* to feed.

Furthermore, he would become immortal.

Rebecca put a vial to her lips and downed a potion meant to keep her from feeling base emotions that might weaken her. She needed her wits about her when dealing with the vampire, and the potion would keep her on an even keel. She wouldn't fool herself as to how dangerous he was—he could kill her if she let down her guard—so she couldn't afford any weakness that he might use against her.

Retrieving Andre's soul wouldn't lighten his spirit, wouldn't change him into a less savage being. The Philosopher's Stone would simply give him the ability to do whatever dark deed he desired with impunity. She had already committed an atrocity by reviving him.

Sweat rolling down her spine from the humid heat, Rebecca lit specially prepared incense and a black cross candle, then as a small sacrifice to the loa poured a glass of aged rum in a small glass. "*Ayza, protect me while dealing with the vampire. Share with me your wisdom so that I can continue to control him. And guide me to find Eric, to know if he's still alive.*" When she closed her eyes and breathed in the sharp scent of the incense, a thought came to her.

Giving the vampire eternal life would be unthinkable.

The alternative was to trick Andre into believing he would get what he wanted—but only after saving her brother. She had to get Andre to heal Danton as soon as possible. Then she could do what she wanted with Andre, leave him here with a spell on the mansion so he couldn't get out, and let him dry up without a blood source, if she so chose. He undoubtedly underestimated her and believed she would do what *he* wanted.

"Thank you, Ayza," she whispered, striking a match and setting it to the liquor.

Then she stared deep into the flame of the black cross candle and willed herself to see through Eric's eyes. Nothing. No matter how long or how hard she concentrated, she got only a void. She found a box that held clippings from Eric's body—hair and nails and dead skin. Taking a few strands of hair, she burned them in the candle's flame and tried again. Still no image, but concentrating with all her might, she heard the murmur of voices.

"*. . . no change in his condition . . .*"

"*. . . let me know if he comes out of it . . .*"

And then the voices were gone, replaced only by faint noises . . . a motor of some sort . . . a clatter . . . footsteps walking away.

Frowning, Rebecca sat back and thought about what she'd heard. It was as if Eric were in a deep sleep, or perhaps in a coma. That was probably why she hadn't been able to connect with him the night before. It was thought coma patients could hear what people said around them, and apparently that was true. But would anyone say anything of use to her in a sickroom? Rebecca wondered. Perhaps. So it was worth checking in on Eric when she could.

She returned to the rooms she'd chosen as her quarters while at the mansion. After cooling down in the shower, she dressed in a white cotton skirt and blouse that were already damp by the time she got back downstairs.

This time, Andre was waiting for her. He sat in a chair at the dining room table where he'd spread out her "puny magical trinkets," as he called them. Did he think he could somehow make them useless to her? His olive complexion was not quite as ruddy as it had been the morning before. He needed to feed again. Another cause for worry.

Surprisingly, he said, "I was trying to amuse myself,

but it seems I don't have the capacity to work with candles and herbs. You'll have to show me how they work."

Eyeing him suspiciously, Rebecca looked for the lie in his words, but his expression for once was benign. No anger. No hatred. Perhaps resignation. Nothing more telling. Had he finally come to terms with her being in charge? No doubt he realized that if he wanted the Philosopher's Stone, he had to stop threatening her.

"Actually, you can accompany me to Madam Erykah's Voodoo Emporium, or perhaps you'd rather not. There are many religious items for sale in the shop."

He grinned at her. "And you think I'm afraid of them? Religious articles are of no consequence. I'll go."

Rebecca glanced out the window. "It's not quite dark yet, but the sun has set. I bought you clothing you might like better than the suit," she said, fetching a bag from where she'd left it near the back door and setting it on the table between them.

She'd bought him black pants, black shirt, black shoes. Clothes that wouldn't show blood, she thought, the potion working to keep her from some useless emotion.

Andre's response was to look into the bag and, without a word, carry it off into the next room.

Rebecca swayed slightly before catching herself, both hands flat on the table. Despite the potion, she couldn't deny Andre's power and her response to it. She'd grown used to the insults and threats. When they weren't forthcoming, she feared he was simply keeping his dark thoughts to himself.

What plans did he have for her?

Chapter 18

Scott did his best to rid his mind of the disturbing images he'd seen in the cave as he landed the Black Hawk in a neighborhood that had been decimated by hurricanes.

Leah had insisted she had nothing to do with the vision, and he believed her for the most part. After he'd told her about the boy and his father she seemed as genuinely confused as he was. In addition, she hadn't known what to make of the rapier, which lay bundled in the Black Hawk's storage locker.

Scott frowned, troubled by a cold suspicion that more was at play here than he'd originally thought. There was no way he could completely discount what had transpired over the last couple days, especially the vision. Was magic really a factor? Obviously there were forces that defied his control and logic.

The troubling questions weren't the only things on his mind.

There was also this crime scene.

Ackart had radioed the Black Hawk shortly after he and Leah had left the cave. Apparently, not long after the major had issued an APB on the escaped fugitive a passerby had reported gunshots to police. Quadruple homicide. There were enough details about the murder scene that seemed to mesh with the perp's MO and warrant a response.

Scott felt a deep, familiar sadness as he guided Leah

from the Black Hawk and toward the line of yellow police tape. He'd seen too many murder scenes like this in the world's backwaters; multiple victims of insurgent death squads or government intelligence agencies. The innocent always seemed to get caught in the cross fire.

"Major Ackart sent us," Scott told a detective at the tape as he flashed his military credentials.

"Other personnel arrived a short time ago, Captain," the detective said, indicating several Humvees parked in defensive positions around the scene. "Take all the time you need."

Scott ushered Leah under the police tape and toward the collapsed, burned-out husk of the FEMA trailer—one more destroyed home in a state littered with them. As they approached, the usual peppery-sweet smell of Louisiana's humid air and flora was undermined by the vague scent of charred flesh. From this vantage point, only scorched appliances and other blackened debris were visible, but Scott knew they'd see bodily remains soon enough.

As Scott moved, his chest wound throbbed ominously under the bandages—the cave tunnel floor hadn't done it any good—but he kept his discomfort from Leah. The last thing he needed was her reporting back to Ackart that he was unfit for the mission. The truth was, he wouldn't rest until he captured the suspect, his own condition be damned.

"Scott, could you tell me what you plan to do here?"

He glanced at her. "Investigate the crime scene. What else?"

She smiled, but he could see the frustration in her eyes. And resolve. "You haven't said one word to me since we left the cave."

"There's nothing to say."

"You don't believe me about the vision, do you?"

"I don't know."

She laid a hand on his shoulder, stopping him. "It's important that we work together on this, now more than ever since things are happening that we don't understand. We very well might need each other."

He looked at her evenly, eyes landing on the soft black purse that held her candles, chalks, and other trinkets. The fact of the matter was that he probably *didn't* need her. All he needed was a fair chance to find the perp—and a loaded MP5 once he found him. Scott couldn't explain how the suspect had sustained multiple gunshots in the lab and survived, but now that he was on the hunt and possessed the tactical advantage, he had no doubt the practical weapon would be effective now. Certainly more than any spell casting might be.

And yet, Leah was sincere in her desire to be of help—he had to respect that. He had to respect her for the courage she'd shown in the cave.

"Okay," he said finally. "What do you want to know?"

"Do you think the creature was here?"

Creature. Scott couldn't help but frown. Leah's magic was tough enough to swallow, but now she wanted him to believe they were after some sort of monster. The killer had displayed powers similar to his Team—that he had consumed blood didn't prove anything. Scott had battled terrorists the world over whose sick rituals of power made drinking blood seem mild.

"I think this *psychopath* is on a killing spree," he said, refusing to pander to her superstition, "and I plan to stop him."

Leah locked gazes with him. Something in her eyes arrested him. "Then you'll need to forget what you think you know about death," she said. "He's not human, though I do think he's working with one."

Scott ignored her second reference to monsters, and started walking again. "You're treading on thin ice,

Leah. My brother has a distinguished record serving this country. He's not a criminal."

"I'm not talking about your brother. Remember what I told you in the hospital room?"

"About Eric's aura?" He could barely say the words.

"I sense the same darkness here."

"So you're telling me the killer and his accomplice are still around, even with cops canvassing the area."

She shuddered. "They're not here anymore. It's daylight . . . the creature wouldn't chance it. But the fact remains that I feel him . . . with energy this dark, traces get left behind."

Her face seemed strained, and she rubbed her arms as though a malignant residue flowed through her. He felt nothing unusual in the air, not even so much as static electricity.

"Traces . . . like the black magic you felt in the infirmary?"

"As black as it gets."

"I can't waste any more time with this, Leah," Scott said. "Not when there's tangible evidence to be investigated. My brother's life is at stake, not to mention the lives of future victims."

Leah seemed to take a mental step back, though she maintained her composure. "I can appreciate your wanting to protect your brother. Truly, I do. But before entering that cave, did you think such visions were possible?"

"Frankly, I'm still not sure what happened. And neither are you."

"If it were my brother in that infirmary, I'd want every possibility explored, no matter how far-fetched it might seem," she said, and then moved away from him.

He watched her for a moment. Her expression strained as she seemed to take the full weight of whatever dark energy she felt. It was as if she'd already forgotten his presence as she headed for a group of trees across the property.

Letting her go, he was relieved that she'd no longer be a burden. But there was something about the way her green eyes held his attention, the way she spoke to him with soft but firm authority. There was sincerity in her that transcended her talk of magic. Despite all logic, he trusted her.

Suddenly, a barb of pain shot through his chest, followed by a shock wave of cold. Icy sweat dotted his forehead. "Goddammit," he grunted, cursing the pain. He shivered despite a sultry breeze that had kicked up. He had to keep it together.

Scott hurried on, and when he reached the burned-out trailer, he stepped through a charred hole into what had once been the living room. The stench of charred flesh was almost overpowering. There was a body on the destroyed couch that had been completely consumed by flame, an ashen stick figure. On the floor was another, curled into a fetal position. Scott couldn't tell whether the bodies were male or female since distinguishing characteristics had been seared away, but he could see very clearly a deep horizontal cut along what was left of their throats—just as the police had reported.

In itself, this wasn't definitive evidence of their killer, but it was a step in the right direction.

He then made his way into the kitchen, which was also a total loss. There was a third body lying on the floor, near the dishwasher. Its head and torso were blackened with the same deep cut across the throat, but the legs—a woman's—were deep red. He'd seen the human body ravaged by every weapon, substance, and torture imaginable during his time in the field, and knew well enough that this flesh had not been burned, but *fried* by electricity.

Scott thought back to the pale man exploding into a

bolt of black lightning. The slashed throats, the electrical burns . . . *Our guy has been here. Now I'm sure of it.*

Turning to leave, he noticed a framed family photo on the wall, somehow undamaged by the flames except for light scorching around the edges. Mother, father, teenage son and daughter. These people didn't deserve to die like this. They'd already lost everything to the hurricane, everything they held dear except one another.

Continuing his search, he entered the master bedroom. A fourth charred body lay inside. A portion of floor next to the body remained intact, and on it was blood and what looked like bits of skull and brain, cooked into a brittle, crimson mass by the intense heat.

Suddenly, a cramp gripped his stomach, one that made the earlier pain in his chest seem like a tickle. Grunting, he dropped to his knees. Crushed his eyes closed. *Jesus.* He took slow breaths through clenched teeth, trying to ride through the agony.

After a couple of minutes, the gnawing subsided, and when he opened his eyes again, he noticed that the blood and brains seemed to shimmer. Almost glow. And then another feeling washed over him, a sort of craving.

Hunger?

Gotta tell BB to go easy on the fucking painkillers.

He struggled to his feet. If he and Leah acted fast, they could coordinate a stakeout of other trailers in the area. Maybe catch the killer in a dragnet.

Scott stepped from the trailer and spotted Leah on the far side of the property. Watching her in the tree line, he wondered how she could possibly use her methods at an actual crime scene. Not in a way that would set back the investigation, he hoped.

Chapter 19

Leah couldn't get away from Scott fast enough. Even though she empathized with him, even though she had felt some attraction for him earlier at the cave, they rubbed each other the wrong way. Stopping when she got to some bushy growth, she glanced back. Though the FEMA trailer and a few members of the investigative team were in view, Scott wasn't. Still, she felt wired, nerves on edge. Her pulse beat swiftly against her throat and she had to think about breathing.

What was wrong with her?

Why did this destruction feel . . . well, so personal?

Undoubtedly because of the perpetrator. The same creature that had slaughtered her father and brother had done the same to this family. Even though she hadn't come face-to-face with it, she recognized its essence, which brought back the painful memory of the attack that was still vivid in her mind even if her other memories of Dad and Gabe weren't.

A coldness enveloped her as she thought about the creature's power for destruction. How many lives would it take before it was stopped this time?

Could she do any less than use whatever weapon she must against it, no matter the personal cost?

Maybe she wouldn't have to . . . maybe she could avoid using magic, thereby avoid losing more memories . . .

Leah took a deep breath and concentrated on finding something tangible that would help track down the creature. Something perhaps connected to the human accomplice.

The brush here was disturbed, as if someone had been tromping around this area. Leah hesitated only a second before stepping through bushes and knee-high weeds.

Her pulse jumped when she spotted a half-burned-out black candle barely a yard away. She stooped to examine it more closely. The moment she touched it her fingers tingled with what she could only describe as a trickle of energy. Picking up the waxy remains, she examined the drawing on the side, distorted from the heat of the flame. Her eyes widened when she realized an X had been drawn across a mouth that contained the name Marthe Toutant, one of the victims.

"Voodoo."

Her heart began to thud and she felt her blood rush through her body. Someone with great power—undoubtedly a houngan or mambo—had cast a Silence Spell over the victims, which would have meant that no one had heard their screams. She closed her eyes and concentrated on the candle, on the tactile and olfactory sensations it provided.

A cloying scent wafted through her. And the sensation of satin against flesh.

A woman. Definitely a woman.

Letting go of the candle, Leah stood and thought about it. Undoubtedly the woman was the person responsible for the dark energy surrounding Scott's brother Eric. Voodoo would make sense. If Eric had been put under a spell—bound to this woman to do her bidding—it would explain the erratic behavior Ackart had told her about. If he came out of the coma, Eric probably wouldn't even remember what he'd done.

Leah wondered what might she be able to get from Eric, even in his current state, if she could be alone with him and really focus. The results might be very revealing.

Picking up the black candle, Leah thought to go back to base. Nothing else for her to do here. She went in search of Scott and saw him outside the trailer.

"Do you mind if I go back without you?" She held out the candle. "I found this. Voodoo. I thought I would give it to BB."

Though Scott didn't say anything as he reached for it, she noted the way his expression darkened as his hand brushed hers. And who could blame him after what had happened to him in the cave. He flipped the candle over, saw the X through the mouth and name and nodded. "I don't know what BB can do with this, but sure, give it to him."

As Leah reclaimed it, she realized Scott winced, then quickly covered. She was concerned, but knew that no good could come of her bringing it up.

"Maybe you should go back, too. Call it a day."

"Can't. Not yet. I'm not done here."

She wanted to argue with him, to find some way to make him take it easy, but she respected him too much to undercut him. He put the mission above self. He would do what he had to, just as she would.

Scott signaled two men in fatigues talking near a Humvee and asked one of them to give her a ride back to base. Then he said, "Leah, would you check on Eric for me?"

Until now, he'd kept her at arm's length, deflecting any personal talk of his brother back to the mission at hand, so the request came as a surprise.

Softening, Leah smiled. "Sure. I'd be happy to." He'd been careful of her feelings in the cave until she'd played her magic card. The least she could do was reassure him if she could. "I'll let you know if there's anything to report."

"Thanks."

As the Humvee pulled away from the trailer, Leah glanced back to get a last glimpse of Scott. He held himself a bit stiffly. She wished she could do something to ease his pain. Good news about Eric would go a long way to making him feel better, she was certain. If only she could find a way to reassure him.

Despite the trials of the day, Leah tried to relax. She had a job to do, a promise to herself to fulfill. She had to stop the creature before more lives were lost. But she was still unsure about Scott's vision in the cave. Could she have triggered it with her Finding Spell?

Once back at the base, she delivered the candle to BB. She wasn't sure what he might deduce from it, but she at least hoped for some interest in what she found.

Slightly discouraged, she changed out of the military garb before heading for the infirmary to check on Eric as Scott had requested. A nurse was in the infirmary, checking Eric's vitals and scribbling something on a chart. Leah waited until the woman was done and had left the room before she entered. She was doing this for Scott, but beyond that, she wanted time with Eric alone so she could use her empathic powers to learn what she could from him despite the coma.

Leah approached the bed and spoke softly. "Eric, I'm Leah Maguire and I want to help you." She knew he could hear her on some level, just as he heard the soft music playing in the background. Sitting on the side of the bed, she touched his wrist as she said, "Your brother Scott is worried about you," and felt a blip in his pulse.

Not taking her hand away from his wrist, she closed her eyes and concentrated, sought the connection that sometimes came to her too easily for her own comfort. Being an empath often took its toll on her. But if she could find something, anything to help Eric, that would in turn help Scott—a thought that sent a warm glow through her.

At the moment, however, she got nothing. Not from Eric. Something else, though, buzzed at the periphery of her awareness like a pesky fly.

Ignoring the distraction, she closed her eyes and concentrated harder on her subject.

"I want to help you," she said, keeping her voice low and soft. "And I want to help Scott—his heart is breaking seeing you like this." Again Eric's pulse rushed a little faster at his brother's name. "How did this happen to you, Eric? Scott says you haven't been yourself. What's been going on with you?" Remembering what she'd felt when she touched the black candle, she said, "A woman?"

Something akin to an electrical current shot through Leah, and it took all her will to keep her fingers connected to Eric's wrist. Emotions so intense they hurt swept through her limbs and left her feeling weak.

Need. Desire. Love.

Gasping, Leah opened her eyes and pulled her hand free. Pity washed through her. Eric so loved the Voodoo priestess responsible for all the deaths and destruction, that when he realized he'd acted under her orders, he would be devastated, if not destroyed.

Leah sat there and stared at the comatose man for a few minutes longer. What was she going to tell his brother, if anything? Would it do any good to share this information? Would Scott even believe her?

A pragmatist, Captain Scott Boulder didn't do well with anything he couldn't see, touch, or smell.

Leah sighed and thought to leave, then hesitated when she had that weird feeling again—stronger this time—like there was something else she should be aware of.

But what?

Standing, she stared down at Eric and opened her

mind. There it was—that internal buzzing. Magic? Eric was steeped with the effects of magic—his aura had confirmed that, but this was something more. Something she hadn't sensed when she'd been here that morning.

Opening herself to discover whatever it was, she felt drawn to Eric's head . . .

Hesitating only a second, Leah slid her hand under the pillow until her fingers bumped against metal, then snagged a chain. A pendant pulled free. Not just any pendant, but an amulet.

Holding the amulet by the chain, she studied the form, a bronze oval overlaid with a *crux gemmata*—a fork-ended cross set with thirteen jewels, standing for Christ and his twelve apostles and representing the Resurrection. Furthermore, the gemstones were sapphires, through the ages regarded as an antidote to black magic.

The question was . . . who here was trying to protect Eric and other than her knew how to turn away evil?

Chapter 20

As they broke away from the loud, sticky crush of tourists on Bourbon Street and cut down an alleyway, Andre wondered what Rebecca truly wanted from the Voodoo shop.

For a moment, he was distracted from the question by the sweet, heady scent of blood. There were so many potential sources of food all around him, yet he could not act to sate his growing hunger. All he could do was follow the witch in forced lockstep like an impotent slave.

Andre tensed his muscles against her magic shackles—not enough to alert her to the effort, but enough to probe the edged, seething boundary. Could he tear himself free? After a pause, he decided it wasn't worth the risk. Fail, and he would destroy the trust he had built with her thus far and diminish his chances to attain the Philosopher's Stone. But how he yearned to dismember her for this insult of control . . . the craving was nearly as strong as his blood lust.

He resigned himself to feasting on the crowd behind them with his eyes instead as he followed Rebecca a few steps more to a peeling yellow door hidden from view in an alcove. On it was a weathered copper placard that read: MADAM ERYKAH'S VOODOO EMPORIUM.

They hadn't taken two steps through the door when the woman behind the counter rushed forward with an expression of nauseating sycophancy. Dressed in a flowing brown caftan and a *tignon* that sat atop a tangled coil of beaded dreadlocks, she exhibited the rigid body language of someone controlled by deference and fear.

So the witch possessed considerable influence among practitioners of her primitive mysticism. Interesting.

"Priestess Rebecca, it is so good to see you again," the woman said. "How is Danton?"

"As well as can be expected, Erykah," Rebecca replied with an impatient edge. Voice harder than he'd heard before. "Did you set aside the ingredients I requested?"

"Of course. Will your guest require anything this evening?"

Andre nearly scoffed at the idea, but again held back. He had to show proper respect if he hoped to continue winning over the witch. But it was not easy.

The shop was filled with tables that held trinkets barely fit for children . . . skeleton marionettes, sweetly scented candles, necklaces hanging with gaudy beads and blobs of amber, flimsy wooden masks depicting the exaggerated howls of restless spirits, T-shirts emblazoned with silk screens of mausoleums and headstones, row after row of glass vials labeled "Love Potion" and "Healing Potion" and "Elixir of Wealth." There was a particularly absurd knickknack that sought to cash in on the ridiculous myth that New Orleans was a mecca for the undead: a die-cast model of Dracula, fanged mouth gaping in anguish as he cowered before a man wielding a wooden stake. On the base it read, "Cease, Puny Mortal!" and below that, clearly stamped aftermarket, "Welcome to New Orleans, Louisiana—Haunt for Spirits and Spooks!"

Indeed.

"He will gather whatever he needs himself," Rebecca said, "while seeing to my needs."

Enjoy your control while it lasts, witch, Andre

thought. For you will pay dearly when I break your hold.

For now, he was content with the minor victory he had already achieved—convincing the witch to allow him to enhance his alchemical powers. Although these powers would not enable him to break her magical hold, they would allow him to battle the military more effectively once they arrived. And they would arrive. It was only a matter of time.

Perhaps more important, after defeating the military and securing the Philosopher's Stone, he would then have the power to make the witch his slave once she finally set him free.

"Very well, Priestess." Erykah motioned for them to step behind the counter and push through a clicking beaded door, but stopped short of following. She knew her place.

In the back room, the mood of cheap tourism was conspicuously absent. It became clear that the tables were simply a front for objects of magic sought by true witches.

Rebecca moved to a small table that was covered by a red cloth. She looked through the bundles of herbs and vials of opaque oils arranged there, paused thoughtfully, then moved to a large mahogany bureau with glass drawers that held more herbs.

Andre tried to discern what spell the witch might be planning from the components, but they held little similarity to what he used to practice alchemy. Challenge her, and she might drop a clue, he thought.

Andre moved to a shelf and picked up a large white candle in a glass holder that bore the ornate, colored drawing of a Catholic saint. "Do you actually believe in the power of these?"

Rebecca glanced over her shoulder, and then went back to her task: opening drawer after drawer and smelling its contents before taking a pinch from some and considerably more from others. "In a manner of speaking, yes."

Her voice carried an edge of defensiveness, a clear indication that she had responded to his tone. Good. But he had to be careful not to overdo it. "And what manner would that be?"

"A manner consistent with my needs. What else?"

Interesting, he thought. From her earlier trepidation about taking lives, he had expected her to say that heart and belief played a part in her decision—and conscience, as well. Apparently that assessment had been wrong. Would she do whatever was necessary to accomplish a goal? If so, that would make her a valuable ally, indeed. "For such a steadfast reason, I would have expected accoutrements that were more"—he regarded the candle with a sneer—"profound."

She moved away from the glass drawers with several more felt bags filled with additional herbs. "Not a big fan of the Church?"

Andre realized she was trying to steer the conversation away from herself—even so, he could not help but respond with another sneer. So much about the Church filled his throat with bile; the way in which it repressed those who might seek a greater truth as it had with his father's order, *Los Oscuros.* The way in which it manipulated the word of God to further its own avarice, and the way it wasted unimaginable treasures on lurid rituals and monstrous cathedrals while common people suffered in squalor . . . while his mother's soul was condemned to Limbo and his father's mind to madness because they lacked the pittance to bribe a corrupt priest.

He felt a rush of blazing anger, and nearly crushed the candle in his grip. "My love for God is separate from the Church's blasphemy."

Rebecca nodded as she carefully reviewed her inventory. "Under fear of death, the old practitioners of Voodoo first hid their true religion under the imagery and customs of Catholicism. Times have changed, of course, but the two are still intertwined, for better or worse. I don't let that fact diminish my beliefs, however." Satisfied with her choices, she began loading the herbs and oils into a white plastic grocery bag. "For example," she continued, "the candle you're holding. In Voodoo, our loas are equivalent to the Catholic saints . . . and loas can act as intermediaries when trying to communicate with God."

"Why do you need an intermediary at all?" Andre said, placing the candle back on the shelf. He was now genuinely intrigued, but still looking for any hint of the witch's purpose. "I am perhaps the last of an order of alchemists who believe that God is in all natural things. Learn to harness these natural things—the elements, natural law—and you not only communicate with God, you are duty-bound to perform His will."

Andre was brought back to his father's alchemical lab, which had been hidden underground to avoid discovery by the Sacred Brotherhood—the Crown's order of knights who had threatened to destroy them. Andre could remember vividly the lab's stone floor covered with animal pelts. The large oaken table, which held the instruments of concoction: glass retorts, each heated from underneath by a small flame and filled with bubbling, ochre-colored stews of rainwater, herbs, animal excrement, and various acids and alkaloids. The retorts had been connected to one another with spiral glass tubing that, in turn, had been connected to tapered condensers that fed liquids into a crucible made of pounded bone ash.

Consuming those potions had been the only true path to enlightenment; to becoming one with the earth as

God had intended. It gave him the divine strength to battle the Catholic Church and infidels the world over.

Andre glanced around the room, saw a few of the necessary glass components, and began to collect them. Rebecca watched him suspiciously, and he held up the components for her scrutiny before she nodded and he placed them into a separate plastic bag.

"Performing God's will," Rebecca said. Now it was her turn to sneer. "Is that what you're doing now?"

Again, Andre found himself taken by surprise. Earlier, the witch had not struck him as one who was in any position to impugn another's beliefs. Her manner had indeed changed after the attack on the family in the trailer. He looked closer and thought he saw the beginnings of a glimmer in her eyes . . . so familiar . . . a glimmer that had been present in his father's eyes before he'd delved into lunacy.

"Once I have what I want, I will do much more. Create others like me. Fight the Catholic Church once again," he said, and moved on to collect the base components for his potions—Salt of Mercury, Salt of Mars, Powder of Saturn. He knew these white, red, and yellow powders were the Trinity of compounds, the foundation of all earthly things and the connecting link between body and spirit that stimulated the body's latent power.

Rebecca's face darkened as she worked. "Once you have what you want . . . you mean the Stone."

"Yes, the Stone," he said, and then moved more clearly into her field of vision. She looked up, startled, and for a moment it appeared she would retreat a step, but she held her ground. He risked another step, and met her gaze. "The Stone," he repeated, "among other things."

Although her magic protected her from his power of Suggestion, Andre found that she was not immune to her feelings as a woman. He felt a sizzling connection between them as her eyes lost their earlier glimmer and gave way to desire . . . and then she looked down hurriedly and busied herself with the contents of her plastic bag.

"To . . . to answer your earlier question," she said, clearly surprised and perhaps flustered by their connection, "sometimes I need an intermediary to pray, and sometimes not. It really depends on what I'm asking for. Channeling a loa is a very powerful form of respect."

"Every religion has great power if you know how to use it," Andre said.

She looked up, eyes seeking his once again. Andre let the smoldering connection last a deep moment until she regained her composure and broke it off. After plucking a candle from the shelf and dropping it into the bag, she stepped from the room, indicating he should follow.

Having found the information he sought, Andre smiled to himself as he complied. Rebecca had purchased a candle to summon a loa—which meant she was planning a very powerful spell. No doubt something that involved the Stone.

Earlier, he'd had his doubts that his manipulation was working. Now he knew that he was well on track to making her his slave.

Chapter 21

Scott glowered as he walked down the lab corridor on the way to the infirmary. The grinding pain in his stomach struck in waves and had chased him away from the crime scene before he'd been ready to leave. He'd wanted to canvass the area, but the pain had been so intense that it interfered with his focus. Better, then, to leave the task to the other responding soldiers.

Now he planned to drop in on Eric before scoring more painkillers from BB and dropping off the rapier.

Leah hadn't left all that long ago, and very well might be in the infirmary with his brother, as promised. Scott was surprised at how easily his thoughts turned to her . . . well, maybe not so surprised. He'd appreciated her willingness to look in on Eric despite the friction between them. He found himself attracted to her compassion, a trait that no doubt grew from her own trauma. She knew what it meant to lose a loved one. She'd been battle-tested at a very young age and survived. Not everyone could have shown that kind of strength in the face of adversity. Despite their differences in method, he found that he respected her obvious inner strength. But did she respect his tactics enough, in turn, to let him accomplish the mission?

As he walked into the infirmary, he found Leah standing over Eric with a necklace in her hands—one that was encrusted with a gemmed cross. She turned and looked self-satisfied. Except that Eric was the vulnerable one in this case.

Scott curled his lip as he thought back to his vision in the cave. The experience had almost pushed him over the edge of sanity when he'd been healthy and of sound mind. God only knew how Leah's methods would affect Eric. "Leah, I thought I made myself perfectly clear—"

"I can explain."

"I don't want to hear it," he said with a wave of his hand, and looked at Eric, who was tucked underneath a light blue blanket and crisp white sheets. His brother's expression was relaxed, serene. Eyes moving behind the lids. Maybe he'd interrupted Leah before she'd had the chance to do anything.

"Please Scott," she said, taking a step toward him. "The amulet isn't mine. It was under his pillow when I arrived."

"You just knew to look there?"

"I . . . I felt its presence, yes."

Scott clenched his fists, frustration coursing through his veins. "I don't care what Ackart says, Leah. You're off the investigation. I gave you a direct order not to involve my brother in your magic, and you knowingly broke that order."

"I know how all this must sound to you, Scott, but I'm telling the truth. Please believe me. Someone placed this amulet under Eric's pillow to *protect* him, not to hurt him. We have to find out who and why . . . it might help us find the creature."

Again with the creature reference, Scott thought disgustedly, and looked back at his brother. He wondered if Eric was dreaming. Wondered if he could feel the warmth of the blanket covering him, or if he was in pain. "We know who placed the amulet," Scott said. "And as for what your reasons were, I could care less. Now please leave before I'm forced to remove you."

"Scott, I can prove I'm telling the truth."

"We've wasted enough time already."

"But this is important!" She glanced at a small black camera in the corner of the ceiling. "This room is monitored twenty-four seven, isn't it?"

Scott's mouth settled into a hard line. If Leah hoped he wouldn't call her bluff, she was sorely mistaken. But as much as he wanted to get to the bottom of the issue, a deep part of him suspected she might be telling the truth. Too much had gone on. Too much he couldn't explain. He'd never worked with someone like Leah Maguire before. In many ways, her dismissal of scientific controls was a hindrance, but in other, perhaps indefinable ways . . . "Leah, if it turns out you're lying to me—"

"I'll leave the investigation on my own. You have my word."

Scott asked the men in the security room to leave and sat down at the bank of monitors. He punched a few keys on a control panel to bring up a live picture of the infirmary. Eric was there, still as a corpse, his body portrayed in crisp black and white. A digital time code shone in the lower right corner. *I'll always be here for you, bro, no matter what . . .*

"What time did you arrive in the infirmary, Leah?"

"Maybe twenty minutes ago."

Scott manipulated a small silver joystick on the panel to rewind the image. The time code wound down rapidly as the black-and-white image didn't change at all—and then suddenly a mysterious figure backed into the room, reached his hand underneath Eric's pillow, and then backed out.

So Leah had been telling the truth after all. He glanced over his shoulder. "Leah, it seems I owe you an apology."

She nodded with no hint of resentment. "You care about your brother, Scott. I can understand that."

He nodded, regretting that he'd accused her again—she'd simply responded with compassion. Turning back to the monitor, he pressed a button on the panel, which made the image continue forward in real time. When the figure reappeared, Scott pressed the pause button, freezing the image. The figure was obviously a man from the shape of his body, but since the camera was positioned behind him, there was no way to see his face.

"Do you know him?"

He shook his head. "Obviously he has clearance on this wing, but so do hundreds of others."

"We might have what we need to narrow it down."

Scott swiveled in the chair and faced her, already suspecting what she might say. Shit, was he beginning to think like her? "The amulet."

"It's worth a try. Another vision like the one you had in the cave—"

"Which didn't make sense," he said, interrupting.

"What if it was a memory, Scott? The rapier you found was part of the vision. Maybe it belonged to the creature."

"In early Spain?"

"I believe BB said the mummy was that old."

"So you think the father and mummy are one and the same."

She shook her head. "You saw through the boy's eyes, Scott. You saw that nightmare because the attack connected you to the creature and my spell triggered the memory."

"He was just a kid."

"Yes, but who knows what else happened to that boy over the years? The amulet is old, probably as old as the rapier. Maybe it can tell us."

Scott could hardly believe he was having this conversation. "What if it wasn't a memory at all? It could have been a hallucination triggered by methane exposure or oxygen deprivation from being underground."

"Only one way to find out."

As it was, Scott knew there was no way they'd be able to find the guy on the monitor in a feasible amount of time. If Leah could induce the same sort of vision in him to narrow down the suspects, then that's what he was prepared to do. "Fine, but for God's sake, lock the door. If BB catches me doing this, he'll never let me live it down."

She did, and then took four candles from her bag. "Are you comfortable in the chair?"

"Comfortable enough."

She placed the candles around the chair, then pulled the amulet from her purse and held it in front of him. The colorful gems glittered with firelight.

"The Finding Spell is no longer relevant, of course, because we're in possession of the object. I'm going to cast something called a Vision Spell instead, which should have a similar effect. Once I make the incantation, it'll kick in as soon as you touch the amulet."

"How am I supposed to get out of the vision once I'm in it?"

"Fortunately, the brain has its own fail-safe. When emotions become too intense, you'll return to the present. That explains why you broke free in the cave."

"Fair enough," he said, although he suspected it might not work a second time. Not when he knew what to expect, and his natural skepticism could kick in.

Leah lit the candles, then stood back and whispered unintelligibly, until finally she said, ". . . link the memories that are now connected."

Her voice was low and mesmerizing. As if hypnotized,

he reached for the amulet swaying in her fingers. He couldn't help touching her, feeling the silk of her skin before the cold of the bronze. The second he made contact with the amulet, he jerked ramrod straight in his chair, then saw only red space as it felt like he was plummeting into an abyss . . .

He found himself in a stone chamber with torches on the walls. The reek of mold and sewage assaulted his nostrils as he looked at a man dressed in crimson robes that matched his own.

What Scott thought he knew about reality flipped on its head as he recognized the man as the father who'd stabbed the priest in his earlier vision. The man was much older now and carried the distinct look of lunacy in his wild eyes. But it was the same guy. Scott was damn sure of it.

"We have found the informant, Andre," the father told him.

Andre. So the perp had a name.

"That is good," Scott heard himself say in a voice that clearly belonged to the boy, now grown.

Scott felt a sickening sense of disorientation. And then he realized with terrified awe that the vision was all too real. He wasn't dreaming. This wasn't some sort of nightmare. Somehow he was really experiencing these things. Not only that, he knew what Andre knew as the man's thoughts flashed by with frenetic speed.

Urged by his father, Andre had joined the Catholic Church to undermine it from within as retribution for what the priest had done to his mother. He'd climbed the ranks quickly, recruiting his father once the opportunity presented itself, and together, with the help of sympathizers, they'd orchestrated the Inquisition to provoke Muslims and Jews into waging a Holy War against the Church and Spain.

Scott could feel Andre's heart roil with resentment. As

in the previous vision, Andre's emotions felt filtered and distant, but it was clear to Scott that Andre hated his father for forcing him down this path. He could also sense that Andre was laden with self-loathing and an undying loyalty to family, which compelled him to obey.

Scott did his best to control his panic and disorientation as Andre turned to look at another man who was naked and bound with leather straps to a high-backed throne covered with metal spikes. The Inquisitor's chair. The man's flesh was scrimshawed and slick with blood, and his long black hair fell in matted clumps around his neck and shoulders. Behind the chair were a half dozen men, also clad in crimson robes. *Los Oscuros,* Scott now knew. The Shadowed Ones. The secret order that Andre's father had founded to fight the Church.

Scott felt a pang of disgust—his own—as he recalled victims of torture he'd found in third-world prisons. The horror human beings were willing to inflict on one another never ceased to amaze him, another reason he wanted out of the military. Those who refuse to learn from history . . .

"Not you," Andre hissed. "Tell me you are not a pawn of the Royal Brotherhood. So many in our ranks have died at their hands!"

"Forgive me," the long-haired man said.

Scott felt an even greater resentment course through Andre's veins. Andre despised the man for his betrayal, but an even deeper part of him despised the fact that he could not similarly buck his father's control.

Scott tried to cherry-pick the long-haired man's name from Andre's thoughts but couldn't. Rage clouded everything.

With a sudden cry, Andre rushed forward and grabbed the man's arm, causing him to convulse violently. He was using electricity. It explained how Andre had escaped the lab after killing Drew and Jonas.

When the current stopped, the man's head lolled to one side, and an amulet slid out from behind his hair, the same amulet Leah had discovered underneath Eric's pillow. "Do you really think the Brotherhood's mark will protect you?" Andre spat.

The long-haired man raised his head, dark eyes glazed with agony. "Yes, Andre. I do."

Just then, Scott heard a thundering boom as the chamber door caved in. Andre trembled with surprise and panic as a dozen soldiers rushed inside, all clad in plate armor and tabards bearing the cross coat of arms of the Crown's Sacred Brotherhood.

Scott now understood, along with Andre, that the long-haired man had lured *Los Oscuros* into a trap, using himself as bait.

The knights unleashed a hail of metal crossbow bolts. The men behind the Inquisitor's chair fell as Andre batted away those bolts aimed at him with a wave of his hand—much in the same way he'd controlled the trajectory of Team Ultra's bullets in the lab. He then retreated to the far end of the room where he opened a secret stone door. "Come, Father!" he called out. "We can still escape!"

His father rushed away from the slaughter when a bolt caught his lower back. The old man stumbled and fell.

Andre cried out to his father, and then cast a look of sizzling hatred at the long-haired man. "A thousand curses on you and your descendants, Juan Gutierrez!" he hissed as his grief exploded and he dashed through the stone doorway . . .

. . . and then came an intense flash of red . . .

Scott realized he was in the control room chair again, drenched with sweat. "I . . . I'm back."

Leah grabbed his hands. "I was so afraid for you. You were moaning and kicking." Her features were tight, as though she'd experienced Andre's painful emotions along with him. "What happened?"

Still disoriented, Scott looked around the room for a moment to ground himself, and then met her gaze. "That," he panted, "was a hell of a thing."

Chapter 22

"How're we doing?" Scott asked.

"About two miles from the exit," Leah replied from the passenger seat as she consulted satellite imagery on a PDA.

He nodded and punched the Humvee's accelerator, rocketing down the weed-covered asphalt of Interstate 10. What he'd really wanted to ask was, How am *I* doing?

His mind was still reeling from the vision. Not only with the intensity of the violent images, but because he was convinced now that something else was going on. He'd be an idiot to deny it. Leah had attributed the vision to magic, which was fine by him. Assigning a label to the process helped him wrap his head around it. Rationalize and deal with it.

In the cave, breaking from the vision had been like waking from a dream, because that's all he thought it was. This time, it had taken several minutes to recover. He'd had to keep telling himself that he was in control of his mind. He'd had to tell himself that over and over again.

And once he'd believed it, he felt good enough to search the lab records for the surname of the man he'd seen tortured through Andre's eyes.

A match had come up almost immediately: Roberto Gutierrez, a member of the janitorial staff. Scott had no idea if this Roberto guy was a descendant of the Juan Gutierrez in his vision, but it was a good bet, and a janitor would have access to every room in the lab. He could move around without suspicion. It was the best lead they had at the moment.

"Can you think of anything else from the vision that might help?" Leah asked.

"I told you everything I remember."

She nodded, eyes still on the PDA. "Well, we have two names now: Juan Gutierrez, of course, and Andre. It's interesting that Catholicism played such a role in Andre's early life. That may come in useful to us. He seems driven to defeat the Church at any cost."

"Seems that way."

"Overall, I think we did pretty well. We should keep the method in mind from now on." She glanced at him. "Is anything wrong?"

He cocked his eyebrow. How could she be so nonchalant about all this? She was acting as though they'd just watched a special on the History Channel. "Leah, I'm not sure that's such a good idea."

"Why not? You said you believed the vision was real."

He nodded, even though he couldn't vocalize his agreement. It was as though saying the words would be giving up his last, tiny bastion of doubt. If he even had any doubt left. Beyond that, the method compromised his control. He'd passed on Team Ultra's genetic manipulation for the very same reason, and wasn't about to consent to becoming some sort of on-demand psychic.

"Look, just because we believe in the method doesn't mean that what I'm seeing is all true," Scott said, weaving in and out of traffic. "We'd be foolish to depend on it as an unassailable method of investigation."

"But we'd be foolish to discount it completely. That's all I'm saying."

He recalled the concern on her face when he'd broken from the vision. The way she'd rushed to his side and interlaced her fingers with his. In that fleeting moment, he'd felt a true connection with her that superseded the violence and horror around them. Had she felt the same way?

"I hear you, Leah, but I still think—" He stopped short when a stomach cramp hit. A gnawing, grinding pain similar to what he'd felt at the crime scene. *What the hell . . . ?* Gritting his teeth, he did his level best to ignore the stabbing pain as clammy sweat broke out across his forehead.

"You were saying?" Leah asked, focus back on the PDA, sounding a little annoyed.

"Nothing," he grunted, thoughts racing. What the hell was wrong with him? Was his chest wound having a more profound effect on him than he was willing to admit?

"Exit here," she said, pointing to a green sign that read MAUREPAS SWAMP.

Scott sped down the exit ramp and then followed more signs down a dirt road lined with towering Spanish oaks that dripped with effervescent green moss.

He knew they were taking a chance confronting Roberto Gutierrez on his own turf. The guy might be insane, prone to violence, one of many assailants—who knew? And if they needed backup, any help from the base would require at least thirty minutes to arrive by helicopter and set up a perimeter in the inhospitable terrain. Which meant they were essentially on their own.

But they didn't have much choice. They needed to operate with autonomy if they were going to resolve the case quickly. He accepted the risks—and knew that Leah did, too, without question.

Scott drove on until the road dead-ended against the edge of the swamp, which was choked with gnarled logs and brown grass. He slid to a stop next to the only other vehicle there: a rusty white Ford pickup truck with a camper shell.

He grabbed the MP5 from the backseat. "Stay here a minute," he told Leah, and exited the Humvee before she could object. If anything dire was about to happen, he wanted to walk point so she'd have a chance to escape.

The humid air was even muggier here near the swamp, wrapping around him like a sodden blanket. Leading with the MP5, he crept to the driver's-side window of the truck. Empty. He then crept around back and peered into the camper shell to find it filled with occult gear. Crosses, pentagrams, candles, statuettes of saints and devils. Satanic worship? he wondered grimly, feeling a chill race up his spine as he thought back to the dark figure looming over Eric's bed.

He returned to the Humvee's passenger door and opened it for Leah.

"What is it?" she asked as she climbed out.

"Apparently, our man Gutierrez is into some heavy shit." He glanced around, peering into the thickly tangled growth. They were exposed here, but the situation wouldn't get much better in the swamp. "Which way?"

Leah consulted the PDA and pointed to a rotting, wooden walkway that extended deep into the swamp—one of many that crisscrossed the area. Moving quickly, Scott took the lead. Stayed tense, ready. Line of sight was blocked in every direction by cypress trees that protruded from the brown swamp water like gnarled fingers, making it perfect terrain for an ambush. He looked and listened for any man-made pattern or sound that might indicate an enemy while keeping tabs on Leah, who kept pace and fed him directions.

"Turn left, Scott, and then take a sharp right," she whispered. "We're getting close."

What kind of guy would live in the middle of a fucking swamp? Scott wondered, when another series of painful chills crested his body. Breathing through the spasms as best he could, he continued down the walkway, boots thumping softly on the rotten planks.

"Scott, are you okay? You seem—"

"How close?" The question came out more abrupt than he'd intended, but he didn't want Leah to concern herself with his condition, as he suspected she might. She was caring, which he appreciated, but they both needed to remain as alert as possible. If she was offended by his tone, she didn't let on.

"The place should be right around here."

No sooner had the words left her mouth than the target came into view—a small, ramshackle house beyond the next cluster of ribbed tupelo trees.

"There," he whispered, pointing with the barrel of the MP5.

"I see it."

Perched on stilts, the place was a confused patchwork of rusty, corrugated metal and cypress shingles. A deck surrounding the house was made of the same rotten wood as the walkway, and was crowded with wilting plants in pots and ringing wind chimes. An adjacent thicket of fragrant purple irises looked out of place against the decay.

Sticky sweat pouring down his neck and back, Scott led Leah toward a side window when a vicious cramp tore through his abdomen. He doubled over as the MP5 slipped from his fingers and clattered onto the walkway.

"Scott!" Leah cried.

He tried to reply when a second cramp hit, shaking him to the core. He gritted his teeth and took a couple of trembling steps, trying desperately to keep his balance on the narrow walkway. He felt Leah grab his arm as he dropped to his knees.

Just then, the door of the swamp cabin burst open and

a heavyset man rushed out. Even in the grips of pain Scott recognized Gutierrez from the employee file.

Gutierrez clutched a wooden staff, which he swung in a vicious, whistling arc at Scott's head. Scott tried to evade, but realized he couldn't move. The cramps had wound his muscles as tight as steel cables. He felt pain explode at the base of his skull, and then pitched headlong into the swamp with a splash.

He felt the warm water close over his head, heard a sharp swoosh of bubbles. Head throbbing and nearly paralyzed by pain, Scott thrashed to the surface in time to see Gutierrez yank Leah into the cabin by her wrist and then slam the door.

"Leah!" he yelled, sputtering bitter swamp water. He grabbed the edge of the walkway and tried to pull himself up, but another cramp tore through his stomach and jarred his grip loose. He flopped back into the water with a grunt. Feeling his sodden fatigues drag against his body, he managed to thrash to the surface again.

It was then that Scott saw a small, grassy island about fifteen feet beyond the deck and the huge alligator that sat atop it. Rushing toward him, it cut through the water like a torpedo homed in on his distress.

Realizing he lacked the strength to escape the water, he lunged for the MP5. His fingers scrambled madly across the splintered wood when a third cramp seized his muscles. He groaned as his body curled into itself again and slid back underwater.

Barely able to move, he peered through the silty murk and saw that the gator was closing fast.

Before Scott could react, the scaled behemoth was on him with lunging jaws and razor-sharp teeth. Adrenaline redlining, he instinctively caught the massive upper and lower jaw in each hand. He fully expected the thing's jaws to crush him, but to his shock, he held them open. The gator should have been able to kill him easily, but here he was, sudden power surging through his muscles, winning the contest of strength.

Realizing it was trapped, the gator began to thrash, its neck and tail whipping violently.

Scott continued to hold the gator steady, marveling at his ability—and then flung the gator back, sending it airborne. The startled creature landed thrashing in the water a few feet away. Clearly not expecting a struggle, it quickly retreated.

Scott felt a flood of relief followed by profound confusion. How the fuck had he defeated the gator? As if in reply, an image of Jonas's smiling face flickered through his mind. *Feels like I'm twenty-two again,* the man had said after his DNA-modified strength took hold.

But Scott hadn't undergone any splicing.

These severe pains, like terrible hunger pangs, and now the burst of strength . . .

Was all this related to the wounds he'd received in the attack?

Fear shot through him. He couldn't tell anybody about this. Ackart would quarantine him for sure. Besides, the stress from his wounds could be fucking with his head, playing tricks on his mind.

He pulled himself onto the walkway, fatigues heavy and dripping. He couldn't worry about the symptoms now. He had to get Leah out of the cabin.

He only hoped he wasn't too late.

Chapter 23

No matter that Leah had dug in her heels, she hadn't been able to stop the crazed man from dragging her into the cabin and throwing her in a chair. Maybe he'd simply panicked out of fear—someone who would place a protection amulet on a man in a coma surely wasn't evil. Worried about Scott, she looked around for a way out.

Cooking utensils sat on a Franklin stove and fishing gear lined up along the wall near a window where Roberto now peered out as if looking for danger. An older man, he had a droopy gray mustache and gray hair pulled back into a ponytail. The only thing that kept her from panicking over Scott was that he'd called out for her after collapsing into the swamp.

Then her gaze lit on an alligator on the floor at the far end of the cabin. It wasn't alive, but there were live gators in the bayou. Her pulse began to thread unevenly as she thought about an injured Scott facing one.

"You have to go out there and help the man you attacked," she told Roberto. "We mean you no harm."

He faced her.

"I want you to tell me what the military plans to do about the vampire."

She started as he confirmed her worst suspicions. "Vampire?"

"Surely you knew what he was after he killed your family."

Her worry for Scott was detoured for a moment—how did Roberto know about any of this? Her heart thudded faster as the significance hit her. "You know who I am."

"I know a lot of things." He rubbed a meaty hand over his brow. A scar like an old wound from a fight cut through his left eyebrow. "I've spent my life knowing."

Just then, she saw movement through the window behind Roberto—Scott struggling in the water toward the dock. She let out a shaky breath. He was all right. Sliding out of her chair, she tried edging toward the door so she could rush out to help him out of the bayou, but with a knowing gleam in his dark eyes, Roberto placed himself in her way.

"He must be stopped. Destroyed. Not easy, though." The man's thick fingers stroked the wooden cross hanging from his neck, framed by a silver-and-turquoise necklace. "*Most glorious Prince of the Heavenly Armies, Saint Michael the Archangel, defend us in our battle against this world of darkness . . .*"

His words faded and his mind seemed to wander off in the middle of the prayer.

Leah noted a glyph decorated each of the four walls as if meant to keep out evil from this place. Three stick figure drawings represented archangels—Saint Michael, the angel of judgment; Saint Gabriel, the angel of mercy; and Saint Raphael, the angel of the Lord. The fourth glyph contained a pentagram. Medieval Christians believed the pentagram would protect them against witches and demons.

On that same wall, a small wooden table was set with a stone slab over which had been placed a white cloth with gilded edging. On the table sat a golden vessel topped by a cross. It looked like the sun emitting rays to all sides—an *ostensorium*, a glass-framed shrine in which the Blessed Sacrament would be publicly exposed during Mass.

Realizing this was a portable altar, Leah said, "You're

a priest," even as she saw a flash of movement outside—Scott heaving himself out of the water.

"Father Roberto Gutierrez."

Hearing the name got her full attention. "I remember a Father Gutierrez being defrocked . . ."

"The Church didn't understand my mission. I only carry on the charge of my ancestors in the Sacred Brotherhood who worked to end the evil during the Inquisition. That's when Andre Espinoza de Madrid began his descent into hell."

Roberto seemed preoccupied again and Leah edged toward the window with its view of the swamp. Heading for the cabin, as if he sensed her, Scott suddenly stopped and looked her way. She made a small motion with her hand meant to tell him to wait, then locked gazes with him, willed him to stay outside until she could convince Roberto they had the same goal, willed Scott to understand she was in no immediate danger.

Nodding, Scott stared back, and she read something unexpected in his eyes. Her heart thudded with the connection. Even from a distance, she sensed his feeling for her was more than simple concern. The thought of it caused a warmth to blossom in her, leaving her breathless.

Then she blinked and he was gone from view.

Behind her, Roberto was muttering, "*May God restrain Him, we humbly pray, and by the power of God, cast Satan into Hell, and with him all the other evil spirits, who wander through the world, for the ruin of souls.*"

Ackart told her the mummy had been five hundred years old, and Scott's visions seemed to verify that. Was it possible? The glyphs on the cabin walls . . . she would swear they were drawn by the same hand that drew the ones in the cave to keep Andre from leaving.

Andre . . . a vampire. It made sense.

She'd seen the destruction the creature had wreaked for herself, first with Dad and Gabe and now with the Toutants. Roberto might be a little crazy, but he might be the only one with intimate knowledge of their adversary. She needed to get as much information as she could from him without further alarming him.

"Are you a vampire hunter?"

"Some would call me that."

"Is that why you have all this . . ." She waved her hand at the makeshift altar. "For the holy water?"

"An old wives' tale! Father Delgado and I sealed the vampire in Cueva del Diablo. We kept him prisoner with religious symbols of One more powerful than he." Roberto shook his head. "The glyphs controlled the evil only as long as man didn't interfere."

Those glyphs *had* kept the creature captive, Leah knew. The military broke the barriers and set the thing free. If Roberto had been able to keep the creature prisoner for all those years, perhaps—crazy or not—Roberto could help them.

"We have the same mission, then," she said. Leah could sense that his lifelong charge had addled his mind, but he had the knowledge necessary to stop Andre. "We're on the same side. We have to find the vampire and destroy it. You must tell me everything you know about him."

Roberto's gaze narrowed. "How can I be sure I can trust you?"

"Think of who I am, of what I've been through," Leah said, stepping closer and looking straight into his rheumy eyes.

She reached out and lightly gripped his arm. His paranoia cut through her painfully, but she didn't react. He was a jumble of contradictions. Sorrow, anger, fear, pride, shame, a panoply of emotion.

The loss of a mind was a high price to pay for using

religious magic to keep the vampire under control. Undoubtedly, he hadn't known it would happen any more than she had known what would happen to her. Undoubtedly, he would have done it anyway.

Leah shuddered. Her memories of Dad and Gabe were fading. If she continued to use magic, would she lose even more? Could she end up like this poor priest?

"If anyone knows how dangerous this creature is, I do," she said, fighting the fear that tried to take hold of her. "I may be the only one who ever survived his attack until recently." She thought of Scott and Eric. "Why do you think I'm here if not to stop him? You saw what he did to those people."

Roberto rolled his eyes and twisted his arm free. "*Heart of Jesus, once in agony, have mercy on the dead . . .*"

"Roberto. Please help us stop him before he kills again, I beg you. Please."

"He's a creature unlike any other, a vampire self-made from alchemy and blood magic."

"Alchemy? What does turning lead into gold have to do with this Andre?"

Roberto indicated she should take the chair at the table. Thinking that would reassure him that she was no threat, Leah sat and wondered where Scott was. She assumed he was someplace where he could hear everything going on, where he could quickly intervene if her interview went bad.

Roberto paced before her. "Alchemists attempted to uncover the mysteries of the physical universe," he began. "They believed God existed in the elements around them, and that to perceive Him as a separate, judging deity was blasphemy. As such, human concepts of conscience and morality became largely irrelevant. If they served to bring man closer to enlightenment, fine. If not . . ." Roberto shrugged. "Andre Espinoza de Madrid began by harnessing the elements. More important, he found ways to prolong his life."

"As a vampire?"

"He traveled to the Americas with Columbus to harness blood magic. That added to the alchemy . . . who knows how long he can live?"

"You're saying he's alive, not undead like the legends."

"Those vampires are long gone now, wiped out by a plague. Andre Espinoza de Madrid is one of the *original* vampires. Andre ages by tiny increments compared to the normal human. He is the last vampire, and if we don't stop him, he will become immortal and breed a new colony of his kind."

"How?"

Leah could feel Roberto lose focus again. He backed away from her, muttering, "*Come to the assistance of men whom God has created to His likeness . . .*"

Frustrated, she cut him off. "Roberto, how can Andre Espinoza become immortal?"

He blinked and focused on her with difficulty. "I took it when we sealed him in the cave."

"Took what?"

"The Stone. The Philosopher's Stone."

"Again a reference to turning lead into gold?" Leah asked.

"It's beyond that. Spiritual alchemy promises extraordinary spiritual powers to whoever possesses the Philosopher's Stone . . . not only will it make Andre immortal, it will restore his soul to him."

"But how?"

"Andre has to become one with the Stone. He hadn't figured out how to do that before we stopped him in Texas. He will need help to do it."

"And now *you* have the Stone?" When he nodded, she asked, "Here?" Again, she could feel his resistance.

Wondering why he hadn't destroyed the Stone, she held out her right palm to show him the brand from the creature's ring. "I bear this always, a daily reminder of how the vampire destroyed my family. You can trust me, Roberto."

The ex-priest fidgeted with his wooden cross for a moment. His features changed and changed again, and all the while, his paranoia came at Leah in waves that threatened to exhaust her. And then, just when she thought she would need a new, more convincing argument, he capitulated. Nodding, he crossed the room to the stuffed alligator, pried open the jaws, and pulled out a cloth-wrapped bundle.

Leah was wondering how much of his tale to believe as he came toward the table and peeled away the cloth to reveal a fist-sized red stone.

She didn't see anything unusual until he stopped next to her and the light shining through the window fell on the stone. Then it lit, as if from within, as if it had a life of its own. Energy emanated from the stone in stomach-knotting waves.

The flesh on her arms raised and Leah felt the same fear she had in that cave so long ago.

The cave . . . the red glow . . . the stone . . .

Realizing that had to be what she'd seen in the tunnel, Leah knew Roberto had been telling the truth. She knew that if Andre got hold of the Philosopher's Stone and figured out how to use it, there would be no stopping him. At that moment the cabin door slammed open and Scott rushed in, wet but sound.

"Scott!" Leah held out a staying hand. Even so, Roberto started and looked around wildly, as if he wanted to trade the stone for a more traditional weapon. Leah placed a hand on his arm, saying, "No cause for panic, Roberto. This is Captain Scott Boulder, my friend. The man lying in a coma in the infirmary—

the one you tried to protect by leaving the amulet—is his brother. He wants to stop Andre as much as we do."

Calming at her words, Roberto said, "I would have destroyed Andre if I'd known who made him. I could have used something owned by his sire, killed him instead of trapping him. Nothing can stop Andre if he gets his hands on the Philosopher's Stone. It will grant the vampire everlasting life."

"Vampire, huh?" Scott said, giving Leah a disbelieving look.

Roberto crossed himself. *"Defend me against the assaults of my enemy, O Lord. Blessed be the hour in which thou were assigned as my guardian . . ."*

"Scott, you don't understand."

"I heard everything, Leah. We'll take him and the rock with us—BB should take a look at it."

When Scott reached for it, Roberto stepped back and hissed, "You, soldier! You hold the curse of the vampire! You are his agent! *Heavenly Father, protect us in these end of times . . ."*

"I'm warning you, Gutierrez," Scott said tersely. "I'll bring you down here and now."

"Scott, please, let me handle this." Leah stepped closer to Roberto's side again, touched his elbow. "It's okay," she told him. "The Stone will be safe with me. I won't let Andre get it, I promise."

Roberto shook his head and Leah could feel his emotions spiraling once more. He was looking around wildly, as if searching for a weapon to use against them.

"Hand the Stone over, man, before I take it from you!"

Leah gave Scott a furious expression she saw mirrored in his own eyes and stance. Then slowly she felt him back down and defer to her, at least for the moment.

"We're in this together, Roberto," she said soothingly, turning to the ex-priest. "You and Scott and me. We've all seen the destruction the vampire leaves in his path. We've all felt his evil. You know me." She held out her hand and his gaze pinned the scar. "You know how much I've lost and how much I want the vampire stopped. You're not safe with the Stone, Roberto. Give it to me, and I'll make sure Andre can't get it. Please let me keep it safe for all of our sakes."

Roberto uttered a sound of anguish and looked deep into her eyes. Leah saw a moment's sanity in them.

Finally, he nodded and placed the Stone in her hand, saying, "All right . . . but will you be safe with the Stone?"

Skin crawling, Leah handled the Stone gingerly, her attention caught once more by the inner pulsing. She looked up—Scott was transfixed on the Stone, as well. What power did it hold? Could it really be used to gain immortality?

Quickly covering it with the cloth and shoving it in her bag, Leah breathed easier. Wanting to reassure Roberto again, she realized he was gone. Somehow he'd slipped out of the cabin while their attention was on the Stone.

"Shit! Where the hell did he go?" Scott headed for the door.

"Going after him would be a mistake, Scott." Fixing her gaze on his, Leah moved to him. "Right now, Roberto is an ally, one that we need. He may be the only one who can help us. If you force him, he'll see you as an enemy."

"If he can help, then he needs to come in."

"Don't do it." She touched his arm and pleaded, "Don't, Scott, please. He's damaged. His obsession with the vampire has taken his sanity. He's another victim, just as we are. As Eric is. Don't let Major Ackart have at him or she'll destroy what's left of him."

Scott nodded, and she knew she had gotten through

to him. The mix of emotions she felt through her connection to Scott confused her. Swallowing hard, she removed her hand from his arm.

He gave her a curt nod. “Let’s get back to base.”

She’d tuned in to Scott’s frustration, to a feeling of respect for her, to his physical attraction to her. But more important was something deeper . . . something darker . . . something she didn’t want to inspect too closely.

Roberto had wondered if she would be safe with the Stone. Part of her wondered if she would be safe with Scott.

Chapter 24

Rebecca connected with Eric several times in hopes of learning what plans the government was making to track Andre, but all to no avail. Thinking to try again since she was alone and could better concentrate with Andre in the other room, she settled down at the mansion's dining table. Shutting out thoughts of Andre, she closed her eyes once more and freed her mind to link with Eric's.

Someone was talking to him. She could hear the soft voice of a woman. Was he awake? Rebecca concentrated, but trying to see through Eric's eyes once more led her to the dark vacuum. Though she could bring him out of the coma, she decided to let him be until she needed him.

"*I'm worried about your brother,*" the woman was saying. "*I don't know what's happening to him. Something terrible. Maybe it's happening to you, too. You have to try to wake up. Scott needs you, Eric. I believe you can hear me. Concentrate on Scott. On his love for you. Find in it the strength to make you whole again . . .*"

The woman's voice faded out, as if she didn't believe in her own words. Not that the stranger could do anything to raise Eric, of course, not while he was under her control, Rebecca thought. Annoyed, she willed the visitor to reveal some helpful information.

As if the other woman were complying with her silent demand, she said, "*The ex-priest who hunted Andre Espinoza and sealed him in the cave knows more about this vampire than anyone, Eric. I wonder if he knows what to do if Scott is really changing."*

That put Rebecca on alert. Who was this ex-priest and what did he know about Andre? Had the man really bested the vampire without using Voodoo or some other form of black magic? She wondered if the ex-priest had used his own brand of Catholic magic to overcome Andre.

A rapid pounding at the back door made her heart bang against her ribs. Now what? She waited, but the pounding didn't stop. "Rebecca, let me in."

"Damn!" she muttered.

Jean Baptiste Neff knew she was in here. She'd left her SUV parked around back. What the hell did he want? she wondered, knowing she would have to find out.

Opening the door, she leaned against the jamb and gave the city councilmember a sultry smile. "Jean Baptiste. I wasn't expecting you."

"Come, chère, you know every favor has a price."

Knowing that sex with her was *his* price, Rebecca murmured, "I'll be glad to pay you . . . later."

"But I need to be paid now." He pressed into her, hard as wood. "And I'm not takin' no for an answer this time."

He pushed her back inside the vestibule. Rebecca seethed with anger and disgust. At the moment, he reminded her of her stepfather when he wanted release.

"Right here, then," she said, unzipping his fly. She had to take care of him and get him out of there before Andre heard him. She didn't want to have to deal with a confrontation.

When he sprang into her hand, she squeezed him so hard he moaned. "Oh, *chère,* show me what you got for me tonight." He tugged her dress up to her hips, then sank to his knees and spread her thighs wide. "What's this? A present for me?" He flicked a finger several times against her clitoris ring.

Despite her caution at being caught, Rebecca felt a tiny thrill shoot through her. And when Jean Baptiste followed the action with his mouth, manipulating the ring with his tongue and teeth, she furtively looked into the dining room.

Don't let Andre come back, she thought.

She spread her legs wider and said, "Get inside me now. Quickly!"

Hopefully he would come fast and then she would throw him out with a promise of more back at the club. After which, she would cast a Forget Spell on him so that he wouldn't even remember her name, let alone that he got her unimpeded access to this building.

Jean Baptiste pushed himself inside her and pumped. "You like that, don't you. Say it."

Her head a little light, Rebecca scraped the tips of her nails along the back of his neck in hopes of finishing him fast. "Come, damn you!"

"Say how you want me to fuck—"

A deep growl was followed by Jean Baptiste being pulled off her.

"Andre, no!"

But the command came too late. Blood splattered her and she had a close-up view of the vampire covering the pulsing stream from Jean Baptiste's neck with his mouth. Her stomach churning, knowing there was nothing she could do, she shoved by Andre and ran straight for the nearest bathroom where she flipped up the toilet seat.

After her stomach emptied, she sat on the edge of the tub for a moment, her head hung low until the room steadied. Then she rose and, turning on the faucets, washed Jean Baptiste's blood off her skin. Her clothing was ruined. She would have to burn it.

Jean Baptiste dead.

Someone she knew well. And more important, he was a city councilman, a citizen of note. When he didn't go home, the whole police force would be looking for him.

Rebecca pulled herself together, pushed away regret. Jean Baptiste shouldn't have come here. He shouldn't have offered himself up as a temptation to a blood-hungry vampire. He'd caused his own death. That she didn't feel sorry for him surprised her a little. It was simply the shock of seeing the vampire at work that affected her physically. By the time she was done cleaning herself, she'd found enough anger that she could go out and face Andre.

But when she returned to the dining room, Jean Baptiste was spread out on the dining table and Andre, now dressed in the black outfit that did its job in hiding any blood, was taking his time draining the body. Maybe Jean Baptiste was still alive and she could use magic to heal him and make him forget.

"Stop!" she ordered. "Now!"

But in the throes of whatever the blood did for him, Andre was able to fight her. Though in the end he did as she said, Rebecca realized Andre was getting strong enough to resist her commands. She needed to use more potent magic.

"He's a prominent member of New Orleans society—a city councilmember." When that didn't stop him, she said, "You're killing one of my best customers."

"From what I saw, he didn't seem all that impressive."

"He was a high roller at the club I own," she informed him. "I don't service him."

Andre aimed a disbelieving expression her way.

"I was doing that *for you,*" she told him, "to pay him for letting me use this place and keeping the authorities away."

Rebecca had never been so angry. Or so determined to

get the vampire to do what she demanded. Going to her altar, she opened an urn that held graveyard dust, and added a few ingredients, including enough oil to make the substance combustible. All the while, she concentrated on bending Andre's will to hers.

She dropped a burning match into the urn. The contents flamed and sent out a thick smoke, which she concentrated in Andre's direction.

"It's time you did something for me now," she said and was relieved when Andre immediately stopped feeding and looked her way.

A rivulet of blood rolled from the corner of his mouth, down his chin. "You want me to take his place between your thighs?"

"I want you to save my brother's life!"

"Not until you get me the Stone."

Was the damn spell working or not? she wondered.

"Getting the Stone would be hard to do since you haven't given me a name."

He licked the blood from his lips and cocked his head, gazing at her steadily, as if she were his next intended prey.

"A *name,* Andre," she said, willing him to do her bidding. "A name and I'll find the man and get you the damn Stone you seek."

"Gutierrez. Roberto Gutierrez. The priest who sealed me in the cave."

"Priest or ex-priest? Do you have any idea of what parish he served?"

"What good would that do if he's not there anymore?"

"They keep records. Probably his. If I knew which parish, I could go there, see what address they have for him."

"I suspect one of the symbols on the wall of my cave along with those that kept me from leaving was related to his parish. It was different from the others—a Celtic cross."

Rebecca's pulse leaped. "That must be Holy Cross Church. I know it. So if I locate this ex-priest—Gutierrez—then you will save my brother Danton?"

He didn't answer for a moment and she had difficulty keeping her temper.

Finally he said, "When I have the Philosopher's Stone, I will take care of your brother. First, I want to meet him."

Not exactly what Rebecca had expected. About to say no, she thought better of it. If she was going to play him to get what she wanted, then she needed to go along with this.

"When you meet Danton, you will treat him with respect. He's a good man, not like us."

"If I do what you want, he will be like me," Andre warned again. "But I agree to your terms." And as if he could hear her next thoughts, he added, "And don't worry, he doesn't need to know what his sister has done to save him."

Andre was being too reasonable. Perhaps her magic had influenced him? Perhaps he'd come to terms with the reality of his situation? Whatever the reason, not having to fight for every inch would be a relief.

Chapter 25

Back at base, Scott ushered Leah down the main corridor toward the lab. His damp fatigues reeked of rotting swamp water, and his sodden combat boots squeaked on the tile floor. He shook his head adamantly. "I can't let you tell BB."

"Scott, it's the truth," Leah said. "Deep down, you know it is."

"Vampires and a rock that grants eternal life? I can't believe you fell for that."

"You've been falling for a lot, too, lately."

For a moment Scott thought she was talking about his growing feelings for her, but then realized she was talking about his new outlook on magic. His rush of strength in the swamp also troubled him. As concerned for Leah as he'd been, it could have been an adrenaline response. He'd had plenty in battle before—kicking in an iron door to free POWs, lifting a burning jeep off a wounded soldier. But marshaling the strength to hold open the jaws of an alligator? That had to have been over two thousand pounds of pressure. "The visions are one thing, Leah. This fairy-tale stuff is another."

"You believed him enough to take the Stone, didn't you?"

"If our killer wants the Stone, then I want to keep it from him. It's that simple. He might make our job easy and come looking for it, who knows? So yes, in that regard, I believe our crazy ex-priest was useful."

"Roberto is more than just a crazy ex-priest to me," Leah said softly.

Scott saw pain in her eyes as she said it. The priest, however deranged, was a link to her brother and father. "Leah, I didn't mean—"

She shook her head, dismissing his concern. "What are we going to tell Ackart about Roberto?"

"The truth. But we'll catch hell for it. I know she would have preferred we bring Roberto back here. Can't say that I blame her. We might have gotten all the cooperation we needed from him with the proper persuasion."

Leah's face fell at that. "I can appreciate that you want to learn everything you can to help your brother, but I wish you wouldn't always rely on a military response to every question."

He frowned at the criticism. He happened to agree with her in this case, but why couldn't she see things from a perspective different from her own?

"Without military responses, this country wouldn't be safe, Leah."

"Unless someone figured out ways to solve conflict that didn't include violence."

"Did you forget that Roberto struck me?" That he was still attracted to her despite her views didn't make any damn sense. In many ways, he thought she was crazy. Still . . . "Regardless, I can't let you tell BB those fairy tales about vampires and immortality."

"Captain, a word." The harsh feminine voice called from behind him before he could respond. Major Ackart was on the warpath—no surprise.

"I'll catch up to you," Scott told Leah.

"I can help explain—"

"Thanks, but I've got this."

Scott watched Leah walk away, and then turned as Ackart approached. "Major."

Ackart met him, ignoring his smell and disheveled appearance, and making no pretense of hiding her anger. "Your performance today was unacceptable."

He wasn't about to make excuses for letting Roberto go. However, he had little tolerance for armchair officers who second-guessed an op. "The man is more use to us free. He'll be more likely to give us intel later on if we don't toss him in a cell."

"That wasn't your decision to make, Captain. You broke chain of command."

"It was a decision I made in tandem with your consultant, Major. It was the right one given the circumstances."

"And those circumstances were?" Ackart asked.

"Expedience of investigation and Leah's safety," Scott replied, and realized what he'd said only after he said it. He snapped his mouth shut, but it was too late.

Ackart cocked an eyebrow. "That's very touching, Captain. But may I remind you that Leah is highly trained for this type of mission. She doesn't need you coddling her."

"I understand that," he said. As much as he'd disagreed with Ackart's initial decision to include Leah, the sentiment had been sincere. If Roberto had hurt her, he wouldn't have been able to forgive himself.

"What you don't seem to understand is that I will use every asset at my disposal to bring about a favorable end to this mission," Ackart said. "You should be just as willing. Or don't you realize what's at stake?"

Scott's anger flared. This robot of a woman cared only about the fate of Project 24, and nothing about the well-being of her so-called assets. "I've served this team and my country with tireless loyalty, as has my brother . . . who, I remind you, is still languishing in a coma. So don't lecture me about what's at stake. I know full well."

Ackart took a step closer. "I want you to keep something in mind, Captain. When you joined the military, you forfeited the luxury of personal motivation. Yes, your brother is in sick bay, and yes, Leah Maguire may not be the optimal team member. But they are the pieces we have in a game we cannot afford to lose. If someone discovers who our subject is, or how we've been testing him, the consequences for this lab, not to mention the country, would be enormous. So you'd better clear your head, and clear it *now.*"

Scott felt an almost insurmountable urge to yell, but dared not push it. Fall on his sword over how to handle the mission, and she could kick him off the hunt. As tough as it was, he had to stay quiet and take this woman's bullshit. He didn't have a choice.

Gritting his teeth, he said, finally, "I'll do as ordered, Major."

"Yes, you will," she replied. "You're one of a few living people who's seen our assailant up close, so I have no choice but to use you if I want to keep this thing as quiet as possible. But put my project at risk again, and I'll transfer you and your brother off base, regardless of condition, no questions asked." Without waiting for an answer, she turned and walked away, saying over her shoulder, "I expect you and Leah in my office for a full debriefing after you meet with BB."

Watching Ackart go, Scott suspected the woman would eat her own young if it served her needs. He pushed away his simmering anger as best he could before continuing into the lab, where he saw Leah conferring with BB at a table, which held beakers and a large glass case in a far corner. As they spoke, BB held an expression of studied concentration . . . and mild incredulity.

Dammit, Scott thought. Leah was telling him about the Philosopher's Stone.

Scott strode through the busy lab and reached them as a tech wearing latex gloves carefully carried away the red stone.

"That's a ravishing scent you have on, Captain," BB said. "Let me guess . . . Eau de Swamp?"

"What did Leah tell you?" Scott asked, not in the mood.

"Just the name of your perp, tidbits about Roberto Gutierrez, and a few very interesting things about the gift you brought me," BB told him with a sparkle in his eye—the same sparkle a child displayed with a new toy. "One that will warrant further study if I'm to prove certain claims."

"Didn't I make myself clear?" Scott told Leah.

"I know I should have waited for you, but we don't have much time."

"C'mon, you two," BB said. "What's done is done. Now, I have a gift to show you as well, but it isn't nearly as nice-looking as the stone. Follow me."

Scott ushered Leah ahead of him, and wondered how the hell he could be expected to achieve success if every aspect of the mission was out of his control.

BB led them to a nearby table, which held a glass case about the size of a shoe box. Inside was a ragged chunk of pale flesh about the size of a T-bone steak sitting in a shallow pan of blood.

"A sample of our guy?" Scott asked, and wished he could tear much more than a pound of flesh from the man for what he had done to Eric.

"That's right," BB said, staring at the sample through the glass. "At first glance, this looks like an ordinary chunk of dead flesh. Cold, stiff, and devoid of any charm whatsoever, right?" He looked at them, eyebrow cocked. "Wrong."

"What do you mean?" Scott asked.

BB turned to Leah. "Moments ago you mentioned

that Andre had acquired the ability to generate and manipulate lightning."

"Through alchemy, according to Roberto," Leah said.

Scott couldn't help but concede that it wasn't only possible, but probable. The phenomenon was no more far-fetched than the powers Team Ultra had adopted from the guy's DNA. "It's true, BB," he said, and noticed that Leah looked at him with appreciation for the support.

"All bodies generate electricity," BB continued, fascinated. "So I suppose it makes sense that a body could generate an extreme amount, given the appropriate circumstances. It certainly would explain the guy's ability to generate cloud formations and lightning, which are just alternative states of energy."

"What other societies used to call mysticism, alchemy, and magic, we now call electricity, chemistry, and technology," Leah offered.

"Exactly. A simple matter of vocabulary and understanding. Who knows what the living body is truly capable of." BB paused, and then indicated the sample with a nod. "But what about a *dead* body?"

"You're not saying the sample is alive?" Leah asked.

"Far from it. It's dead as dead can be. But our tests indicate the electrical impulses are off the chart. I mean more than a living person, even more than my entertainment system at home. You wanna know the really weird part?" He lowered his voice to a conspiratorial whisper. "The cellular composition of the sample hasn't changed since we scraped it off the floor."

Scott watched Leah close her eyes and take a deep breath. Clearly, the news came as validation to her that Roberto had been telling the truth. "This is nuts," he said, realizing where the conversation was headed.

"This flesh is dead," BB said. "And always has been."

"I can't believe I have to say this, but the guy isn't some walking member of the undead, okay?"

"Look, Scott, I've been known to tell a lie or two. Or three. Especially to beautiful women. But the tests we conducted don't lie. However we choose to define it—undead or whatever—it's the truth."

Scott frowned, exasperated. Couldn't believe they were talking seriously about movie monsters. "For all we know, the guy could have been in some sort of weird cryogenic state when we found him . . . a state weird enough to alter the composition of his flesh and throw off your calibrations. Hell, Ackart could be conducting tests about reviving people from stasis behind our backs."

Leah said, "I certainly wouldn't put it past Ackart to be keeping us in the dark on some things. But my suspicion is that cryogenics doesn't begin to explain what's happened."

BB nodded in agreement. "And I haven't gotten to the really, really weird part. I conducted all the standard stress tests to see what would reduce the sample's composition in case you met this guy again. Extreme heat and cold had no effect. Neither did acids or alkalines. And then I remembered what happened when the subject was shot. Now watch this." The scientist slid his tattooed forearms into a pair of nitrile safety gloves affixed to the glass case from the inside, plucked a syringe that lay near the pan, and injected the sample. Almost immediately, the flesh shuddered, and its radius expanded a quarter inch.

"What the hell was in that syringe?" Scott asked.

"Antimony."

"Antimony?" Leah asked.

"We melted down a few standard rounds of ammunition," BB replied.

Scott shook his head slowly in amazement. "No wonder the guy used magnetism to pull our rounds into his body during the attack. Fucker was healing himself."

"I didn't think lead was magnetic," Leah said.

"You're right about that," BB said. "But lead bullets are blended with antimony to make them stronger—and antimony is highly magnetic." He crossed his arms. "Aside from lead, I haven't found anything else that has an effect. Doesn't make any damn sense."

"It may make all the sense in the world," Leah said. "Try gold."

BB shook his head. "Gold is a typical ingredient in salves. I don't think—"

"Lead harbors earth energy, lifeblood to the undead," she added softly. "Gold harbors ethereal energy, which would be toxic to a creature who's forsaken its soul."

BB looked at Scott quizzically, waiting for his go-ahead. In turn, Scott looked at Leah, and she held his gaze. About to say no outright, he sensed a depth of sincerity in her that went beyond the talk of monsters. "Go ahead, BB."

BB nodded to an assistant, who hurried away and returned a short time later with a second syringe filled with liquid gold. BB took the syringe, placed it into the glass case, and then used the protective gloves to administer the injection.

Almost immediately, a wide circumference of flesh around the needle hissed sharply and dissolved into ruddy slush with a wisp of black smoke.

"Geez!" BB exclaimed, leaping back.

Leah, who stood by with a strained expression—as though wrestling with terrible memories—suddenly grabbed a scalpel from the table, and walked underneath the skylight, where her body was bathed by the sun. "There's one more thing that can hurt him," she said, and angled the blade until it reflected a spot-beam of sunlight onto the flesh sample. The illuminated area burst into flame.

Scott approached BB as the man snuffed the flame with a nitrile-gloved hand. The scientist looked as confused as he felt, which didn't exactly fill him with confidence.

"Regardless of what's going on, we need something that'll put this guy down." Scott paused as he looked at the sunlight-cooked flesh. The investigation kept getting weirder and weirder. "Based on what we've learned here. . ."

"Twenty-four-carat and lethal," BB nodded. "Got it."

Scott watched the scientist rush away, feeling a growing sense of dread. If the killer's flesh had such bizarre properties, there was no telling what could be happening to his own body if the guy had indeed infected him.

Chapter 26

"Ready to get out of here for the night?" Scott asked as he left the infirmary.

Leah looked at him closely. His face was expressionless, but waves of what felt like anguish—and something else she couldn't yet define—battered her. "How's Eric?"

"No change."

"I'm sorry."

Stepping closer, she reached out to Scott, touched his arm so he would know he wasn't alone. He covered her hand for a moment, and the warmth of the connection surprised her. Then he smiled sadly and let go and she suddenly felt hollow inside.

"Go on home, Leah. Get some rest."

"You need to get out of here, too." She hesitated only a moment before saying, "I could use a good meal. We both could. Why not have dinner together?"

Scott shook his head and looked back toward the infirmary. "I don't know."

"You'll be in no condition to help your brother or deal with a killer if you're hungry and exhausted."

The day had exhausted Leah, yet she had no desire to dive into her bed at the motel where Major Ackart had put her up temporarily. After everything that had happened, she couldn't stand the thought of being alone just so she could relive it all in her head.

"My place is just a few minutes down the road," he said. "After being in that swamp, I need to clean up before going anywhere."

Scott touched the back of her arm to get her moving out the door and toward the parking lot, now dark but for mercury-vapor lights. Under the weird blue glow, Scott looked like a bloodless corpse. After all that talk of vampires, the thought made her sick inside. She shuddered and Scott gripped her more firmly, binding her to him, unleashing something new and strange inside her.

A little woozy, she moved with difficulty as if through something as thick as the swamp, but Scott held her steady. Stopping at a jeep, he opened the passenger door for her. Leah climbed in and the moment her head hit the rest, she let her eyes flutter closed.

Scott Boulder made her feel as safe as was possible, considering the circumstances. Just as important, they had an equal stake in the outcome of the assignment. A personal stake. She'd never before met anyone who might be able to understand what had happened to her in that cave. Scott had survived the vampire's attack just as she had, the difference being she'd simply been branded whereas he'd been badly wounded.

Though come to think of it, he hadn't been acting like he was hurt the last few hours.

Belying his pale appearance, Scott seemed way too vital for a man who'd been wounded and had lost so much blood less than forty-eight hours ago. Could painkillers really be that effective, or was something else going on? Who knew what kind of scientific or medical Voodoo was being practiced at Miescher Laboratories in the name of Project 24?

Feeling the vehicle slow, Leah realized they must be there already. Through slitted eyes, she peered Scott's way. Though it was dark, apartment complex lights let her see his face, which had relaxed, softened, making his rugged features more appealing. She couldn't deny her attraction. She was looking forward to getting to know Scott Boulder, the man, rather than the captain.

"We're here."

He pulled into a diagonal parking space alongside a gray three-story apartment building that looked to hold a couple dozen units, all of which seemed to have balconies overlooking Bayou Foncé. Whatever the inside of his apartment was like, the outside setting was certainly premium.

"Not bad for government issue," she said, knowing the building was home to Miescher Laboratory scientists and Special Ops guys.

"It's a decent place. I usually sleep on base, though. I can keep better tabs on things that way." They climbed an inner stairwell to his apartment on the second floor, where he said, "I'll shower and change as fast as I can."

"Take all the time you need," Leah said, looking around as he headed into the bedroom.

Scott's apartment was every bit as efficient as the man. Not a thing out of place. Not much furniture, either. The brown couch, chair, and ottoman in the living room were accompanied by a stark coffee table. A small dining table with two wooden chairs sat outside the kitchen. Nothing on the taupe walls, but Leah didn't miss the framed photograph on the entertainment unit holding a television and sound system, the only thing she imagined Scott had added to the government décor.

Picking up the photograph, Leah studied a younger Scott and Eric on motorcycles, arms slung over each other's shoulders. She felt their brotherly affection for each other as sharply as if they were here with her. She could only imagine the torture Scott was going through not knowing if Eric would live or die. If only she could reassure him . . . if only life weren't so fragile . . .

Thankfully, she had photographs of Dad and Gabe, so she would never totally forget them. Not that having photos was the same as having memories. She would be able to see that Gabe had red hair and green eyes like she did, but she wouldn't be able to hear his laugh or remember the way she felt when he teased her. It made her feel so alone.

Scott returned with wet hair and wearing a pair of worn jeans and a faded House of Blues T-shirt. The casual clothing suited him better than black fatigues, which reminded her of military conflicts, something she wanted to avoid being part of. As did he, she knew, if he would allow himself to change.

"I'm blind tired," Scott said. "Would you mind if we ate here? I have steaks in the fridge."

"Here would be great."

Relieved that at least getting a meal would be easy, she followed him into the kitchen where he immediately began digging into the refrigerator. "What can I do to help?"

"Throwing a couple of steaks in the broiler and potatoes in the microwave isn't rocket science. You could pick out some music, though."

"All right."

His collection was mostly blues and heavy metal. In deference to the T-shirt, she picked out a couple of CDs featuring New Orleans blues musicians. By the time she had the player loaded and the music adjusted so it was soft in the background, Scott already had the steaks in the countertop broiler and was putting the potatoes in the microwave.

"I'll set the table," she said, and when he indicated the correct cabinet, she fetched the plates. "Thanks, by the way. Being alone tonight would have been difficult."

"You've been through a lot in one day. Are you sorry you took the job?"

"No." She came back into the kitchen where Scott was fixing a salad. "The vampire has to be stopped, and I want to be the one to do it."

Noting the way Scott's spine stiffened at the word vampire, Leah stopped herself from going on.

She'd raised his hackles—Leah could feel it. That and something else. Something that made her want to keep her distance even as she wanted to get closer. What was wrong with her that she couldn't read Scott any better than this? Or maybe she was getting carried away. There really wasn't a bogeyman around *every* corner. She was too tired, had gone through too much in a single day. Her imagination was working overtime, confusing her into thinking she might not be safe with Scott.

But of course she was.

Staring down at the scar on her palm, she felt ready to shatter. Calloused hands slid around her damaged one. She looked up into Scott's worried gaze.

"Leah, are you all right?"

For a moment, time stood still. Leah felt her pulse speed up and her senses come alive. This felt so right—their being together, his touching her. She felt something else, too, that reminded her of the vampire's energy . . .

Suddenly nervous again, she slipped her hand free and backed off, into the wall. The kitchen suddenly seemed too small and narrow. Or maybe it was that she had this weird sense of something being off, like she had earlier in Roberto's cabin. Disappointed that the moment had been spoiled by such thoughts, she pushed them back. She didn't know why she was torn about being close to Scott. Didn't want to know.

"Just thinking, is all." She tried to make a joke of it. "I seem to live in my head most of the time. Meeting you is . . . well, kind of weird."

"Because we both survived attacks?"

She nodded. "You understand. You don't blame me for what happened to my father and brother . . . for surviving."

"No one could possibly blame you for that."

"Mom does. Since that day, she's been . . . well, inaccessible. She's waiting to die so she can join Dad and Gabe. But I'm here . . . and I'm alone." She shook her head. "I don't really matter to her. I don't matter to anyone."

"Don't say that. Your mother obviously is broken. Mine was, too. She used Vicodin to dull her pain. I remember the time I came home from baseball practice and couldn't find Eric. I tried asking Mom where he was, but she only stared at me with glassy eyes. After running around the neighborhood, I finally found Eric at the corner market trying to buy himself dinner. He had a shopping cart filled with boxes of macaroni and cheese and chocolate ice cream. I actually laughed when I first saw him . . . pushing that huge cart with his broomstick arms. I mean, how did he expect to pay for all that stuff?" Scott clenched his jaw. "From that day until Mom left for good, I was the one who really took care of Eric."

The roughness in Scott's voice made Leah want to open up further, to voice the truth to someone who would get it.

"I go through days and weeks and months without ever feeling the normal connections most people feel," she admitted. "I can't form a viable relationship with anyone. I'm constantly hoping to find something I can't quite touch. But today we connected . . . and . . . it was different."

"Different how?"

"Like I know you. I'm starting to feel like I've always known you, even though we met yesterday morning."

"I could say the same about you."

Scott stared at her. Her pulse picked up. She needed someone in her life she could talk to, someone she could turn to when the past caught up to her.

"But your work," he finally said. "You're so invested in it."

"Apparently I intellectualize too much. I haven't been able to do what it takes to bring everything I know together. I tried to help a little girl who'd been raped." She shook her head. "I couldn't do it. I could only identify with the way she felt." Her throat felt clotted as she whispered, "At least she had a mother waiting for her with open arms."

Scott didn't say anything, merely stepped closer and slid his arms around her.

Startled, Leah froze for a moment, then let herself go. Emotion flooded her and she swayed into him. Softened. Felt her pulse humming through her. As he pressed his cheek to her forehead, he murmured something soothing, and she realized this was the closest she'd gotten to another human being in . . . well, maybe ever since that fatal day.

He pulled away to look down into her face. His expression serious, he said, "Leah—"

She pressed her fingers to his lips. No words. Nothing to spoil this moment. Whatever he wanted to tell her could wait. She wanted to put the horror they had to stop out of her mind just for a little while.

He covered her hand with his, rubbed her fingers against his lips, then groaned and pulled her hand back, up against the wall over her head. His fingers laced through hers and once more she felt the deep connection. And something scary, as well. The breath caught in her throat. Pinned between the wall and him, she couldn't move, didn't want to. Maybe Scott's scary side was as attractive to her as the rest of him. She didn't know. She only knew she wanted to be with him now. In the moment.

Her gaze roamed his face mere inches from hers, traced every angle and curve and plane. Familiar . . . so familiar . . . like they were a part of her . . . like she and Scott were meant to be together . . .

The distance between them closed and his mouth covered hers, not gently, but with the passion of a man who didn't know how to live otherwise. Heat seared her as she returned the kiss with a breathless excitement that turned her knees to rubber. If Scott wasn't pressed against her, she might slip down the wall to the floor.

Wanting to touch him, she slipped her hand along his neck, but he pulled it free and slammed it up against the wall next to her other hand so she was arching into him and breathing hard. With a groan that lit her inside, he slid his mouth along her cheek, down her neck. She watched as he trailed his mouth over her breasts. Her nipples were already hard and extended. He let go of her hands to cup the full flesh, to mouth the sensitive tips through the material of her blouse.

Her world tilted and she closed her eyes. It had been so long since she'd felt this close to anyone. She went through her days and nights and weeks alone, living in her own head, pretending it didn't matter. Other men had held her, but none had ever made a true connection with her before.

Scott was different. He made her feel and want and hope. He might scare her at times, but she would face it down . . . whatever it was.

She ran her hands down the front of his body until she found the snap and zipper on his jeans, practically ripping them open. Slipping a hand inside, she found him, stroked him, yearned to feel him fill her.

As if he could read her mind, he freed her breasts and dipped his hands under her full skirt, easily removing the only obstacle. His hands spread under her buttocks, he lifted her easily and she parted her thighs, wrapping her legs around his as she sank onto him.

He backed her against the wall again, hands flattened

on either side of her head. He let her set the rhythm, and she could tell he held himself back. She watched his face, took in every nuance of expression, waited for the moment when she knew he couldn't hold on longer. Only then did she let herself go, her voice breaking as she cried out, and took him with her.

The toaster oven timer went off with a *ding*.

Neither moved.

Scott's deadweight pressed Leah into the wall and, her arms and legs wrapped around his body, she held on to him for as long as she could.

Chapter 27

Are you goddamn crazy? Scott railed at himself as he looked at Leah in bed next to him. Purple dawn streamed through the bedroom window and illuminated her pale skin. She looked even more beautiful now than she had last night.

He started to smile, then caught himself.

He knew better than to get involved with a team member. A civilian no less. What the hell had he been thinking?

Still . . .

It had felt damn good to be with her. Not just physically, though feeling her writhe against him and hearing the sweet sound of her moans had tested his endurance almost as much as a Special Forces training test.

It had felt good to be *with* her.

He'd never experienced a connection like that with a woman before. Even though they'd argued, she instilled a feeling of profound calm in him. Her company was like the home he'd never had, the home he'd always wanted—peaceful and loving.

Feeling this way made him want to leave the military behind that much more.

Frankly, it felt like he'd known Leah Maguire his entire life. Or for many lifetimes, as she might say. That she didn't hold the burned steaks against him was a definite plus. Add a sense of humor to her attributes of savvy and strength. He thought back to the kitchen with a smirk. And spontaneity. Couldn't forget that.

Which is why an episode like this could never happen again. Ever.

He simply couldn't afford to let feelings come into play here. Doing so could compromise his judgment and the mission. Not to mention put Leah's life in danger as well as his own. He had to keep his mind clear and focused.

Yet, despite himself, he found himself reaching for her—when she opened her eyes.

He snatched his hand away as she rolled toward him, sheets rustling. She smiled. God, she was beautiful.

"Good morning," she said.

He climbed quickly out of bed, snatched his boxer shorts from the floor, and pulled them on. "Morning," he grunted.

"Is something wrong?"

I made a huge mistake, but other than that, things are goddamn peachy. "No."

She sat up, holding the sheet against her breasts. "I don't have to be an empath to know you're uncomfortable."

"I'm just putting my focus back where it belongs," he replied, stepping into his jeans and trying his best not to dwell on what he could feel for her if the circumstances were different. "Back on the mission."

He saw an expression of hurt flicker across her face—an expression that pierced his heart. But he was doing what he knew was right, and not only because of the mission. He'd felt something in addition to desire last night. Darkness deep inside that he couldn't quite describe . . . a cold heaviness that had grown more intense since leaving the swamp. He didn't know what it meant, but couldn't risk exposing Leah to any more danger. For whatever reason, he hadn't been able to stop himself from being with her last night. But he'd damn well better stop himself now.

"I don't consider this a mistake," she said softly.

"Neither do I," he replied with an affected shrug. "We needed to work off frustration . . . needed someone else to hang on to for a while. Understandable considering the circumstances."

She looked directly into his eyes and it became clear that their connection was still very much present. "The mission doesn't have to suffer for what happened between us. You don't always have to be ready for a fight."

"I'm proud to be a member of the Special Forces."

"I'm not saying you shouldn't be proud. I'm just saying there might be a different way to approach things. Both in terms of this mission—and personally."

"Touchy-feely tactics may work in your world of magic and fairy tales, Leah, but take it from me—in my world, they'll get you killed." He felt a knot in his throat as he said the words. He was picking an argument as a diversion. Worse, he knew that she knew it, too.

Apparently, the fact that he'd resort to such a tactic seemed enough for her. She turned her head, peered out the window.

He already missed the connection they'd shared. Well, it was his own damn fault. He never should have gotten close to her—and couldn't allow himself to lose control like that again.

"Would you like breakfast?" he asked finally.

"Okay," she replied, still not looking at him. "Now would you please close the door while I dress?"

He did. Still shaken, Scott walked into the kitchen where he filled a couple of bowls with grapes and slices of cheese. It seemed as though idealism and practicality rarely, if ever, had much in common with each other, in matters of war and in matters of the heart.

Carrying the bowls from the kitchen, Scott noticed that his body felt . . . off. Like he was coming down with the flu, maybe. He tensed. The sensation was similar to what he'd felt in the swamp before the violent stomach pains hit.

His hands felt very strange; tingling and light, almost like they were asleep. And then he noticed that he no longer felt the bowls.

He looked down in time to see the bowls fall and shatter against the tile floor.

"Scott?" Leah called out. "Are you okay?"

"Fine, just clumsy," he answered.

But he wasn't fine. His hands had been replaced by clouds of gray mist. Hearing Leah climb from the bed, Scott dropped behind the counter and tried to scoop up the bowl shards and scattered grapes, already forgetting the state of his hands.

Scott stared in horror. This was the power Drew had inherited . . . but how the hell had he adopted it without DNA splicing?

When Leah walked around the counter, he whisked his arms around his back to hide his hands.

She regarded the mess. "Do you have a broom and dustpan?"

"In the utility closet near the front door. Thanks."

"Did you cut yourself?" she said, indicating his hidden hands.

"I'm fine."

As she left to get the broom and dustpan, Scott pushed aside his shock and racked his brains—and then remembered what Drew had said once about his transmogrification power. *I visualize my body the way I want it to be, and voilà!*

Sweat dotting his forehead, Scott looked at his smoky hands, and concentrated on seeing palms and fingers there instead. His flesh began to materialize slowly like a ship through ocean fog, but nowhere near fast enough. His hands were still a little transparent when Leah returned, but she was too busy with the broom to notice.

However, what Leah did or didn't see was the least of his worries.

He was certain he was becoming *something else* now. Cold dread nearly overcame him as he feared for himself . . . and, more important, for Leah and Eric.

If Drew's and Jonas's condition after the DNA-splicing procedure were any indication, his body and mind—his very effectiveness as a soldier—would be at the mercy of a transformation he could not stop.

Chapter 28

Major Ackart swooped down on Leah the moment she came into the lab the next day. "Where's Captain Boulder?"

Tearing herself away from BB, who was getting ready to run an experiment on the red stone, testing its strength with a diamond-tipped drill, Leah said, "In the infirmary with his brother."

"Good, you and I need to talk alone. In my office."

Ackart spun on her heel and took off. Leah gave BB a questioning look, but the scientist merely shrugged, so she took after the other woman, asking, "Is something wrong?"

"It's Boulder."

Filled with dread, Leah reluctantly followed her down the corridor. No doubt having noticed something was wrong with Scott, the major wanted confirmation. Could Leah really admit to seeing Scott's hands turn to smoke? She couldn't betray him without telling him that she'd seen what was happening. Leah couldn't be sure how far things had progressed with Scott, but it was obvious to her now that the wounds he'd suffered in the attack were transforming him. For now, he still seemed to be himself. According to vampire legend, to transform completely, Scott would have needed to swallow Andre's blood, too.

Roberto's accusation about Scott being an agent of the vampire haunted her. What if Scott really was inching over to the dark side? She'd felt something scary in him and had chosen to ignore it. What did she do now?

Upon entering the office, Ackart got right to it. "I've noticed that you and the captain have gotten close in a very short time."

The major's words were clipped and her tension was palpable as she fingered a pendant around her neck. Leah feared that Ackart was going to ask her to turn on Scott.

"Scott and I are in a high-pressure situation," Leah said, "both with a personal stake."

"That's not what I meant—I'm talking about a *personal relationship*." Ackart scowled at her accusingly. "You left the base together yesterday. You went to Boulder's apartment."

Did Ackart have someone spying on them? Surely she couldn't know what had gone on in the apartment between them, couldn't have seen what had happened to Scott this morning.

"We had dinner together."

Ackart sat forward as if she were trying to press Leah into submission. "Mixing your personal life with your professional life would be . . ."

Leah was surpised to realize that Ackart did not want to talk about what was happening with Scott. She might even be oblivious. Ackart might put the fear of God in the hearts of her men, but Leah had scarier things to fear.

"Major Ackart, let me make this clear. I am an employee of the government and as such have signed a nondisclosure agreement about what's going on in these facilities. I did not sign over any other rights, certainly nothing that makes me answer to you about my personal time."

The major sat back and stared at her, and Leah got the distinct feeling she was trying to regroup. But what was so important about this? Leah wasn't sensing any jealousy or possessiveness from this woman. She wondered if her motives were anything other than standard.

"Your getting personally involved with Captain Boulder would be a mistake," Ackart said, her fingertips worrying the pendant, her voice softer, as if she were merely trying to give a friend good advice.

Not that Leah believed it.

"I don't usually talk about my family history, Dr. Maguire . . ." Ackart paused for a moment and her expression reflected distaste. ". . . but I'm worried enough about the situation that I'm going to make an exception." A flicker of emotion softened her features when she said, "My grandmother Rachel gave me this caduceus when I was a child—the only thing my grandfather ever gave her. She was a brilliant woman just like you. She was highly educated for her time—a medical researcher and nurse who spoke five languages. A very important operation in the European theater rested on her shoulders, but she unexpectedly got careless."

Not knowing if she could believe a word that crossed the major's lips, Leah said, "You're saying this happened because your grandmother got involved with a man."

Ackart nodded. "Romantic notions clouded her judgment. She made a grave mistake and people died. My grandmother Rachel never really got over the consequences of her actions and devoted her whole life to working with the military, trying to make up for it. She still is."

Highly unlikely that an elderly woman was still working with the military, Leah thought.

"I don't want that same error happening here on my project, Dr. Maguire. We're at war with an unknown hostile right now. I need every member of my team to focus on the mission alone so we can successfully contain the creature."

"We *are* focused."

"Good. I need you to stay that way." The girlfriend act over, Ackart stood and her tone changed into that of an officer in charge once more. "I trust you won't make the same mistake as my grandmother. You won't let your emotions rule your head."

"I'll be careful," Leah said.

Not that an empath could make any promises where emotions were concerned . . .

Ackart's story did impact Leah, however, so when she met up with Scott a while later in the break room for a brainstorming session about how to track down Andre, she mentally took a step back from him. He was a colleague, her partner, and it would serve them both better—it would serve the *team* better—if they kept their relationship on a professional level. And from the way he kept his distance and a scowl plastered on his face every time he looked at her, he was doing the same.

She didn't want to examine her deeper feelings, didn't want to feel the hurt.

"I think I know how to find the vamp . . . Andre." Uncertain of how Scott was going to react, Leah tightened her grip on her coffee mug. "After what Roberto said, I think he'll be looking for the Philosopher's Stone."

"To make him immortal?"

That Scott's tone was caustic didn't surprise her.

"Whether or not *you* believe has nothing to do with what *he* believes. And if he believes what Roberto told us, he'll want the Stone. He probably assumes the man who walled him in is still a priest and would search for him at his old parish."

"And how would he figure out which church Gutierrez served?" Scott asked. "The man was excommunicated shortly after he sealed this Andre in the cave."

"The glyphs. The answer was there right in front of him as he starved to death. Holy Cross in New Orleans." She'd done the research when she'd studied the photographs of the glyphs the year before. "I've never been to the parish, but maybe that's exactly what we should do. Go to the church and wait for Andre to show up. And if he's already been there," Leah said with a shiver, "I'll know. Maybe I can figure out how to follow him."

A way that didn't include magic, wouldn't destroy more of the past for her.

To his credit, Scott didn't comment on her ability to sense things. He informed Ackart about what they were going to do and told her to have backup at the ready.

Tension wired Leah all the way into New Orleans. Telling herself to keep her distance from Scott was one thing, actually doing it another. The night before they'd gotten so close that she now mourned the loss of that openness. But she wouldn't be responsible for any more deaths if she could help it. What she wanted—needed—was nothing when compared to the greater good. As she'd promised Ackart, she would be careful to keep her focus until the vampire was dealt with.

It seemed Scott was in line with that. He hadn't said anything personal to her since leaving his apartment.

Even so, Leah kept sneaking glances at him as he drove in silence, wanting to be close to him, wondering if she would notice anything else wrong with him. He seemed totally in control of himself, and when she tried to delve deeper psychically, she couldn't. He'd created a mental barrier between them, one she couldn't penetrate. That was almost as unnerving as seeing his hands turn to smoke, something she simply couldn't bring herself to mention.

Though it wasn't all that far from the French Quarter, the church sat in a dilapidated neighborhood of mostly small shotgun houses, half boarded up, all still showing damage from the hurricane. A waterline about four feet up imprinted the walls of Holy Cross itself, and the bell tower had been damaged by high winds, the famous Celtic cross sitting crookedly atop its dome the result.

"We should stay close," Scott said as they left the jeep. "If you see or hear anything, warn me. Don't try to do anything on your own."

"Of course." When Scott touched her arm to guide her to the door, Leah flushed and avoided looking at him.

Once inside the vestibule, Scott hesitated only a second to scan the nave before striding toward the altar. Watching his every move, Leah dipped her fingers in the font of holy water and crossed herself.

"In the name of the Father, the Son, the Holy Spirit . . ."

This was a house of God.

Could a vampire actually enter here?

Moving into the church after Scott, Leah gripped the strap of her soft case holding her tools and concentrated on finding out if magic had been used here, but she sensed nothing amiss, no trace of the vampire or of the human who served him.

"I think I saw something back by the chapel," he said. As he quickly unbuttoned his sports jacket, she got a glimpse of a shoulder holster. "Let's check it out."

Wanting to put some distance between them, Leah hung back. Until she talked to Scott about what she'd seen, she simply wasn't comfortable being too close. Slipping into a pew near the back, she knelt and said a quick prayer for her father and brother.

When she opened her eyes and looked around, the church suddenly took on a life of its own.

Voices lifted from the empty choir loft overhead and the ghosts of parishioners lined a second-story balcony. The hair at the back of her neck rose. To the right of the sanctuary was a large open doorway—was that really an altar boy running up a staircase to ring the bell in the tower? Along the lower walls, a penitent she hadn't seen enter made his way along the stations of the cross toward the wooden confessional tucked into a corner.

Something was terribly wrong.

As they had for seventeen years, the Blessed Virgin and the saints looked down upon her with pity in their eyes from stained-glass windows and statues in niches surrounded by votive candles.

The candles . . .

Staring at a burning bank of votives, Leah became mesmerized by the flames. She heard tinkling laughter as they danced within the red glass holders.

Before her eyes, they shifted and gradually changed . . .

Suddenly the candles were black and inscribed with mouths and names, both crossed out so their namesakes couldn't call for help.

The church building itself seemed to inhale, to breathe, to moan.

A chill pebbled the flesh along Leah's spine as she became aware. Magic whispered through her, paralyzing her.

Leah fought it, fought the inertia that made it nearly impossible for her to get to her feet. What was being done to her? What was making it so difficult to move? It must be some kind of dark spell, cast in a church of all places. Standing and clinging to the back of the pew in front of her, she felt shaky and unsure of herself as footsteps echoed around her.

Closing her eyes, she concentrated as she had at the kill site the day before. Again, a cloying scent filled her, the same odor she'd encountered outside the FEMA trailer. The same sensation of this being a woman. The human who served Andre Espinoza.

She had to get to Scott, to warn him, but when she checked the front of the church for him, he was still nowhere to be seen. Struggling for focus, she knew she would have to face this Voodoo priestess head-on and alone.

It took her forever to turn, to see who'd entered the church.

It wasn't a woman, but instead a man.

Leah's eyes widened and her heart beat painfully against her ribs at memory seemingly turned into flesh and bone.

He wore jeans and a flannel shirt half-covered by a vest with a dozen pockets, most bulging with their contents. On his head, a helmet's light shone directly into her eyes. The spelunker's headlight blinded her, but not before hope cascaded through her.

No, it couldn't be. Impossible.

But denial didn't make the phantasm disappear.

This was black magic.

Even recognizing it for what it was, Leah couldn't help herself.

Stumbling out into the aisle, she cried out, "Dad!"

She couldn't help wanting to believe the vision was real, if only for a moment. She couldn't help wanting to hug him, to tell him how sorry she was that she had been responsible for leading the terror straight to him and Gabe.

They locked gazes and Leah knew at once he wasn't there. She was trying to connect with an illusion. No matter how hard she tried to shake it off, she couldn't. Quaking inside, she thought quickly as the illusion turned from her and gazed around the chapel as if looking for something.

This was her fault. She should have stayed with Scott.

She'd been tricked.

With effort, Leah moved to the votives, picked up a holder, and dumped out the candle. She would use the power of the church itself to break the spell that had been put over it. At the font, she filled the votive with holy water.

The realization that using this magic would make her lose more of her precious memories froze her for a second. But there was no choice. She couldn't let her emotions get in the way.

"Dad," she called, even as she forced herself forward.

The thing that looked like her father turned and for a moment, gazing into the face she so loved, Leah faltered. She could do this, she told herself. She had to.

Stumbling closer, she grabbed his arm and threw the holy water over him.

"I adjure thee by the living God that thou torment me not!"

Her fingers tingled with an unnatural energy that threatened to overcome her, but she clung tightly to that arm. Her father's visage flickered like a television with a bad antenna, and she glimpsed a dusky female face twisted into an angry expression.

"Per Dominum nostrum Jesum Christum . . . through Our Lord Jesus Christ . . ."

The image flickered between the male-female visages and when the flickering stopped, Leah's breath caught in her throat. This time when she saw her father's face, it was twisted and tortured, a gory red as was the rest of him, blood spurting from a wide gash in his neck.

"No!" she cried out and tried to finish the adjuration. But she was so transfixed by this terrible sight that had been hidden from her by the darkness of the cave, by those who'd found her afterward, that the words refused to come forth.

Her stomach twisted and her gorge rose and from her

throat came a wild cry that echoed her horror through the recesses of the church.

Unable to fight the sensations swamping her like a physical blow, Leah let go, and defeated once more, helplessly dropped to her knees.

Chapter 29

Clutching a broken shard of wood, Andre scratched a large circle into the dirt floor. The large toolshed tucked into a corner of the courtyard behind Magic Nights was not the optimal location for what needed to be done, but the witch had bound him to the nightclub grounds while she went to hunt the priest. So be it.

"*Por la ayuda de este fuego divino* . . ." Andre intoned as he proceeded to draw a square inside the circle, making sure the four points touched the circumference, and then drew a triangle inside the square, and then an open, lidded eye near the pinnacle of the triangle—the centuries-old symbol of *Los Oscuros*.

It denoted true, alchemical enlightenment, which he would now attempt to recapture fully after having nearly lost it when the priest trapped him in the cave. Enlightenment exercised through manipulation of lightning and magnetism.

His powers were sorely lacking. That had been clear during the attack on the trailer. His body would have to be reminded of its latent elemental powers. Reinitiated. Shocked agonizingly into accord like the atrophied muscles of a coma victim.

But dare he take the risk? The attempt might kill him in his weakened state—as his initial transformation had very nearly done.

"Papi, I beg you . . . give me the courage to make this decision . . ." Andre whispered through clenched teeth.

He'd been only nineteen years old when his father had presented him with his first alchemical potion in the ossuary of the cathedral in Sigüenza where he'd studied to become a priest to infiltrate the Crown's Catholic order. Scattered throughout the ossuary had been several stone sarcophagi, their lids carved with the likenesses of the false saints enshrined within. After leading him into the torch-lit darkness, Papi had smashed in the head of one of the saints with a mace so that he could retrieve the cremation vase from within. Papi had then poured a silky gray heap of ashes onto his palm, spit into it, and then drew a symbol on Andre's forehead with the desecrated remains—an all-seeing eye to cover the cross drawn in black ash by the Catholic bishop only an hour before.

"You are now a member of *Los Oscuros,*" Papi had said. "From this moment forward, you will use your standing as a priest to help us strike at the Church from within."

Andre remembered the hellfire glow in his father's eyes. He had watched it grow with Mama's passing to consume the man in lunacy and grief. Seeing this lunacy had filled Andre with such terror that he'd refused to drink from the corked vial his father had offered until forced to do so by the point of a rapier with a medallion in its hilt that had once graced Mama's neck. The very rapier that Papi had offered the corrupt priest.

Moving around the earthen circle, Andre placed a lit red candle at each cardinal direction, upon which he'd scratched the symbols of Air, Earth, Fire, and Water.

He moved to the makeshift still he'd cobbled together with liquor bottles, glass piping, and rubber tubing—a functioning mockery of what his father's lab had been—and picked up a soup bowl now filled with the viscous, cloudy reduction of plant extracts, manure, soil, and pulverized stone. To this he added the Salt of Mercury and Mars and the Powder of Saturn that he'd acquired at the Voodoo shop. The liquid turned red, then orange, and then became marbled with white.

Preparation complete, he stepped into the circle and brought the bowl to his lips. Felt a bolt of fear as he closed his eyes and inhaled the potion's tilled-earth aroma.

"*Papi, give me strength,*" he prayed again.

If the potion killed him, his body and soul would be lost for eternity.

However, if he survived, his enlightenment would allow him to rescue his parents from Limbo—an aim he'd hidden from the witch. The Philosopher's Stone would indeed grant him eternal life, but with enlightenment it would also allow him to cross the astral boundary and snatch his beloved parents from the maw of death itself. Together they would then usher in a new vampiric age, and wage a final war against the Catholic Church and those who refused to embrace the tenets of divine alchemy.

He knew there was really only one choice to make. For Papi and Mama. For himself.

Pushing aside his terror, he continued his earlier intonation, ". . . *pueda sea encontrado digno ser llamado en la iluminación del justo.*"

He then titled his head back and drank the potion. As he remembered, the potion tasted of spoiled wine and crackled on his tongue on its way down his throat.

At first, he felt nothing. And then he collapsed as it felt like acid was being pumped through his veins . . . as it had when his father had first given him the potion in the ossuary long ago. His flailing arms and legs knocked the candles askew and erased the symbol of enlightenment that he'd rendered in the dirt. He roared and the sound was covered by the thumping music and commotion of the club upstairs, but the intensity of it vibrated the walls. He continued to roar in helpless, churning agony until his throat was raw, and then for a terrible moment, he believed he might be enduring the horrible pain for nothing. Had he blended the wrong chemical proportions? Had he just poisoned himself?

Terrified, Andre scrambled to his hands and knees, not knowing what to do or how to save himself, when he noticed that the tools on the walls around him were trembling violently. They shook with a loud, discordant clatter—and then jerked free of their wall-mounted storage hooks and flew at him. Dozens of saw blades and hammers and screwdrivers and hedge clippers sliced through the air and then swirled around him in a vortex, propelled by his growing magnetic influence like satellites around a planet.

Struggling to his feet, Andre screamed in agony as acid continued to pump through his veins, the cry echoing in concert with the swirling, clanging steel. He then felt the core of his body swell and crackle with energy like an overloading reactor core, an energy he could not keep in check. With a groan, he let the black energy streak from his body in jagged bolts and strike the flying tools in a massive shower of sparks.

A grin cut Andre's face as he stood in the eye of the crackling storm of steel. He was confident now that he could endure the agony of enlightenment and survive to claim victory.

An hour later, after removing all traces of alchemy from the basement, Andre moved through the thronging nightclub with satisfaction, his body humming with new power. His alchemical side was back to full strength, and his vampiric side would soon be as well with only a few more feedings.

That meant he would be in a prime condition to strike

back at the witch once he possessed the Philosopher's Stone—even if he did not yet know what to do with her.

He considered sparing her life once he attained immortality, particularly after witnessing her spell-casting ability. She was skilled and powerful, and he could use her considerable talents to further his own ends. But did that excuse her affront against him? Should he kill her out of spite?

He would suspend judgment.

Climbing a flight of stairs carpeted with red velvet, he walked down a hallway and entered a room opposite the witch's own. The bedroom of her brother.

The place was cloaked in shadow, smelled thickly of disease. Across from the bed, French doors opened onto a balcony. He could hear the faint rumble of passing cars, the birdlike squawks of conversation. Occasionally, the wind carried in a hint of perfume or cigarette smoke.

He moved silently to the bed and looked down at the thin figure who slept under a mountain of blankets. The man's flesh was as pale as his had been before feeding.

So this was Danton. The motivation for the witch's every act of terror.

Andre suspected that she had left him within striking distance of her brother without fear. No doubt she believed that his desire to obtain the Stone superseded any impulse to seek revenge for enslavement.

She was wrong. Danton was a new vulnerability. An opportunity. A shortcut to defeating her, perhaps. Andre considered that if he killed Danton, the witch would suffer terrible anguish, possibly enough to weaken her hold over him. He could then search for the Philosopher's Stone on his own. It was an option.

As he took a step closer to the bed, his foot pressed on a warped section of hardwood, causing the floor to creak.

Stirring, Danton looked up with a start. "Who . . . who are you?"

The man's voice was weak. Clotted. Andre didn't answer the question as he considered taking the man's life.

Danton shrank away wide-eyed, and then relaxed. "Wait . . . you must be Andre. Am I right?"

Andre decided to entertain the man's questions. They may be the last he would ever have. "Yes. I am Andre Espinoza."

Moaning, Danton struggled into a sitting position and rested his back against the cherrywood headboard. "My sister said that you might be able to help me. Thank you." Danton extended a pale hand. Andre took it. Shaking Danton's hand was like shaking the hand of a child. It would take no effort at all to kill this man.

"Would you mind handing me that glass of water?" Danton asked.

Andre plucked the glass from the night table and gave it to him. Danton drank, swallowing thickly. "Are you a doctor?"

"Your sister did not tell you who I was?"

"Only that you could help."

So the witch had not told her brother how his life might be saved. Or what he would turn into. Interesting. "I can help," Andre said. "That much is true."

"Well, like I said, thank you." Danton took another sip of water. "If you don't mind me asking, is your family originally from Spain? Somewhere near Sigüenza?"

Andre took another step closer to the bed as he wondered what the witch had divulged. Had she given this man enough information about his history to divine a weakness? One that he himself had forgotten during his long sleep? He clenched his fists.

"How would you know?" Andre asked.

Danton smiled. "I'm studying to be a linguist. Or at

least I was before I got sick. There's a very distinct inflection in your voice."

Andre nodded, stood down. "You have studied well."

"Thanks." He paused. "You don't like my sister very much, do you?"

Andre cocked an eyebrow. This young man was astute, much more than he had expected. Perhaps he would let him live a few moments longer. "Why do you say that?"

"I don't get the feeling you want to be here. Does Rebecca have dirt on you or something?" he asked, smirking at the half-joke. "If you want to leave, that's okay, no hard feelings. I'll take full responsibility. Believe me, I understand what it feels like to deal with something unpleasant and unexpected."

Andre was again impressed with the young man's discernment. Indeed, he deeply resented the witch's control over him, yet at the same time, part of him felt an attraction to her that went beyond magic. She carried unique intelligence and inner strength. She might do well by his side. "Thank you for your offer, Danton. But as you are well aware, sometimes we have no choice but to do things that are difficult."

Danton cleared his throat. "Well, if my sister does have something on you, please don't judge her too harshly. She's been though a lot."

"Haven't we all?" Andre said.

"True enough. I can only tell you, when we were kids, we had a stepfather who . . ." Danton stopped, took a sip of water. He gripped the glass so tightly it shook. "She didn't deserve what happened to her, Andre. I protected her when I could, but . . ." He looked down.

"You fought, Danton. That is what matters."

"I lost my sister after that happened, you know? Who she used to be got buried. I wish every day that I could fix her . . . bring that part of her back to life. She gets so sad sometimes . . . so sad I don't even recognize her." He coughed wetly into his fist, and shrugged. "I guess that's why I study languages. My futile attempt to communicate with her."

Andre felt a sudden and unexpected swell of respect for this man. His courage—as well as his sickness—reminded him of Mama during her last days. Even ill, Mama thought of others. She strove to take care of those she loved until her dying breath. "What would you say to her?"

" 'Look at what you're doing. Please look.' I mean, take what she does for a living. There's nothing wrong with it, I guess, but I can see the resentment in her eyes. At men, at the world. It's obvious she's most angry at herself for not being able to let go of the past, you know? She deserves more than all this."

"What does she deserve?"

"To be free."

"Freedom from pain and earthly restraint exists for those bold enough to take it," Andre said. "Do you trust your sister?"

"Implicitly. She has a kind heart, Andre. Truly, she does. She would do anything for me, and has, for as long as I can remember."

Andre paused. So his suspicion in the Voodoo shop had been correct. The witch's temperament had changed from one of tolerance to one of hostility.

A variable he could not ignore.

At first, he hadn't thought her peasant Voodoo powerful enough to adversely affect her. But according to Danton, it had—as did any power of consequence.

His own vampiric powers had robbed him of tactile pleasures, most notably of taste and touch. How he longed to taste the sour-sweetness of an apple, to feel the tickling, warm caress of a lover. As it was, he could only taste the coppery bitterness of blood, and any touch, no matter how hostile or loving the intent, was but cold pressure on his flesh. His alchemical abilities had their own costs, making him vulnerable to compounds and symbols that were harmless to ordinary human beings. In his case, he believed the end justified the means.

Did the witch? Did she even realize that she was changing? The magic she so coveted was altering her personality as she grew more powerful. She was growing harder, losing her humanity. He'd fought battles throughout the birth of North America with soldiers like her. They were best unleashed against an enemy and then killed once the day was won. Otherwise, they might turn like rabid dogs. Would the witch change so much as to not be of any lasting use?

"People can make choices that result in more harm than good," Andre said.

Danton thought for a moment. "I trust she's doing what she thinks is best. I'm not saying it's necessarily the right choice. We don't ever have a way of knowing that, I guess. What she's doing is good enough for me."

Loyalty to family was important, Andre knew. He also knew that it could have tremendous consequences, however worthy. Centuries of pain and solitude. Of thankless struggle.

"Danton, your sister and I have an arrangement that should conclude soon," Andre said. "After that, we will deal with your ailment." It was not his place to tell Danton what was in store for him. That was his sister's responsibility.

Danton nodded, eyes heavy. "It was nice meeting you, Andre. Now if you don't mind, I think I need a little more rest."

Andre took the glass from Danton, and watched as the man slid back under the covers. In less than a minute, he was asleep.

Andre looked back toward the billowing curtains. He

may not have been able to save his parents in life. But he could help this honorable man.

When the time was right, he would help Danton live, Andre decided. As a vampire, Danton could become an ally against the Church, and perhaps even against his own sister, if she refused to comply with her fate.

Chapter 30

Heart pounding, Scott strode quickly through the chapel door, leading with the SIG. Was it the killer he'd seen? Or his accomplice?

The place smelled faintly of incense, wood polish, and melted wax. Sunlight beamed through stained-glass windows that depicted the Stations of the Cross, splashing the pews with pools of red, blue, and green. Forty feet above, arched crossbeams supported a gilded ceiling decorated with a painted blue sky populated by angels.

After scanning his lines of fire, he moved into the center aisle, and continued toward the altar, senses on high alert. He hated to draw his weapon here. The lessons he'd learned while attending church with Eric as a kid still echoed in his head. This was a house of God. A house of peace. Although his childhood had been rough in plenty of ways, he missed believing that the world was a good place. He wished he could lay down his arms and learn to embrace that innocent view once again.

The only sounds were the quick tread of his boots on carpet, and the faint hum of distant traffic. As he moved, he peered down each row of wooden pews—maybe twenty in all—in case his quarry was hiding among them.

His heart rate surged as he stepped onto the chancel. There were blind alcoves on either side—one for altar boys, the other for the choir. There was no way he could cover both at once. If he guessed wrong, he could be a sitting duck.

He decided to veer left. He slid around the marble wall, fast. There were two rows of empty chairs and he was clear. Whirling to the other alcove he saw a figure.

Adrenaline surging, he dropped to one knee, aimed center-mass, and realized he was about to shoot a marble statue of Saint Francis. He exhaled sharply, and continued past the lectern to the white marble altar where a huge crucifix hung. Clear. Nobody was present, not even an altar boy.

Then whom had he seen from the church?

Heading quickly off the chancel, he wondered if Leah had found any sign.

Scott stopped mid-stride. Canted his head as his vision blurred. He wondered if the pain he'd experienced at the swamp was coming back, but that pain had since settled into his gut; a dull, manageable throb. This was different. Like an outside force pressing in. He blinked, shook his head to clear it.

Vision pinwheeling, he holstered the SIG then stumbled forward and clutched a pew for balance, grunting as the very mass of his body seemed to jerk away, like he was BASE jumping into an abyss. His vision whirled end over end—red carpet, pew, painted ceiling, carpet again—and he felt nothing but the tactile sensation of his hand on wood.

I'm smoke! he realized with horror. Looking down at himself as best he could in his present form, Scott saw that his body had transformed into a churning mass of gray mist. Only his hand remained solid, and it grasped the back of a pew, keeping him anchored to the floor.

He had to stay in control, but it was too late, he realized, as his fingers dissolved next.

He tried yelling to Leah for help as the carpeted floor

of the church drifted away beneath him, but he couldn't make a sound. He had no mouth. No lungs. No body.

Panic tore through him as he continued to rise, the pews shrinking. He felt errant breezes slide though his smoky form, swirl and shift his very composition, which triggered a new burst of panic. What if his body blended? Jumbled? He had a terrible vision of himself reconstituting like the victim of some roadside bomb, a confused mess of organs and limbs.

He floated forty feet to the ceiling and then nestled against a crossbeam. Painted angels around him looked on compassionately.

Calm down, he said to himself. You rematerialized your hands last night, you can do the same now.

Remembering again what Drew had said, Scott visualized his body as whole. Concentrated. Focused. Slowly he felt the weighty bulk of his torso return, followed by the broadness of his shoulders, the mass of his arms and legs.

Suddenly whole again, he dropped three feet to slam painfully against the top of the narrow crossbeam. And then began to slide off it. He scrambled back onto the foot-and-a-half-wide surface, cursing himself for his carelessness. He was forty feet up with no way down. Would he have to turn into smoke again?

He was about to call for Leah when he heard her scream, a pitched sound of anguish muffled through the wall.

"Leah?" he called out. "Leah?!"

He had a terrible thought of losing her, and it shook him to the core. Feeling a surge of adrenaline, he looked around for a way down from the crossbeam, but there was none. He concentrated again on becoming smoke, saw himself floating to the ground as a gray cloud. Nothing. Fear for Leah hummed through his veins, shattering his focus.

He thought about jumping to the floor below, but knew he'd likely break a leg or much worse. But he had no choice. He had to take the risk.

He positioned himself over a patch of carpet and prepared to jump when he heard Leah scream again. The plaintive cry triggered another burst of adrenaline—and with it came a surge of power.

It was the same power he'd felt in the swamp with the alligator.

Climbing shakily to his feet, he strode along the narrow beam as quickly as he could until he reached the chapel wall. He then angled his shoulder like a linebacker and rammed the wall as hard as he could. With a *poom!*, the plaster cracked at the point of impact and fell away, revealing faded red brick.

Gritting his teeth, he rammed the wall again, harder this time, punching through the brick completely with an earsplitting *crash!*, creating a two-foot hole. He heard raining thumps as the debris hammered pews on the other side.

He peered through the hole, saw Leah clutching the back of a pew, staring at the altar, her entire body trembling.

"LEAH!" Scott cried.

He followed her gaze to the altar. There was a woman there. Dark skin, dressed in strange robes. Surrounded by blazing black candles. What the hell was she doing to Leah?

Another blow with his shoulder, and Scott was through the wall, debris crashing down again. He stepped onto the nave's complementary crossbeam, drew the SIG, but couldn't get a clear shot. The woman on the altar was swaying and chanting . . . chanting that reminded him of what Leah had done to help trigger his visions.

It occurred to him that this robed woman might be able to bring her own spells to bear, but he didn't give a shit. Leah was in trouble. His own safety a distant concern, he nearly ran along the beam to get a closer bead. "Leah, hold on!"

He saw Leah look up at him. She seemed to wave him away. He stopped, line of sight to the altar clear, and aimed the pistol. The woman was small, doll-sized. Despite his smashing through the wall, it seemed she had no idea he was there.

But she whirled, suddenly, and her body flickered like a strobe light.

Her appearance had completely altered. She was now clad in a pink bathrobe. She peered up at him with glazed eyes behind ratty blond hair. Scott's mind reeled. His muscles trembled as the strength leached out of them. This wasn't possible. It just wasn't possible.

"Mom?" he whispered.

His mother glared at him, eyes alight with flame from the black candles, and then he heard her yell to him, though her mouth didn't move. "Do you think you're better than me, Scotty?" Her words slurred together in drug-fueled anger. "I raised you and Eric for years after your scumbag father ran off!" She tore thick clumps of hair from her head as if overcome with rage. "Now look at the job you've done with your brother! You should be ashamed! Do you hear me, Scotty? DO YOU HEAR ME?"

Scott closed his eyes, her voice echoing in his head. Guilt tore at him as he saw Eric in the infirmary, followed by a deep, childlike longing to embrace her. He wished she could be a loving mother just this once.

Gritting his teeth, he pushed the emotions away. This was some sort of fucking trick. Magic. However unlikely, it had to be magic, there could be no other explanation. Leah had explained her own brand of magic was based on nature, light, and purity. But it was clear that whatever was emanating from this woman came from a dark place, a place as black as any evil he'd know. She must be the one Leah thought responsible for Eric's coma.

The initial panic Scott felt at acknowledging a force out of his control was immediately overwhelmed by rage.

He opened his eyes as sweat poured down his forehead, but seeing his mother—right there in front of him, so goddamn real—had taken its toll. Drained, he tottered on the beam, dislodging clouds of dust and grit, before he caught himself with a jerk and regained his balance.

He had to keep it together.

Below, he saw Leah writhing on a pew, tears streaming down her face. Her agony brought him agony. If only he could reach down, scoop her into his arms and whisk her out of there.

Scott saw his mother turn away on the altar and continue to gesture frantically, looking like some trailer park sorcerer's apprentice; the back of her pink robe dotted with dime-sized burns from times she'd fallen asleep while smoking and rolled onto her cigarettes. She continued to rant, "YOU'LL NEVER AMOUNT TO ANYTHING, SCOTTY! YOU'RE A FAILURE AND ALWAYS WILL BE! JUST LIKE YOUR BROTHER!"

Hands trembling, Scott tried to zero her with the SIG. He did his best to visualize the woman with the robes instead of his mother so he'd have the strength to do what needed to be done. His hands shook even more violently, messing with his aim. He glanced down at Leah—she was in a fetal position now. Not moving.

"YOU'RE NOTHING, SCOTTY! NOTHING BUT A FAILURE!!!"

He tensed his arms, steadied the SIG as best he could. His strength was gone. So was his will. Almost.

He had no choice. He had to act now if wanted to save Leah's life.

"NOTHING!!! DO YOU HEAR ME???"

"Yeah, I fucking hear you," Scott whispered, and pulled the trigger.

The pistol kicked, threw off his balance, and he pitched over the side of the crossbeam.

Twisting once in midair, he saw the bullet tear meat from his mother's left arm before he slammed into the pews forty feet below.

Scott woke up to see Leah kneeling over him. Her beautiful green eyes were filled with tears and edged with fear; possibly fear for him, but there was more. She was clearly suffering from shock. God only knew what that bitch on the altar had done to her.

"You're alive!" she gasped.

"I guess I am," he said, sitting up and glancing at the shattered pews around him, and then back at her. His heart was thundering and his body ached. She was okay. Thank God she was okay.

"Thank God," she whispered, throwing her arms around him as if she were trying to anchor herself to him.

She sobbed against his neck and he wrapped his arms around her back, felt himself wanting her despite the danger they'd faced.

She said, "When I saw you fall, I thought . . ." Her voice trailed away and she pulled back to look into his face. "Are you hurt?"

Already missing the warmth of her body pressed against him, Scott looked down at his arms and legs.

"I'm not sure." He tilted his neck, then his pelvis. Oddly, he hadn't sustained injury. Nothing he could feel, anyway. And then he noticed his chest.

The fall had torn a fist-sized hole through the front of his shirt and the bandage covering his right pectoral. He should have been able to glimpse the messy, sutured remains of his wounds. Instead, there was only smooth, flawless skin.

He felt a swell of deep panic, a swirling sensation of chaos as any control he thought he had spiraled away. His body was transforming without DNA splicing. He could no longer deny it.

Vampire. Despite himself, he thought back to storybook legends and compared them in a new light with the powers given to Team Ultra. Strength, Smoke, Suggestion. They'd all been the traditional powers of the creature. The final piece of the puzzle could have been when the assailant had bitten him in the chest. Transference of bodily fluid. Saliva and blood. The possibility filled him with even greater terror when he felt Leah's hand on his chest.

"I *feel* you, Scott," she said. "Over the past three days, I've felt you change, get darker and more desperate."

Had it only been three days? He could hardly fathom that. He stayed quiet, knowing her observation would be useless to deny. She already knew him so well, even without her power as an empath.

"I saw your hands back at the apartment, Scott," she continued. "I didn't want to tell you because I didn't want to believe it myself. I'm assuming the same power took you up to the crossbeam. And your fall . . ." Her voice trailed away before she composed herself. "How far have you turned? Did Andre force his blood on you?"

"No."

Leah closed her eyes and took a deep breath of relief. "But you're afraid anyway."

He shook his head, ignoring her sentiment. Ignoring his own realization. "We have a psycho on the loose. That's all I'm concerned about."

"We have a vampire on the loose. You know it now. You fear becoming like him just as Roberto did."

"I'm nothing like that motherfucker."

"But you are changing."

Scott glared at her, but she wouldn't back down. Meeting his gaze, she placed her hand over his heart and he felt it kick-start into a faster rhythm. From her strained expression, he could see that she felt every iota of his fear and desperation. He tried to move her hands to spare her the pain, but she held them in place.

"I lost my father and brother to that monster, and each time I feel him, I feel them," she said. "In the church, I saw my Dad . . . the way he looked after Andre was done with him. That horror will be with me always."

This woman always offered her heart and honesty. She deserved his in return, at the very least. Vampire. Was the notion any more incredible than magic? Any more incredible than the other events that had transpired since he'd joined Team Ultra? He sighed as the idea finally took root. Likened his acceptance to watching a badly wounded soldier finally pass away—after the initial trauma, it was almost a relief to accept what was happening.

He slipped his hands over hers. "You haven't told anyone about what's happening to me, have you?"

"No."

"Don't. Ackart would bounce me from the team." He paused. "I realize I was wrong about everything. The magic, this vampire. The proof was everywhere, but I refused to see it." Looking back at the altar, he was struck suddenly by the terrible memory of what he'd done to his mother. Or might have done. "That robed woman . . ."

"You saw what she wanted you to see, Scott." She looked at him evenly, touched his cheek. "Do you understand? Anything else you thought you saw up there wasn't real. It was a Voodoo spell, judging from the robes and candles. Nothing more."

Scott believed her. "We have to follow this through to the end, Leah."

Now it was her turn to show fear. She withdrew her hands. "I don't know if I can."

"What are you talking about?"

"You nearly died."

"How is that possibly your fault?"

"I was too weak to stop her."

"My transformation is to our advantage, don't you see? Now we can fight these people—or whatever they are—on their own terms. You and me."

"I don't want to take the chance it could happen again, Scott," she said, shaking her head. Too consumed with her failure to hear him. "Next time, you could get seriously hurt, or worse."

He stopped her sentence with a kiss. It was the best way he could think of to pass the confidence she'd instilled in him back to her. At first she leaned back, startled, but he followed her motion, never breaking contact. And then he felt her delicate fingers slide along his stubbled jaw as she kissed him back. Her lips were soft and warm, safe and loving. Again, foreign sensations invaded him, making him wish they could freeze like this, insulated from the violence of the world.

Before long, he forced himself away. That morning

he'd made a vow not to let his feelings get in the way. Too late for that. He only hoped it wouldn't cost them.

"Together, Leah," he said. "We'll do it together."

She locked her fingers with his, and for the first time since the entire ordeal began, he felt a profound sense of hope, and knew she did as well.

Chapter 31

"Don't worry, you'll be safe with me," Rebecca said as she drove Andre to the swamp cabin where Roberto Gutierrez lived.

"Not if he's protected himself against me."

"I told you I would take care of it."

If the ex-priest had protected himself with more magic like the glyphs that had kept Andre in his tomb for all those years, then the vampire would be ineffective without her help. Rebecca imagined Andre had endured such pain many times while trying to escape Cueva del Diablo—undoubtedly until his body had desiccated into nothing.

Rebecca could only hope that her magic was stronger than the ex-priest's.

She parked and they set out across the bridge on foot toward the cabin, Andre quickly circling out of sight. A wrinkled face peered through the window at her. The abject fear it reflected filled Rebecca with confidence. Clearly, Roberto knew his magic was about to be tested and was uncertain as to the outcome.

Before he could bolt the door against her, she opened it and stepped inside, then blew a small handful of dust in his face.

Roberto rocked on his heels and frowned as she shoved by him. His confusion would last only a few minutes, so she quickly assessed his protective magic. A glyph on each wall—three angels and a pentagram. Taking a container and chalk from her pocket, she splashed her potion on the first glyph and drew a large X through it. She quickly took care of the other three religious symbols, then went to the door and signaled Andre, who slashed through the window at the speed of light, penetrating the glass without shattering it. After returning to his corporeal self, he loomed over the ex-priest, who fell back in fear, his mind apparently clear.

Cowering, the man clutched a small metal cross in one hand, and a white candle in the other as he peered skyward in plaintive supplication. "*As darkness is upon me, so are you my Lord . . . I am but a sheep in your flock . . . in need of your divine guidance and protection . . .*"

"Roberto Gutierrez, do you know who I am?" Andre said, slapping away the candle to disrupt the prayer. "Do you know why I am here?"

Roberto kept his eyes pointed toward heaven as he brought his free hand to the crucifix. "*I beseech you, O Lord . . . light of the world . . . always and ever-present in the darkest of valleys . . .*"

"Of course he knows," Rebecca said. "Otherwise, he would not be so afraid."

Andre gripped Roberto by the throat and lifted him from the floor. The priest gagged, but didn't release the cross.

"Andre, stop. Killing him won't help us."

The vampire eased his grip and let the man's feet touch the floor, but he didn't let go. "The Sacred Brotherhood must have been desperate indeed to recruit someone such as you."

"Tell us where to find the Philosopher's Stone," Rebecca said, "and I won't let him kill you."

Roberto's eyes sparked with terror—but also with the conviction and resilience of his faith. "The Holy Father will protect me from your evil."

Andre sneered. "It is you who blaspheme God with

your idolatry and blood rituals. Now give me the Stone."

"You are unworthy of such a treasure," Roberto rasped. "Only one who has truly suffered in Christ can—"

Andre tightened his grip, cutting the sentence short. "What do you know of suffering?" he boomed. "Your church condemned my mother to Limbo! Your cursed Brotherhood butchered my father!"

Roberto's eyes rolled back into his head. *"Lord, I pray that you lighten my burden, and strike down all my enemies . . ."*

In a burst of rage, Andre flung Roberto across the room. The ex-priest slammed into a makeshift altar that held an *ostensorium,* his body shattering the glass-framed shrine with a crash before thudding to the floor. The cross he had held slipped from his limp fingers.

It was all Rebecca could do not to react in anger herself. If Andre killed the priest, they wouldn't get the Philosopher's Stone and Danton would be the one to suffer. She had to keep her temper.

Stepping between Andre and Roberto, she asked the downed man, "Where is the Stone?"

Dazed by the impact, Roberto didn't answer as he struggled to his hands and knees. His face a mask of fury, Andre started across the room toward the man again.

"Andre! Stop!" Rebecca feared he would kill the man in anger before they got the information they came for.

Rebecca glared at him and stopped him dead in his tracks. He gave her a foul expression but he didn't move. Instead he warred with her silently, his gaze boring into her as though he thought he could control her rather than she him.

"Heavenly Father . . ." Roberto mewled.

Rebecca noted his right leg was bent underneath his

body at a hideous angle. Blood poured from a large cut on his forehead. He had to be in agony, yet she felt nothing for his pain. The more magic she used, the more powerful she became. And power seemed to relieve her of base emotions like pity.

"Do you want your brother cured or not, witch?" Andre sounded as if he was losing his patience.

"You know I do."

"Then let me do what I must to get the Stone."

She didn't want Roberto dead, but she did want him to cooperate even more. "Do what you must," she said, moving out of the way.

Andre crossed the room, knelt, trapped Roberto's head in his hands. "You will tell me what I want to know."

Glancing over his shoulder, he concentrated his will on something. Rebecca followed his gaze to the metal crucifix that Roberto had dropped earlier . . . felt the air go thick. Somehow Andre willed the metal trinket across the room, and it sailed quickly and smoothly toward him.

"I will tell you nothing!" Roberto rasped, staring at the crucifix that hovered mere inches from his face.

"As you wish." Andre pried open Roberto's right eye, and the next thing Rebecca knew, willed the stem of the crucifix deep into it.

Roberto howled and thrashed, but Andre held him steady. "Tell me what I want to know, and the pain will stop!"

"The w-woman has the Stone . . ." Roberto whimpered, blood and milky eye fluid running down his cheek.

"What woman?" Rebecca asked. "Her name!"

Roberto trembled in Andre's clutches. "L-Leah . . . her name is Leah Maguire . . . may God have mercy on my soul . . ."

"Too late for that," Andre hissed, and slashed the man's throat open with this ring. Roberto gagged as Andre drank from the spurting fountain of blood—and then Andre used the ring to slash open his own palm. "Now you will pay for the blasphemous treachery of your Brotherhood," he said as he pressed his bleeding palm to Roberto's lips, and forced the man to drink. "Now you will know true suffering . . ."

Roberto grabbed on to Andre's hand as if trying to push it away from him. Rebecca watched, more than a little thrilled by the power Andre exhibited.

"No doubt this woman was the one in the church," she said. "That means the military has the Stone."

Another obstacle to overcome before Danton was cured.

Chapter 32

"Chili again?" Gabe complained as she set the coffee can on the grate over the fire.

Leah glared at him. "If you don't like it, then you cook."

"Guys set up tents and gather dry wood and build the campfires. You know, man things. Girls are supposed to provide the food."

"*Da-a-ad,* Gabe's being sexist again!"

Their father unzipped the tent and stepped out. "Do I have to referee or can we just enjoy this beautiful night?"

Leah stirred the contents of her disposable pot. "Gabe's not eating with us."

"Hey, I didn't say that!"

"He's going to go find himself a snake to cook."

"I'm going to find one that has your name on it, Le-e-a-ah."

Leah squealed and launched herself at him . . .

And then what?

Snapped back to the present by the blank, Leah fought to remember as she and Scott sped toward Roberto's cabin to warn the ex-priest. Javier had been correct about sacrificing her memories being her price for using magic. The incident in the church pulled her further from her past, stole more of the details of that night and every other memory she tried to recall. How much more would she lose before this was over?

"Are you all right?" Scott asked.

Leah didn't miss the concern in his voice. Remembering the kiss they'd shared in the church, she grew warm all over. "I'm okay now thanks to you." All except for the memory loss. His drawing out her emotions with such close physical contact had eradicated the remnants of the spell the Voodoo priestess had cast.

A glance in his direction assured her all body parts were intact. Those were flesh-and-blood hands on the steering wheel. For how long? Could he learn to control the physical shifts?

"I hope Andre doesn't find Roberto before we do," she said. "And that Roberto agrees to come with us so you can put him under protective custody. Even if he doesn't agree, he has to come with us—it's the only way he'll be safe."

"If it comes to that, I promise I'll try to do it without hurting him."

Leah shuddered at the thought of more violence. Of Scott having to use force on the old man just to save him. But his promise told her he was obviously in tune with her thoughts. She regretted his having had to wound the woman in the church, but she understood why he had. While the woman hadn't physically harmed either of them, she had terrorized Leah mentally by using black magic—and undoubtedly she'd done the same to Scott.

Could her own magic that she used for healing hold up against Voodoo?

Suddenly Leah had to remind herself to breathe.

Still heartsick because of the illusion that had trapped her in her own mind, she once again felt as if she were ready to jump out of her skin. That last image of her father was burned into her—his bloody visage would forever be part of her memory now.

Worse was the realization that, faced with black magic, she hadn't been strong enough to fight it successfully. Her failure at the church had once more illustrated her inability to defeat real evil.

What would it take to give her the strength she needed to fight and win?

"We're here," Scott said, slowing the Jeep and parking it next to Roberto's rusting pickup. "Keep your eyes open for anything out of place. I don't want us to get ambushed again."

Her stomach in a knot, Leah forced herself out of the vehicle and toward the plank walkway bridging the swamp to Roberto's cabin. Hesitating, she focused mentally and then felt frozen to the spot by the sensations that suddenly deluged her.

"What do you see?" Scott asked.

She shook her head. "Feel."

Evil touched her like an invisible hand latching onto her insides. Once more her father's visage swept through her. Only now, Dad was the way she remembered him . . . and he was with Gabe . . . both gone as quickly as the blink of an eye. This wasn't the work of the Voodoo priestess. Leah's very blood pulsing strangely—the same sensation she'd had outside the FEMA trailer—gave her fair warning.

"The vampire . . ." Horror at what they might find in Roberto's cabin nearly stole her breath. "Scott, he's already been here."

Scott drew his pistol and took off across the walkway at a run. Leah forced her legs to move and ran after him, ignoring the groaning and cracking of the boards beneath their feet.

What if the vampire was still in that cabin? He would kill Scott and her. No gun would stop him. No knife. No mortal weapon in Scott's possession. And despite his thinking that his transformation would be in their favor, Scott didn't know how much power he had or how to control it yet.

She could liken Andre Espinoza to no other vampire mythology she had studied. A dark creature of blood and alchemy. Even if she knew more about what he was, how he had been made, she would need the power to go the distance, and nothing that she'd done to this point convinced her that she could do so.

Upon their reaching the cabin, Scott stopped cold and, indicating Leah should stay, slid his back along the wall as he inched toward the window. When he looked in, he stiffened. His physical reaction ricocheted back at Leah, and she knew it was bad. If Andre was still in there, Scott was dead, but even if she warned him, he would go in anyway.

"Wait there!" he ordered, moving fast and kicking in the door.

Crouching, holding the gun two-handed, he turned from side to side, obviously checking out the interior to make sure it was safe before going in.

Right behind him once he crossed the threshold, Leah gasped at the destruction around the fallen man in the middle of the room. Even in the dim light, she could see the place was wrecked, and the ex-priest wasn't moving. His leg was bent under him at an unnatural angle. Even more macabre, what looked like a crucifix stuck out of one eye, a sight that made her stomach churn.

"Roberto!" she cried, rushing to his side.

Leah fell to her knees next to him. Ignoring the blood oozing from the gash in his neck, she felt for the pulse that trilled weakly against her fingertips. Suddenly Roberto opened his one good eye and gaped, fear oozing off him and sliding over her.

"Scott, he's alive!"

But for how long? She felt something in him, in his very essence—his soul?—flicker weakly. Was his soul dying? Her heart began to thud.

Scott crouched behind the old man and slid his hands

under his shoulders to help raise his head, causing him to cry out in pain. "We need to apply pressure to stop the bleeding."

"No use!" Roberto rasped.

"I'm not going to let you die," Leah said, ripping part of her underskirt and pressing it to the wound in his neck, then tying it in place. She could hardly look at his face, especially not at the crucifix in its unholy employ. Had the tip entered his brain? If so, how was he still alive?

"There's worse than death to fear." Roberto's good eye rolled. *"He descended to the dead, but on the third day He rose again and ascended into Heav—"*

Leah interrupted. "What is it you fear? Did Andre force you to drink his blood?"

Roberto held out his hand. Sparks popped from the fingertips and an electrical current ran from one finger to the other. Leah gasped and a low curse escaped Scott. Roberto's gaze wandered to the shattered altar. *"He is seated at the right hand of the Father and will come again to judge the living and the dead."*

"He's changing, becoming like the creature," Scott choked out.

Leah's own blood surged, the feeling weak but familiar. She sensed the vampire's blood pulsing through Roberto's veins. Felt Dad and Gabe, weaker than what she felt from Andre, but still there. Horrified, she could only pray that it wasn't too late, that they could stop the transformation before it was complete.

"We'll find a way," she whispered. "We have to."

"A way to satisfy the blood lust?"

Fear came at Leah in waves that took away her breath. Not from Roberto this time, but from Scott. He appeared as stricken as she felt.

Roberto could hardly go on. "Andre Espinoza . . . d-damned me for eternity."

"Let's get him to the lab," Scott said, his voice low and hoarse. "Maybe there's something BB can do before he changes completely." He grabbed a couple of pillows from the floor and shoved them behind Roberto's back. Then he stood, fumbled with his pocket, and pulled out his cell. "I'll call for evac."

"And I'll get you some water, Roberto. Hang on."

Leah got to her feet and rushed to the sink in the kitchen area, where she was able to take a long breath. Dear Lord, what now? What could they do—what could *she* do—to save Roberto? They needed his help—he'd stopped Andre once and hopefully he could figure out how to do it again. But if he turned . . .

Her hand shook as she filled a cup with water.

Scott stepped away to the other end of the cabin to find a signal for his cell, saying, "BB can fix this."

"Only God can fix this," Roberto countered. "*Grant that I may prepare for death, that I may fear Thy judgment, escape Hell and obtain Heaven, through Christ our Lord. Amen.*"

Leah turned from the sink, and to her horror, Roberto was crawling along the darkened floorboards toward the shaft of late afternoon sun streaming through the window.

Her eyes widened as she realized what he was doing. The cup fell from her suddenly nerveless fingers. "No!"

Too late . . . sunlight bathed his broken body.

Like a match to kindling, the sun combusted the ex-priest like a flaming torch. His flesh bubbled and charred as his soul-searing scream bounced off the cabin walls and echoed through Leah's mind. As something dropped from his burning hand, she grabbed the altar cloth to beat back the flames.

Likewise, Scott grabbed a blanket and dropped his cell.

Flames ate Roberto's clothing, leaving his flesh bubbling as if he were covered with infected pustules that wept blood and yellow fluid together. Leah and Scott beat the flames down, but Roberto was dead, body curled on its side, flesh blackened and seared to his bones, what was left of his face contorted in a scream of never-ending agony.

Leah's eyes filled with tears. Dear God, would the nightmare never end?

"Miescher Laboratories," came a tinny voice from the cell on the floor.

She looked at Scott but he appeared to be shell-shocked. Was he envisioning a like end for himself?

Though Leah thought she was going to lose whatever food was in her stomach, she bent to retrieve the phone, and in doing so, saw the shiny silver object near the corpse.

A ring.

"Oh my God," Leah said, staring down at the floor.

"What is it?" Scott asked as he draped the smoldering body with the blanket. The reek of charred flesh was so intense he could practically taste it. But the terrible smell didn't seem to bother Leah. She was fixated on something else.

He followed her gaze and saw a ring. Its silver face winked in the sunlight that had just killed Roberto. For a moment, he didn't understand Leah's strong reaction to it, and then he knew. To make sure, he plucked the ring off the floor and gently turned up the palm of Leah's right hand.

Sure enough, the ring design matched her scar perfectly: a triangle inside a square that held an open eye.

"It belongs to him," Leah whispered. "To Andre."

"He's not here, now," Scott said, squeezing her hand. Hoping like hell he didn't sound as freaked out as he felt. He still couldn't believe what he'd just fucking witnessed. Roberto burning like he'd been on the business end of a flamethrower—except that he'd only been exposed to sunlight.

As a boy he'd read comic books and knew the supposed rules of the undead. Sunlight killed vampires . . . vampires like the one Roberto had become. Like the one he was *becoming.*

Icy dread sent his mind in a thousand directions. If he continued to change, was he doomed to the same fate? Would he be forced to skulk in the shadows? Drink blood to survive?

"You're not at that stage yet, Scott," Leah said, looking into his eyes. No surprise that she'd known what he was thinking. His fear must be emanating in waves. "Andre forced Roberto to drink his blood. That's what has to happen to make the transformation complete."

"Okay," he said, shoving his fear aside. If Leah said he wouldn't turn into a monster yet, he believed her. The alternative was too terrifying to contemplate. "I'm getting tired of this guy being one step ahead of us, Leah. It's time we turned the tables."

"The ring," she said. "I was thinking the same thing."

"The amulet and rapier gave us some good intel about what makes the guy tick. But a ring . . . it could be more personal. It might tell us how to kill the bastard."

"Are you sure you're ready for another vision, Scott?"

"Do we have a choice?"

He saw a flicker of concern cross her face at his bravado, partially because she knew as well as he did that some of it was bullshit. The gentle reaction reminded him again about why he'd fallen so hard for her. She understood him, allowed him to be who he was. Allowed him to do what he had to do.

He handed her the ring, and then ushered her out of the cabin. It was nearly dusk. Encroaching shadows cast the swamp in shades of deep blue and green. He sat on the rough wooden planks as she pulled candles from her bag and placed them around him.

"Are you ready?" she asked, lighting the wicks.

"Let's do this."

She whispered a now-familiar chant, and then offered the ring.

This time he was ready when he reached out to touch the silver band that had been warmed by Leah's touch . . . ready when he was abruptly flung into deep red space.

He actually whooped, relieved that the spell had worked—that they had a chance to gain the upper hand—as he plummeted far and fast, feeling like he was on some supernatural roller coaster, and then found himself sitting naked on a throne made of branches and woven palm fronds.

Through Andre's eyes, he saw a dozen native women writhing together as one, their sweaty, coffee-colored flesh glistening in the campfire light of the large hut. Through Andre's nostrils, he detected the musty scent of sex.

Scott could feel the man's consuming resolve—and fear.

Andre ignored the orgy performed to curry favor with him and looked at his hands. They were wrinkled and worn, as was the rest of his body. Scott knew that Andre considered himself not simply old . . . but too old to continue the quest for the Philosopher's Stone.

After traveling to these Caribbean islands with Columbus years ago, he had searched high and low to no avail. Although he knew there had to be a New World beyond this one that held the treasure, it was too late. He had spent far too much time searching in vain.

Time had run out for all options but one.

Andre stood and walked across the hut to a small metal chest half-buried in the sand floor, and then knelt and opened the creaking lid. Inside was a corked test tube lined with a cracked, ruddy substance that Scott couldn't quite make out. Hands trembling, Andre pulled off the cork, and Scott detected a faint, coppery scent. *Dried blood.* But there was something wrong with the sample, Scott realized. Through Andre, he could feel malignant energy flowing from the mouth of the tube, a dark static that swirled around him like poisonous fumes.

Any information about the blood that Scott tried to pick from Andre's consciousness—purpose, source—was clouded by Andre's growing dread.

"My God," Andre intoned softly. *"Forgive me for what I am about to do."* He looked around for a knife, but not seeing one, slit his palm with the edged, triangular design on his ring instead. *The* ring. And then he let blood from the wound drip into the test tube.

Scott expected the vision to end with the use of the ring, but it didn't.

Instead, he watched Andre drink the mixture. Scott expected a warm, salty sensation down Andre's throat, but an icy chill raced to the pit of his stomach instead.

Andre looked around in desperation as the cold began to spread across his body. Suddenly, Scott could no longer feel the warmth of the campfire on Andre's naked flesh.

A buxom woman who had disengaged from the group came up behind Andre, slid a willing hand between his legs. Panicked, Andre whirled and grabbed her by the shoulders. The warmth of her flesh did not pass to his. Panicked, Andre smashed his lips against hers, aching for any kind of warmth as the cold inside him continued to spread like ice water through his veins. The woman tried to break free, but her struggles were no match for his strength. He kissed her hard, but there was no transference of warmth between them, no true sensation of human contact.

Dread gouged Andre like gaffing hooks as he yanked the woman's head back and slit her neck with the ring, desperate to feel the hot gush of her lifeblood. Scott nearly retched with disgust as he tasted the fiery, salty rush this time and heard the other native women scream and flee from the hut. And then he trembled as he felt absolute cold plunge deep into Andre's heart like a spearhead, threatening to freeze the part of him that possessed everything he held dear. The part of him known only to God.

His soul? Scott wondered with awe.

"No!" Andre whimpered. "I did not know it would be like this!"

And then a stark image of a man crystallized in Andre's mind . . . seven feet tall and clad in white plate armor that shone as brightly as virgin snow. He had long blond hair that fell across broad shoulders in sheaves and framed crimson eyes that flickered with the intensity of funeral pyres. The man's flesh was as pale as his armor, ghostly pale, the sallow flesh of a corpse, and his upper lip was drawn in a sneer to reveal gleaming, sharp canines.

This was the creature who'd appeared as an ally against the Catholic Church shortly after Andre's father had been killed. The creature who'd given Andre the poisonous blood magic. Scott heard the creature say its own name in Andre's memory, the voice deep and resonant, but hollow, too, like the distant, echoing cry of the damned.

"My name is Tepes," the creature had said, slitting his own wrist with a fingernail and draining the blood into the tube. "If there comes a time when you no longer have the strength to search for the Philosopher's Stone, drink this."

Andre had taken the tube, fixated on the creature's mouth. "Your teeth . . ."

"Do not worry. I must bite you for you to inherit them. My bloodline will die with me, just as another bloodline may begin with you."

Tepes, Scott thought, searching his own memory now. Why did that name sound so familiar?

And then Scott felt Andre's mind pinwheel with terror as the cold from the consumed blood dove deeper still . . . into his heart . . . deep, deep inside . . . icy and ruthless until Andre uttered a croak of bitter resignation as the warm connection he'd always felt with God was unceremoniously snuffed out . . . the dark implosion total and abrupt, like being dragged underwater into inky, arctic depths . . .

Andre covered his face and sobbed violently, icy tears streaming down his cheeks. What had he done? And then the man noticed his hands. The wrinkles covering them had smoothed. The same was true with the flesh all over his body. His hair was no longer gray, his muscles and penis were no longer flaccid. He felt fresh power infuse his body. Dark, cold power that caused him to tremble.

Andre clutched the ring in his fist as he vowed to always fight on his father's and mother's behalf, vowed to find the Stone and save them from Limbo, vowed to destroy the Church. He made vow after vow while clutching the ring tight enough to cause blood to pour through his fingers in a desperate attempt to stave off his spiraling terror . . .

. . . Scott was still screaming when he realized he was back on the dock with Leah cradling him. She rocked him while whispering in his ear. "It's okay . . . it's okay . . ."

He grasped on to her, needing her and not just physically. She gave him the courage to face things he didn't want to know existed. Gently releasing himself from her arms, he leaned back and told her what had happened.

"Your instincts were right," Leah said. "Andre lost

his soul when he drank the blood. The same thing happened to Roberto."

And might happen to me, Scott thought, even more committed to wiping Andre off the face of the earth. There was no way he'd give the creature a chance to doom his soul that way—or anyone else's.

"And did I hear you correctly? The vampire's name was Tepes?"

"That's what the he called himself, yeah," Scott said, and watched Leah turn white as a ghost. "What is it? What's wrong?"

"The people of old Hungary knew him as Tepes . . . Vlad Tepes . . . the legendary warrior king who battled the Ottoman Turks," she said, trying to compose herself. "We know him as Dracula."

Chapter 33

Shadows crept through the mansion as Rebecca worked her spell to awaken Eric from his coma. Night winds buffeted the windows, rattling the glass in their frames, sending a current of unease through her. She sat at one end of the dining table and stared through the smoke made by a fat red candle and a combination of incense and burning pubic hairs that she'd taken from the man while he'd slept next to her the week before.

Focusing on her subject, she said, "Eric, it's time to wake up." She kept her voice both soothing and seductive as she concentrated on putting the thought in his mind. "Open your eyes and sit up." Sharing his struggle to throw off the dark, she intensified her mental energy to help him. "It's time to come to me. To be with me again."

Suddenly his eyes opened and, through the haze, Rebecca could see ghostly paraphernalia surrounding the hospital bed. She felt panic rush through Eric and was quick to calm him.

"You've been unconscious, Eric, but you're all right now. Listen to my voice and stay calm." When she felt him settle down inside, she said, "First shut off the equipment, then remove the monitors and the IV."

Rebecca watched him work. He'd been out for forty-eight hours and he seemed confused and clumsy. Still, he did as she bade. Then his gaze swung around the empty room and focused on the far windows. She could see vague movement out in the corridor and a nursing station that appeared abandoned for the moment. Through him, she'd heard that scientists were testing the Philosopher's Stone. She only hoped it was out in the open tonight—easily seen, easily stolen.

"Get to your feet, Eric, and walk out of the room." Concentrating, she sent that image to him, so that he could see himself do it. "Don't let anyone stop you. You have to get to the lab as fast as possible."

Rebecca bit back the scream she wanted to let loose. Eric was looking down and she saw that he was hanging on to the edge of the bed, white-knuckling the mattress. Now that he was awake, he was undoubtedly trying to take command of himself, complicating things for her.

Not willing to let Eric free himself of her power, Rebecca picked up a red taper that she'd covered with remnants of his semen. She lit the candle, then ran her tongue up its length and in her mind saw Eric's penis. The easiest way to control a man was through sex, even through imagined sex. She felt Eric's will weakening. He let go of the mattress.

"Get to your feet," she urged.

He stood, his knees bouncing slightly for a moment.

"Good. Now leave the room before someone stops you. You must get to the lab. Find the Philosopher's Stone." She projected the image of the red pulsing stone into his mind. "Protect it and bring it only to me. Only to me and you'll have everything you want!"

"I only want you," Eric mumbled. Still he was hesitating, looking confused.

To reinforce the command, Rebecca visualized what she wanted him to do as she licked the taper all the way to the tip, then plunged the flame into her mouth and closed her lips around it, dousing the flame with her saliva.

With the choked sound of a highly aroused man, Eric made for the door, his wobbly gait quickly straightening as he entered the corridor and headed in the direction Rebecca assumed held the lab. Relief made her limbs go weak. She smiled and set the doused taper on the table.

The sound of the door slamming open made her start. She whirled around to see Andre standing in the doorway, a limp bloody body slung over each shoulder. She'd allowed the vampire to go out to feed alone, but she hadn't expected that he would bring home his food.

He dumped the dead men on the table, where blood still oozed thickly from the gashes in their necks. Not that she felt anything for the victims, but Rebecca still didn't want dead bodies lying around.

"Andre, you interrupted my connection with the man who is bringing us the Philosopher's Stone."

"Then reconnect."

She blocked Andre from her thoughts and looked back into the tendrils of smoke and concentrated until she could see through Eric's eyes again. He was entering the lab. Only one scientist was working this late. Rebecca's pulse picked up when she saw the object of his attention.

"That's the Philosopher's Stone," she told him. "The one that man is working on."

"BB," Eric mumbled.

The man in the white lab coat turned when he heard his name. His eyes widened and he jumped back. "Eric, you're awake!"

Fearing that Eric might say the wrong thing, Rebecca concentrated on making him respond simply, putting the words into his mouth. "Yeah, awake."

The scientist looked around nervously as if for backup. "You've been checked out by the docs, right? If so, no one told me."

Rebecca urged Eric to say, "Hey, I'm fine, good as new."

"You were in a coma, for God's sake—"

Again, the door slamming broke her concentration. Again, Andre carried in two fresh corpses—one an older woman whose head dangled from her body as if almost severed. Again, he threw them on the table.

Rebecca gave him a dark look. "Why are you bringing your leftovers here?"

"They'll have their use," Andre said. He stared at the candle. "Does he have it yet?" His features were pulled into a frown as he tried to see what she'd been seeing.

"No, not yet." Rebecca gathered herself together and looked back at Eric through the tendrils of smoke. She made Eric say, "Scott sent me to check on the Stone. Is that it?"

He was looking at a red stone at the bottom of a deep Pyrex pan of water where it glowed eerily, casting beams of crimson light. Multicolored wires snaked from the bottom of the pan and a huge lens the size of a paper towel roll hovered above it.

"Uh, yeah, that's it." BB continued to watch Eric closely. Rebecca urged Eric forward to look through the lens so she could see what looked to be swirling, crimson cobwebs interspersed with glowing orange disks and spheres on a sea of sparkling black. *The Grand Grimoire* was right. Andre was right. The Stone had some supernatural power.

She made Eric say, "Scott wants to talk to you."

"Right now?"

"The sooner the better."

Rebecca expected the scientist to leave the room, but instead he backed off and pulled out his cell.

"Take it!" Rebecca urged. "Eric, take the Stone now while BB is distracted."

For some reason he was resisting her again. Rebecca's

stomach tightened. BB wouldn't be on his cell long. Eric had to get the Stone and now.

"For me, Eric, do it for me. I'll explain it all when you get here! Take the Stone, cher, now!"

Eric quickly pulled the dripping Stone from the Pyrex dish and wrapped it in a nearby piece of cloth.

"Hey, what are you doing?" BB asked. "Eric, put that down!"

The scientist stepped toward Eric and tried to take the Stone from him.

"Don't let him take it!" Rebecca ordered. "Don't let him stop you!"

Eric responded with a punch that sent the scientist flying backward. He bumped into an equipment table and went down.

"Get out of there now, Eric!" she urged him. "Don't let anyone get near you. If you do, they'll take the Stone from you. That Stone is the most important thing to you . . . because it's most important to me."

"Stop! Eric, stop!"

Ignoring the scientist, Eric moved forward, opened a door, and started down the corridor.

"That's it, Eric. Bring the Stone here . . ." Rebecca envisioned his path from the base to the mansion, implanted the virtual map in his mind. "I'll be waiting for you . . ."

"How long?" Andre asked. "How long until I can hold the Philosopher's Stone in my hands again?"

"Hopefully he'll be here within the hour."

"Good. Another body to put to work."

"No!" she said sharply. "If Eric disappears, his brother won't stop until he tracks us down."

"Let him. Once you bind the Philosopher's Stone to me, I'll be immortal."

"But *I* won't be immortal."

"You'll be under my protection."

If she could trust that promise . . . not that she was going to argue about it.

"I don't want Scott Boulder after us," she said, keeping her tone steady. "I'll cast a Forget Spell on Eric and send him back to base to buy us time." Enough to do what was necessary.

Enough time to see that Danton would be cured.

"If you feel that strongly about it . . ."

Hopefully Andre would remain reasonable when she insisted he take care of her brother before she did anything more for him.

She said, "I need to concentrate on Eric until he's off the base. In the meantime, get rid of these bodies."

"But I brought them for you. And I have more outside."

Knowing what he wanted of her, Rebecca nodded. "For now, just put them someplace where I don't have to see them."

Surprised when Andre complied, she still wondered at his motives for being so accommodating.

Once Andre and the Philosopher's Stone were bound, not only would he be immortal, he would no longer have the need to feed. A case for her going through with the ceremony, she thought, reconsidering sending the vampire back to his hell.

He was powerful . . . would be more powerful with the Stone implanted . . . and he could be her ally . . .

Rebecca turned back to the smoke just as Eric came face-to-face with the two from the church—his brother Scott and the woman who'd accompanied him. Eric stopped and when Scott called to him, she felt him slip away from her influence in response to his brother.

"No, stay focused!" she commanded.

"What's going on?" Andre asked as Eric backed off, seeming confused, as if he weren't sure what to do.

Scott and the woman moved closer—they were getting too close too fast.

"Listen to me . . . only to me!" Rebecca ordered. "Get away from them! Now!"

Her command was punctuated by a braying mechanical sound. The scientist must have pulled the alarm.

Chapter 34

Eric bolted.

What the hell? Scott turned to Leah in stunned confusion. What he saw in her didn't make him feel any better—she'd gone utterly pale, her expression twisted. "I sense black magic around him Scott . . . the same as I felt earlier . . ."

Scott took off after Eric before she could finish.

"Scott, no!" Leah called after him. "You don't know what Eric might do to escape!"

He ignored her, running full speed now, holstered pistol bucking against his thigh. He wouldn't let that Voodoo bitch control his brother. Not again.

He saw Eric about thirty yards ahead, the guy's bare feet squeak-slapping the tile as he hauled ass down a long hallway . . .

Scott flew around a bend and nearly collided with a gaggle of lab techs and soldiers who'd backed Eric into a corner. Any time one of them stepped close, Eric would chase them back with a howl as he wielded the cloth-wrapped Philosopher's Stone like a weapon.

"Everybody back off!" Scott ordered. As the group retreated, Scott moved past them and raised his hands in a calming gesture. "Eric, it's Scott. Can you hear me? Step toward me if you can."

Eric didn't answer. Instead, he whipped his head around like he was confused, and then finally peered in Scott's direction . . . in his direction, but not at him. More like *through* him. Scott realized with horror that his brother had the same expression now as he had when freeing the killer from the Plexiglas cell. There was no recognition behind Eric's vacant eyes. No knowledge of who he was, where he was, what he was doing. That Voodoo bitch would pay for this.

Scott took another step forward. All he wanted to do was hug his brother tight. Tell him things would be okay. "Eric, it's me . . . Scotty . . ."

Eric bolted again. In reply, a soldier raised his assault rifle. Took aim.

Scott smashed the soldier across the jaw with his fist. "Anybody fires on my brother, and they'll answer to me! Is that understood?"

Before the startled man could answer, Scott took off in pursuit again. He'd sooner take a bullet himself than watch Eric be shot in the back. If Ackart had a problem with that, she could kiss his ass.

The Klaxon continued to sound, plangent and harsh, causing dread to thrum through Scott's veins. The chance that Eric would be shot had just risen exponentially.

Scott followed Eric's tiny, bobbing figure as best he could, running hard, doors and details a blur. From their direction, Scott knew Eric was headed for the main entrance, but because of the alarm, the doors would be triple-guarded. His brother had nowhere to go.

Even so, Eric would reach the front entrance a good twenty seconds before him. And if he charged the guards, they'd take him down without hesitation.

Scott felt a cold pit in his stomach. He couldn't let Eric die that way. Wouldn't. He pushed himself to run faster, legs burning.

As Scott rounded the corner leading to the front entrance, he readied himself to hear the crack of automatic gunfire. To see Eric's bloody, bullet-ridden body sprawled on the floor. Instead, he saw Eric standing among five guards who lay in a circle around him, snoring deeply. His brother stared at and spoke softly to the sixth and last guard, who then slumped to the floor, also asleep.

Suggestion! Scott remembered a second too late. In the chaos of the last three days, he'd thought of Eric only as his little brother. Not as a supernatural member of Team Ultra.

Eric whirled and Scott tried to mask his eyes with his hands, but Eric met his gaze first, pupils blanching cue ball white. Scott heard a grotesque, thundering hiss in his head like hundreds of bodies sizzling under napalm.

"You—" Eric began, voice cutting through the din before stopping abruptly. Scott saw his lips twist hideously, as though he were struggling not to speak. Although Eric managed to stay silent, winning the war of wills for the moment, the message in his anguished expression was crystal clear to Scott: *This isn't me! This isn't me!*

"I know it's not," Scott hissed through clenched teeth, feeling like he'd failed again. As the drill bit hiss cut through his concentration, he dropped to his knees. Reached out an imploring hand, desperately trying to help his brother wage his terrible, inexplicable battle . . . when Eric's face suddenly collapsed into an expression of defeat and profound sorrow.

"I won't let you follow," Eric mouthed in hideous caricature, voice a weak echo of its true self. Tinged with a feminine lilt. The Voodoo woman? "Do you understand, soldier? I won't let you hound me ever again. Now draw your gun."

Scott felt his right hand tighten into a claw. He strained to keep his arm in place, but his fingers scrambled for the holster nonetheless and yanked the SIG free.

"Put the gun to your head," the androgynous voice commanded as Eric's cue ball eyes narrowed in horror. Helpless to stop what was going on.

Scott's arm made a pendulum swing to press the barrel of the SIG against his temple. Gritting his teeth, he strained to lower his arm, but it simply wouldn't budge. It was as though his muscles were rusted in place.

"Squeeze the trigger."

Scott felt his finger tighten on the trigger, and there was nothing he could do about that either. He saw tears flow down Eric's cheeks as his finger continued to tighten.

"It's okay, Eric, we'll be okay . . ." Scott whispered, with deep melancholy that things would end like this. He and his brother had so much life left to live outside the military. Now they'd never get the chance.

And then in what he assumed were his last seconds, his thoughts focused on Leah. The way she made him feel and the way she felt. The way she tasted. The way they'd connected at the apartment. In the kitchen. In the kitchen . . . *where he'd dropped the bowls.*

Scott forced himself to concentrate on his right hand, on the image of a ship disappearing into fog. He'd rematerialized his hands in the kitchen—why not the other way around?

"My hand is nothing," he muttered through clenched teeth. "My hand is nothing . . . my hand is nothing . . . my hand is nothing . . ."

He felt a tingling along his wrist as the sensation of his tightening trigger finger became lighter and then almost an afterthought. From the corner of his eye he saw only gray smoke where his hand used to be. The gun plummeted and clattered on tile.

With a cry of anguished relief, Eric whirled stiffly, and then dashed out the front door, the Stone glowing underneath his arm.

Scott scrambled onto his feet in a lame attempt to follow, and then collapsed and blacked out.

He awoke sometime later to BB slapping his cheeks. Leah stood behind the scientist, face creased in worry.

"Scott! Man, you had us worried!" BB said, hoisting him into a sitting position.

Scott looked around. The sleeping soldiers were gone, presumably up after the Suggestion had worn off. His right hand was whole again, thank God. It had been a dicey situation, but at least he knew he could control the smoke ability.

"Eric got away," he said, rubbing his arm. His muscles were sore from being frozen in place.

"Then let's send a team after him!" BB said.

As much as Scott wanted to bolt out the door, find Eric, and kick vampire ass, he shook his head. "Too risky without visual contact or prep." He knew they had to prepare to go against such a diverse range of dark powers. No way around it. "That said, let's get a Predator drone in the air, pronto. I want my brother's location zeroed and a strike force scrambled within the hour."

"I may be able to track him faster using other means," Leah said. "I'll let you know the second I do."

Scott nodded, trusting her implicitly. "Meanwhile, BB and I are going to have a little chat."

BB nodded like he'd had the same idea.

BB led Scott quickly across the Special Weapons Depot, a yawning warehouse teeming with lab techs and holding an assortment of gadgets, machines, and weaponry in various stages of development.

"I owe you an apology, Scott," BB said.

"For what?"

"I should have been able to keep Eric from taking the Stone, but he took me down with one punch. One punch. Stopped me as cold as an easy-looking blonde who owns a liquor store." He shook his head disgustedly. "I'm pathetic."

"No, you're a vital part of the team, BB," Scott replied. "You're not supposed to be combat-ready. That's what lugheads like me are for."

"Thanks for saying so because I feel like a real dope," BB said. "Look, I know we're in a time crunch, but I wanted to give you a handful of face cards before you run into this Andre guy again."

Scott nodded, willing to give BB a little space, but frustration still coursed through his veins. Putting him on edge. What was that Voodoo bitch doing to Eric? To make matters worse, he felt a familiar twinge in his stomach . . . a hint of the razor-blade gnaw he'd first felt at the FEMA trailer and then again at the swamp. Should he tell BB? Would the man quarantine him as a contagion risk?

Presently, they reached a twenty-yard target range enclosed on three sides by concrete walls. At the end of the range was a standing mannequin outfitted with black satin clothes, plastic fangs, and a bat-wing cape.

"We're in the Vampire Area now," BB said.

"I can see that."

On a card table in front of them was an M4A1 assault rifle, a black Kevlar vest, a black ceramic cylinder about as long as a road flare and twice as wide, military goggles, and what looked like a tube of pepper spray in a black canvas slipcase.

Scott indicated the assault rifle. "Let's start with this."

BB nodded, picked up the weapon. "We pimped out the rounds. Instead of regular old 7.62-millimeter, we developed 7.62-millimeter liquid-gold mimetic polyalloys. But that's not all. Keep in mind the mannequin's synthetic skin has been treated to react like the real thing."

He aimed the rifle downrange and fired a short, thundering burst. Predictably, three fist-sized holes were blown through the mannequin's torso in flashes of vaporized plastic and molten gold. But left behind the bullets, floating midair and delineating their precise paths, were gossamer lines of gold dust.

"Tracers?" Scott asked.

"Keep watching."

When one of the gold lines drifted into the mannequin's arm, the synthetic skin flared bright red and bubbled like a flame was being held to it.

"Even near misses will hurt the guy," BB said proudly.

Scott nodded impatiently. He knew BB's weapons would help in the coming assault, but he couldn't take his mind off the fear that had clouded Eric's face as he ran out the main doors. "And this?" Scott asked, picking up the ceramic tube.

"Twist the top, then throw it."

Scott did. The tube landed mid-range with a clatter, and then BB pressed a button, which lowered a Plexiglas blast shield. For a moment, nothing. And then the tube spun madly, like a compass hand gone haywire, spraying golden, foot-long spikes that riddled the mannequin and ricocheted with terrifying force against the concrete and Plexiglas.

"From bloodsucker to porcupine in two seconds flat," BB said, raising the blast shield again.

Scott nodded again, but swallowed thickly. The scraping abdominal pains cut deeper now, like knives. He felt a trickle of sweat trace down his temple, rubbed it away with his palm before BB could notice. "Is that mace?"

"Our own special mix." BB pulled the tube from the canvas sheath, walked through the mess of gold spikes to the skewered mannequin, and then sprayed a thick burst in its face. The affected area hissed and smoked and bubbled, then sloughed away in a viscous glop.

"Gold-infused for use on the discriminating undead. And in case you're worried about the guy's powers, the Kevlar vest is insulated against electricity, the goggles are filtered to disrupt ocular connection, and all this stuff has been coated with a special, anti-magnetizing agent. Only thing our vampire will be able to attract is a serious ass whooping, excuse my French."

"Looks like you thought of everything," Scott said.

BB returned to the table and placed a hand on his shoulder. "Including what's happening to you."

Scott looked at him. "How did you know?"

"It doesn't take a genius—even though I am one—to figure the vampire's bite would have an effect."

"I'm manifesting smoke and strength."

BB nodded. "You really should have told me, Scott. I could have taught you how to handle the powers, not to mention the initial disorientation."

"Honestly, BB, I thought you might turn me in. I couldn't let that happen when I was fighting for Eric's life."

"Point taken."

"You tell Ackart about this?"

BB shook his head. "I know how important this investigation is to you. Besides, Ackart scares me, man. She scares me the way hot dogs are made scares me, you know?"

"What can you tell me about these powers, BB?" Scott said, finally deciding to keep the stomach pains to himself. BB might feel compelled to quarantine him regardless of his feelings for Ackart. "Give me the Reader's Digest version."

"Focus on any part of your body and it'll turn to smoke. Turn your entire body to smoke, and you can will yourself in the direction you want to go."

"Strength?"

"Adrenaline will enhance your strength up to ten times, at which point, you can bend steel bars or open ketchup bottles. Your choice."

Scott nodded and moved to leave, hoping like hell

that Leah had been able to find Eric as fast as she'd claimed.

"One more thing, Scott."

"Make it quick."

BB walked to what appeared to be a large vehicle covered by a green canvas tarp. With a sharp yank, he tugged the tarp away to reveal an M2 Bradley Fighting Vehicle. "Insulated, coated, and the 25-millimeter chain gun is loaded with its own gold polyalloy rounds. You know, in case your guy doesn't answer the door when you knock."

"Speaking of which, BB," Scott said. "It's high time we found out where that fucking door is."

Chapter 35

"You're sure you know what you're doing?"

Leah had expected the question to come from Scott, not from Ackart. More agitated than Leah had ever seen her, the major was clinging to the caduceus pendant her grandmother had given her like a lifeline.

"If you're asking if I've ever done this before, then no, but I have seen the spell work."

Javier had done something similar while she'd worked with him. Rather than a raven like the one she'd taken from the animal lab, however, Javier had used a hawk and magic to find an unconscious woman in the wilderness. He'd saved her life just as Leah hoped to save lives now, no matter the cost to her.

"Too bad Eric wasn't wearing his gear. No tracker on him. But I put out an APB," Scott said, sounding tense. "And he's driving a Humvee, not exactly an easily hidden vehicle. He'll be found."

"Not if she doesn't want him to be," Leah said, noting he was all business with her. He'd found it easier than she had to ignore the personal shift in their relationship. "The Voodoo priestess. Remember the spell in the church."

Her fluttering stomach made Leah remember that she'd been bested by the other woman. But the spell she was about to cast was simple . . . straightforward . . . she hoped.

"Hopefully Leah can find Eric faster," Ackart said. "The faster the better."

They'd gathered in the war room, as Ackart called it—the major, Scott, BB, and Leah. The conference room was equipped with every electronic device imaginable, as a dozen soldiers in dark fatigues and armed with gear BB had designed grouped together on the far end of the room waiting for orders. The one thing Leah would use in addition to her magic lay before her on the table—a tiny GPS tracker in the form of a backpack that she would attach to the raven via Teflon-treated ribbons.

Science would allow the team to track the bird.

But first, magic would allow the bird to track Eric and the woman who controlled him.

And using magic would take more of her memories, Leah knew.

She'd had a half hour to herself while the major and Scott organized the new team. She'd spent that time with a digital recorder, preserving as many memories of Gabe and Dad as she could muster.

Not enough memories.

None of them nearly complete.

They would have to do.

"Leah?" Ackart said with a questioning expression.

Leah focused and looked to Scott. "I need something of Eric's."

"Like what?"

"Something small and light that the raven can carry."

"His things are still in the infirmary. Come with me—you can pick what you need."

She nodded. Ackart's gaze bore into her back as they left the war room. Leah ignored her.

"Why do you need something of Eric's?" Scott asked.

"It'll have his essence just like the black candle I took from the church. The more personal objects I can use, the more powerful the spell." A cornerstone of the Native American shamanistic ritual she'd been studying.

When they entered the infirmary, they went straight

for Eric's bed. "Can you use one of these?" Scott asked, indicating the tubes and wires Eric had pulled free that still hung in a jumble.

"I'm looking for something more personal." Leah opened the drawer in the bed stand and from it pulled a comb. "Like this." She removed some of Eric's hairs from the teeth and slipped them into a pocket.

And then she realized Scott was staring at her intently. She opened herself to him and his mixed emotions flooded her. He wanted to take her in his arms . . . and at the same time, he was holding himself back. Personal desire and duty tore him in two.

Why couldn't he have both, if only for a moment? Why couldn't *she*?

If things went wrong, this could be their last chance.

Leah stepped into the shelter of Scott's body and felt his arms circle her back and his heart hammer against her breasts.

"We have to believe that we're going to get through this," she said. "We have to believe in each other, Scott."

"I do believe in you, Leah."

"And I believe in you." She looked up into his face, touched his beard-stubbled cheek. "I believe in *us*. Together."

Too aware of the camera that was recording everything that went on this room, Leah thought to break the embrace and step back. But she couldn't move, couldn't leave the safety of Scott's arms just yet. Couldn't stop looking at him, drinking him in with her eyes, making new memories to replace the ones she'd lost.

With a groan, Scott lost the tight control he held over himself and kissed her. Leah raised herself on her toes and threw her arms around his neck and kissed him back for all she was worth. She wanted him, needed him. Instantly, her body came alive . . . her heart . . . her soul . . . She'd never felt so close to any man, and at the same time, she'd never felt such a deep sense of panic.

Nothing could happen to him. Scott couldn't be taken away from her, too.

Her heart pounded, a mix of desire and fear.

As if coming out of a trance, Scott raised his head and set her away from him. "That'll have to hold us for a while. But we aren't through, Leah. We have to believe that."

Leah smiled and nodded and let him lead her back to the war room.

Once there, Leah ignored Ackart's piercing gaze and moved straight to the table where she'd been working. She set Eric's hair and the black candle in the midst of the objects she'd already arranged before her.

To the north, a rock for the earth.

To the east, incense that she lit to represent air.

To the south, a crystal symbolizing fire.

To the west, a seashell for water.

Then she made a triangle inside the square by adding her own power object—the digital recorder containing her memories represented Dad and Gabe as her spirit guides. There was a shift in energy around the room as unvoiced questions arose in the others.

Pain hit Leah so deep that she couldn't move for a moment. Her eyes stung as she called up what she could remember of Dad's and Gabe's images and silently asked for their help. When this night was done and her magic was spent, the recording and some photos might be all she had left of them.

Finally, she lit the remains of the black candle and then placed the birdcage inside the triangle of power objects.

She closed her eyes and imagined the bird in flight.

"Fly swiftly, black raven . . . ascend to the heavens . . . fly to my bidding."

She saw Eric, pale and confused, the Philosopher's Stone in his hands.

"Find the one who is lost and the woman who holds his mind captive."

The dusky-skinned woman she'd glimpsed in the church glared at her.

"You are my black scout . . . descend from the skies and lead us to those we seek . . ."

No site image came to her. No clue as to where Eric and the woman and Andre, she assumed, would be found.

Leah opened her eyes and for a moment doubted herself, as she had so many times before. Then she told herself she would see the site when the raven zeroed in on it. After slipping the recorder back into one of the pockets in her black camouflage, she picked up the metal open band that she would place around the bird's leg. She rolled the band in the melted wax from the black candle. While the wax hardened, she secured Eric's hair to one of the transmitter's ribbons. Then she took the raven from the cage. The bird fluttered in her hand as she fixed the band on its leg and squeezed the metal so the opening closed. Careful to keep the ribbons from tangling in its wings, she fitted the bird with its miniature backpack.

Done.

Leah looked straight at Ackart, hoping she would see reason now that she'd had time to process everything. "As I told you, Major Ackart, it's dangerous to send the team in at night. We can get their location now but we really should wait until daybreak to go in. That's only a few hours away, and Andre will be more vulnerable with the light." An argument the major had earlier ignored.

"Leah's right," Scott said. "Eric's going to be in there.

We should go when the hostile's most vulnerable, least likely to do damage."

"We will not squander this opportunity," Ackart said to Scott. Then to Leah, "Release the bird now."

"I'll pull my men before I lose them!" Scott warned her.

"I'm in charge of this operation, Captain." Ackart's tone was icy. "In charge of you. You'll do what I say, or be escorted to the brig. Don't think I won't do it. How will you save your brother then?"

Her stomach in a knot at the thought of more unnecessary deaths, Leah stroked the frightened bird, wishing she could calm the rapid beat of its heart as well as her own. Ackart had made up her mind, and obviously nothing was going to change it.

BB beat her to the window. "Magic and science used together. Now why didn't I think of that?" He removed the screen. "Something to keep in mind for future experiments."

If they had a future.

One last glance back at Scott bolstered Leah's courage. He wouldn't fail. *They* wouldn't fail. She held the bird in both hands as she moved it through the opening and tossed. . .

The raven flapped its wings furiously, then caught an air current and smoothed out its flight.

"It's headed south, toward New Orleans," Leah said.

She glanced around and saw that Scott had already turned on the GPS tracking system. He and Ackart were looking at a handheld monitoring device.

For some reason, BB was still at the window with her. He was gazing at her with a new respect, even before they had results. Leah smiled sadly and slipped a hand in her pocket and wrapped her fingers around the recorder.

Keeping her voice low, she said, "BB, can you do something for me?"

"Name it. Anything."

Hand trembling, she freed it and held out the recorder. "Take care of this for me."

The question in BB's eyes went unspoken. He nodded and took the recorder from her, slipped it into his own pocket. "I'll keep it someplace safe, Leah, I promise."

"The bird is flying over the Mississippi," Scott said. "Right along the river."

"The river is the way to go," Ackart said. "We can move fast and avoid unwanted attention that way."

Leah took a deep, nervous breath.

Now they just had to sit tight and wait to see where the raven landed.

Rebecca breathed a sigh of relief when the Humvee finally pulled behind the mansion.

Eric had arrived with the Philosopher's Stone and before Andre returned from his latest foray. Hopefully before the vampire appeared, she could secure the Stone, make Eric forget, and send him back the way he'd come. Andre had sounded reasonable earlier, but he could change his mind.

She opened the door just as Eric approached.

"Rebecca!"

His loopy expression was due in part to the spell she'd cast on him, in part to his true feelings for her. He looked lovesick.

"Come in, cher." She held out her arms but felt nothing but impatience when he stepped in close and kissed her. Making him feel wanted would keep him cooperating. "You weren't followed, were you?" Not that she had a sense of trouble seeing through his eyes. "You took so long."

"An accident on the road into town."

"Come inside." Already knowing about the delay, having seen it through his eyes, she asked, "You have the Stone?"

Eric followed her and pulled a bundle from his pocket. He peeled away the cloth to reveal the brilliant red stone she'd seen through his eyes in the lab. Rebecca took it from him and marveled that it seemed to pulse with a life of its own.

"I missed you," Eric said, wrapping his arms around her. He kissed her again, longer this time, and then asked, "Why here instead of at the club?"

A sound from the other room alarmed her. What was that? Not Andre—he hadn't returned from feeding. She listened more intently but didn't hear anything more. The wind must have kicked up and blown something through the broken window.

"Did you just buy this house or something?" Eric was looking around, his expression puzzled.

"This place has privacy the club doesn't."

"Yeah, privacy." He smiled and cupped her bottom with both hands.

"Let's not rush things. We have all night."

Rebecca pushed away from him and went to the sideboard and her stash of magical tools. From a box, she took a cloth sack large enough for the Philosopher's Stone. Once she slipped the Stone inside, she tightened the sack's strings and bound them to the chain around her waist under her dress. She wouldn't chance leaving the Stone around for Andre to find. Not that she thought he would take off with it. He needed her Voodoo to bind the Stone to him.

"You must be hungry."

"For you."

She smiled. "Food first. Sit. I've prepared something for you. I want you at full strength when you bed me."

Still under her influence, Eric did as she suggested.

The scraping of the chair legs almost covered the noise. This time fluttering was followed by clicking.

Frowning, Rebecca said, "I'll be right back."

But when she stepped into the front parlor, she saw nothing amiss. Still, the hair at the back of her neck stood at attention, so she waited, frozen, waiting for some movement. When none came, she checked the other rooms and returned to Eric and her plan to wipe his memory of her away and send him back to the base before Andre returned.

"Your favorite, cher—crawfish étouffée." She ladled a good quantity into a bowl and put it before him. He immediately spooned it into his mouth like a starving man. "I'll get you a cold drink." One that she'd prepared earlier, liberally laced with a potion meant to make him forget.

Halfway through filling his glass, Rebecca heard the weird noises again. Rushing back into the other room, she cursed. The room was empty!

Or was it?

"Pruk-pruk-pruk."

The odd sound echoed through the room. Rebecca looked up and her eyes widened as she met the gaze of a large black raven. The bird was perched on the curtain rod over the broken window.

"Kraa-kraa . . ."

The low guttural rattle grated on her nerves.

A raven.

And not just any raven, but one that had been used to cast a spell. The magic stink it carried was unmistakable.

Suddenly having trouble breathing, Rebecca ran back into the dining room.

"Hey, this is great stuff," Eric said. "Can I have more?"

She slammed the half-filled glass in front of him instead, saying "Drink this," before fetching a closed basket from the buffet. She emptied the contents on the table.

Eric picked up one of the small doll-like figures. "Hey, what are these?"

Simultaneously fearful and furious, she yelled, "Drink the damn potion!"

"Potion . . . what . . . what are you up to?"

Before she could force him to it, the back door opened and Rebecca knew it was too late. Andre strode into the room draped with corpses once more.

Eric jumped out of his seat, knocking over the glass and spilling the potion all over the table. "What the hell!"

Ignoring him, Rebecca turned to Andre. "We've been discovered."

Chapter 36

The spotlight on the bow of the airboat cut through the night like an errant finger, illuminating their way as they rocketed east along the Mississippi River at sixty miles an hour.

Scott tried to concentrate on the humid slipstream and warm spray the boat kicked up, on the way his body jerked as the flat aluminum hull thumped over cross-tides and floating clumps of flora.

Anything to keep his mind off the pain.

The gnawing in his stomach was extreme now, like a living, ravenous thing trying to claw its way out. He'd chewed a handful of industrial-strength painkillers before departing; he might as well have downed Junior Mints.

Glancing portside, he saw the other airboat keeping pace with its own complement of six soldiers armed with BB's modified M4A1 assault rifles and other gear, and not far behind was the massive hovercraft that carried the Bradley, powerful engine thrumming. Ackart's Black Hawk swooped overhead, its dark, tumorous shape like some nightmarish guardian angel.

"Are you sure you're okay?" Leah said. Scott could barely hear her over the howl of the airboat's propeller engine, and more gleaned what she'd said from the movement of her lips, which were the color of dark rose petals in the moonlight.

"I'm good," he lied, and indicated her handheld monitor. "How's our feathered friend?"

Leah regarded the tiny glowing screen. "Hasn't moved." And then she looked back at him, placed a hand on his wrist.

"Everything will be all right," he said for her benefit, knowing full well it wouldn't. Lives were always lost in situations like these—he'd seen it time and time again in conflicts around the world. All he could do was protect Leah as best he could, and pray it wasn't too late to save Eric.

"Thirty seconds!" the airboat driver yelled as they flew past the French Quarter, kicking up a wall of wake.

Seen at this speed, the Quarter was a gas-lit, kaleidoscopic blur. Hot, sparkling colors cascaded across the muddy water to glance off the amulet hanging from Leah's neck—would its magic be strong enough to protect her?—and flush the armed men and machines, making it look to Scott like they could have been part of a holiday parade rather than a strike force.

He closed his eyes, relishing the Quarter's delirious sounds of life—sounds the airboat engines could do nothing to mask—an eclectic, euphoric chatter of tourists and blues bands and howling, drunken revelry that floated thick on the humid air. He squeezed Leah's hand as he thought about how he'd give anything to be in the Quarter tonight as a civilian with her and Eric enveloped by a million heady scents: gumbo and spiced meat and flavored liquors and incense and over-ripened fruit and oil paints and worn, well-traveled cobblestones, with their biggest concern navigating the labyrinth of neon-splashed side streets and trying to jump into as many blues clubs as possible before last call.

"Ten seconds!" the driver yelled. "Lock and load!"

Scott opened his eyes, let go of Leah's hand. They'd already been swallowed by the deathly stillness of the Ninth Ward, the transition from light to dark blunt and abrupt. The sounds of mirth were replaced by the metallic clacks of rounds being chambered into the M4s.

"Ready?" he asked Leah through clenched teeth as he chambered a round in his own weapon. She carried Andre's rapier in a leather sheath strapped across her back—in the hope his weapon could be used against him.

Noticing that Leah could no longer hide her fear, he took her hand again. "I won't let anything happen to you, okay? Just remember to keep your goggles on and your wits about you. And don't leave my side."

She smiled nervously. "How will I protect you if I do?"

Smirking, he moved her hand to the cage housing the engine. "Hold on."

"Landing!" the driver yelled as his final warning, and then the engine cut. Propelled by momentum, the airboat shot up and trembled across the embankment.

Scott glanced over his shoulder in time to see the front ramp of another hovercraft splash down. With a six-hundred-horsepower roar, the Bradley lurched from its iron womb, headlights beaming, treads whipping muddy water and silt before gaining purchase and speeding forward.

Their hovercraft continued a short distance more past buildings, many of which were abandoned, before grinding to a halt. Without the boat's movement, the humid air became gluey and suffocatingly thick. Scott felt himself immediately covered in sweat. He jumped from the craft, making sure Leah was behind him, and then raised a fist to call the remaining ten men to him before rushing ahead.

Now the enemy knew they were here.

The Black Hawk thundered past, the spotlight on its nose flashing a huge, trembling beam onto the front of their target: the mansion. A dilapidated, three-story structure with a peeling pink facade and haphazardly boarded windows. Scott saw an eerie, orange flicker through the boards not washed out by the spotlight. Somebody was definitely at home.

We're coming, little brother . . . hold on . . .

With Leah at his side, Scott sprinted past the moldering, soiled wrecks of other houses and leaped onto the pillared porch of the mansion. The door was heavy oak, and was locked. The other men took up position along the left wall underneath a boarded window, ready to go in when ordered. Scott glanced over his shoulder as the Bradley lurched to a halt underneath a huge oak tree to cover the door, and then looked up. The Black Hawk had climbed to a higher altitude for a better view of the grounds.

"How're we doing?" Scott said into his headset, and then clenched his teeth against another stabbing pain in his gut. Would it ever stop?

"No movement around the perimeter," came Ackart's crackling reply. "Commence full breach, I say again, commence full breach."

"Full breach," he whispered to Leah and the rest of the team.

A man approached from down the line with a portable battering ram, but Scott waved him away. If anything was going to happen, he wanted it to happen to him first.

Wiping the pouring sweat from his forehead, Scott took a step back and aimed a savage kick at a point on the door just above the knob. With a crash, the door tore off its hinges and went flying end over end into the darkness of the entry hall. The enhanced strength certainly had its benefits, even if he hadn't gotten the hang of gauging it just yet. But the other soldiers didn't seem to notice. When Scott rushed through the shattered doorway, they followed him without question—a twelve-person serpent bristling with automatic weapons.

"Talk to me, Leah!" he said, rushing into a large, tiled reception hall and keeping his eyes peeled for movement.

"Right behind you!"

He continued, leading with the M4, heart in his throat. If something happened to Leah . . .

They progressed down a carpeted hallway, which presently opened up into a massive, yawning parlor that reached all the way up to a spectacular domed skylight—through which he could see the Black Hawk hovering far above—and boasted a grand, carpeted staircase with oak banisters at the opposite end that led to the second floor.

But that wasn't what struck Scott most. The room was furnished with decrepit antique furniture—every surface of which was covered with blazing black candles. The source of flickering light he'd seen earlier.

"Leah?"

She was trembling, eyes darting up to the second- and third-floor railings. "We're not safe here, Scott . . ."

"Stay with me," he said, capturing her gaze. "Where's the bird now?"

He could feel fear emanate from her in waves before she regained her composure and consulted the handheld. "I'm sorry . . . the raven is upstairs . . ."

"We'll get out of here as soon as possible, I promise," he told her, and then to the team, "Keep moving!" Scott led the men over moldered, debris-strewn Oriental rugs to the foot of a grand staircase when he felt Leah clutch his elbow.

"Scott . . ." Her voice was paper thin, barely there.

He followed her gaze to the head of the staircase. A man was there, partially concealed by shadow, dressed in a business suit. Scott immediately brought his M4 to bear, as did the rest of the team. "Put your hands on your head, and walk slowly toward us!" he ordered.

The man did not reply. Or place his hands on his head. He simply started down the stairs with slow, thumping, deliberate steps. Scott couldn't make out the man's features in the half-light, but it certainly wasn't Eric or their quarry. "I said put your hands above your head!" The man continued to ignore orders, but when he was halfway down the staircase, the candlelight finally caught his features . . . dark eyes and matted dark hair, square jaw.

Scott recognized him immediately. Councilmember Jean Baptiste Neff. The front of his white shirt was soaked with blood. Scott's anger flared. How many other victims had Andre taken?

"I sense black magic all around him," Leah said, fear back in her voice.

Scott looked at the man's eyes. They were vacant, but not white, which meant he wasn't being Suggested. "Controlled like Eric?" he asked. "Or turned into a vampire?"

"Something else . . ." she replied, clearly struggling to divine the nature of the spell that had Neff in its grip. "Something horrible . . ."

Scott couldn't afford to wait for Leah's recommendation, nor could he afford to bypass the man and leave him to the mercy of the psychos that dwelled here. A rock and a hard place. "Go get him," he ordered the soldier next to him. "But stay frosty."

The soldier rushed up the staircase, took the councilmember by the arm. "Don't worry, sir. I've got you now . . ."

Neff lunged. Bit the soldier savagely in the neck. For a moment, they struggled—a brief, terrible dance. And then Neff reared, tearing free a bloody, ragged chunk.

Gagging wetly, the soldier tumbled down the stairs in a heap.

The attack took less than two seconds. The team's response was just as quick.

Scott yanked Leah out of the way as the team opened fire. Neff convulsed as the gold alloy rounds—just as effective against ordinary human beings—blew splattering holes in his body. He crumpled and slid down the staircase to land against the dead soldier.

Suddenly, Scott felt himself drawn to the blood pooling around the bodies. It glowed as the pain in his stomach redlined, making him gag. He sucked a breath, did what he could to force the agony away. "Cease fire! Cease fire!" he rasped.

Barrels smoking, the team did. Leah wept softly. He wanted to comfort her, to take her away from the horror. She shouldn't have to witness this. Instead, he did his duty. Stepped forward to inspect the body . . . the blood pooling around both bodies shimmered like oil in water.

"Vampire . . ." one of the team members breathed.

"No, he was already dead," Leah said, voice edged with sudden realization. *"Zombie."*

And then Neff spasmed. Rolled over onto his hands and knees.

Scott stepped back. *Jesus!*

Neff shambled to his feet, body perforated by ragged, seeping holes as a length of intestine lolled from a wound in his abdomen like some horrible tongue. His movements were jerky, unnatural. Like he was being controlled by marionette strings. The team stared in disbelief.

"Scott, please, we have to get out of here now . . ." Leah said.

Scott nodded. There were too many unknown variables now to argue the point. He turned to give the order when the parlor door slammed closed behind them with a bang, and metal bars slid into place by themselves to seal them in. Clearly under the influence of magnetism.

"Welcome to my home, Captain," hissed a cold voice from the second-floor landing.

Scott looked up. Andre Espinoza was there, eyes blazing. Next to him, also on the landing, was the Voodoo woman from the church. She clutched several tiny, black felt dolls in one hand. Scott's rage exploded. "Where's my brother, you rancid motherfucker!" Andre only smiled as a dozen people took up position around the Voodoo woman. Necks bloodied, they wore business suits, blue jeans, nurse uniforms, and dresses, and moved with the same unnatural gait as Neff. Possessed the same vacant gaze.

More living dead!

Scott was about to give the order to fire when the Voodoo woman waved her free hand, streaking the air with some sort of black ash.

Suddenly, Scott realized he couldn't breathe. He tried to suck air, but it felt like his nose and throat had been sealed with hot cement. Around him the other men gagged, clawed at their throats. Leah dug frantically through her bag as her face turned blue.

"Leah!" Scott rasped, and tried to raise his M4 as Neff shambled toward her trailing a thick swath of blood, the yawning holes in his body providing wet glimpses of organ and bone. But it was no use. His arms felt like rubber.

From the corner of his vision he saw the Voodoo woman wave the dolls, and then the zombies descend the stairs in a rotten, tottering phalanx.

Scott tried like hell to turn himself into smoke, to muster his enhanced strength—anything to break free from the black magic—but his oxygen-starved brain couldn't put two thoughts together. The best he could do was stagger in between Leah and Neff and then watch in horror as the team was overrun.

Two zombies wearing construction flannels and dirty jeans bowled into a gagging soldier, knocking him off his feet. One tore the M4 from his hands as the other yanked off his Kevlar vest. Before the soldier could stand again, jagged shards of metal lanced across the room and skewered his chest, pinning him to the floor like a moth to a corkboard.

Nearby, a shrieking nurse clawed at another soldier. "Please! Get back," the soldier rasped, but she managed to tear the goggles from his face. Without them, Scott knew the man would be susceptible to Andre's Suggestion. Sure enough, in the very next instant, the soldier's eyes went cue ball white, and he blew out his own brains.

Scott reeled as Neff lunged and clawed his fatigues, gagged as the reek of decay and blood washed over him, causing his stomach to cramp in agony, the pain like knives digging into fresh wounds. Struggling to remain conscious, he tried to keep the man's snapping teeth from his throat when he heard a clap. He threw a look over his shoulder and saw Leah on her knees, lips moving silently in an incantation. She clapped again and a small cloud of glittering white puffed from between her fingertips.

When she clapped a third time, Scott felt the hot, terrible pressure in his throat dissolve. He sucked a sweet lungful of air.

"Way to go, babe!" he called out as his strength surged with adrenaline. He slapped away Neff's hands, then grabbed the man by the shoulders and tossed him across the room like a tattered rag doll where he landed in a heap. When Neff clambered back to his feet, Scott opened fire with the M4. Neff's chest ruptured with bloody holes before his head exploded in a fan of red slop. The decapitated body dropped to the ground. Lay still.

"Aim for the fucking head!" Scott yelled to his men, and then turned back to Leah.

His heart caught in his throat as a man wearing a bloody mechanic's coveralls appeared from behind her and raked her right cheek with his fingernails before freezing, then slumping to the ground. Roberto's amulet, he realized. It must have the ability to cancel the zombie magic—but only on contact. Which meant the creatures would still be able to get in a strike.

He had to get Leah out of here.

Far to the side, he saw another soldier under assault by two men in bloody business suits and a woman in a torn yellow sundress. The soldier managed to get off a single shot from his M4 that turned the woman's head to pulp before his goggles were torn off. Scott couldn't see his eyes, but the man stood statue-still, not lifting a finger to defend himself as the remaining zombies tore him apart with fingernails and teeth.

More Suggestion. He had to take Andre out of the fight.

Scott brought his weapon to bear on the vampire, fired full-auto. Andre dodged the armor-piercing rounds with supernatural speed—but in doing so grazed the gold sparkling tracers. They lashed his face and neck like acid, leaving bloody red streaks. Roaring in pain, he dissolved into a wisp of gray smoke.

Scott knew this would give him the time he needed. He raced over to Leah, who was searching through her bag again, maybe trying to find a spell that could duplicate what the amulet had done, and clutched her hand. She looked up in wild-eyed terror.

"Forget it, let's go!" he told her, then turned to his men. "Everybody out! Fall back!"

Leah grabbed up her bag and Scott pulled her along as they bolted for the sealed parlor door. He could batter through it using his enhanced strength and free his men . . . God, he hoped he could.

"Sitrep! Give me a sitrep!" Ackart yelled in his ear. He ignored her. Couldn't bring himself to say that most of the men were dead . . . slaughtered because she'd sent them in prematurely.

And then Scott faltered as wave after wave of agony tore through him. Drained his strength. There was so much blood around him . . . glowing, shimmering. It was as though the blood's mere presence was making the pain worse.

Through the pain, he felt Leah thrust her arm around his waist to buoy him. To help him keep going.

Metal shrapnel whistled through the air. Cleanly decapitated three men as they ran. Andre had zeroed them. The last man looked around frantically as his comrades dropped around him, then was bowled off his feet by a pair of zombies. A bride and groom streaked with blood.

Scott felt shrapnel pepper the back of his vest—*thup-thup-thup!*—as he moved Leah in front of him to shield her. A bigger piece of metal slammed into his helmet, nearly pitching him onto his stomach. They'd never make it to cover in time.

"Keep running, Leah! For that room over there!" He pointed to an open door near the sealed parlor.

"I'm not leaving you!"

"Go!" He pushed the M4 into her hands. "Please, Leah . . . I'll be right behind you . . ."

"Come with me . . ."

"You know I can't."

"And I can't lose another person I care about. I sent you here, I brought you to the vampire like Dad and Gabe—"

Refusing to let her blame herself, Scott pulled her close and kissed her hard. Tasted her sweat, her fear. But also her strength, which eclipsed his pain for the briefest moment. He would not lose her, either. She deserved better than to die like this. "We'll make it out of here. Together. Now go!"

Eyes welling, she sprinted away.

He turned. The zombies glared at him as they stood over the bloody corpses of their prey. Racked with pain, he would never be able to protect Leah from them.

Scott knew what he had to do. But first things first.

As metal shrapnel sliced into his Kevlar vest, he yanked a Spinner from his belt. He could see Andre just beyond the second-floor railing above him, a savage grin cutting his face.

Scott twisted the top, lobbed the Spinner straight up. Timed perfectly, the gadget whirled and sprayed its ordnance in midair.

Andre raised his arm in protection, got a forearm full of gold spikes. He howled in agony, then exploded into a bolt of black lightning that arced up through the skylight.

"Suspect is on his way to you," Scott rasped into his headset, hoping Ackart was ready for the attack.

The surviving zombies converged, shambling toward him.

A tsunami of pain tore through his body and he collapsed onto his hands and knees, no longer able to fight it. He felt his strength drain away completely. The entire room shone with blood.

Eric, I'm sorry for letting you down . . . "Bradley crew," he rasped. "Fire on my location."

"Say again, Captain?" came the crackling reply.

He knew the crew had his GPS location. They would know exactly where to aim the chain gun's high-explosive rounds.

Only fifteen feet away, the zombies kept coming.

"Fire! On me!" he yelled.

"Jesus, Captain—"

"Do it!"

Scott took a deep breath, closed his eyes. Did his best to block out the ravenous groans of the zombie horde. Concentrated.

Heard a rash of approaching footsteps, then felt fingers clawing his fatigues.

When the wall exploded behind him with a deafening roar.

My body is nothing . . .

Volley after volley of high-explosive rounds streaked through the shattered wall and then streaked through *him,* intermittent tracers flashing with blinding intensity. The torrent punched through and buffeted his dissolving body, before slamming full-bore into the zombies, liquefying them on the spot. Bones and muscle and organs and flesh were transformed in the blink of an eye to fans of clotted, ruddy mush. The barrage continued, tearing apart the grand staircase beyond as viscera rained down with wet, hideous plops.

And then there was silence.

Scott rematerialized on his hands and knees. *I'm alive . . .*

He looked around. The air was thick with a hot charnel stench. So much violence . . . total and neverending . . .

Blood was everywhere. Soaking the floor, coating the walls. Over the past few years, shedding blood in the name of freedom had started to make him sick. So much that he could barely stand the sight of it.

But now the stuff shimmered and shined, iridescent, dazzling . . . captivating . . .

His mind reeled. There was nothing but pain humming through his veins and the shimmering blood . . .

I need it, he thought suddenly as a terrible hunger unfurled inside him and flickered to life. *I need it now.*

Trembling, arms and legs seeming to move of their own accord, Scott crawled to a nearby pool of blood like a man dying of thirst in the desert.

And then he lowered his lips to drink.

Chapter 37

The earsplitting noise of an explosion added to firing guns ceased and a spooky silence got to her.

Shaky hands clutching the gun Scott gave her, Andre's rapier still laying across her back, Leah couldn't wait any longer—she had to find out if he was all right. The scratches on her cheek smarted, reminding her of how innocent people had been used for evil. The soldiers hadn't had a choice but to defend themselves. Still, the tragedy sickened her. Terrified at what might be awaiting her, she cracked the door to make sure there was no imminent threat before stepping out of her hiding place.

The sight that met her was like a physical blow, stopping her dead in her tracks. Her heart thumped against her ribs and her pulse sped like a train gaining momentum. The interior of the mansion was destroyed. The soldiers were dead. The unholy army that Andre and his Voodoo priestess had mounted had been blasted to pieces, reminding her of the dark slaughter in the cave.

Trembling from the memory, Leah tried to pray, tried to find the words that would banish the most awful of images, the only piece of her past that she could recall in its entirety. When that didn't work, she tried to draw on that one perfect night when they had all been so happy. Though she remembered the conversation with her father and brother, she couldn't call up the emotions. Not anger or joy, not frustration or love. What was left was like her photographs, flat and two-dimensional.

Looking around, she couldn't believe that God had

abandoned her again, that every surface was covered with body parts or blood, nothing moving.

"Scott!" she cried, looking around frantically.

Movement from the corner of her eye made her turn to see a man lifting himself to his knees.

Scott . . . he was alive!

She took a few steps toward him and then stopped again when she saw that he was covered with blood. His clothes . . . his face. He licked his lips and then wiped at his mouth with the back of his hand as if he'd . . .

Leah dropped the gun and backed up.

The horror of the sight sent her reeling back to the past.

She should try to stop the Voodoo priestess from using any more black magic, but her soul was sick of death.

Scott was looking to the fallen staircase, as if seeking a way to the second floor, where renewed shots and screams made the flesh along her spine crawl. He seemed flushed with power, as if he were ready to find and save his brother . . . ready to continue the fight, no matter the human cost.

Leah shook her head and backed up. Scott couldn't help himself, she knew that but couldn't bear to look at him covered with blood. And then his body dissolved into a cloud of gray smoke that streaked to the skylight.

Her stomach churned and her head went light. She'd brought him here. She'd brought them all here. Her fault. She'd led them to their deaths.

She'd led Scott to much worse.

Brokenhearted, she knew there was no escape. Not for Scott, not for her.

Her back against the wall, Leah sank down to the blood-splattered floor and waited for the death that should have come seventeen years before.

Chapter 38

On the rooftop's highest gambrel, Andre howled in pain as he tore the gold spikes from his right arm. The puncture wounds were ragged and deep, and would not heal until he cleaned all traces of gold from them. Nor would the bloody gashes that marred his face.

He glanced down through the skylight. The ruined parlor shimmered with the gory remains of the massacred zombies, and the witch was gone. Perhaps she was taking cover. Or making sure the Stone was safe. She was not dead, of that he was certain, since he would have felt free from her control. He scowled.

He could have created vampires to fight the military—more powerful than zombies by far—but they would have been independent-minded, and may not have joined the battle. Zombies were easily created and controlled, but were also easily destroyed. The witch should have compensated by creating more slaves from the bodies he'd provided.

But none of that mattered now. All that mattered was defeating these military dogs—especially Scott Boulder, the man the witch had identified as the captain of the military unit. Clearly, Boulder had acquired powers from the wounds he'd sustained during their last meeting. It mattered little, Andre knew. He would flay the very flesh from his bones all the same.

And the woman with Boulder? He recognized her from long ago. She'd been but a child in the cave while he was searching for the Stone. So now she was back to claim her revenge. He would make sure to give her the same fate as her father and brother.

Moving to the edge of the gambrel, Andre searched for the best way to stage a counterattack on the armored vehicle below when the Black Hawk swooped out from the darkness, and cast its beaming spotlight on him like an all-seeing eye. It hovered close, fifty feet away. Close enough that the thundering rotor wash whipped his long dark hair, and he could see the four-person crew inside. It swayed back and forth in the air like a bully angling for a fight.

He narrowed his eyes against the bright light.

"Andre Espinoza! My name is Major Wallas Ackart!" a voice boomed from a loudspeaker on the Black Hawk.

Andre splayed his fingers. Felt the Black Hawk's hull and instrument panel somehow resist his magnetic influence. And then a surprise . . . not everything in the craft was protected.

"Surrender and you will not be harmed," Ackart continued. "You have my word on that! We can work together, you and I!"

Work together . . . the words made him sneer. Only those who wished to control him had benefited from their alliances. Like the others, this woman believed she had power over him. Tactical superiority with her technical magic and duplicity. How wrong she was.

He stepped to the roof's edge to make the major think he was conceding to her wishes. To bring the Black Hawk closer. As he had done with the witch, he would make this woman believe she had the upper hand.

"That's it, Andre," Ackart said as the bobbling helicopter slid closer. He could see her peering at him from the murky belly of the craft. "We can resolve this without further loss of life! We'll lower a basket to pick you up . . . just stay where you are!"

He nodded, and then reached out. Felt his magnetic web snare something small, but very strong. Now he would make these military dogs think twice before hunting him again.

Andre whipped his hand to the side—and the major tumbled out the side door.

He then stayed his hand, and her fall halted abruptly. She gagged and kicked as he suspended her in midair by the only piece of gear that was vulnerable to his magnetism: a metal chain around her neck that carried a caduceus pendant.

Andre knew the crew would not fire on him for fear their Queen would plunge to the ground. Now the Black Hawk was nothing more than a castrated guardian angel.

"We can help one another! Please!" the major cried, cheeks wet with tears. Her hands clawed at the chain, digging furrows in her flesh. A prisoner strangled by her own noose.

"Help?" Andre growled. "You imprisoned me. Made me the subject of your experiments. Siphoned my God-given powers for your own ends!"

Continuing to hold his hand aloft, Andre began to curl his fingers slowly. With a cry of alarm, Ackart thrashed harder, eyes bulging, foam speckling the corners of her mouth. A pencil-thin line of blood welled up where the chain met her neck. "Did you believe I would let you rob me of immortality? Your caduceus will not be able to heal you now . . ."

Andre clenched his fist. Ackart's screams cut abruptly as her body dropped away from her head in a spurt of blood. He kept the dripping head aloft a moment longer so the crew could behold their dead Queen before letting it fall, too.

There was a hissing roar as the Black Hawk fired a

missile. Andre stepped back to brace himself, then shoved forward with his palms as though he were forcing open a heavy door.

Suddenly, the missile turned in a tight arc—passing close enough for him to feel the heat of its engine—and then flashed down to strike the Bradley. The armored vehicle exploded in a massive orange-and-black fireball that rolled into the sky.

The Black Hawk veered away, quaking in the throes of the shock wave. Andre sneered as the concussion rippled harmlessly around him. The soldiers had not coated the missile, clearly thinking it would be too powerful to control.

Andre's victory was cut short as a metal bar burst from his chest. He roared, agony blossoming around the wound, razor sharp. Whirling, he saw Scott Boulder. The man's uniform and face were drenched in blood.

Scott followed up with a vicious blow to the jaw.

Andre pitched back, feet crushing slate tiles. Glared back with blazing eyes. "So you discovered how blood can enhance your powers," he growled. "That will not save you." He yanked the bar from his chest with a wet sucking sound. The wound began to iris shut immediately.

"Where's my brother?" Scott yelled, and leaped forward.

Andre met him with a blow to the gut. Scott gagged, doubled over, but twisted away and was up again in a flash.

Scott aimed a vicious blow at Andre's jaw, but Andre willed his head into smoke and the man's fist passed harmlessly through it. Momentum from the missed blow pitched Scott forward, throwing off his balance. Andre took advantage by grabbing the back of Scott's neck and tossing him hard into the gambrel's iron trim.

Scott grunted as his head and shoulders slammed into the bars and bent them out.

Scott recovered quickly again, stood and whirled. Andre grappled with him in the moonlight. Where Andre had easily bested the man at the lab who had inherited his strength, blood had made Scott much stronger. Clenching his teeth, Andre tried to tear Scott's arms from their sockets. But the man resisted him like no one ever had. It was like trying to change the course of a river.

"Where is he?" Scott growled. "Tell me or I'll fucking kill you!" Andre saw crazed determination in Scott's eyes. But there was fear there, too. Not of dying . . . but of himself. The vampire sneered. This terror would be the man's undoing, a harbinger of the price he would ultimately pay. "Tell me what you've done with Eric!"

"Your brother," Andre said, "will not recognize the monster you have become."

To Andre, the result was all too predictable. He saw Scott's expression falter, then felt the corresponding ebb of strength. Pathetic.

He wrenched Scott's arms around, pinning them, and then lifted the man above his head and flung him toward the skylight. But at the last moment, Scott lashed out and grabbed his wrist, pulling him along.

They crashed through the skylight together, plunging back into candlelit, esophageal darkness . . . and then slammed into the parlor floor with a meteoric *THOOM!* as raining glass shards exploded around them.

Scott rolled onto his back, dazed. Andre straddled him, pinning his arms against his sides with his knees. Smashed his fists into Scott's face. Again. Again. Crushing bone faster than it could heal. Gouts of blood flew from Scott's mouth and nose as his head whipped with each blow.

"Do you feel that?" Andre hissed. "It is nothing compared to what I have endured over the centuries! Nothing compared to watching my mother and father die in front of me!"

Andre felt Scott groping through the thigh pocket of his fatigues. Too late. Scott snaked his arm free, thrust something into his face. A hiss . . .

Burning! Andre reared, shrieking. His hands flew to his face, came away with clotted smears of gold-tinted gore.

Fury exploding, Andre jammed his fingers between Scott's lips and teeth. Wrenched open his jaw. Suddenly, he sensed the woman from the cave. Sensed her crawling fear. She was close. Let her try to deal with what this man would become, he thought, as he slid his bleeding face over Scott's open mouth. Her horror would be far worse than death. As soon as the raining gore hit Scott's tongue and slid down his throat, he convulsed violently. But Andre held him fast.

Now Scott Boulder was truly damned. They had traded blood. And without the Philosopher's Stone, Scott's soul would be lost forever. A deserving fate for one who had schemed to ruin his plans.

Andre stood. "Your brother will not recognize you now. Nor will you recognize yourself." Scott moaned beneath him, barely able to move.

Glancing past the demolished stairway, Andre saw the witch on the second-floor landing. Somehow, a badly injured soldier—the last one surviving, from what Andre could see—had climbed onto the second-floor landing. He had his hands locked around the witch's throat. She kicked at him, but was clearly too weak from her earlier wound to escape.

For a moment, he looked on with satisfaction. Let the witch suffer. But he knew he could not let her die without first obtaining the Philosopher's Stone.

In a burst of black lightning, Andre streaked to the witch's side, and snapped the soldier's neck with a brutal twist. He tried to help her up but she slapped away his hands and struggled to her feet on her own.

"Did you kill them all?" she asked, voice raspy from the choking attempt. "I don't want any survivors coming after us."

"It's taken care of."

"What about Eric's brother?"

"I did much worse than kill him." He quickly looked her over, searching for injury, but saw only a lump under her robes below her waist. The Stone—she'd hidden it on herself. Clever, because he couldn't steal it from her while she still was protected by her potions.

"Time to live up to your side of the bargain," she said.

"As it is yours."

He followed her from the mansion, feeling a swell of triumph. Soon he would have everlasting life and the means to bring his mother and father back from Limbo. And the witch would die in pain, as she deserved.

It was all he desired.

Chapter 39

Scott gasped for air and an electrical current passed through him with a bluish-white glow, so that his limbs trembled in a macabre dance. Another manifestation of the vampire's powers, Leah realized.

Andre's evil had tainted Scott's soul . . . after which Andre had become one with the night as only evil could.

Forcing herself away from the wall where she'd surrendered to her fear, expecting a new threat any second, Leah moved stealthily toward Scott, all the while jerking her gaze in every direction. When the combatants had crashed through the skylight and landed a few yards away from her, she'd been unable to make her limbs move. Not that she could have done anything against such a powerful vampire. The fight hadn't lasted long—only a moment or two—still enough time for Andre to brutalize Scott.

Though the building was dark now, light reflected from the street and the vehicle out front allowed her to see how Scott's face had been pulverized. Not only was his flesh torn, but jagged bone poked through skin in several places.

Leah's insides twisted as she murmured, "Scott, Scott, hold on." Though she desperately wanted to hold him, she dared not touch him lest she put him in more pain.

"Nothing . . . can do . . . I feel cold. Am I dying?" The last word squeezed from wheezing lungs.

"No! You'll be fine."

She couldn't tell him he was losing his soul. Even so,

his fear was thick and cloying. It threatened to suffocate her, battered her in waves, consumed her. If his soul did die, Scott would be condemned to feed on human blood and to walk by night just as Roberto had predicted. He would become part of the evil that had destroyed her father and brother.

She couldn't let that happen.

Even as she stared at his poor face, the mutilation seemed less extreme, the bone fragments less obvious, smoother, as if he were already healing. And his eyes seemed to be dulling, as if he were losing the spark that lit his humanity from within.

Dear Lord, it was happening before her. His soul really was dying.

Scott rasped, "Kill me . . . out of control . . . too weak to do it myself . . ."

He tried pushing a knife into her hands, but Leah wouldn't take hold of it. "No!"

She couldn't do it, wasn't willing to take his life. She couldn't let him go over to the dark side without fighting for him, without trying to save him using healing magic. Scott's despair warred with panic—Leah sensed every nuance of emotion as if it were her own.

He said, "No other course—"

"Yes, there is." Though Leah knew what that meant for her personally.

She could try . . . but could she succeed?

And could she really sacrifice what was left of her memories of Dad and Gabe? For surely she would trade all for magic of this magnitude.

For Scott, she thought. For Scott she could do it.

Fumbling with the soft-sided pack she wore at her waist, she took out the things she'd brought from the war room—rock, incense, crystal, and seashell. As she placed them around Scott, doing her best to set them in the correct directions, Leah tried not to think too closely on the price she would pay for this night's magic, but she couldn't stop the images that flicked through her mind.

Dad twirling her around through the air . . .

Gabe picking her up from the sidewalk when she fell learning to skate . . .

Dad and Gabe and her surprising Mom with breakfast in bed.

Fragments of memories . . . all she had left . . . and not for long.

Scott suddenly convulsed and Leah experienced his pain as if it were her own. He was trying to hold himself together, but his flesh was trembling and his face was twisted as he swallowed a cry of sheer agony.

"Hold on, Scott, hold on just a little while longer."

Leah placed his knife at his feet to represent the fight ahead, after which she took off one of her bracelets and wrapped it around a lit candle that she placed above his head so his mind would follow hers into the light. Then she scrabbled back so she could look directly into his face, which had changed yet again.

His flesh was continuing to heal—how much time did she have left?

"We're going to take a journey together, Scott, into the light," she said, laying Andre's rapier on the floor next to him. "You need to concentrate, to help me, to project yourself there. Take my hand and I'll lead you."

His fingers trembled as they laced with hers. She shared his desperation. He couldn't turn. She couldn't let him. A life without him was impossible. She didn't know how this had happened in such a short time, but Scott had become everything to her. If he turned, Scott Boulder would be forever lost. In his place would be a creature of the night.

"Close your eyes and relax . . . let go of your fear. . . be bold. Take a leap of faith with me."

She was ready now.

She would do it for Scott.

"Let your body go light . . . lighter . . . you're floating now . . . with me . . ."

For a moment he was with her, and then he tensed, gagged for breath, Andre's evil power washing through him and over her this time. She lost concentration for a moment and Scott clutched her hand harder . . . so hard she thought her fingers might snap.

"Can't!" he rasped, his body jerking.

Beating down her own panic, she said, "Scott . . . Scott, listen to my voice."

But it was as if he couldn't hear her. The struggle was increasing and his body was shaking with an electrical current that passed through him to her. Leah closed her eyes and held on and tried to deny that Scott was losing the battle.

She couldn't fail again. Not this time.

She couldn't fail the one person who had sacrificed everything for what he believed in, the man who had become part of her in such a short time.

The man she loved.

Love . . . yes, she did love him.

The thought stunned her. How was it possible? They were so different. It had happened so fast. But it had happened. The thought of losing Scott left her feeling hollow, dead inside. She couldn't lose him, too.

But how could she best Andre's power over Scott?

Then it came to her . . . the way Scott had reached her in the church. She remembered the kiss, the unspoken feelings it had brought to life in her. He'd unknowingly used *himself* to bring her back from the edge. If he felt even a fraction of what she felt for him, then surely this would work.

"Scott," she said, touching his feverish face. His flesh was hot and damp. "I'm here for you, because you need me the same way I need you."

She moved alongside him, curled a leg around his, hung on to his waist though he tried to push her away.

"Sh-h-h," she whispered, lying half over him, tucking her head into the curve of his neck. "Together. We can do this together. I won't let you fall."

The beat of Scott's heart pummeled her chest, his limbs tried to disengage hers. Leah refused to let go, refused to give up.

"Release everything that belongs to Andre," she said, gently touching his battered face. "Release the power he put into you. Think of the way you used to be. The man you really are."

A fist tightened around her heart. She couldn't let Scott lose himself.

"Let go, Scott," she whispered, kissing the corner of his mouth. "Banish Andre from your mind and think of me instead."

Closing her eyes, she stroked his face, his neck, his chest with her free hand. "Let yourself float . . . with me . . . wrapped in me . . ."

Entering the trance state, Leah could see them threaded together in her mind, floating in deep space, a million stars and a handful of planets. Could sense his emotions growing stronger. Could feel his lips softly brushing against hers.

"Let yourself go . . . open yourself to me . . . let me see what's inside you . . ."

His lips nudged hers open and he kissed her deeply like a drowning man searching for air. She gave over to the kiss, imagined them twined tightly as one, mouth to mouth, breasts to chest, flesh to flesh.

Sensations that went beyond the stars shot through her as she whispered, "*Now,* Scott, give yourself over to me . . ."

Still struggling, he complied, and for a moment, she imagined their souls merging. Mired in her trance, eyes closed, she could see him clearly as she backed away. Sweat poured down his face and his chest began to throb and glow. The glow burned red like fire, but with each second that passed grew infinitesimally darker, like a dying sun.

He was turning even as she was trying to save him.

She had to do it now, before it was too late. Before Scott was forever lost.

Heart thudding, she called, "Scott!" and whirled to see him even farther away, the glow now a crimson black.

Trying not to panic, she imagined herself at his side and suddenly she was there.

Now.

It had to be now.

Dad . . . Gabe . . . I'll always love you . . .

Knowing she could never tell Scott about the sacrifice she was making to save him, Leah plunged both hands into the glow that was his dying soul and took that leap of faith to call upon the God she had doubted for so long. She knew she was putting her own soul at risk, but how could she do otherwise?

"In the name of God, the All-Powerful, let the evil spirit that would take this soul be banished so this good man can heal and live."

Though the dark glow set fire to her hands, she didn't so much as waver.

"Let the evil pour from him into me and let him see the mercy of Your Light."

As she imagined Scott's soul lightening, the darkness inched its way up her arms, creating a halo of electrical current around her entire body, shocking her over and over. The pain zapping through her was excruciating, and Leah almost invited the fear back inside herself, but losing Scott to Andre's evil trumped everything, including death itself.

"In the name of God, let the evil lose its power and be banished back to the demon from whence it came."

Leah held on and rode out another attack . . . this one aimed at her . . . at her own soul. Determination stoked her. She would not be left behind. She imagined her soul gaining radiance and strength . . . the current diminishing . . . gradually losing its bite until it sparked in fits and then suddenly flickered out.

After which, a light so brilliant that it banished the night sky nearly blinded her while Scott's chest glowed with a soft radiance echoing her own.

Chapter 40

Scott sat bolt upright. When he realized Leah was on his lap, he enveloped her in a tight embrace. "I don't know what the hell that was," he rasped. "But thanks."

"I owed you one," she said softly into his ear. "Well, more than one, actually. And you're welcome."

He remembered only bits and pieces after crashing through the skylight. Bone-crushing pain as Andre struck him again and again . . . and then a very particular scene of horror of came rushing back . . .

He went rigid with panic, and Leah homed in again, voice soft but firm. "What Andre did to you doesn't matter, Scott. You have everything you need to overcome any obstacle on your own terms now," she said. "Deep down where it counts. Deep in here." She slid her hand over his heart. "You are *not* like him."

He nodded, believing her, even though he could still taste the cold, spoiled flow of Andre's blood down his throat.

"You were losing your soul, Scott," Leah went on. "But it's okay, now. You're okay."

Mention of his soul brought back bizarre images . . . deep space . . . intense flashes of light. Leah's magic, no doubt. Saving his ass. Or, in this case, his soul.

Still disoriented, Scott let the touch of Leah's skin, the weight of her body, the warmth of her mouth pull him back to the present. Which proved to be a nightmare. He glanced around at the candlelit carnage as the acrid stench of cooked flesh assailed his nostrils. So much blood. So much death.

Eric!

He quickly but gently guided Leah from his lap, and then clambered to his feet. "Do you still have the GPS tracker?"

She pulled it from her pocket, consulted the glowing screen. Then she picked up Andre's rapier and slung it across her back again. "Eric is in a second-floor bedroom."

Scott catalogued the sensations rushing through his body—the surging strength and swirling smoke capabilities were still present. But there was no sign of blood thirst as far as he could tell. That didn't mean it was gone, he knew. It could simply be dormant, sated by his earlier feeding. Suddenly, he felt something else coursing through his body. A sort of crackling energy . . .

He held up a hand and saw tiny filaments of black electricity arc between his fingertips. "Jesus!"

Leah looked up from the tracker, regarded the lightning with awe. "You must have adopted another of Andre's abilities by consuming his blood."

There was no time to indulge his panic. Not with Eric close and possibly in trouble. "Another way to kick Andre's ass when we find him."

"Exactly what I was thinking."

"Let's go." Scott swept Leah into his arms, sprinted to the foot of the grand staircase, and jumped—easily clearing the splintered ruins thanks to his enhanced strength. She clutched him tightly and buried her face in his neck as they sailed through the air. "I've got you," he told her, wishing he could say it again in a more intimate context. But also knowing that he should break things off with her after this mess was resolved. As a soldier, he couldn't afford the distraction. As a civilian, she couldn't afford the risk.

Landing, he put Leah down, and the two of them followed the monitor to a room at the end of a long, carpeted hallway.

Scott kicked in the door, ready to take on whatever threat lay beyond with his bare hands. But there was only his brother, who sat on the floor, right wrist chained to a radiator. Apparently uninjured.

"Thank God," Scott uttered, then rushed forward and easily snapped the chains with his bare hands.

Eric looked up. For a moment, he didn't seem to recognize his surroundings, and then his eyes focused on Scott's face, and he smiled weakly. " 'bout fucking time . . ."

Scott hefted Eric off his butt, wrapping him in a bear hug. He fought back tears of joy as his brother hugged him in return. "You asshole . . . I thought we'd lost you . . ." He kept hugging Eric, mentally vowing never to let him down again. No matter how much of a stubborn little shit Eric could be, Scott knew how lucky he was to have his brother with him nearly every day. How many people could say the same?

After more hugging, Eric began to squirm. "Hey, man, ease off . . . you're about to crush me. Literally."

Scott let go. "Sorry, I don't know my own strength anymore. Long story."

Having given them space for the reunion, Leah moved into the room. "Eric, I'm so happy to see you well, but we don't have much time. It's imperative we find the man and woman who brought you here."

Eric looked at her quizzically. "Yeah, sure." And then he leaned close to Scott. "Who the heck is that?"

"Her name is Leah," Scott whispered back. "You saw her in the lab after you woke up. She helped save your life."

"Man, I must have been really out of it not to remember her. She's cute."

Scott cocked an eyebrow.

Eric hands raised in mock surrender. "Okay, okay."

"Go ahead, Leah," Scott said.

"Do you remember anything about them?" Leah continued. "Anything at all?"

Eric frowned. "Not very much. I remember being in the lab a couple days ago . . . arguing with Scott . . . feeling strange after our raid on the airplane." He paused. "I remember entering the lab somehow, and then an explosion of red smoke . . ." He paused again, and then shook his head. "Not much else, I'm afraid. Not even how I got here. Speaking of which, how did I get here, anyway?"

"You were under the influence of a Voodoo witch."

Scott was surprised that Eric didn't laugh at the notion. Instead, he nodded in apparent understanding.

"That would explain all the weird statues and symbols in her room. It could have been Voodoo gear."

Leah asked, "Whose room?"

His face fell. "Rebecca Dumas. The woman I was seeing. I remember Rebecca. Absolutely."

Scott thought back to the church as Eric gave a description of Rebecca—it fit the woman who'd attacked them to a T.

"You mentioned Rebecca's room. Where is it?" Leah pressed.

"In Magic Nights. It's . . . um . . . a strip club on Bourbon Street."

"I see."

Eric blushed. "I used to know where the room was exactly." He paused, then shook his head. "Sorry, I'm still a little groggy. Can't remember."

"That's okay. We'll find it."

Scott said, "I'll call a medevac for our casualties, and then we'll take a Humvee to the club."

"I'm not going with you," Eric told him.

"What are you talking about?"

"I'm done with the military."

"We don't have time for this, Eric," Scott said. "Get your ass outside."

"I'm serious, Scott. As of right now, I'm done. I keep thinking about Rebecca," he said, face clouding.

"Are you kidding? That woman doesn't deserve one second of your pity."

"That's just the thing. She had a good heart before all this happened, you know? She looked after her sick brother in the same way you looked after me these past few days. And then something happened to change her into a heartless woman I can't even recognize now."

"Her use of black magic is responsible, Eric," Leah said. "Losing her humanity was the price she had to pay. She's sick from its use."

Again, Scott was surprised that Eric took the mention of magic in stride. Even so, he couldn't believe what he was hearing. "How can you possibly compare us to that woman? She used you in the worst way. Killed innocent people."

"I almost killed you, too, Scott, remember? Back in the lab, it was my power of Suggestion that nearly made you pull that trigger."

"You were under control of the very woman you're feeling sorry for!" Scott said incredulously.

"Maybe I could have fought harder, Scott. And who knows? Maybe she could have, too, against the black magic."

"And maybe we wouldn't have been in this mess in the first place if we'd grown up in better circumstances." Scott looked at Eric evenly. "The point is it doesn't matter. You never have to explain yourself to me. Beneath it all, I know you're always trying your best."

"Then let me go."

"You're nuts if you think I'm leaving you behind after all that's happened," Scott said. "I'm giving you a direct order."

Without another word, Eric started past him. Anger boiling, Scott intended to use his enhanced strength to grab Eric by the scruff and drag him to the Humvee by force. Instead, he felt his anger drain away, suddenly, as he realized that what his brother had said had struck a chord. He wasn't quite sure how, but it made him feel lighter somehow. Even free.

After Scott let Eric leave, Leah took his side. "Are you going to be all right?"

"You know how out of control I've felt with these new powers?" he replied, trying to keep the tremor from his voice. "That's nothing compared to this."

"But somehow it's okay."

"Somehow."

As Scott ushered Leah to the door, he threw one last glance over his shoulder at the chains that had bound Eric. *Guess I'll see you around, bro.*

Chapter 41

"The Philosopher's Stone," Andre said the moment they entered her quarters above Magic Nights. "I want it now."

Stopping at her altar, Rebecca opened her vial of Commanding Oil and sprinkled a bit on her hands. "I need to prepare—"

"No time. If the soldiers find us before my transformation is complete, I don't know that I can save you again."

Nodding in agreement, she moved to Andre. "Yes, time is of the essence."

She kept her gaze locked with his as she touched the back of his hand, keeping the transfer of the oil to his skin casual, so he wouldn't be aware. "You must take care of Danton as quickly as possible. *Now,*" she emphasized.

He glared at her for a moment, and then nodded. "Yes, all right. Now."

Her thoughts went back to the massacre at the mansion and her own part in it. So many dead. But not Danton. She smiled. Danton would live!

Leading Andre to her brother's room, Rebecca felt a sense of triumph. Andre might be a powerful vampire, but he was a man, as well, one she could manage using Voodoo. She could see herself aligned with him, using his power for herself.

Once inside Danton's room, Rebecca stopped before his bed. Her brother looked so frail that it made her heart hurt. "Cher, wake up." She stroked his face until his eyes fluttered open.

"Rebecca." Danton's lips curved into an affectionate smile.

"Andre is here to make you well," she told him.

Danton looked past her, his smile not diminishing as his gaze met Andre's. "You have the cure?"

"One you must choose to accept."

"Whatever will get me out of this bed for once and for all—I'll take it. I don't care what I have to do."

"Very well, then."

Knowing that Danton didn't truly understand what he'd just agreed to, Rebecca held her breath as Andre slashed his ring against his other wrist and held it out to her brother.

"Drink."

"What?" Danton gasped, looking confused.

"Drink his blood, cher, please."

His pale features reflecting his confusion, Danton looked from her to Andre's wrist. His expression turned to disgust and he shook his head.

"Drink and be stronger than you ever imagined," Andre said, pressing his bleeding flesh to Danton's mouth.

Rebecca hardened herself when her brother tried to tear himself away. Obviously impatient, Andre held his head in place. Danton was so weak that he quickly succumbed to Andre's strength, eyes rolling in fear the only indication that he wanted to fight this particular cure.

"Danton, don't fight him!"

Andre held Danton in place a moment longer before easing him back to the pillow. "You're going to feel things you never imagined. But once you've . . . become like me . . . a whole new world away from this bed, away from this room, will be opened to you." Eyes widening, Danton gasped as his body began to spasm. Andre grabbed Rebecca by the arm. "Time for your part of the bargain."

Though she knew her brother was suffering, she had no time for pity. Whatever he had to go through would be worth it in the end. Rebecca let Andre pull her to the door. Danton cried out and arched so high in the bed that she thought his back would break.

She'd known her brother would need to drink Andre's blood. Undoubtedly there was nothing she could do to help him get through the pain.

"The Stone," Andre said.

"Yes, now." Rebecca led the way back to her quarters.

Hearing Danton cry through the walls, she closed her mind against what was happening to him and headed for the bathroom, saying, "Take off your shirt and sit there." She indicated the thronelike chair in the corner. "I'll be ready in a minute."

Andre grunted as if he were irritated, and yet he did as she commanded. Once out of his sight, she slipped out of her dress. To do what Andre asked, she would have to conduct a very difficult ceremony, one she couldn't do alone. She would have to become a vessel for the Voodoo gods. The loa would ride her, speak through her. An exhausting, soul-searing process, and she needed to be fully prepared.

She already wore body jewelry studded with blood-red rubies. The bag with the Philosopher's Stone still hung from the belt around her waist. After coating her body with a prepared oil meant to increase her power during the ceremony, she pulled on a diaphanous red gown and rejoined Andre.

She could feel the vampire's impatience as she crossed the room, stopped before a crucifix which she'd set to one side of her altar, and began with a Catholic prayer.

"O Lord God, by the Precious Blood which Thy Divine Son Jesus shed in the garden, deliver that soul amongst them all which is most destitute of spiritual aid; bring it to Thy glory, there to praise and bless Thee forever."

She opened a vial and poured a special potion into a chalice, which she then offered to Andre.

"What is this poison?"

"It will aid me in joining you to the Stone. Drink."

Andre did as she commanded and held out the empty chalice. Rebecca took it back to the altar where she began lighting candles and incense that she'd placed all around the room earlier. She inhaled the scent—jasmine and lily and coconut—meant to set an uninhibited mood.

She then moved to the front of the terrarium and stepped out of the diaphanous material so that, except for her body jewelry, she was nude. Despite trying to keep her thoughts from her brother until the ceremony was done, a roar from the direction of his room made her see Danton in her mind, struggling with the effects of the poisonous blood. She turned on a recording of drumbeats meant to move her through the ceremony, but which would also muffle things she didn't want to hear. She drank a potion meant to bring her closer to the loa. Finally she retrieved Ami, her eight-foot-long albino python, and standing before the statue of Saint Patrick on her altar, hung the snake around her neck.

Closing her eyes, Rebecca swayed and switched her prayer from Catholic to Voodoo. *"Damballah-Wedo, serpent god, most supreme and powerful of the loas, hear me. I appeal to you for your help in my joining Andre Espinoza de Madrid with this magical Stone."*

Opening the bag, she removed the Philosopher's Stone and set it on a small table to the left of Andre. A deep red-black against the gloom, it softly pulsed streaks of lighter, brighter red as if it were alive. As she watched, mesmerized, Ami wound her way around Rebecca's arms and the potion quickly had its way with her. Her head went light as did her body. She began to sway to an internal rhythm.

"Get on with it!" Andre demanded.

When she ignored him, Andre attempted to get up but of course couldn't move his body.

"What the hell! What did you give me, witch?"

The rhythm inside her was stronger now. The room was expanding and contracting. Spinning. Her flesh rippled in tune with Ami's and she danced harder. The snake dance symbolized the merging of the present world with the beyond as the dancer and snake became one. Damballah-Wedo would speak through her. She convulsed with the rising pulse of the drumbeat. Her feet moved faster and she tossed her head from side to side, her hair whipping out like wings as she welcomed the oncoming trance. Welcomed the loa that would ride her. The room around her was shifting, changing, the seated vampire her focus and the only constant. Her breathing grew shallow, her heartbeat fast. Every inch of her flesh quickened. Sweat coated her flesh as she shimmied in between his thighs.

"Your skin is tight." The loa spoke through her. "It pulls and stretches and throbs . . ."

Andre's chest began to pulse and ripple visibly, but the rest of him was frozen in place. He couldn't move. His eyes glowed red, revealing his agony, and the part of her that was still Rebecca shuddered with apprehension.

"You'll know pain such as never before," the loa continued. "That which is inside you must find its way to freedom."

Indeed, Andre howled as his flesh moved and twisted and finally split down the middle. Snakes crawled out and over and down his body only to disappear into the dark corners of the room. His chest lay open, both flesh and protective ribs stretched out of the way to reveal blood oozing over and around his heart. The power of what she'd done filled Rebecca, and she had a hard time tearing her gaze away from the beating organ.

Ignoring Andre's glowing red eyes that tried to drill through her, Rebecca picked up the Philosopher's Stone. But she didn't instantly follow through and do with it what Damballah-Wedo bade.

First she wanted to make sure to bind Andre's will to hers forever.

Her body still shaking, eyes turning back in her head, uttering sounds that made no words, she rubbed the Stone over her skin to coat it with her sweat. She rubbed it between her thighs where her inner dampness surrounded the tip. Her thighs splayed, her nether lips opened to suck the Stone, her hips thrust in an imitation of the sex act. Damballah-Wedo was riding her, pumping his potency into her, granting her the power to take the Stone and with one sharp shove, drive it into Andre's exposed heart, splitting that vital organ in two.

Andre opened his mouth and howled.

And then no sound at all but the drums and Rebecca's moans as her body shook and her hips thrust and she convulsed from the inside out.

Within seconds, the room began righting itself again, allowing her to focus. Allowing her to see the pulsing Stone as bone surrounded it and flesh miraculously healed before her eyes. Andre was coming to. Breathing. Limbs moving. His expression lightened and then grew amazed, and natural color flooded his exposed skin.

"My soul! I can feel it returned to me!" he shouted, sounding triumphant.

Damballah-Wedo had heeded her request.

Smiling at her success, Rebecca was about to return Ami to the terrarium and retrieve her red gown from the floor when she changed her mind. She could use a man to finish what she had started.

And Andre could use a woman who knew how to please. A woman with enough power to complement his own.

Moving to him, she stood over him, her legs around his. She covered his perfect, scarless chest with her hand. Ami slithered down her arm and around the back of his neck. His heartbeat was strong. His penis was rigid and so large that gazing at its purplish-red tip took away her breath. But when he raised his gaze to hers, she started, for his eyes still glowed red.

"You're angry. Why? You have what you want."

"Not all." He grabbed her and pulled her to him. "Do you think I haven't been aware of the way you've been controlling and manipulating me? Now it's my turn."

He jerked her down on him, and with a hard thrust, filled her. Though she felt as if she were split in two, Rebecca couldn't resist the power surging inside her. With Ami slithering around their bodies, binding them together, Rebecca rode Andre the way she practiced her Voodoo.

Uninhibitedly.

Chapter 42

Leah led the way into the courtyard behind Magic Nights and stopped at the fountain, then looked at the second- and third-floor balconies with cast-iron railings all around them.

"Damn!" Scott said, keeping his voice low. "Too bad Eric couldn't have been more specific about where to find Rebecca's room."

All had French doors, some open, some closed. Soft lights danced in most. Thrusting, grunting sounds from several directions assailed her, and Leah imagined patrons of Magic Nights had found their way upstairs with girls who worked for the club.

"If we choose wrong, we'll alert Andre and Rebecca and they'll get away again," Scott said.

Adjusting the sword still strapped across her back, Leah stooped and opened her bag on the ground. "Good thing I brought this." She held out the ring. "Hold on to it for a minute."

Scott's hand brushing hers flooded Leah with emotion. His features were taut and filled with worry, his eyes told her the worry was for her. So far they'd survived the night, both their souls intact. She had to believe together they could once again face a Voodoo priestess with a powerful vampire who might now be immortal, and yet come out of the confrontation alive. Both of them. She wouldn't want to survive without Scott . . .

"Hurry up," he urged.

Realizing she'd checked out for a moment, Leah quickly set out four lit candles in a circle around them. Then she took the ring from Scott and set it on a stone on the ground.

Concentrating on the design of the scar on her hand, she murmured an incantation that was really a prayer, ending with ". . . *link the Eye of* Los Oscuros *with the one it serves.*"

Instantly, a hazy purple line flashed from the ring to her palm to a second-floor room to their right. Scott was already taking the stairs two at a time, an M14 assault rifle loaded with gold bullets in hand.

Leah put out the candles and followed.

She was halfway up the stairs, when, like a crazed man, Scott drove straight through the closed French doors as though they were made of paper rather than wood and glass. Leah heard a woman's shriek and a male curse, then gunfire. A gut-wrenching breath of silence was followed by an explosion of splintering wood that came at her as both men—Andre nude—flew out on the balcony and straight down the stairs.

"Scott!" she screamed, her heart feeling as if it had seized.

Both men hit the landing below without any seeming mishap. Then they were moving again, down the last of the stairs, body to body, rolling one over the other and throwing punches that might have killed a normal man.

She had to trust that Scott's newly enhanced powers would make him an even match with Andre, that he would be able to hang on while she found a way to stop Rebecca Dumas from adding her black magic to the fight. Sensing a wave of strong emotions behind her, Leah flipped around to find the Voodoo priestess in the doorway—she wore a diaphanous red garment and a furious glare.

"You are fools for coming after us."

"I don't die so easily," Leah said, tamping down the fear that tried to wrap itself around her. This wasn't the time for hesitation, not if she wanted to live. Her success at saving Scott's soul bolstered her courage. "I survived your vampire seventeen years ago."

Rebecca's expression suddenly held a hint of fear. She backed into the room and Leah saw that she was headed for her altar with her tools.

Quickly following, Leah said, "My magic is stronger than the vampire, Rebecca . . . stronger than your Voodoo."

Rebecca shrieked as she turned and splashed some kind of oil over Leah. "You are now in my control, you pathetic excuse for a witch!"

Leah felt nothing hindering her and knew Roberto's amulet was protecting her from Rebecca's black magic. But how much could it do for her? Needing to touch Rebecca to know how to defeat her, Leah boldly stepped forward and reached out.

Rebecca backed up. "What do you think you are doing?"

Then Leah latched on to her arm. Waves of darkness flowed from the priestess and threatened to suffocate her.

"Let go!"

When her command didn't work, Rebecca seemed confused. Her eyes widened and she struggled to free herself. Infused with the strength of someone determined not to die, Leah hung on, concentrated and sifted through the dark energy.

Fury . . . a taste for power . . . a need for revenge . . .

Leah felt all of these wrapped around an emptiness that reminded her of death. She let go.

"You're soul-sick, Rebecca, and it's destroying you."

"And you're mad. You've crossed the wrong woman."

Rebecca whipped around to gather ingredients from her altar.

"So many deaths . . ."

"I've killed no one. *Yet.*"

"You're wrong." Realizing what she had to do now, Leah removed the amulet from around her neck. "Your hands are covered with blood."

"I don't need to draw blood to kill."

When Rebecca turned around, she held a small doll in her hand. Suddenly she lashed out and tore hair from Leah's head. She then wrapped the strands around the doll's neck.

"Baron Samedi protect me by taking the breath from this witch." Rebecca twisted the strands of hair tightly.

Leah couldn't breathe. Even though she knew clawing at her throat wouldn't help her, she couldn't stop herself.

Rebecca grinned. "See whose magic is stronger now!"

Magic . . .

Tightening her fist around the amulet's chain, Leah knew she had to act now or die. Rebecca was turning back toward her altar when Leah lunged forward and threw the chain over Rebecca's neck. Startled, the priestess dropped the doll and, her throat immediately opening, Leah sucked in as much air as she could manage.

"Lord, those who die still live in Your presence . . . their lives change but do not end," Leah whispered, beginning with part of a Catholic prayer, since Roberto had undoubtedly used magic based in Catholicism on the amulet. From her case, she took a vial of holy water and tossed the contents over the other woman. "Heal Rebecca Dumas and let her see the error of her ways. Restore her humanity and reacquaint her with the lives lost in her pursuit of power."

She watched the other woman's furious expression turn to one of fear and then horror.

A wave of sensation washed through Leah, and she

imagined she could see them—dozens of the dead—closing in on the Voodoo priestess. The panic in Rebecca's eyes told Leah the other woman saw them, too.

"Noooo!" Rebecca cried, her eyes filling with tears.

But the parade of ghosts didn't stop. Every person who had fallen victim to Andre through Rebecca's black magic surrounded her. All of them—whether soldier or civilian, those dying for their country and the innocents.

All of their seething final emotions bombarded Leah. It was all she could do to hang on to their essences long enough for Rebecca to experience them.

Shaking her head in denial, Rebecca backed off toward the doorway. "I didn't kill them . . . I didn't."

The tears started to fall, drenching her exotic face with misery and despair. She looked around in panic, as if looking for a way to run from the truth.

"You can't run, Rebecca. You have to face what you did, help us undo it." The most difficult words Leah had ever uttered hesitated on the tip of her tongue. She kept in mind that while Andre might have recovered his soul, he hadn't really been human for centuries. "Help us destroy Andre Espinoza de Madrid."

Looking as if she'd lost her mind, Rebecca frantically ran onto the balcony, screaming, "Danton! Danton, I need you!"

Then she tripped and rocketed forward, and as if in slow motion flew over the railing with a soul-wrenching scream.

Even as Leah ran out of the room, she flashed her gaze to the balcony floor where an eight-foot-long albino python slithered into some greenery. She was down the stairs as fast as she could go, but before she got to Rebecca, a man dropped down from the balcony and ran to the fallen woman.

"Rebecca!" he cried, taking her in his arms.

"Is she conscious?" Leah asked.

The man turned her way and the look he gave her made her stop short. "You've killed her!" He looked around at the candles, the remainder of the spell she'd cast. And the amulet. He ripped it off Rebecca's neck and threw it at Leah. "You killed her with your magic!"

Leah couldn't deny it. Even though the priestess had tripped over her own snake, she'd done so because Leah had healed her, had restored the humanity she'd lost.

A soft moan got Danton's attention. "I'll get you help, chère. Your friend Andre, where is he?"

Rebecca shook her head and blood dribbled from her lips. "The Stone . . . ," she choked out, reaching up to touch her brother's face. ". . . get the Philosopher's Stone from him . . . only thing that can save you now . . ."

With that, her hand dropped and her head lolled. Her eyes remained open and aimed at Leah as if in accusation.

Leah grabbed the amulet and backed away from the scene as, crushing his sister's body to him, Danton wept.

She had to find Scott and help him destroy Andre.

Chapter 43

Scott didn't move fast enough to dodge the blow. Andre's fist slammed into his jaw, pitching him down a hallway where he crashed through a door that led to the club's main showroom.

Shaking off dust and debris, he stood to meet the confused stares of the topless strippers and their patrons. "Everybody get out of here! Now!"

But the people continued to stare, clearly thinking he was drunk or crazy or both.

Scott moved to hustle people out when suddenly, in the blink of an eye, Andre was next to him. Slammed a fist into his stomach. Scott doubled over with the force of the blow, his enhanced strength helping mitigate the pain.

"I do not know how you survived with your soul intact," Andre growled. "But it does not matter."

Scott struggled to stand, when Andre delivered a brutal uppercut to his solar plexus that sent him sprawling into the mirrored wall behind the main stage with a deafening crash.

Dazed, Scott saw only flashes of sequins and breasts and business suits as the strippers and their patrons began screaming and finally rushed toward the exits. Beyond them all he saw Andre. Stalking toward the stage, fists clenched. Murder in his blazing red eyes.

Scott clambered to his feet, trying to prepare himself for Andre's next assault, when he saw movement in the corner of his vision. His heart leaped into his throat . . . *Leah!*

He looked at her in alarm as she stepped through the shattered hallway door, rapier clutched in both hands. If Andre spotted her, he could kill her easily. Her face was etched with fear and concentration as she tried to move as quickly as possible without making a sound.

She glanced at him, then looked at the blade and indicated Andre with a nod. He didn't know what she had in mind, but had to trust that she knew what she was doing. It also meant he had to bring Andre close, fight him hand to hand to give her a chance to spring her trap.

"Hey, Andre, looks like you did your job too well!" Scott yelled as he tried to push his concern for Leah aside. "I've got strength, speed . . . everything that's yours!"

Andre vaulted onto the stage with a hiss. Scott lunged to meet him and the two slammed into each other, trading blows, causing the stage to tremble.

Scott then felt a rush of dark energy flow from Andre's body to his, which he countered with his own. There was a thundering crackle as fingers of lightning swirled and danced around them. Gelled spotlights suspended on the metal grid above the stage shorted out, showering them with white sparks.

That's it, Scott thought. Stay nice and close until Leah reaches you. And then Andre broke contact and slipped past Scott's defenses to land a blow to the side of his head. Scott staggered back, but kept his footing. "My drunken mother can hit harder than you—"

His voice caught in his throat when he saw Leah lose her footing. Nothing major, a subtle misstep on the shattered remains of a table. But the crackling of wood underneath her boot sounded through the air like a gunshot.

Andre whirled. Saw her. Scott leaped but sailed past

the vampire, missing him completely. Too shaken from his beating to be accurate.

Andre raised a hand.

Fired a bolt of lightning that struck Leah in the chest.

She collapsed, not moving.

On the floor of the stage, Scott blinked through the sweat in his eyes. Could hardly believe what he'd just seen. Simply could not process the reality.

Leah was gone. Killed in a second's time.

In *less* than a second.

His mind reeled in horror as heady, surging power flooded his body. "Goddamn you!" he yelled, and rushed Andre like a linebacker.

Tears streamed down his face. He should have taken Leah away from here when he had the chance. He'd made the same mistake with Eric. He'd never learn . . .

Andre charged at him in return, moving so fast he blurred. Raising his fist as he ran to throw the entire momentum of his body into the blow. Scott knew if that blow connected, that would be it. Game over.

Part of him wanted it to be over. Without Eric and now without Leah.

Movement behind Andre caught his attention.

Leah used the rapier as a crutch as she climbed shakily to her feet. He hitched a breath . . . God only knew how she'd survived. As she dragged herself forward, Scott felt a surge of renewed determination. They could still beat Andre. They still had a chance.

Scott leaped back onto the stage. Closing the distance between them, Andre delivered the blow with vicious resolve. Scott made no attempt to avoid it.

He knew Andre could cancel his power of dissolution. Something in his DNA, something about conflicting magnetic fields . . . whatever it was, the bastard had done it to Drew back in the lab, turned the man's stretched, smoky body into bouillabaisse.

If Scott tried to do the same now, his power would be canceled out as well.

Which was exactly the idea.

As Andre's fist homed in, Scott focused on his shoulder. Told himself his shoulder was nothing, nothing . . . its weight dissolving and then relinquishing altogether as it transformed into gray smoke.

Scott felt Andre's right fist punch through the smoke, and then a fraction of a second later, felt the muscles and tendons and bones stitch together to trap the fist like a saber-toothed tiger in a tar pit.

Joining them like some sort of demented Siamese twins.

Andre grunted in surprise. Yanked back his arm to tear his fist free. But Scott gave up resistance and let himself be pulled forward like a fish on a line, ruining the man's leverage. For Andre, it was like losing a hand and being chained to a 180-pound deadweight. For Scott, it was a golden opportunity to show Andre how he felt.

Scott slammed his elbow into Andre's face over and over. Andre's head whipped back with each blow as blood shot from his mouth and lips. Scott saw Andre's pupils go white with Suggestion, and closed his eyes. He didn't need to see the vampire to hit him. Punching him was like shooting a big, murderous fish in a barrel.

Eyes cinched tight, Scott kept punching Andre repeatedly in the face . . . *this is for Eric, you goddamn leech . . . for Leah . . . for me and all the people you've killed . . .* When he judged Andre to be sufficiently on the ropes, he opened his eyes, yanked the vampire to his feet, and then shoved him back against the wall.

"LEAH, NOW!" Scott yelled.

But as Leah rushed forward with the sword, Scott knew the vampire still had the capability to kill her. Even after being run through with the sword, Andre would have a chance to dole out a final act of vengeance before Leah had time to act.

Unless he did something to stop it.

As Leah approached, Scott let Andre tear his fist free. He grunted as bloody chunks of his shoulder went flying. The wound irised closed.

Scott imagined his entire body consumed by crackling light, which triggered a searing-hot surge of voltage up his spine. He had no idea what effect his plan would have. Hopefully, it would distract Andre for a few precious seconds.

Scott knew the attempt could kill him. But Leah had risked her life to save his soul.

Scott watched Leah rush past and plunge the sword into Andre's chest with all her strength. The blade sliced straight through Andre and bit into the wood behind him, pinning him like meat on a spit. He howled in pain and surprise.

God, I hope this works, Scott thought, as his body began to flash and shimmer and then collapsed into a jagged, pulsing bolt . . .

Chapter 44

Leah could hear the rush of her pulsing blood as Scott's body transformed into pure lightning.

"God be with you," she whispered as the bolt jumped onto the sword blade and, with a blinding blue-white light, arced through the vampire.

Scott was temporarily incapacitating Andre, alchemy leaving him powerless and vulnerable to her magic—the same alchemy that had made Andre the vile creature he was. As the vampire's screech at being paralyzed echoed through the club, Leah turned inward, seeking a trance.

Mentally, she entered a maw as bleak as the vampire's black soul. He floated some distance away in the absolute dark, the arcing electrical current outlining his body her only guide to his location. Knowing what she did about his past, she chose to use his obsessive hatred for the Catholic Church against him.

"In the name of Almighty God—The Father, The Son, and The Holy Ghost," she said, drawing closer, *"I adjure the spirit of evil in this creature to be vanquished now and forever."*

"YOU THINK YOU CAN DEFEAT AN IMMORTAL?"

Ignoring the shout that threatened to puncture her eardrums, she sped toward the electrical current, knowing that while he could speak, he couldn't move, couldn't strike her down because Scott was holding him fast from the inside out. *"To that end, I pray that Almighty God will see me as his righteous soldier. . ."*

"IF I DIE, THE LAST VESTIGES OF YOUR FATHER AND BROTHER DIE WITH ME."

An empty threat. Though Leah already mourned the loss of Dad and Gabe, she couldn't help but be affected by the reminder of her sacrifice. She went cold inside, and she had to force herself to keep going. Had to prepare herself to commit violence, even if it was to be cloaked in her execution of apotropaic magic. This was her biggest test—using her knowledge to turn away evil in a way that wasn't benign. A more telling sacrifice, perhaps, than losing her memories. An act that might change her forever . . .

Stopping directly in front of the vampire, she focused on calming herself, on slowing her rapid pulse and swallowing the bile that crept from her stomach up to her throat, on reminding herself that he'd chosen to turn away from humanity. If violence was necessary to stop this creature made from alchemy and blood from destroying everything in his path, then she had no choice.

Hoping that Scott could keep Andre frozen for a moment longer, she said, "*Lord Jesus, guide my hand to pluck the evil from the demon and to heal him. . .*"

With that, she drew back her arm and, with all her might, punched the vampire in the chest.

Which did nothing more than make him laugh at her.

She wouldn't give up. Nothing—not threats or her own fear of failure—would stop her. This was their only chance to defeat Andre. Centering herself, she drew on all her psychic energy and imagined her hand as an arrow of purest gold—the only substance that could defeat a creature of alchemy. Then saying, "*Andre Espinoza de Madrid, you shall no more dare to deceive the human race . . . persecute the Church . . . torment God's elect!*" she struck at him again while visualizing that arrow burrowing deep into his chest.

His skin split . . . flesh tore . . . bone broke.

Blood from his wound doused her.

His blood.

The blood of his countless victims.

Their essence whipped through her, their faces flashing through her mind so fast that they were all a blur. The horror of their combined agony made Leah feel as if the very life were draining from her. She dug farther into the hot, pulsing mass of flesh that was Andre's heart. Even as her fingers surrounded the beating organ, she once again sensed Dad and Gabe. The flashes in her mind slowed and, for a brief moment, she thought she saw her loved ones. Suddenly unable to breathe, she stopped what she was doing. Crying out in desperation, she sought to capture their memory, but they slipped through her mind like leaves in the wind.

Andre laughed at her misery, the triumphant sound cutting through her.

When she realized the current around Andre was growing fainter—which meant Scott was growing weaker, less capable of keeping the vampire paralyzed—Leah tugged at Andre's heart, but it wouldn't budge. Her own heart began to thunder.

"Scott, get out!" she cried, fearing that if Scott waited too long, he would be unable to free himself from Andre and would therefore die. "Get out now!"

The electrical current flickered and began to withdraw from Andre's body and spark back up the sword. Though she tried again, she couldn't budge the heart. Dear Lord, she couldn't fail Scott. If she didn't manage it now, even if he did free himself, he would surely die anyway.

"I beseech you, Lord Almighty, give me your strength to end this evil."

Focusing the power of mind and healing magic into her hand again, she gripped the heart hard so that it pounded at her. Imagining a fist of gold, she tugged and tugged and tugged, hot blood oozing through her fingers as she squeezed harder and harder until she finally tore the organ free of Andre's chest. Just then, lightning separated from the sword and morphed back into Scott.

Soulless once more, Andre howled in anguish, his arms thrown out, his head aimed upward, as if he were begging God to spare him.

In Leah's hand, Andre's heart pulsed red against the blackness of his soul.

Andre's grief at the realization of what he'd become stunned her. A part of him had still been human, after all. His sorrow surrounded her, his anguish pierced her, and for a pain-filled moment, she shared heartache with a man who had chosen to become a monster.

Then the heart in her hand morphed back to Stone . . . and the Stone morphed into a sun of blinding light . . . and the monster at last met an enemy he couldn't conquer.

Shafts of sunlight beat at him until his skin bubbled and split.

Feeling the turmoil and agony of those he'd murdered, Leah concentrated on them. "*O Lord, grant eternal rest unto his victims. Let Your Perpetual Light shine upon the souls of all the faithful departed through his evil. Through the mercy of God, may they—and he—rest in peace for eternity.*"

Gradually the turmoil in her slowed and then stilled.

Before her, Andre's flesh burned with a low black flame as if in alchemical reaction to the sun.

His features twisted, his mouth wrenched open. Guttural sounds of agony escaped him as he once more raised his arms to the heavens as if begging for mercy. Lightning bolts erupted from every orifice—eyes, nose, ears, mouth, chest. Then the lightning transformed into fire that grew hotter and hotter.

Black flames turned red . . . turned orange . . . turned yellow . . . turned white . . . turned blue.

Then one unearthly scream and Andre imploded, flesh collapsing inward, bones breaking and folding in on one another . . . his remains pulverized and then gone.

Limbs trembling with relief, Leah gasped, "It's over!"

She blinked her eyes open and the world righted itself. Andre's smoking skeleton lay at her feet and the Philosopher's Stone in her hand.

Was she different now? Had the violence changed her? Yes, Andre had turned away from the world, but within that monster she'd recognized a spark of humanity that had never died.

She turned to embrace Scott and realized he lay on the ground, moaning.

"Scott!" Dropping the Stone, she moved to him and knelt at his side. "Say something. Talk to me."

"You did it, Leah," he forced out, his face a mask of pain.

"*We* did it. Together."

She was helping Scott into a sitting position when she sensed someone behind her. Whipping around she got a quick glimpse of Rebecca's brother Danton in the doorway. And then he was gone, as was the Philosopher's Stone.

"Rebecca's brother took the Stone!"

"I should go after him."

Scott tried to stand, but nearly fell on her.

"You're in no shape to go anywhere. You're lucky to be alive. Let it go. He won't be able to use it."

Scott wrapped an arm around her shoulders and Leah leaned into him, supported him, relieved that they were both still alive. At least she could be content in her belief that all those souls she'd sensed in Andre—including her father and brother—were finally at peace.

And the hollow feeling in her eased. Scott was alive. They'd both made it through the horror. She hadn't lost another person she loved.

They'd only known each other for a few days, but she couldn't love Scott more and sensed that he felt the same about her, even if they couldn't yet voice those feelings.

What they'd gone through together had forged a connection that would never be broken. It had changed them both—they had learned to respect each other's skills and had stepped out of their comfort zones in a crisis.

But what about the future?

Where would they go from here?

Epilogue

When Scott drove the Humvee to the Miescher Laboratory front gate, the attending MP asked him to please wait and then went back into the guard station to make a call. This can't be good, Scott thought. Had they learned about Eric? Had BB told them about his powers?

Leah threw him a look of concern. "What do they want?"

"We'll find out soon enough," Scott said wearily, settling back.

Now that they were well clear of Magic Nights and the chaos of Bourbon Street, he realized how exhausted he truly was. He also felt the crackling aftermath of the lightning throughout his body—as well as a series of strange side effects. His vision was tinted green, and his mouth tasted thick like peanut butter. Also, his skin was extra sensitive, making the simple contact of his fatigues feel like sandpaper.

Although the effects had faded since he'd morphed back into human form, their presence was disorienting nonetheless. But not nearly as weird as coursing through Andre's body had been.

Even as lightning, impact with the rapier had felt like slamming into a brick wall, and streaking down the edged steel toward Andre's heart like plunging from a skyscraper window. Once he'd entered muscle and tissue, his superheated energy had fused with Andre's, neutralizing it. He'd felt the guy fighting him on a molecular level, but there was nothing Andre could do. Since he'd been re-created in Andre's image, the vampire was, in essence, at war with himself. The resulting stalemate had given Leah a chance to deal the final deadly blow.

He glanced at her. "How are you doing?"

"Tired," she said, making an effort to smile. "You?" She reached for his arm, but he moved it, pretending to rub the side of his face in weariness.

"I'll be fine," he said, and noticed that his gesture of refusal was not lost on her. As usual, she had an uncanny way of tuning in to his feelings. She frowned slightly, but respected his distance.

Part of him wanted to stay by Leah's side as long as possible. She was incredible, no doubt about it. But, realistically, he couldn't make her a part of his life, a fact that left him cold inside. Empty. He needed Leah, needed her warmth and love, but he couldn't have her until he was sure it was safe. He cared about her too much to put her at risk again. First he needed to resolve the obligations he felt to the military, especially with Eric going AWOL. And more than that, he needed to make sure his new powers weren't a danger to anyone, especially not to Leah.

The guard came back. "You're to come with me, sir."

"What's this about?"

"I don't know, sir, but I have my orders. This way, please."

Scott looked at Leah, whose face had not released any of its consternation. "Very well, soldier."

Leaving the Humvee at the gate, Scott and Leah followed the MP into the lab and then down a labyrinth of corridors to a section of the base Scott hadn't seen before. Alone, that wasn't cause for alarm—the place was so big that there were plenty of areas he hadn't yet visited. It was the tense attitude of the MP that worried him.

From the look Leah gave him, he suspected the same held for her, as well. "Should we be worried?" she asked.

"After all that's happened, they might want to bury Project 24. If that's the case, it would make sense that they debrief us in secret," Scott said to put her at ease, even though he wasn't so sure. The last pure remnants of DNA had died with Andre, but there was still the adulterated strain humming in his veins—a fact he would keep secret if he could. Project 24 had wreaked enough havoc already. It was time for it to be buried.

They filed into an elevator, and took it two levels down. There seemed to be several levels belowground.

"I didn't think you could build down in this part of Louisiana because of the water table," Leah said.

"Neither did I," Scott replied.

Once out of the elevator, they headed through a subterranean tangle of corridors until they finally reached a red steel door, which led into a windowless control room filled with computer equipment. Two more MPs were there to greet them. Along the ceiling were monitors set to rooms occupied by people—anywhere from one to a few dozen—some of whom were restrained in hospital beds and hooked up to medical equipment.

Scott turned to the MPs. "Okay, we're here. Now what's—" His voice caught in his throat when a man walked into the room from another door: much older, wiry build, snub-nosed, gray hair carefully trimmed and khakis pressed.

"Good to see you again, Captain," the man said, saluting.

"Colonel Harriman," Scott replied with profound surprise, nearly forgetting to salute back. He knew Project 24 had advocates in the top brass, but James Harriman? The man had trained him and Eric years ago at

Fort Bragg in North Carolina, had been like a father to them both.

"I'm sorry about what happened to your team a couple days ago, son," Harriman said. "Beyond that, I reviewed the battle transmissions sent back by the Black Hawk and the Bradley Fighting Vehicle." A look of regret crossed his face. "I'm afraid you're under investigation."

Scott wondered just how much the man had seen. It was possible neither transmission had captured clear evidence of him performing any superhuman act. "On what grounds, sir?"

"You suffered total casualties in the assault, Captain, including that of your superior officer. I'd be remiss not to put you under investigation. Also, you allowed your brother to go AWOL."

"He carried out an impossible mission under impossible circumstances," Leah said. "If not for Scott, things could have been much, much worse. You should be thanking him."

"I'm prepared to take full responsibility," Scott replied. So Harriman hadn't changed after all this time. Still tough as an Abrams tank, with a razor-thin tolerance for bullshit. Scott felt Harriman's admonishment cut deeply, the way a true father's might, even though he sensed the colonel had an agenda beyond chewing him out.

The colonel nodded. "Consider yourself suspended from duty until further notice."

"Are you planning to detain me as well, Colonel?" Leah said. "I was a part of the raid."

"I haven't yet decided," Harriman said quietly.

Scott was tempted to take the charges at face value, thought maybe at worst he was headed for testimony in front of a military tribunal. But he suspected there was something else going on. They were being manipulated with threats to their freedom. It was a feeling echoed in Leah's face as she grasped his hand.

"There's one more issue we have to discuss," Harriman said. "The Philosopher's Stone."

Dread sizzled through Scott as Leah's hand tightened around his. The accusations of recklessness were clearly pretense now. So Harriman knew about the Stone, which meant he likely knew about Scott's powers as well. But had he seen him drink blood?

"What's going on here, Colonel?" Leah asked.

"That Stone is a matter of national security."

"It's long gone," Scott said, wanting to write the object off. Its existence had only brought violence and pain.

"We want it back," Harriman said. "Yes, we experimented on the mummy—excuse me, the vampire—with the intent of using its DNA to create Team Ultra. But then we learned the vampire wanted the Philosopher's Stone to become immortal. We'd heard of the stone, of course, but we never imagined that you would recover it. Now that we know it exists, we're not going to let it go."

Scott realized that a hidden cabal with unknown goals had been at work all along. One that very much believed in vampires, magic, and immortality. Was the top brass involved across the board? Was Harriman the point man or merely a pawn, as Ackart clearly had been?

"Truth be told, we were close to figuring out how to use the Stone until the Dumas woman got Eric to steal it," Harriman continued. "We lost the prize, but only temporarily. Our goal now is to find the woman's brother, Danton, before he goes underground. Or worse, learns how to use the Stone himself."

"And if we refuse?" Leah asked tightly.

"I'll be in touch" was all the Colonel said.

He nodded and the MPs ushered Scott and Leah out another door into a hallway lined with white steel doors set with small grilled windows. Cries of frustration—or pain?—echoed throughout.

"Scott, we can't let the military gain possession of the Stone," Leah whispered. "God only knows what they'll do with it."

"We may not have much choice," Scott said, knowing the tactics the military sometimes used when they wanted something. If Harriman pressed the point, he'd have no choice but to comply, for Leah's safety. He suspected that Leah would have the same motivation toward him.

Scott glanced through each of the cell windows in turn, and felt sudden, crawling horror.

Did he know some of these men? Some looked like soldiers he'd trained with, men he'd served with on other black ops . . . hooked up to medical machines he'd never seen before in his life . . . faces twisted in pain, bodies warped and bloated and malformed into caricatures of what they'd once been.

What the hell was this place?

Whether Harriman sent them this way to illustrate what happened to people who disobeyed orders, or whether it was to show them what was at stake, the effect was the same. His stomach turned to ice. And then he glimpsed a thick smear of blood underneath one of the doors—from God-only-knew what. The smear shimmered like oil on water.

"Scott, I'm frightened," Leah said as their footsteps echoed in the hallway, competing with the cries.

"I won't let anything happen to you," Scott said,

wrapping his arm around her back as his heart began to beat faster and faster.

Truth was . . . he didn't know if he could protect any-body.

The blood thirst was back.